THE BALTHASER WOMEN

Life Among the "Worldly"
Pennsylvania Dutch

SHIRLEY
ZWEIZIG
NESTLER

THE BALTHASER WOMEN

Life Among the "Worldly" Pennsylvania Dutch

by Shirley Zweizig Nestler

Biblical references are taken from the Authorized King James version of the Holy Bible; London: Eyre and Spottiswoode Limited; New York: Harper & Brothers Publishers.

For more information about special discounts for bulk purchases, please contact Masthof Press: 610-286-0258, orders@masthof.com

Cover Artist: Anne Marie Scharf
Interior Artists: Anne Marie Scharf and Marvin C. Zweizig

Library of Congress Control Number: 2023933671
International Standard Book Number: 978-1-60126-848-8

Masthof Press

219 Mill Road | Morgantown, PA 19543-9516
www.Masthof.com

TABLE OF CONTENTS

In loving memory
of the greatest farmer ever—
my dear, dear daddy
Herbert Balthaser Zweizig
(1903-1993).

DEAR READER

(21st Century)

21ST CENTURY

Dear Reader,

How many times have you heard someone expand and expound upon a personal experience and say, "Someday I'll write a book." Yet, they never do. I take exception.

When I prepared the script for The Balthaser Women, I couldn't imagine how I'd include all I wished to say between two covers and still have it fit comfortably on a person's lap as they read. So, I applied my traveling philosophy, which I learned the hard way. When I fly, I lay everything out that I think I need for the journey. Next, I cut it in half. I cut that in half. And again. That's what I did with this book.

There's a slim line between fiction and nonfiction. The stories in this book are a work of both and span a time period from 1916 to 1993. Some stories are based on events in my life, others are a product of my imagination, while still others are from the lips of my father. All in all, with the exception of historical figures, any resemblance to persons living or dead is coincidental.

My father, Herbert B. Zweizig, was a truly remarkable person in the eyes of his youngest daughter. One to be proud of in the Pennsylvania Dutch farming community in northern Berks County where he lived his entire life. I dedicate this book to his memory.

You say, "What do you mean by life among the 'worldly' Pennsylvania Dutch? I always thought the Pennsylvania Dutch were anything but worldly and associate only with their own kind, travel by horse and buggy, string wash outside to dry, and read by gaslight?"

So glad you asked. "This, my Dear Reader, is the main purpose of this letter so that I can explain. First, some history."

The Pennsylvania Dutch (Deutsch anglicized to Dutch) are descendants of early German-speaking people from Germany's Rhineland and Palatinate regions as well as parts of Switzerland. They came to

America in the late 1600s and early 1700s to escape religious persecution, a shortage of land, and a crumbling economy. A suitable climate, fertile soil, and four rivers attracted a host of these Swiss-German immigrants with a hard work ethic to settle in William Penn's colony in the New World called Penn's Woods. These Deutsch-*speaking people became known to* Englischers *as the Pennsylvania Dutch.*

I'll break down these people of similar ethnicity into two groups: The "Worldly" and the "Plain." "Plain"Dutch are Amish, Mennonite, and other Anabaptist groups—people in the world but not of it. For purposes of comparison, I'll address only the Amish. Tourists in Amish country get the chocolate box version. You, Dear Reader, get the Nestler unfiltered, unsweetened version.

From the time the Amish settled in the new land, time has stood still as far as advancing with the rest of the world. To this day, they shun modern convenience of any sort—electricity, radio, cars, telephones, TV, and anything else with tangible ties to the outside world. (Though, in all due respect, these folk deserve credit as forerunners of clean energy, i.e. solar and wind power. They call it a clothesline. Wesch *line in Dutch.)*

Amish life focuses on faith, family, and community. Major occupation is farming; minor are carpentry and handcrafts. They travel by horse and buggy. Clothing is homemade and plain (buttons, no zippers). Schools are private and stop at the eighth grade. Conscientious objectors in time of war. Amish have strict religious codes and conduct worship services—no musical instruments—in the home, alternating bi-weekly within respective church districts. Bishops teach that to get to Heaven, an Amish must obey all local church rules, of which there are many and some quite severe, else he/she risks eternal damnation after death. Verboten *is a common word. Amish farm communities are located throughout the United States and Canada. Yet, regardless of where these people reside, they are known as Pennsylvania Dutch. Major tourist attractions are in Lancaster County, Pennsylvania.*

The other Swiss-German immigrant group—Lutheran and Reformed—are labeled the fancy or "worldly" Dutch. Since arriving at the start of the 18th century, while retaining their Germanic culture and faith ideals, these people continue to advance with the rest of society in dress, lifestyle, education, and technology. Like the former group, major occupation is farming. Unlike the former group, they worship weekly inside churches and play musical instruments. They support charities and mission work around the globe. They voluntarily engage in the Armed Forces and sacrifice sons and daughters along with the rest of the populace in defending America against aggression and preserving its freedom. "Worldly" Dutch are concentrated in the southeast region of the Keystone state.

What's unique about the Pennsylvania Dutch people, whether plain or worldly, and, unlike other immigrants whose tongue, with time, absorbs into the English vernacular, both groups continue to speak the fodderlond's Platte Deutsch dialect. [Were it not for our brave men and women in uniform winning the war in Europe, EVERYONE would speak German today.]

A minor postscript: Sad to say, with the birth of my generation, the worldly people's dialect has slipped into a second language. To keep the dialect alive and well, there's the Pennsylvania German Society, several local/annual Ponsylfawnish Deutsch Fersommlings, Pennsylvania Dutch family reunions, and special church services where senior ministers preach and choirs sing in Dutch. There are even Pennsylvania Dutch courses offered in local colleges. And there's the ever popular Kutztown Folk Festival held each year during the week of the Fourth that attracts tourists from around the world.

Well, there you have it. Everything you needed to know about the Pennsylvania Dutch but were afraid to ask, Yah? Nay! You'll discover there's much more to learn as you join Hannah, Sarah, Grace, and Jennie in their numerous adventures and challenges with life. Read on and enjoy the journey!

-Shirley Zweizig Nestler

P.S.: The author's personal proceeds from the sale of this book are donated to: Alliance Defending Freedom—For Faith and Justice, 15100 N. 90th St., Scottsdale, AZ 85260 (1-800-835-5233).

HANNAH

_____

(Nineteen Hundred-Sixteen)

CHAPTER 1

I t was a dark and stormy night. The shanty creaked and moaned from an icy wind blowing around the corners, flickering the kerosene lamp at the kitchen table where Hannah peeled potatoes. A rap sounded at the door. It's probably Cousin Emma, she figured, bringing leftover stew or roast from the big farmhouse kitchen. She did that quite often since Uncle Thurman took them in.

Hannah glanced over at Mem who's sitting by the fireplace for its light and heat, darning holes in the hand-me-down stockings her brother's *frau* gave the young-uns. Her right foot misses not a beat rocking the wooden cradle next to her rocking chair, the one with the squeak she says Dawdy never gets to fix.

Another knock. Louder this time. Little Levi whined, and John and Howard, shooting marbles across the wooden floor, cried out that someone was wanting to come in. Didn't anyone hear? Hannah dropped the knife and wiped dirtied hands on her bib apron as she went to the only outside door to their home. When she opened it, two strange men stood in the cold, icy darkness.

The older of the two removed his cap and, placing it over his heart, spoke up, *"Es deine mem da haem?"* (Is your mother at home?) Hannah opened the door wider and stepped back, allowing Mem to pass. "Are you Mrs. Balthaser?" this same man asked. Mem answered affirmative in a like Pennsylvania German dialect. The man cleared his throat and said, "It's Wilmer, ma'am. He..."

Mem cut him off. *"Ach!* Now what's he done?"

The man continued as if he hadn't heard, "Got caught under the forge coming down to the No. 2 Furnace."

It was vague as to what followed. There was confusion and shuffling of heavy feet, the small room suddenly spinning in circles. An old wooden cupboard stood behind the door, and Hannah leaned against the solid support it offered. Her knees buckled as she slid downward into a frozen heap on the cold floorboards. In a haze, she watched as the men laid her father on the worn fainting couch beneath the window where tiny ice particles attacked the glass from outside.

The bearer of bad news said something like, "He was new on the job and didn't act fast enough to step aside when the hammer got pulled. It's happened with others." These words came to Hannah thin and distant. Not screaming, not crying, she made ghastly noises somewhere in between. The men disappeared into the cold night.

The crude pine coffin was supported by apple crates turned upside down and topped by right side up crates filled with chunks of ice Hannah chipped from the crick's edge. Despite the fireplace, the room was cold, but not cold enough to keep the ice from dripping. Drip, drip, drip, it made throughout the long night and next day. Outside the black drape on the door flapped in a raw wind, scratching as if the devil himself tried to enter.

On the third day, two men came, the earlier spokesman and one other. The wind had died down some, and snow that fell during the night turned into a freezing rain. The men assisted Hannah's older brothers Ralph and Billy haul the box of death across the slippery walkway. Hannah, little brothers John and Howard, and Mem carrying Levi, followed. Their somber footsteps crunched into the rawness of the day, stiff and mournful steps that moved toward the waiting hearse and carriage. The small caravan took Hannah's beloved Dawdy to his final resting place, a place where the topsoil was not yet hardened next to it.

Barely two weeks before, the family stood around the same gravesite. They lived near Penn Valley back then on the other side of the mountain. Landlord Aaron Stitzel and his two teen-aged daughters stopped by their house early one evening with a horse-drawn sleigh. They were on their way to sledding beyond the bend and invited Hannah, John, and Howard to squeeze in beside them. The yet unnamed three-week-old baby was fast asleep in her crib on the second floor while little Levi, still in diapers, stayed with Mem.

Mem was busy making *Faschnachts* for Shrove Tuesday. According to later telling, she dumped a batch of raised dough squares into a pot of sizzling lard on top of the coal oil stove when some *spritzed* to the side and ignited. She grabbed the burning pot and ran out to the yard. By then, the flames had spread to the kitchen ceiling. There was barely time to rescue Levi for, in minutes, the rented frame house was gone. So was the baby. As was with everything that went wrong, Hannah's father took the blame. Mem said if they had lived in a beautiful thick-walled sandstone house like her brother Thurman's instead of an old dried-out shack, it would not have caught on fire.

The day after the fatal blaze, the Balthasers accepted the charity of Mem's brother Thurman. The family moved to the Seifert dairy farm and into their summerhouse that had a ground cellar below and loft above. The family slept in tight little rooms. The accommodation was temporary until *der dawdy* could relocate them. This, of course, depended upon sufficient income from his new job at the Jalappa Plow Works. "See if he can hang on to this job, which is more than we can say for the others," Mem complained. Mem always complained. These new living quarters were small and cramped and offered Hannah little escape from Mem's constant whining about their impoverished lifestyle.

Here they were again, what was left of them, on the hillside cemetery above the little red brick Church in the Valley. Once again, it was the Reverend Hiram Goodlich delivering a Balthaser eulogy.

The *parrah* (preacher) had driven to their house the previous day to ask what words he could say over their departed loved one. Mem admitted she didn't know much about such things. Hannah said she didn't either, but she did know her father well and told the good minister in her fourteen-year-old way that he loved the Lord and talked to Him all the time. Now, the good Reverend led the few mourners in song:

> *What a friend we have in Jesus,*
> *All our sins and griefs to bear!*
> *What a privilege to carry,*
> *Everything to God in prayer....*
> *(Joseph M. Scriven, 1877)*

After a long, flowery prayer, the small group disbursed and departed for their buggies. Except Hannah. She chose to walk instead and shuffled listlessly alongside the black hearse and carriage that slowly made their way down the hill and toward the guttered road. A road all full of itself with a slippery film of white and gray on top.

A dark hat appeared from inside the hearse. "Young *maedel*, are you sure you don't want to ride? This weather's nasty, and it's a long walk back," called the undertaker through the sleet. Hannah waved him on. They passed the little red church and gradually faded from view.

Not a sound broke the silence but for the mournful toll of a bell. In the way of the Pennsylvania Dutch, next of kin did the tolling to spread the news over the countryside that a beloved in the neighborhood had died and was buried. Hannah's father had no siblings. Cousin Mahlon Balthaser did the honors and pulled the rope in the small church's bell tower. Slowly, forty-two times, one for each year of his dear blood relative's life on earth.

The walk home was far, Hannah agreed, but the cold was less sharp from earlier in the day. Not that it mattered one way or the other. She was numb anyway, and the thin freezing raindrops dried quickly enough into snowflakes that swirled through the air before touching the hardened winter earth. A somber peace hung over the fallow fields, as though they, too, felt the grasp from the ice and stretched themselves in their long winter sleep underneath the white cover. The same white cover that now blanketed her father's grave.

Hannah thought back to the song they sang as they had lowered the coffin and wondered where Dawdy's friend Jesus was the night he fell under the forge. He was nowhere near the Plow Works that was for sure. She kicked at a stone that jutted out of a frozen rut in the road and, tightening the borrowed mantle about her head and chest, quickened the journey home. Home, where things would be different from now on. Not better, most likely worse. But surely different.

CHAPTER 2

I t was early March. Hardly spring since the onion snow hadn't yet arrived, but the weather was decent enough for a leisurely Sunday afternoon walk. It was also little Howard's fifth birthday. Hannah took coins out of a tin drinking cup salvaged from the fire and put them into her coat pocket. Pulling Howard on a wooden wagon that had been Cousin Roy's when he was little, she made her first visit to the general store in the small village of Bern, a couple of miles away and on the other side of the Schuylkill River. At the store, she parked the homemade wagon underneath the long bench on the storefront and cautioned Howard to wait, promising a surprise on her return.

Three bells at the top of the huge, heavy glass-paneled door jingled when she entered the store. Inside was so crowded with things that, except for a narrow path to the counter and some sitting space around a potbellied stove, there was hardly room to move. Heavy winter jackets and work boots of varied sizes, muskrat traps, glass washboards and wooden buckets, and just about anything else one could imagine hung from the thick wooden beams in the ceiling and along the walls. Odors were rampant from damp gloves drying over the stove door and of dry wool and cotton from shelves stacked with pants, overalls and long underwear for men, and finer undergarments for women and children. On the floor in front of the stove was a pan of yellow water that gave off a rank smell from cigarette butts, cigar stumps, and tobacco juice.

From behind a row of shelves, popped an elderly man of medium build. He had a heavy, pear-shaped frame that moved surprisingly adept amongst the barrels and layers of wooden boxes and crates lining the aisle. The storekeeper ushered Hannah to the candy bins next to the cracker barrel.

"New here?" he asked in Pennsylvania Dutch. Hannah nodded. The man fingered his white goatee and watched Hannah contemplating the various sweet offerings of penny candy in the tin bins. She chose black licorice strips for Howard and pink wintergreen lozenges for herself and gave the man a nickel.

After a final ding of the cash register, Hannah returned to the porch, but Howard was no longer there. Across the road, a group of people skated on the frozen millrace. There, she spotted little Howard targeted by a speeding man who skated backwards, his hands interlocked behind—obviously not a care in the world.

"Howard! Howard!" she yelled, sprinting across the slushy road and up the bank. Her warning was too late. Howard and the skater collided, both skidding clear across the ice, knocking down two others in the bargain. The little boy screamed as he rolled back onto his heavy shoes. When he appeared unhurt, Hannah scolded, "Howard Walter Balthaser! Didn't I tell you to wait for me on the porch? A fine birthday you made it turn out to be!" She stooped down and tenderly wiped his hiccupping face with her rough mitten, then looked up into the most sparkling blue eyes she'd ever seen.

"*Ach,* I'm awfully sorry, Miss. I didn't see him there," said the young man, his focus settling on the leather straps that secured blades to his shoes. His gloved hands moved toward the pockets of his woolen knickers that were let down at the hem. When they didn't fit, he fiddled instead with the gray woolen muffler that was wrapped around his neck.

Hannah straightened and placed both hands on her hips. "Well, now! How could you see him? You certainly weren't watching where you were going!" Having said that much too bluntly, she bit her lower lip and cupped a mittened hand over her warm face. Her mother said she was mouthy. She was beginning to believe it. The young man shuffled awkwardly and began to skate away when Hannah called out, "My name is Hannah Balthaser."

The man pivoted and, with a lopsided grin, responded like-
wise in dialect, "My name is Jonathan, Jonathan Hunsberger." His
eyes were full of gleam from the sunlight reflecting off of the frozen
surface beneath their feet. They stared at one another until Howard
tugged at Hannah's coat. She looked down at the little round rosy
face that focused on the brown paper bag she had picked up from the
ice. Laughing, she excused herself from Jonathan Hunsberger with a
hurried bow. There didn't seem to be anything else to say anyway. She
took Howard by the hand. Together, they walked cautiously over the
smooth frozen surface and across the road to the storefront where the
little wooden wagon awaited.

Hannah made frequent visits to the general store. Usually Sunday afternoons when the store opened a few hours so the neighborhood could get the Sunday paper with its funnies and other special
treats. Occasionally, she ran into Jonathan. When they met, they talked only of Howard. How's Howard? Did he ask for blades so he could
skate on the millrace? No, never. He was scared of skaters, but he was
not afraid to come to the little village where he might get more penny
candy. Then they'd laugh.

She guessed that Jonathan knew by the modest clothes she wore
that conditions with the Balthasers were not all that favorable. Even
though it was spring, she continued wearing the black worsted over-
coat, adjusting to the changeable weather by how many buttons she'd
close or let open. It was a coat that, in its outgrown condition, hung
a few inches below her knees, not long enough to cover the faded
muslin skirt. The brown skirt, though clean and ironed, had a large
mended tear just above her ankles. Braided red hair done up in the
German way was covered by a blue woolen cap, a recent hand-me-
down from her brother Ralph.

On the second Sunday in May, Jonathan extended himself.

"We're needing someone to help out in the kitchen and the garden. Mom is all alone."

———————————

Hannah was strong and responsible for her fourteen years. Of the children at home, she was the only surviving female, her sister Ellie being married and Margaret off goodness knew where. A major load of housework such as befell a grownup was hers. Though the family frequently moved, they always lived in the country. She chopped wood for both the cooking and heating, dug up dandelion in the fields in springtime for sweet and sour salads, and picked wild berries during the summer, mushrooms in the fall. She pumped and carried water to the house, fixed the beds, swept the house and scrubbed the floors daily by her mother's stringent standards.

Cooking was another of Hannah's many chores. Though there was seldom meat for the table, there was usually a variety of vegetables from a garden her father cared for wherever they lived at the time. Dawdy wasn't able to keep the weeds under control, so that task, too, fell to Hannah. She did what she had to do what with Mem occupied with the *young-uns*. "Your father's busy enough making babies," she'd complain, "but never around to help and pay for their keep." Hannah wasn't exactly sure what Mem meant by that, the making babies part, so she complained, too, but only in her thoughts.

There were two strong influences at work in Hannah Balthaser's mind. From the first time she stared into Jonathan Hunsberger's blueberry blue eyes, she knew he was her man. The other impulse that drove her forward was to be anything but poor. Now that Dawdy was gone, money was surely in need. Since Billy and Ralph were hired out, Hannah felt she could as well. Surely, getting Mem's approval would be easy enough considering the dire need for money.

There was one bothersome thing. Teacher said that since Mr. Woodrow Wilson is President, children are not allowed to hire out like before, and that even those who do are limited to eight hours of work time in a day. After some thought, Hannah decided she didn't give a fig about child labor laws, and that, being country folk, it shouldn't matter none one way or the other. After all, who would know? Her repeated plea to Mem was, "If I help at the Hunsbergers, that's one less mouth to feed, and, at the same time I can help you with expenses." *Not that I'm willing to help with expenses, but it's one reason you might give in.* Mem finally gave in.

———————

Hannah finished her last ten weeks of the eighth grade at the little one-room Naftzinger School. This last day of May, the afternoon of the final examination, was also the frightening interview.

She dressed up special this special day. Despite the unseasonably warm weather—a heat wave Teacher called it—she wore a starched dark green jumper over a clean, slightly faded, but freshly pressed, paisley print dress that had been Cousin Emma's before she outgrew it. Thank God for Cousin Emma for the pretty straw hat also came from her. It had a fancy pink silk ribbon banded around the brim that ended in a bow with two generous streamers dangling elegantly down the back. The air was breezy, and the hat controlled the fine coppery hairs escaping the braids that still wrapped her head in the old-fashioned way.

She walked through a covered bridge and from there onto a road that followed the river on its east side. It was a pleasant walk. The spring peepers were busy with their mating or whatever they did in the lowland this time of year. Trailing arbutus decorated the edge of the tree line where she walked, while a flock of Canada geese flew overhead in V formation, pointing the way to the Hunsbergers.

She turned up a long dirt lane ending in a thicket of tall trees surrounded by freshly painted outbuildings of various shapes and sizes. Black and white Holstein cows, a dozen or so, plus a red Guernsey, waited at a gate across from a big red barn with colorful *hex* signs on the front. To the right, a large sandstone farmhouse, with green and white wooden shutters that gleamed in the lowering sun, looked warm and safe. Humming nervously, Hannah let herself through a whitewashed picketed gate into a yard fenced to keep out the numerous chickens scratching dirt in the lane.

Suddenly from nowhere, a black and tannish dog rushed past her and over the fence, scattering the chickens to kingdom come. He no sooner accomplished this feat when he returned to the yard and stood between her and the walkway to the porch. He'd evidently been having a glorious time in some mud puddle for his legs, all three of them, and chest were caked with the stuff. Jonathan had told her about him and not to be afraid when she came. "Just say his name, and you'll be okay" he'd said in *Deutsch*. "What's his name?" she'd asked, and he answered, "Froch Een" with a grin. "You mean, I'm supposed to ask him?" she said. "*Ach*, you talk too dumb." And then she got it. Silly name or not, the dog responded to her greeting with a wag of his hairy tail. Still, she walked cautiously around him.

The wooden walkway was edged on both sides with daffodils that barely hung on from the recent warmth. Here and there cultivated beds grew mountain pinks that alternated with lamb's wool and heather. Except for the lamb's wool, a routine planting along walkways for the brightness it gave off at night, the flowers' perfume filled the late afternoon air with the delicate fragrance of springtime. Overhead the maple trees began to leaf, partially shading the well-kept yard. A path led up to a wooden porch with Victorian pillars—an obvious modern addition to this late 18th-century home.

At the screened front door of the farmhouse, Hannah paused and managed a deep breath before gently tapping while her other hand toyed with a jeweled brooch pinned to her jumper. For an instant she was tempted to turn and run away, but then she noticed the iron horseshoe above the doorjamb. The good luck sign drew her on. When the door opened, she scarcely knew what to say, even though she'd rehearsed it a dozen times.

"Hello. I, I'm Hannah. Hannah Balthaser," she stammered. The farmer held a bucket of sweet-smelling stuff that steamed. They stared at each other in silence before she quickly continued. "It wonders me if you need a maid yet." The man said kindly enough that he'd just come into the house to heat starter mash for the new chicks and that he'd have to go get *die frau* to talk about something like this. He asked her to sit and left.

A warm evening, the kitchen windows were open to the many sounds of the barnyard before feeding time. *"Hupta, Hupta, Hupta!"* came the familiar voice of the farmer's son bringing the cows in from pasture. There was the farmer's voice itself, calling Mrs. Hunsberger from the springhouse where she was readying cans and buckets for milking.

While waiting, Hannah surveyed her hopeful place of employ. Everything was spotlessly clean and functional. The kitchen was spacious and high-ceilinged. Bonneted little maidens sprinkling yellow dahlias bordered the wallpaper above the wainscoting around the big room. A Red Rose Feed & Fertilizer Calendar torn off to May 1916 hung over one of the doors that opened to either the cellar or pantry, she couldn't tell which. Potted geraniums and coleus drawn toward the outside sunshine filled each of the deep windowsills facing south. Preparations had been started for the supper. Reflecting an errant shaft of sunlight from a side window, a scrubbed black cook stove diffused the sweet aroma of roasting pork into the room. Potato peelings and onion shells domed abundantly on top of the sink board while a tin kettle planted under the sink pump's outlet held the yet-uncooked vegetables.

On an inside wall, numerous pots and pans hung from hooks, and, to the right, a burnished wood chest below served as a bench for a long table that had four spindle-back chairs around the other three sides. A gas lamp flanked by long sticky flypapers that warned of the approaching hot summer and its dreaded pests hung from the ceiling. In a corner next to the parlor entrance stood a tall cupboard, which most likely stored books, papers, and varied odds and ends.

On the other side was a stuffed rocking chair with a pillow that was thin from wear and tear. It looked comfortable and inviting, and Hannah decided to accept the farmer's earlier invitation. Just then, her eye caught a portrait hanging on the stairway wall and above the family Bible stand. She walked slowly toward it and gazed at a young light-haired man who stared back at her from a gilded frame. Her freckled hand reached out tentatively to touch the familiar face when the screen door opened, and the sound of hurried footsteps entered the kitchen.

"*Yah?*" a woman's voice asked heavily.

Hannah's own small feet pivoted so quickly that her straw hat tipped and one of the braids came undone, falling to her shoulder. She curtsied awkwardly, lowering her eyes toward the floor as she did so.

"G-good evening, ma'am. My name is Hannah Balthaser."

The stout middle-aged woman had dark brown hair, peppered with gray. There was a great mass of it pulled straight back and coiled above her neck. She glanced hurriedly at the stranger in her kitchen and flexing a dimpled hand in a wave, proceeded to the sink where she pumped water over the potatoes. "Can you cook?" were her first words as she carried the full pot to the stove.

"Yes, ma'am. I can cook and clean, and I..."

"*Sehr Gute!* Fifty cents a day. That's almost half as much as the hired man gets," Mrs. Hunsberger said proudly, tilting her double chin. She poked around at the wood with a stove plate handle and coaxed the flames back to life. "I'll show you to your room just as soon as I rev up this fire." Inwardly, Hannah was relieved with her reception, since it was obvious Jonathan prepared his mother for the impending visit. But outwardly, she shifted nervously. Behind the woman's back, she pulled a hairpin from under her straw hat and adjusted the fallen braid.

"Oh, thank you, ma'am. I, I didn't bring my things, but I can be back first thing in the morning though," she said in one quick breath.

CHAPTER 3

T he upstairs wallpapered room was clean, sparsely furnished, and practical.

A multi-paned window with a blue curtain swept to one side was held in place by a length of cord string. Beneath but nearer the corner was a white chamber pot. A double bed with an oak headboard was draped with a flowered patch quilt and centered against the south wall. That was a good thing, Hannah decided. Granny Moyer said the body sleeps best with the head of the bed facing north. Next to the bed stood a smoking stand that apparently served as a night table. A coal oil lantern rested on top.

Hannah brought few belongings. Two changes of clothing besides what she had on. Except for the work dress—the dress she wore when they sledded and the house burnt down—they were hand-me-downs from Cousin Emma who was four years older and had fortunately outgrown them. Optimistic for long-term employment, Hannah brought her worsted coat, cap, mittens, muffler, and galoshes that she'd also worn the night they sledded. The remainder of her wardrobe, though never plentiful, had burnt in the fire.

Opposite from the bed and above the chair rail was a rustic length of wood with eight dowels. On one hung a small calendar with a picture of Jesus knocking on a door from the outside. Hannah hung her outer garments on the other dowels. Everything else was neatly folded and placed in a small bureau. A bureau with a mirror on top. How nice was that!

When packing things into a burlap bag the night before, she took possession of her father's Bible. It was not a large Bible, not at all like the one the Hunsbergers had on the stand below Jonathan's por-

23

trait. Nor was it like the large black leather-bound one lost in the fire. In that one had been recorded the family's full names and birth dates, as well as those of each member of the Seifert family with births, baptisms, marriages, and deaths down through her mother's side of the *freundschaft*. Going way back to when Silas Seifert and a host of other Swiss-German immigrants came to America on the Ship *Molly* that docked some place named Philadelphie or something like that. Except for personal entries, Hannah never recalled seeing the Bible opened. It was written in *Hoch Deutsch* (High German). Nobody could read *Hoch Deutsch*. Not even her father.

Unlike the Seifert Bible, Dawdy's was small and printed in English. His Bible, along with a few other items, had been stored in a walnut box lined in tin and salvaged after the fire. Frequent penned notes marked the narrow margins. Some of the pages were worn and dirty as if weathered by the elements. Hannah planned to read these notes someday, hopefully clearing up many questions she had in mind. For now, she carefully placed the book on top of the smoking stand. The Seiferts had one of these in their parlor, and that's what they called it. Surely she wouldn't be smoking but it would serve quite well for storing Dawdy's Bible.

Hannah also brought her father's journal. It, too, had been salvaged by the insulated box. "Might as well take that, too," Mem had said, supervising the packing. "All he ever wrote in there anyway was nonsense." She went on mumbling something about if he'd have spent as much time working as he did daydreaming, they'd be well-off like her brother Thurman. Hannah was certain her mother would never know if it were nonsense or not since she never even read the Bible. Nor the journal book. Mem didn't put much stock into reading and things like that. Hannah wasn't even sure Mem could read.

Mem called Dawdy lazy when he sat down to read. More than once, Hannah saw him slip the Bible inside his coat before leaving the house. Hannah was sure, too, that on some of those evenings when he came home late he'd been reading somewhere instead of drinking like

Mem accused him of. Now, during this first night in the Hunsberger home and in the privacy of her very own bedroom, Hannah stooped to the faint light of the coal oil lantern and made her first entry in Dawdy's journal.

"Dawdy. Oh, Dawdy. Why? Why, did God take you away? Why did you have to leave us? Why? Even Mem misses you. She never says so, but last night her voice quivered when she told me to take your Bible. She said that as tender as I ever heard her talk...." Hannah's pen didn't move. In these strange and lonesome surroundings at the Hunsbergers, she broke down and sobbed uncontrollably, barely hearing the soft tap on the door.

"Something wrong in there?" It was Warren, the hired man. He slept in the room next to her's. It was a big house.

"Nay," she answered between hiccups. "My head hurts something awful, but it often does. It doesn't last long ever, though."

That seemed to satisfy the man, and his footsteps quietly retreated. Hannah closed the journal and placed it next to the Bible inside the smoking stand, extinguished the light, and lay down, the corn husk in the mattress rustling beneath her. She had the first undisturbed sleep since the fire and her father's death in February.

———

Hannah absorbed into the Hunsberger household routine and took her new position seriously. There was lots of work to be done. But the atmosphere was pleasant enough, and she was capable in performing her newly-assigned duties. Where she wasn't, Mrs. Hunsberger was kind and patient and showed her how to do things in spite of her own hurried tendencies.

On her first Sunday with the Hunsbergers, Hannah rode along to church. Inside, she was ushered to the left side of the sanctuary where other unmarried girls were seated. Jonathan sat with other boys and young men on the balcony. Married couples filled in wherever.

Jonathan told her later that men and women used to be separated, up and down, but when his Mom and Pop married, they stayed together down below and soon others followed this break in tradition.

Throughout the service, Hannah was careful to stand and sing and sit when others stood and sang and sat, and cocked her head at the right tilt when listening to the preacher. Yet her mind wandered all over the place with the newness of it all and concentrated little on spiritual presence.

After the service, Mrs. Hunsberger stayed behind in the sanctuary to conduct Ladies' Aid business with a wife of one of the church elders. Hannah waited alone in the crowded vestibule and overheard one of the women in a lowered voice, say, "The girl sitting next to the Mengel girl must be Martha Hunsberger's new *maut* (maid)." Another said, "*Yah,* I believe so, too. I'll bet Sally Hepner's Mary won't like that." She giggled. Hannah wondered who this Mary was they mentioned. She was relieved when Mrs. Hunsberger finally joined her in the vestibule, then outside to the sheds where the men waited with the buggy.

The following Tuesday, Hannah accompanied Mrs. Hunsberger to the Ladies' Aid meeting, which this month was held at the home of Mrs. Klopp. She lived on a small farm somewhere in the area. There, she met the mother of this Mary who was apparently threatened by her employment at the Hunsbergers. She was the last arrival.

Sally Hepner, a woman of great size, squeezed past two older women seated in the second row of chairs set up in the parlor off to the side of Mrs. Klopp's long kitchen. "You'll never believe why I'm late," she said. She took a seat as the women waited for more. "Mary had me drive special to the store to get chicklets. She has a tooth here." She pointed to one of her own on the lower left side of her mouth and turned so everyone could see where she pointed. "It's got a black hole in it, and she uses gum to cover it up."

"*Oi*, Sally. Now I heard everything!" her neighbor said. "Ain't she being pretty stuck on herself?" She unconsciously fingered her own mouth. Hannah, sitting behind them and to the left, thought it looked like her teeth could use patching as well.

"*Yah*, she's vain alright! But she's at the age, you know. Boys are looking hard." She chuckled and smoothed her dress before putting her baggy pocketbook on the floor at her feet.

Hannah hoped with all her heart that Jonathan wasn't one of those who looked Mary's way.

The meeting opened with a vesper prayer and ended with Hymn No. 65 in the Sunday School Song Book. A portly woman they called Helga Bagenstose led the group with a loud aggressive soprano while she energetically pumped away on the organ. Hannah mouthed the words since she wasn't familiar with the song. Even if she would've been, her heart wasn't into it, her attention focused primarily on the grotesque growth the size of an apple that hung off of Mrs. Bagenstose's neck. The veins in the goiter pulsed purple, bluish red while she sang. After the singing, Mrs. Klopp collected the songbooks and asked Hannah and the others would they mind taking their chairs along into the dining room.

"*Ich hawwe yuscht zwelfe schtiel ins gansa haus.* (I have just twelve chairs in the whole house) so we must do with that," she apologized.

"*Kum now, du huscht au der schockelschtul dot,*" (Come now, you have also the rocking chair there), said Thelma Wentzel, pointing to a wooden rocker by the pump organ.

"Shhhh," puffed Mrs. Klopp, placing an index finger in front of her lips. "We don't count that one. That makes the unlucky thirteen." She laughed and returned to her kitchen to prepare the goodies.

A quilting bee. Hannah had been to several at Granny Seifert's. One of the quilts she helped with had all kinds of farm animals on it and was on Levi, John, and Howard's bed that burnt in the fire. She hoped that wasn't a bad omen for one she'd help with tonight. This one here was in the makings of a Granny's Flower Garden pattern and was stretched out on a rack that, except for a folded table against the wall and a sideboard too heavy to move, occupied the entire room. One could barely squeeze around the rack with one's chair.

This was the third of four quilts the women planned to display and auction off at the county fair come September. Somebody said they were certain to finish this quilt tonight with such a good turn-out. Another joked they might even catch up on the neighborhood goings-on in the process. It was then that Hannah first heard of the gypsy woman.

"Do you know that someone moved into the old Schade place over by the river?" The hefty Amy Naftzinger reached for the well-worn and yellowed instruction paper in the center of the quilt. She used it to fan herself under one arm and then the other. It was a warm evening. "Maude Metz told me her husband heard it at Grange. Name's Frog. No, Toad, or something like that."

"*Yah*, I heard so, too," said Sarah Hartman, looking thoughtfully at two red square patches before her. The petite woman, sitting on a big fat cushion, held them up toward the ceiling lamp, squinted, and decided on the gingham, angling both artfully into the tip of the rose petal, which her arms could barely reach. "They say it's an *auslander* (foreigner)." Another of the women agreed and nodded worriedly to her neighbor.

Hannah had the notion Helen Schnell might have something to add to this. She was right. "*Yah*, a woman they say lives alone, and a gypsy at that! Come down from a camp the gypsies have over the mountain, and, you know how they are!" Helen gave her needle such a thrust that it knocked Hannah's spool of thread down and across the carpeted floor. "My son Willie, he saw those gypsies coaxing people into their tents at the carnival last summer. *Yah*, he did!"

Hannah never heard of a gypsy. Mem said that children couldn't help but be seen sometimes, yet they should never talk in the company of grownups. She wouldn't dare ask what a gypsy was. And, for sure, one didn't start with the likes of Mrs. Schnell, she decided, retrieving her thread from the floor. Silently and with a skillful twist learned from old Granny Seifert, she pressed her needle into the colorful fabric and continued to weave it in and out of the padded cloth, listening attentively to the older women.

"Is it true they have special powers?" Hannah was surprised to hear Mrs. Hunsberger's question. She didn't know her employer very well, but guessed she wasn't disposed to idle gossip.

"It's for sure so," confirmed Helen. She nodded as if that settled the matter. "Devil's work, I'd say!"

Hannah recalled bits and pieces of the hymn they sang earlier and thought this comment quite judgmental of this Mrs. Schnell. But, on second thought, perhaps she, too, was being judgmental for she couldn't help but think about what the women said behind her back after church last Sunday. Helen was seen in Jerome Muller's covered buggy at a farm *fendue*. A woman had said her husband bid on and got a small pig's trough and a sausage stuffer, and, while the sale was still going on in the barn, he carried his purchases to his wagon at the far end of the muddy field. That's when he passed the Muller carriage and saw Jerome and Helen embracing on the back bench. He swore it was Helen Schnell. Another woman had said, "I hear Helen has a bun in the oven. I'll bet Jerome's *der dawdy*."

Hannah's own *dawdy* taught that, when you point a finger at someone, there are three that point back at you. For now, Hannah decided she'd forget that after-church conversation.

"What *fer* sound is that? Is it thundering outside?" asked Flora Stoudt. The women looked up, and Helga stepped over to the closest window.

"*Ach*, you just imagine things," Helga said, pulling back the curtain. "*Ai yi yi*, Flo! It's only a cat batting at the bugs on the screen."

Hannah wondered if it was the same cat, big and black as the darkest of nights, that had come out of nowhere and crossed in front of them on the boardwalk coming in. Hadn't she had enough bad luck? She shivered in spite of the warm room.

"*Haurry Yamma Noch Amoll!* (It makes awful in here!) Sounds like a fox got in the hen house," Mrs. Klopp said good-naturedly about all the chatter going on in her house. Hands and arms were loaded with food. She started with Hannah and held a platter heaped with layers of egg sandwich squares, prettily embellished in a bed of spring garden lettuce. In the other hand was a plate of *Lebkuchen* sliced into triangles. "Your coffee's behind on the sideboard," she said.

Hannah took one of the sandwiches and a small piece of cake and laid them in her lap. For a moment, she thought of having a cup of coffee. She tried it once and thought it bitter. How could grown-ups drink such stuff? She said, "Thank you, ma'am. But, I don't drink coffee yet." She thought she heard a couple of snickers and wished she hadn't admitted to that. Her youth was an irksome matter, especially since she promised Dawdy she'd wait until after Confirmation before thinking of boys. That was a whole year's wait after her fifteenth birthday in August. There goes Jonathan.

CHAPTER 4

Hannah flipped through Dawdy's journal and stopped at February 8. This had been the last of their many nature walks together. The long entry was penned in a flourishing hand of fine English, as was all of Dawdy's writing. He was an educated man, having gone to normal school and all that. It was written just two nights before his fatal accident at the Plow Works.

"*February 8. It snowed all day, a light, peaceful, steady snowfall. I told the missus that Hannah and I would shovel the walkways to the stables for her brother Thurman. Of course, she didn't trust I'd get it done. I was counting on that, so I didn't. Instead, Hannah and I walked down to the canal. Hannah loves when we walk the towpath, and this Sabbath eve, because of the snow, it was especially beautiful. We stopped by that huge elm where we often sit in milder weather and, brushing the snow off an overturned trunk alongside, sat down and let the cool moist flakes flutter around us. 'It's so pretty and peaceful here,' Hannah said after a while. 'Why can't it always be like this? Why must we die? Why does God take away innocent little ones like Baby Sis who never even had a chance to see snow? That was so cruel. Sometimes I think I hate Him.'*

"*Hannah never talked about that terrible night so this came out of nowhere and took me by surprise. Cupping her uplifted chin in my cold hand, I looked into her eyes and in my most humble words, tried to explain. 'You are so young, my child, and hard for you to understand. There are a lot of things I don't understand either, but we must put our trust in the*

31

Lord. Death is all part of His divine plan for the universe. Everything is precious and perishable, including you and me and Baby Sis and…. Yes, my dear, death seems cruel, but it is not always so. God knows the end from the beginning. I trust that He took your little sister to Heaven when He did so He could save her from something far more cruel down here on earth.'

"It broke my heart to see Hannah's heart so troubled, a heart that is still so child-like and loving and naive, yet enveloped in a body that's maturing and dedicated to hard work much beyond her 14 years. Much as someone who's had to take on grown-up duties long before her time. Far more responsible than her father could ever be…."

It had been that same evening when Dawdy surprised Hannah and pulled out of his pocket the amethyst brooch—an oval-shaped purple gemstone set in 14-karat gold and gilded in Florentine. Hannah remembered well the words he said as he pinned it to her coat. "This brooch was my mother's and my mother's mother and way on back. We don't know when the tradition started, but it was somewhere back in Germany, long before the Moyers came to America. The pin was handed down from generation to generation to the youngest girl in the family." He choked up when he said that and looked far into the white darkness. Hannah knew he was remembering Baby Sis.

Hannah thought of Mem and how she blamed Dawdy for their loss. She'd said, "Our baby's surely gone to hell now and so will you for not coming home that night…drinking at the *watshaas* (hotel), you was, while your daughter burnt…." Then he said, "I was not out drinking, and our baby girl did not go to hell. Our God is a loving Father. He takes innocent children to His bosom." Then she said, "Oh, you and your flowery language! That baby went to hell because it wasn't baptized yet!" Then he said, "The Bible says nothing about baptizing little babies. Jesus says if we believe, we'll be saved. Now what does a little baby know about believing?" Then Mem said, "I swear I don't know where you come up with this stuff. Always saying the Bible says, the Bible doesn't say, it says in the Bible that...I tell you, Wilmer Moyer Balthaser, I'm sick of it. You want to be so religious and goody-two-shoes, yet you're the one who's going to pay for it and go straight to hell with her when you die. Good, at least she'll have company there...." And so they went round and round until Dawdy left the house.

Hannah had known a little of the family legacy. Granny Moyer Balthaser, or Granny Moyer as the family called her, said not long before she died that, having no daughters of her own, she'd give the brooch to her only son. That, of course, would be Hannah's father. She also told Hannah confidentially that the brooch had special powers. What those special powers were, she never said. What she did say was that Dawdy said the pin was beautiful, but he'd be more than blessed to pass it on to his youngest. At the same time, he denied that it held special powers and that a break in tradition might be a good thing to stop such nonsense belief. "Curses are just silly superstitions left over from the Dark Ages and the Bible shuns such sorcery," he'd said to his mother. "Mind me, son," she'd countered, "your Great Aunt Sadie never believed in curses neither, yet she was cursed as surely as I stand here. Both her twins turned out to be funny in the head. Folks say she passed them through a worn horse collar three times to cure them, but that didn't help matters neither. After that, she kept the children in the attic so that people wouldn't know they were growing up funny. But word got around. People knew anyhow."

Hannah's thoughts returned to Dawdy. After they'd started walking again that snowy night, she had said to him, "It wonders me already why you're giving this brooch to me? Mem still might have more babies and goodness knows, maybe another girl or two." She herself thought of coming womanhood. Of a husband. And children. Why, she loved children, but, and then she'd suddenly turned to him and, with a giggle, said, "Oh, Dawdy, you should give this brooch to sister Ellie instead. After all, I may never have children of my own to pass it on to. How would I? I'll never get married because no boy can ever take your place in my life." She'd said the latter to Dawdy dozens of times before, and it always made him laugh. When he didn't this time, she realized the seriousness he attached to his formal presentation.

At a sideways glance, she noticed his stooped figure that seemed small and shriveled in that big shabby coat of his, which in spite of the cold and the snow coming down was open in the front. Like the scarlet oak saplings they walked next to, he was gaunt and thin and spent. His clothes, normally loose-fitting, had that never-made-to-order look. Once when Mem accused him of looking like a vagrant, he dismissed her comment by saying, "Since Eve brought sin upon man, clothes have little more importance than for covering the body. What does it matter how they look, as long as they're clean!" Clean they were. *Mem* made sure of that.

Now that she read the journal entry of their last night together, Hannah realized Dawdy never did answer her question of why now? It was as if he knew he was leaving. As if he knew that God rescued him from something more cruel that would happen down the road, just like with Baby Sis. *I'll never, never understand that,* she mumbled and closed the journal in frustration and opened the Bible instead, hoping to find some answers there. The light in the lantern flickered, sputtered, and quickly disappeared into the darkness of the room. "*Oi, Nay,*" she muttered, and closed the Book, laying it next to the journal inside the smoking stand. She'd resume her search another time. She slipped between the cool clean bed sheets and fell asleep.

CHAPTER 5

Friday was baking day. At home Hannah baked whenever there was a need and then only if there was enough creamy milk available to make the butter she needed for cakes and pie crusts. Here at the Hunsbergers, she baked every Friday. Today, she cleaned out the pie safe in the cellar and slopped the pigs with last week's leftover fruit pies that turned sour. She saved the dried loaf of bread that could still be used for gravy dunking.

At Mrs. Hunsberger's direction, Hannah spent the morning baking fresh bread, plain and wheat grain, three marbled pound cakes, and four rhubarb pies. And two small milk tarts with lots of sugar to use up the extra pie dough. She scooped up all the molasses in the kettle and made six shoofly pies, one for each breakfast table during the coming week. Only six fit in the cook stove's oven at one time so Sunday's breakfast would be cake instead of shoofly. But she wasn't finished. She was elbow deep in flour again when Jonathan with an odor of barnyard clinging to his clothes came into the warm kitchen.

"Hey, what's it making?" he said checking out her baking dish.

"Angel's Food Cake." Hannah cracked four eggs into a small bowl, carefully removing the yokes, and poured the whites into her mixture.

"I like Devil's Food Cake better." Jonathan chuckled at his joke and, with his fingers, scooped the sticky remains of rhubarb syrup from another bowl. Wiping his hand on his trousers, he moved to the water bench on the far side of the long kitchen and got the dipper hanging above the bench. He dipped it into the white enamel bucket filled with spring water.

Hannah observed by a side glance as she worked and smiled to herself when she recalled the lengthened knickers Jonathan wore that day on the millrace back in March. She knew then that he must be somewhere past the age of sixteen for it was customary that boys go from knickers to full-length pants following Confirmation. One was not confirmed until sixteen or later, anyways that's what Dawdy said. She mixed all the ingredients together and set the bowl aside before retorting, "That figures. Angel's Food Cake is made for angels, and Devil's Food Cake is made for..."

"Devils," finished Jonathan, turning around. A shock of sandy-colored hair haloed his sunburnt face that was partially shaded by a broad-brimmed straw hat, slightly cocked. He took a swallow from the dipper, making a slurping sound, and, from out of nowhere, said, "*Yah*, Hannah, I'll have to teach you how to cultivate. It's a real trick to gee and haw the horses so they walk between the rows instead of treading on the plants." Jonathan spoke a lot about horses. It was easy to tell he had a fondness for working with them.

"*Yah*, and I'll teach you how to bake cakes," Hannah said, stacking the dirty dishes to one end of the table. At the other end, she placed a huge tin tray and took the blue agate dishpan down from its hook on the cellar door and placed it on the tray. She checked the clock on the mantle. Time to take out the shoofly pies. She did this now and slipped the Angel's Food Cake into the hot oven. Jonathan watched.

"Well, how 'bout it?" he asked.

"How 'bout what?" she said looking up from wiping the table where she'd spilled sugar earlier.

He gave Hannah one of his big lopsided grins. "Cultivating."

"And what's your mom to do then if I help you men on the fields? Seems to me she's the one who needs the help around here, be-ings you're all such big eaters!" she chided, stifling a giggle.

Jonathan gulped the rest of the water and replaced the dipper on its hook. "Ah, that makes good and wet." He made a gratifying sound and wiped his mouth with the back of his free hand and withdrew a pipe from his breast pocket with the other. At the screen door, he paused and scooped the pipe into a pouch of something or other, then pressed it down with a square thumb. *Pipe smoking already? My goodness*, Hannah thought. She watched Jonathan's strong husky back with a sigh as he disappeared through the doorway and past the kitchen window as Mrs. Hunsberger came in from the garden. She pushed the screen door open with a shove of her elbow, while carrying an apron-full of red beets with two ground-dirtied hands.

Martha had a square face and nice, wide blue eyes that, unlike her son's, were shielded by eye glasses and set under a serious brow. She managed her household in an orderly and expedient way. "Get me that bucket under there," she commanded, aiming her double chin toward the water bench. She dumped the beets into the pail after Hannah brought it, then asked her to run to the store following dinner.

Hannah washed up the baking dishes and stored the pies and cakes in the pie safe down in the cellar, then reset the table. The noon meal would be steamed apple dumplings served with chilled milk from the springhouse and sprinkled with lots of sugar and cinnamon. Sliced summer sausage on the side with freshly baked wheat bread. Jarred horseradish to relish the top.

She changed into a fresh bib apron and put on her sunbonnet. Untacking Mrs. Hunsberger's store list from the medicine cabinet door above the wash stand, she gave herself a hurried glance in the little mirror. It was set so high in the door she could barely reach on her tippy toes. She adjusted the bonnet over her braids, then counted out three silver dollars from the jelly jar on the corner cupboard shelf and put them in her apron pocket. With the market basket swinging over one arm, Hannah set out for the general store in Bern.

The sun shone warm and bright in a cloudless early afternoon sky. Hannah removed the bonnet and placed it in her basket. Without it, she could more fully absorb sunshine through her pale skin, normally very sensitive to the elements. But it was so worth the exchange for the freedom she felt as the light breeze brushed her face. A breeze that carried in it the sweet, heavy scent of cut clover drying in the meadow. South of the meadow and below the orchard, the cows lay peacefully, swishing their tails at flies and chewing their cud in a picture of contentment. Open fields and rolling hills with pleasant patches of woodland were everywhere on the horizon. "Dawdy told me once that one could find something beautiful to love everywhere one goes. I love it here!" she announced to the world. Even the river was calm and quiet as it meandered beneath the covered bridge she crossed to get to the other side. A great day to be alive!

On the far side of the river and piece-ways up the road, the store lay straight ahead. But curiosity got the best of Hannah, and she checked out a seemingly untraveled dirt lane that forked off to the right. A thicket of trees and brush barely hid a stone wall of a barn or some such that sagged haphazardly in front of an old elm tree. The only sound was the noisy chirp of a mockingbird from above.

Next to a break in the wall was an overgrown path. Hannah set her market basket down in the brown weeds, which crackled mysteriously, and climbed through the hole, carefully avoiding the mixed bramble of poison ivy and thorny blackberry vines. The brush grew even more bountifully inside. Grass, spare in spots, was long and rangy as it stretched off to a terrace of sorts. There, an unkempt garden looked strangely peopled with dark shadows from the towering locusts overhead. In the midst of this wilderness loomed a large gray house with weathered clapboard siding. Its windows were shuttered against the western sun that hovered over the trees.

Hannah thought she heard a voice coming from the house, but it was only the breeze changing direction of a rusty weather vane perched on top of the gable. Was this the old Schade place the women referred to?

"Who's there?" a voice in accented English called out from somewhere.

Hannah jumped and looked around in bewilderment at a tall, slender woman standing on the other side of the wall. She was dressed in a loose, long black skirt with a flowery bodice. Hooped golden earrings dangled brilliantly through a flowing crop of thick black hair that was topped in a silk kerchief, also flowered. From her position near the elm, Hannah saw the woman's dark eyes staring inquisitively at her out of a slightly shining face. *She's clearly not one of us*, thought Hannah. *Could this be the gypsy the women talked about?*

The woman stepped closer to the opening in the wall and said this time, "I help you?"

Hannah shook her head. *No, I was just snooping.* What she heard herself say was, "I, I don't think so ma'am. I was just on my way to the store when I saw this nice house." The house was out of her way to the store, and was hardly visible from the road. And it was hardly nice, at least not from the looks of the outside. She catapulted her body over the top of the stone fence and fumbled for her basket that now lay next to a big white sack with a red rose painted on it.

"You help, please?" asked the stranger who talked kind of funny. She appeared pensive for a moment, touching a long slim finger to her olive-complected chin. "I should not get much flour at one time. Too heavy. But I need plenty to bake." She looked at Hannah while pointing to the bag. "You help fill flour bin?"

Hannah fumbled with her basket she had just retrieved. The church women said that one should be suspicious of foreigners. Especially gypsies. "I best be going, ma'am. R-right away," Hannah stammered and walked backwards quickly before turning to go out the lane. Suddenly, she remembered something, something her father once said. It was about Jesus' parable on the Good Samaritan. Jesus would make no distinction between Pennsylvania Dutch and gypsies, now would He? When she turned around again, the dark woman was struggling with the heavy sack.

"I'm sorry, ma'am," Hannah said. "I'll help you." She jiggled the market basket up her left arm and cradled one end of the cloth bag while the woman took the other. Together, they carried the flour and let themselves into the yard through a rusty wicket gate that barely clung to its post by an iron hand. They entered the house through a set of wooden steps that led into a mudroom, then into a big square kitchen with a tall white Hoosier against one wall. A tin flour bin was in the midst of its cubicles.

"We put here," the woman said, moving toward a small end table below the window. "I fill bin later." Hannah turned to leave. "I thank you!" The woman said most pleasantly.

Hannah faced her, curtsying, then bolted for the door, but was stopped once more.

"Stay and have tea?" As the woman spoke, she took a copper tea kettle from the back of the coal oil stove and poured water into it from a hand pump in the sink. She placed the kettle back on the stove.

"Well, ma'am, I don't know now." Hannah's eyes fell upon a long crack in the spotted linoleum.

"What your name?" The woman lit a match to the burner.

"Hannah Balthaser," was whispered.

"I Ebey."

"Ebey?" Hannah repeated. She shifted her basket to the other arm while waiting for a family name, but the woman disappeared into a walk-in pantry on the far side of the kitchen. Moments later, she returned with a handful of green leaves. As the water steamed, she put the leaves into the pot. Hannah watched until Ebey caught her doing so and moved her stare back to the floor. A ladybug traveled aimlessly over the worn mat in front of the stove before it moved purposefully over the door sill and disappeared.

"We let steep. Come, Hannah. We go to parlor and get acquainted." Parlors were for notable occasions, like working on quilts or like Christmas time, funerals, or for when the preacher and his family called, or for other special company. *I must be special,* Hannah thought, as the woman led the way into the next room where it was a wee bit cooler, but not much, and dark.

"It warm last days. I close to keep sun out." All of the windows were closed, and she lifted the shades and opened the two windows on the south side of the room. A slightly wilted fern on a stand in front of the closest pane strained for sunlight that now filtered through thin lacy curtains. The air smelled musty and thick as if the room had been closed for a very long time.

In a hurried glance, Hannah noticed the room's walls were painted the color of dark moss and chipped around the shuttered windows on the far side where a highboy stood majestically between them. In the middle of the parlor, a kerosene lamp hung from the ceiling above a library table covered in colorful tapestry. A huge fancy vase held a dried flower of some sort in the center. Otherwise, furnishings were sparse except for a wingback chair and spindle rocker bordering the table.

A cat, curled in a large furry ball, snoozed in the rocking chair. Where Hannah came from, dogs and cats lived in barns or sheds, maybe underneath the porch. Only people lived in houses. As if she knew what Hannah was thinking, Ebey shooed the cat out of the rocker. Hannah jumped back. No, no, not another black cat crossing in front of her!

"Jezebel think that her chair," Ebey smiled lovingly after her pet as it disappeared. "Have seat, and I be back with tea." She left the room.

It was hot. Hannah used the hem of her clean apron she'd put on for the trip to the store and fanned her face, then removed a hairpin and used it to pick a bottom molar that harbored an irksome morsel of food her tongue discovered. How embarrassing if the nice lady saw such in her smile.

Moments later, Ebey returned with a steaming tea kettle and two matched cups and saucers and placed them on the library table. "It comfrey, brewed from herb leaves. It have wonderful mending value." Smelling vaguely of sweet lavender, Ebey bent over and poured the tea. Without further explanation on healing attributes of herbal tea, she sat down in the vacant chair across from Hannah. "Where you live, Hannah?" she asked.

Hannah sat still and cleared her throat. It was times like these that something got caught inside there and minced her words. "I, I live across the river and then some the hill over." She withdrew her moist hands from her apron pockets, folded them in her lap. There was nothing else to say.

"You still go school, Hannah?" said the lady.

"*Oi, nay,* ma'am! No, ma'am," she quickly corrected. She wasn't going to be one of those dumb Dutchmen who didn't talk English right. "I already took the examination," she said, relaxing her back to better fit the curve in the rocker.

"You try tea, yes? It good for you. Should be cool now."

"Yes, ma'am." Hannah swallowed some of the unsweetened liquid and coughed, spilling it onto her skirt and the Oriental throw rug beneath their chairs. "*Oi, nay!*" she said again. She wanted to disappear through the floor, down into the cellar, and through that floor, too.

Ebey calmly replaced her own teacup and saucer on the table and took Hannah's. "Don't worry. I clean skirt," she said.

"*Oi, nay,* ma'am! My dress makes no never mind. It's old, but I am sick for your carpet." Hannah froze to her seat as Ebey moved gracefully across the floor to the kitchen.

Ebey returned with a dish rag, and gently wiped the wet stain on Hannah's lap. Completely ignoring the spill on the floor, the woman reclaimed her seat. "You wonder where I from?" Ebey said this time. "I new here in Bern, as you see from scarce furniture. I live in America twelve year. I born in Hungary. My family come to America when I pretty young lady like you, Hannah." She looked past the wilting fern, sighed, and took a sip of tea.

Hannah bit her lower lip in concentration. She knew of Hungary from her geography book. Why, it was not so very far from the Palatinate region of Germany where her many great *grossdawdy* Balthasers came from. She searched for the words to tell Ebey this, but they were quickly lost when the clock on the mantle chimed three.

"I thank you for the tea, ma'am. I must go fetch yet some stuff at the store, and I have to fix the supper right quick before the men come home from the fields." She rose to leave but not until a statue on the side wall caught her attention. Ebey stood, too.

"It called Crucifix," said Ebey, placing a warm hand on Hannah's shoulder.

Together, they advanced toward the hanging object for closer inspection. The Lord's bloodshot eyes penetrated down into Hannah's from a thorn-encircled face, a face that seemed to reflect her own suffering and pain of the last several months. All she could think of as she stared back at the wooden figure was her father's story of Jesus on the cross and how Jesus had asked His Father why He forsook Him. She couldn't remember God's answer and barely heard Ebey inviting her to drop by again, soon.

"Soon" was a couple of weeks later. On a Sunday afternoon after visiting her mother for the first time, Hannah went out of her way to pass Ebey's on return. The shutters were still closed in the big gray house. The place looked deserted, except for Jezebel sleeping on the outside step. That was okay. She didn't know what to say to the lady anyway.

CHAPTER 6

June, July, August were busy times on the Hunsberger farm. The garden work continued in earnest. The endive and spinach plants, now browned and exhausted from the hot summer weather, were pulled and thrown into the chicken coops of which there were three. In that space, Hannah and Mrs. Hunsberger planted a second crop of peas and shelled and canned the first crop. They weeded and hoed onions, pinched off the tops to keep them from sprouting, and snatched the monstrous green horny worms from the ripening tomato plants and bugs from the string beans and deposited them into kerosene.

Lima bean plants were limed, and yellow gage plums and bull's eye cherries picked, washed, and cooked into jams and jellies and, what was left over, jarred for fruit salads come next winter. Sweet corn was husked, cut, cooked, and canned. Maiden's Blush apples, the first in the season to ripen in the orchard, were carried by the basketsful to the summerhouse kitchen. Later, jar after jar of golden applesauce lined the shelves next to the canned pears, peaches, and vegetables on the stone wall inside the ground cellar.

On days when the gardening was caught after and Mrs. Hunsberger was off helping the men in the fields, which she often did, Hannah tended to the flowers. Hannah loved flowers. There were varieties of colorful plants spread in beds beneath trees and alongside walkways. Roses climbed up and down trellises alongside the washhouse. Rows of hollyhocks of every size and color grew inside and outside the garden wall. Above the garden and next to the grape arbor flourished bush after bush of peonies—pink, lavender, and white that bloomed until the middle of June. A bed of bachelor's buttons, snapdragons, and dusty millers bordered the front porch, and, later small

45

crimson, blue and gold delphiniums and asters of every shade in the rainbow popped up. Lamb's wool brightened the wooden walkways from there to the summerhouse and the smokehouse where more red roses climbed the brick walls, competing for light and space with the English Ivy.

Hannah was not at all fond of hoeing and weeding vegetables, but pulling weeds to free the flowers was "Count it all Joy" to use one of her father's favorite expressions from the Bible. Her father said weeds that encroached upon beautiful flowers were likened to the devil trying to smother the soul. Dawdy often spoke of how beautiful the Garden of Eden was before sin came and the weeds took over. "Soon, Hannah," he said one day as they walked through the woods—the violets in full bloom and trees in foliage, "soon, mind you, there will be another Garden of Eden. It will be a place of such beauty that nothing bad can ever be present. No weeds, no bugs, no dead leaves. Maybe no snakes." He looked down at her and grinned when he said snakes. She hated snakes. "There will never be any sickness or death of any kind. God's presence will be so bright there will be no need even for sun, yet the flowers will grow, living on and on and never die." She hoped Dawdy was right. Life on earth could sure use some improvement.

The men were busy, too. The corn was cultivated for the second time and missing stalks replanted. They cut the first crop of alfalfa, timothy, and orchard grass. Dried, raked, loaded, and hauled it by wagon loads into the big red barn. Everywhere grain stood straight and ripe. Barley and oats harvested in July, wheat in August.

"I walked to the back woods field yesterday and the heads on that wheat are ready," Samuel said one morning at breakfast.

"*Yah*, Sam, you have to start today," said the old man, accenting the word "have" as he dipped his bread into the sausage gravy bowl. A generous portion of it tracked back to his mouth. "*Dunawetterl!*"

he swore, spitting out both breakfast and dentures. He frowned at his plate, then slipped the teeth back in and squinted at Hannah under bushy eyebrows. Pap didn't believe in eye glasses. "Why didn't you warn me that was hot?" he barked. Everyone ignored Pap like they usually did.

Mordacai Hunsberger, 69, was Samuel's father and, in his mind, still in charge of the farm, Hannah observed. And perhaps physically able, too, if it weren't for a bad limp he suffered since falling off of the hay wagon ten years before. His right leg had broken and was never reset, making it difficult to help with the farming ever since. Yet, it was no trouble climbing up into the buckboard to join Sam and Jonathan to the store weekday nights to play cards.

Overall, age was catching up to Pap. He was hard of hearing, selectively so, the family concluded, and always asked "*Wos?*" (What?) whenever someone spoke to him. But his long-term memory was excellent. If someone asked what he ate for breakfast that morning, he couldn't recall. But he remembered clearly events that occurred years ago. When he laughed, which wasn't often, he pushed air out of his mouth in "puh," pinching stale air through his lips as he did so.

Pap was born in 1847 and started farming for himself on the farm handed down from his father. Consistent with Pennsylvania German tradition, he'd pass the farm onto his youngest son, Samuel. When Samuel and Martha married, they moved into the big house, and Pap and the missus moved into the *grossdawdy's haus* (grandfather's house) next door. Two years before Hannah's arrival, Eleanor died of *wasser sucht* (water over the heart), and Pap moved back into the big house with Samuel's family. The *grossdawdy's haus*, or summerhouse as it was later called, was used only for canning and butchering from then on.

Pap, in spite of transitions, maintained his position as homestead boss and claimed that no one could farm like he did. Hannah frequently heard him complain that Samuel couldn't plow half as straight a furrow as he did. Martha couldn't cook at all like his

Eleanor. Jonathan didn't get the right training for handling horses, "…even though he thinks he's good with them…" Warren, the hired man, was only wasting Samuel's hard-earned money. So was Hannah…. "My Eleanor raised seven boys and helped in the milk house besides and didn't need no maid," Hannah heard him say one time when she was polishing the china closet in the next room.

Samuel wiped his mouth on his rolled-up shirt sleeve, pushed his chair back from the table, and rose. "Warren, harness up King and Prince and meet me behind the barn, and we'll pull the binder out of the old shed."

Jonathan's father was tall and clean shaven, a lean and industrious man, given to bursts of vigorous activity around their productive and well-kept farm. Hannah suspected that much of Mr. Hunsberger's energy was to prove to Pap that he was just as successful a farmer as he had been in his hay day. Normally a soft-spoken man with quiet authority, Samuel did on occasion explode when something went awry. There was the time just a while back when Hannah heard a string of biblical names drifting from behind the chicken house, including such words she doubted even a preacher used. She was hoeing onions in the garden at the time, and Froch Een, his tail tucked tightly between his hind legs, jumped clear over the picket fence by the lane, immediately seeking refuge by her side in the garden. She guessed he'd been chasing chickens. Again.

Samuel grabbed his hat off the wall peg by the front door. "Coming?" he said to the others at the table.

"I'll be right along after Mom and I finish milking," said Jonathan. He tilted his saucer and slurped the coffee that had slopped into it and left the table. Warren stood, too, to leave.

Hannah announced that she'd bring peppermint water out to the fields, since it promised to be a sweltering hot day. "But not until after dinner," she said. "Can you hear the bell from the back field when I ring?"

"*Nay*, we can't, but the horses can. You can bet they'll let us know!" said Jonathan, putting on his straw hat. He told her before there was no sense trying to go around the field once more because the horses would trample down everything in their haste to get to the barn once they heard the bell. It was their dinnertime, too. Jonathan winked at Hannah and nodded toward his grandfather's back, "Don't ring, though, until dinner's cooled off."

Hannah got it and smiled. That's all she managed to do when Jonathan looked at her.

After everyone left, Hannah set about removing the dirty dishes but was careful not to take the leftovers until Pap was finished. Pap stayed at the table until good and ready.

"*Yah*, wheat shoulda started a week ago," he mumbled, as he sponged his plate with an end crust of bread. "Now when I was farming yet I had all the wheat cut and shocked by this time." He finished, struggled to his feet and grabbed the cane hanging on the back of his chair. "Mind you, it's gonna rain. I can feel it in my bones." Pap limped his way out of the house.

———————

Mid-afternoon, Hannah set forth across the fields. She took a shortcut through the orchard and walked up the slope, then through rows of corn before coming to a field of stubbles that were left behind where the binder cut through. A wagon and horses were at the far end of the field. A figure leaning forward thoughtfully on a pitchfork grew larger. At first she saw her father, but as she drew closer, it was Jonathan. When Jonathan saw her, he stuck the pitchfork into the ground and walked slowly toward her, all the while wiping his face and neck with a big red handkerchief. It sure was a hot sticky day.

"You're like an angel, Hannah Balthaser. *Yah, Gawiss!*" Jonathan said, relieving her of the bucket. "Come now, we sit ourselves awhile." At his invitation, they both sat in the shade of the wagon that was almost fully loaded with wheat sheaves. Jonathan smelled of horses and dirt and sweat, but sweet nonetheless. He helped himself to the peppermint water that had been chilled by the dwindling ice buried in wood shavings in the *kelterhouse* on the north side of the old shed.

"Ahhhh, that makes cool and wet!" he said after gulping down the first dipperful. "Hey, the horses need this rest as much as I do, because it sure is hot!" he added as if to justify his break. He wiped his face and neck again, and pushed back a damp lock of hair with the brim of his straw hat.

"Appeared like you were already resting onct I come up here!" said Hannah. She broke into a giggle and flashed a bright smile in his direction. Butterflies fluttered.

"*Ach*, now, Hannah, I was just thinking how I should load the last row on top so the wagon wouldn't throw over the lane all the sheaves."

The lane was full of stones and washed-out gutters. More than once, she heard at supper how a wagonload of something or other had upset from the bumpy drive coming off the hill.

Jonathan looked down, blinking at her brooch. Small yellow chaffs of wheat fluttered in his sun-bleached lashes.

"Mom never wears pins except on her Sunday best, or if she's expecting the preacher for dinner, but I see you wear one all the time. It's wonderful nice, but aren't you afraid you lose it?"

"*Nay*, I better not! It was my granny's and her granny's before her and yet even further back than that yet. Granny Moyer gave it to my father, and he gave me it just before he died so it stays in the family." She'd mentioned briefly about her father's death while she helped Jonathan pick up fallen crab apples in the orchard, and they'd got talking.

"I thought you said your father died quick. Then how comes he knew to give it to you just before he died?"

Hannah tensed. She wasn't the only one who questioned a coincidence. "I guess he just knew it was time to give it to me. It has a superstition attached to it, that's why." She was sinking deeper.

"Superstition?" Jonathan's eyes sparkled with amusement. He reached into his pocket, withdrew his pipe and stuffed it with tobacco from a Standard Clippings pouch. He lit a torch into the bowl, sucked hard on the stem and let loose a cloud of smoke. "What kind of superstition?"

Hannah thought about the supposed special powers that Granny mentioned the brooch held. She said, "It's queer what things one remembers and what things one forgets." She picked herself up off the ground, smoothed out her cotton dress and apron, and picked up the water bucket. A team of horses pulling the binder around the east end of the field came into view. "It's time to serve the others some cool drink now." As she walked away, she heard Jonathan clucking to his horses to move ahead. Jonathan had a way with horses!

That night Hannah reread her father's entry in the journal about the evening he presented the brooch. Then, for some odd reason or other immediately dismissed thoughts of anything but coincidence. After all, how could he possibly have known what the future held for him and that he'd be gone two days after he put that brooch in his pocket? Yet, Dawdy did seem to have conversations with God, something she could not and would never understand. She reread Dawdy's entry and recorded one of her own.

Not sure of the date, she wrote:

> "*Summer 1916: It wonders me what Jonathan would think if he knew I was not old enough for boys. Dawdy said young people should give themselves to the Lord in Confirmation before thinking of marriage. Goodness knows, I have over a year yet before I can even attend Catechetical Class. It matters not much anyway. Jonathan doesn't even know I'm around. He goes puffing on that stubby pipe of his and acting big all the time. And, well, too, there's Mary.*"

CHAPTER 7

Pap was right. A steady land rain came in from the east toward the middle of the following week, which was welcomed for the growing corn and second crop of alfalfa. The rainy weather came at a good time. It was right after all the wheat was bindered and stacked and covered behind the barn, ready for thrashing sometime soon. The ground was too wet for plowing the wheat stubbles under, so the men did maintenance on implements, repaired harnesses, and manured out the pig stable and chicken coops. When it wasn't actually raining, they mended fences and trimmed fence and fence corners with the German scythe.

Hannah and Mrs. Hunsberger, too, had plenty of work during rainy weather. Carrots, cucumbers, celery, and lima and green beans had already been picked and in baskets down in the ground floor arch outside in the yard. Onions were drying on the loft over the pig stable. Only sweet red and green peppers awaited picking for chow chow, but that was easy enough between rain showers. While she cleaned and chopped the vegetables, Hannah asked out of the clear blue what a Crucifix was, but Mrs. Hunsberger simply looked up and repeated the question, going on with slicing corn off the cob like she never heard. But Pap, napping on the couch, did. He gave a short laugh, but there wasn't any humor in it.

"I'll bet the girl's been hanging with those Catholics down the river," he grumbled.

Hannah continued scraping carrots, diced them with the fancy slicer, and filled the crock with cool water, then grabbed a basket to pick the peppers in the garden. When she returned, a cricket leaped over the threshold and into the kitchen. In a panic, Hannah dropped the basket and plunged after the insect as it hop-scotched across the floor.

Pap yelled, "Shut the door! You let the flies in!"

I will as soon as I chase this darn thing back out, Hannah replied in her thoughts. *Don't you know a cricket indoors is a sign of death?*

Mrs. Hunsberger was assembling ingredients for pickling. "Oh, *shupkarrich* (wheelbarrow)!" That was the closest Mrs. Hunsberger came to using barnyard language. "We don't have enough alum. *Yumma Yay!*" she added, giving her dilemma more emphasis. "I guess it will just have to do. We're in the middle of this now."

"I can fetch some at the store," Hannah offered as she closed the screen door. She'd given up on the little critter. "I'll be quick." The store was only a mile or so away and across the river.

"*Gute.* I'll do the peppers and start cooking some of these things until you get back. And better pick up more mustard seed, too. And an extra box of jar lids and rubber rings while you're there. They won't go to waste if we don't need them all today. And why don't you get...oh, never you mind, I'll write all this stuff down so you don't forget." She wiped her hands on her apron and hurriedly penciled the items on the back of last month's calendar sheet.

Froch Een scattered the ducks splashing in the wagon ruts that had become miniature ponds in the lane. He then retreated and Hannah continued toward the store. Almost before she knew it, she crossed the river through the covered bridge and came to the fork in the road that led to the old Schade place.

At the path's entrance, she carefully pulled aside wet, thorny blackberry vines to see whether the woman who had called her a pretty young lady was anywhere about. No one ever called her pretty before. Growing up, she was teased by Ralph about her red hair and that she should wash her face with water collected from a tombstone to rid herself of freckles, said he'd heard that works, then he'd laugh. Billy even called her plump. How she cried. But now, upon recent examination, she seemed thinner. And taller. After all, she was still growing, not too much though she hoped. When she was little, Billy made her lay flat on the ground while he walked over the top, saying that now her growth would be stunted. Her cheeks were no longer so chubby, and her hair most definitely was darkening.

With her free hand, Hannah twisted unconsciously at her braids. A dark figure from the front doorstep saw her and motioned her in.

"*Oi, Nay*, ma'am. No!" Hannah protested as Ebey reached for the wet umbrella.

"Hannah? What wrong?"

"It's bad luck!"

"Bad luck? What bad luck?"

"The open *bumperchute*."

Ebey laughed. "I no understand."

"It's bad luck to have a *bumperchute* open in the house. The umbrella," she corrected. This time Ebey didn't laugh and folded the umbrella, propping it against the closed door. She invited Hannah to sit in the same spindle rocker she sat in last visit. She had just made tea and how nice it would be to have someone as nice as Hannah to share it with. The room was stifling and sticky, and the steaming hot tea made the air even more humid as they once more sat across from each other in Ebey's parlor.

"Hannah, how you been? I no see you good while."

"We're very busy on the farm."

"You live on farm?"

"Why, yes. I live with the Hunsbergers."

"Who the Hunsbergers, Hannah? You told me name is Balthaser."

"I help the Hunsbergers. I'm their maid."

"I understand you people do that here," Ebey said, nonchalantly. She sipped her tea and gracefully returned the cup to its saucer on the table. "I mean work as hired help on farm to earn living."

"Why, *yah*," Hannah agreed, losing some of her earlier timidity. "My brothers Billy and Ralph are also farmed out. We're helping my Ma out. She's very busy with my younger brothers and can't work out herself." Hannah swallowed some of the bitter tea to please her hostess and went on, surprised how talkative she'd become. "But not my sister Ellie, she's married, and Margaret, well, she don't help none neither. Took off with a pots and pans salesman onct and never came back. They said she was in trouble." She couldn't believe she said that. She didn't even know what that meant.

"The Hunsbergers. Tell me. They big family?" Ebey asked in an interested voice.

Hannah hesitated, and shook her head, drawing in her lower lip. "Why, no. Not big a'tall. There's just the Mister, and there's Mrs. Hunsberger and their son Jonathan and his grandpa. There's also Warren. He's the hired man." She paused and reached for her tea but drew back. "Mrs. Hunsberger says there's too much work. They shoulda had more boys to help the mister in the fields." She observed her worn buttoned shoes performing semi-circles on the faded Oriental rug that still had the stain from spilled tea. She lined up her toes, then smoothed out the carpet and added, "Mrs. Hunsberger, she says it just never happened." Heat crawled up one side of her neck and down the other.

"This Jonathan. What he like?" the woman asked this time.

Hannah looked back down, contemplating an answer and nervously fingered her amethyst brooch. Even in the faint kerosene light, the crystal sparkled in various shades of lilac, purple, and gold like the stained-glass window in the church where the Hunsbergers went.

Ebey noticed and asked, "You have pretty jewel. You wear each time you come. It have special meaning?"

Hannah was relieved she didn't have to answer the question about Jonathan and only too happy to switch the topic.

"I wear it every day since my father gave it to me. It's a family legacy, handed down from generation to generation on Dawdy's side."

She paused, then slowly continued, "My granny said it has special powers."

"Special powers?"

Hannah wished she hadn't mentioned that. After all, Dawdy didn't believe in the special power thing. He said its sole value is that it's a family heirloom. To own and to wear and to hand down to the next in line. A beautiful stone to be worn and admired, but just a stone.

"I'm not sure what Granny meant," said Hannah, hoping to drop this subject as well. The blood rushed to her already warmed face, and she wiped the moisture forming above her lips with a hand-kerchief.

Ebey seemed not to notice and this time asked, "How old Jonathan?"

"Sixteen, seventeen. Maybe eighteen, I'm not sure," she answered, *rutching* forward in her uncushioned seat.

"Aw," Ebey said softly, gazing toward a spot on the wall as if re-membering. "I have how you say, suitor, when I eighteen. His name Johnny Todt. He older. And charming as you Americans put. I not give up until he marry me." Tiredness crept into her voice. Her dark eyes grew small, and a little wrinkled strain formed between them and her brow. "You never mention father, Hannah. What he do? He farmer, too?" She took a sip of tea.

Hannah set down her cup and looked out the window where the curtain was slightly drawn. A ray of sunshine strained to penetrate the heavy clouds. A song sparrow, landing on an oak branch, show-ered a mist of rainwater over the unsuspecting turf below.

"Ma'am, it stopped raining. I best be going," she said, standing up.

"Please call me Ebey. We friends now, and friends call each other by first name, yes?" Ebey opened the front door and handed Hannah the folded umbrella. Hannah thanked her for the tea, said goodbye, and headed out the path. She heard Ebey call out after her, "You have chickens on farm? I buy fresh eggs."

Rainy weather continued into Saturday. The garden was too wet to work so Mrs. Hunsberger helped Hannah with the cleaning. After sweeping and scrubbing the house from top to bottom, they set about making dinner. Earlier, old man Bagemstose came racing past the farm with his Buick touring car and hit a White Leghorn. Today the menu would be Chicken *Boi Boi.* Pot pie was Jonathan's favorite meal. Not to Hannah's liking, however, was the task of cleaning chickens.

"We must do this to make it bleed proper," Mrs. Hunsberger said as she placed the head of the injured chicken between two nails on a wood block she had set up out in the middle of the dirt driveway. She swung the hatchet with the accuracy of a practiced lumberjack. The chicken, still having some life in it, flopped aimlessly around the driveway *spritzing* bright red blood toward its retreating assailant. "Now fetch me a bucket of hot water quick."

Gladly, thought Hannah, *I'm more than happy to depart from this awful scene.* On her way to the house, Hannah noticed Jonathan crouching against the pump house wall, holding Froch Een by the collar. In spite of leaving one paw behind in a muskrat trap, the dog was still a menace to anything of a lesser nature that moved about the driveway.

Jonathan laughed then said, "You looked awful funny standing there with your face in your hands. I thought Mom was trying to show you how it's done."

"Seems to me, Jonathan Hunsberger, you weren't watching either one time when you shoulda," she hissed in return.

"Then we're even?"

"Even!" Hannah drew herself to full height and, passing him without missing a step, went to the house for the water boiling on the kitchen cook stove. When she returned, both Jonathan and the dog were gone.

Hannah helped Mrs. Hunsberger pluck the feathers, poke out the stubbles, and reluctantly gut the innards, then they stuck the bird back into the hot boiling water. While things simmered, Hannah stood by the table and followed Mrs. Hunsberger's directions in making the noodle dough, a task she much preferred over the former. Flour, a little shortening. Water. Eggs. She decided that maybe now was as good a time as any.

"You mentioned the hens are laying heavy right now. Why not sell eggs to Keimey?" She rolled out a thin sheet of dough on the floured oilcloth, spun it around carefully, and rolled again from the other direction. She was getting good at this. "Says he has some new customers at the store," she lied, and looked over at Mrs. Hunsberger. She was slicing strips of noodle from the one sheet of dough. Hannah guessed from her expression that she wasn't listening. She had several excuses lined up just in case she met with resistance, and, this time, said, "I could easily carry eggs along in my basket when I go to the store. It would be no trouble."

"*Yah, Yah. Gute.*" Mrs. Hunsberger made an impatient gesture toward Hannah and added the squares of dough to the pot. She wiped her sticky hands on the bib of her apron. "Now some parsley and onions yet, and you can clean up this mess while I peel potatoes."

That evening at supper, Hannah was proud to serve the pot pie. When she went to place the big bowl in the middle of the table, she accidentally tipped it. The hot fatty broth dripped generously down Jonathan's neck and right shoulder.

"*Ai du sztu schtann!*" Jonathan said, jumping up and pulling back his chair. He added quickly, "It's alright, Hannah. It was getting chilly in here anyway." He winked and pulled his chair back into place.

Pap wagged his fork at the air and said, "Now look what the girl's done! Never does nothing right!"

Hannah blinked back tears that threatened to come and went to the dry sink for a dish rag. Afterward, Jonathan stayed on to talk to her when she shelled lima beans out on the porch glider.

"Whatcha doing?" Jonathan asked, hoisting himself up on the railing. He propped his body against the post and planted one foot on the banister while the other reached down to the floor. He pulled his pouch of tobacco from a back pocket. With the other hand he dumped the contents of his ridiculous pipe over the railing and scooped the pipe into the pouch for more.

Hannah thought, *you can easily enough see what I'm doing. I can certainly see what you're doing.* "I'm shelling lima beans for vegetable soup," she said. "We're doing up vegetable soup tomorrow in jars."

"Oh, that means we're having vegetable soup for dinner tomorrow." Even in the dusk, she could see his brilliant blue eyes gradually dim as he spoke.

"I take it you don't like vegetable soup."

He shrugged. "Mom always made me eat it. From little on up. Said it would make me grow fast."

"Well, did you?" she asked, not knowing what else to say, but guessing soup might work better than pipe smoking.

"I guess so," he said without much interest.

Out of the corner of her eyes, Hannah noticed him sucking and puffing while looking into the twilight, his six-foot frame silhouetted against the gray dusked horizon. A mourning dove cooed from somewhere and a heifer called longingly from the back pasture to its first calf that was stalled in the barn.

"Sure is sticky this evening. Hope the weather clears up soon so's we can get on with the thrashing." He swatted at a mosquito on his neck. They were bad.

"I thought all the grain was in?" Hannah knew little of farming except for her day-by-day experiences at the Hunsbergers. When she was little, they lived on a small farm for a short while. It was a one-horse farm. At least that's what she overhead Mem call it, screaming at Dawdy after the landlord left one night. "...You can't even make a living for us on this one-horse farm...." She could never figure out for the life of her why Mem called it that. They didn't even have a horse. Only some chickens, two pigs and a goat. And her father never thrashed that she knew of.

"*Yah*, it is, but now it has to be thrashed. That big stack of wheat behind the barn and the one of oats behind it, that all has to go through the thrash machine yet. The machine shakes out the heads of the grain into bags, which we haul into the granary, and it blows the straw up into the mow." He looked down at her and smiled. "Don't worry, you'll know soon enough. The neighbors all get together and go from farm to farm until everyone is done with the harvest. You'll be plenty busy cooking for fifteen people when that happens here."

The evening was quiet except for the cicadas. It was August, and the locusts were in full chorus. Hannah watched her busy hands snapping the plump white beans from their green pods while her rehearsed speech, thick and stupid, stuck in her throat.

"I'm sorry I spilled the pot pie all over you at supper," she finally said. She was so *doppich*, but now she felt the better for apologizing. Jonathan swung himself off the porch railing. He reached down, petted Froch Een who had parked between them, and disappeared behind the screen door.

That's it? Not even an, oh, never you mind, it didn't matter none?

CHAPTER 8

It was Sunday. Hannah went to the Smoke Church with the Hunsbergers as usual. But what wasn't as usual was the way they'd get there. Normally the six of them, including Warren, went to church in two conveyances since they didn't all fit in one. Today, Warren and Pap weren't going so the Mister and Missus and Jonathan and Hannah were privileged to drive Pap's three-door Ford Model T—Tin Lizzie they called it—with Samuel at the wheel. Hannah had never been in a road machine before. How exciting was this!

She was dressed in her best for this special occasion. The freshly ironed paisley dress and green jumper and the pretty pink banded straw hat. She sat in the rear seat next to Jonathan who was dressed in a dark brown suit and white shirt with a celluloid collar. Earlier, she heard him grumbling in the house that he couldn't find his collar button, but noticed now that he had it on. His trousers ended slightly above his white socks, and his black Sunday shoes kept time on the floor boards to the engine's putt putt putt as they rattled over the bumpy road.

On the way, Jonathan explained to Hannah how the Smoke Church got its name. "When the first settlers came here, there were still a lot of Indians living back there." He pointed toward the Blue Mountains on the north horizon. "One Sunday morning the Indians came down and, when the people were inside singing, they set fire to the log church."

"*Ach*, how awful!"

"That's just one story. Another one is that the sexton who farmed the property and took care of the church itself fired up the stove one Sunday morning but forgot to open the flue. When the peo-

63

ple came for church, they held services outside in the cold cause there was smoke like everything inside." He sucked on his pipe, thoughtfully. Short gray vapors of smoke puffed into the air before disappearing behind them. "Pap says that none of those is so. The Smoke Church got its name because it had a side room where the men would go to smoke when the preaching got too long. No one will ever know the real truth, I guess." With a thumb, he smothered the warm tobacco in his pipe and stuck it in his vest pocket just as they pulled into an open area where other machines were parked.

The Smoke Church was a union church—Lutheran services one week and German Reformed the next. Mr. Hunsberger was a confirmed Lutheran member and Mrs. Hunsberger, Reformed, hence, the family went each Sunday. Hannah wondered which one of these two denominations Jonathan joined. After all, he was surely confirmed by now?

Today was Lutheran. It was also Harvest Home. Members of the congregation brought their nicest fruits and vegetables—fresh and canned, cured summer sausages and smoked hams left over from last winter's butchering. Eggs and recently cooked applebutter. Jugs of cider pressed at the local cider mill were also displayed on the table up front. It was a well-known fact that cider was the *parrah's* favorite beverage. Especially the hard cider kind that was frequently offered when he visited folks of his congregation.

Those who didn't farm displayed store-bought goods such as salt, sugar, and flour. Or they brought loaves of bread and other home-baked goodies including a wide assortment of fruit pies. Everyone had fruit trees on their property. Following the service, the Reverend Benjamin Schweitzer took the produce home to his own pantry to supplement his meager wages.

Smoke Church was only one of the good minister's charges. He preached there every other week at a late service, coming directly from the Kissinger Church several miles distant. Alternate Sundays, he preached at Beckeman's and in Geigertown, and twice a month he held afternoon services up country. For all his activity, he was not a slight man. Jonathan told Hannah one time that people said the *parrah* could eat the produce from five Harvest Home celebrations within a month's time and have none left over to preserve for winter. But that was only hearsay. He was a single man, and the church women took turns preserving things and keeping him in baked goods. Sundays and holidays, he ate dinner with whomever invited him. One always wondered what the preacher ate the rest of the time though it never appeared he was starving. Nor did his stained shirt fronts attest otherwise.

Not only was the Reverend's stature large as a result of his voracious appetite, but also his voice box. Folks said that one didn't have to come to church when the *Parrah* Schweitzer preached. They need only sit on their front porches and watch and listen for the fire and brimstone that bounced off the long, stained-glass window panel.

Today, he asked the Lord's blessing over the fruits of the harvest and went directly to his favorite topic. "Sin!" he thundered in *Deutsch*. "It's sin that's brought you here today, for without sin you wouldn't need to come to church. The serpent tempted Adam and Eve to eat of the forbidden fruit in the Garden of Eden, and, hence, man fell from the grace of God. Now it's damnation for each of you when you break even one of His Commandments....!" He leaned over the pulpit and pointed an index finger, waving it back and forth across the tense congregation below, all the while shouting so emphatically the candles on the overhead chandelier sputtered. Two blew out.

Hannah was sure he spoke directly to her. She had uttered some swear words last Monday. She couldn't help it. *"Heilicha Dunawetter!"* (Holy Thunder Weather) spewed out of her mouth when boiling hot wash water *spritzed* her arm.

———————————

If they weren't expecting company, Mrs. Hunsberger napped on Sunday afternoons. Hannah was free to go home, though she seldom did. Sometimes she went for short walks. Sometimes she just doodled. Today, she picked up her father's Bible. Holding it close to the window, which was the only illumination one had indoors during the day, she searched diligently for the Ten Commandments. She had never heard all ten in sequence like the minister put it that morning. Maybe because they rarely went to church while she was growing up. Mem always said church was too far to walk no matter how close they lived to one at the time. She said it was because Dawdy didn't provide. "If he'd spend as much time working as he does dreaming and *putzing* around, we'd have a horse and buggy like normal people and go to church."

Dawdy, it certainly wasn't that he downed religion. He said the Lord created Heaven and earth in six days and rested on the seventh. Church or no, that's exactly what he did. Mem said he just used that as an excuse not to work. But in spite of her constant bickering, Dawdy faithfully, morning or afternoon, rain or shine, winter or summer, took a nature walk on the Sabbath where he could be "closer to God."

Often Hannah accompanied Dawdy on these walks, like through the woods or across the fields or along the canal towpath. On these excursions, she learned about God and Jesus, and how Jesus loves all the children and the beasts of the field, the birds, the bees, the trees. The flowers. And that God forgives each one of us if we ask for forgiveness, no matter how much we sinned. This was puzzling to Hannah, but Dawdy taught school for three years before she was born, so everything he said must be so. And yet? It always came back to the same questions she had about Dawdy's leaving so soon. For now, though, she'd focus on the minister's sermon.

Following a frustrated search, Hannah found the Ten Commandments in the Book of Exodus, Chapter 20. After reading, it appeared she was innocent of sin except for swearing the other day. That is until she came to the Fifth one that said: "....honour thy father and thy mother that thy days may be long upon the land which the Lord thy God giveth thee." This was perplexing. Hannah was quite familiar with this particular commandment while growing up, hearing it repeatedly from Mem. Only, she noticed now her mother eliminated the father part. It was always after she'd been bad, which was often. She never brought in enough kindling with the wood when she filled the wood box and her fault the fire went out. Or, she dumped the ashes in the wrong place out on the bank, or there were streaks on the floor after scrubbing. The babies' diapers weren't washed properly. Once she was locked in the attic as a rebuke.

She was eight. It happened on one of those long hot, humid evenings when Dawdy hadn't come home yet from his job on the railroad where he worked at the time. She misjudged the time for the wild strawberry jelly to finish and burnt the pot, ruining both jelly and pot but good. Mem went into a rage and sent her up to the attic to get another pot that was stored in a chest of unused wedding gifts. By the faint light of the evening sky through a little window in the eves, she found the chest and retrieved the new pot. But when she came back down, the door at the bottom of the closed stairway was locked. She was certain it was accidental. But when no one answered her shouts, she knew the door was locked on purpose.

Later that night, left weak and trembling in the darkness, she heard her parents' voices rise and fall, rise and fall. Their bickering kept her alert far into the night. Then a handle turned and a light appeared at the bottom of the steps. She didn't recall what happened, except the next morning she awoke in her bed she shared with Levi. There was never a mention by anyone. Maybe it was just a dream?

Hannah took a fourth steaming hot kettle from the wood furnace in the corner of the washhouse and poured the water into the galvanized wash tub on top of the wooden bench. She threw in several chips of homemade lye soap and hand swished to make sure everything was spread around. Mrs. Hunsberger laid a reed basket filled with dirty and grease-stained clothes alongside, clothes that in better days were worn for church and now condemned to work. All the while, she grumbled it was high time Jonathan found himself a wife. After all, she didn't wish to go on farming forever.

Mrs. Hunsberger's flair of romance had long been gone, Hannah decided, if, indeed, it had ever been there to begin with, but her own interest quickly peaked when Mrs. Hunsberger went on.

"I believe, though, he might like that oldest Hepner girl, the one he was confirmed with last year." *Confirmed? I guess that puts a period where once a question mark had been,* thought Hannah. The woman took a pair of Jonathan's overalls from on top of the pile. Following close inspection, she hand-scrubbed the greasy spots on the glass washboard and then slipped them into the washer with the rest of the dirty clothes while Hannah turned the washer wheel. "She'd make a good wife," she added. "The Hepners are hard workers."

Hannah was afraid that maybe Jonathan might think so, too. Yesterday in church, she turned around and looked up at the balcony. Jonathan was staring at Mary Hepner in the choir loft instead of keeping his eyes on the pulpit like he should've. And then there was the Sunday School picnic in Cleaver's Grove. Hannah was still unacquainted with others her age at the Smoke Church and ended up hanging around with the older women and helped in the cleaning up. Yet, she was well aware of the young folk's goings-on.

The boys pitched horse shoes while the girls played croquet or some such. Then the clumsy Miss Hepner tripped over a ball and twisted her delicate little ankle. There she was, prettily stretched out on the grass with all the boys standing around offering to help. It was Jonathan who received the honor. His strong arms picked up the damsel in distress and deposited her on a wooden picnic bench. Hannah wondered if Mary felt all tingly inside like she felt when Jonathan touched her. They sat on the bench at least fifteen minutes before rejoining the rest of the gang, all the while leaving Hannah curious as to what they talked about. Did Jonathan notice her tooth with the chicklet patch?

Well, for now, Hannah decided to dismiss all thoughts of the prissy Princess Miss Mary and get on with the washing of Prince Charming's dirty clothes.

Warren came into the washhouse to fetch Mrs. Hunsberger. "The mister wants you to help with the spraying while the weather's holding."

"*Yah*, I think," was what Mrs. Hunsberger replied and shook out wet hands and wiped them on her apron. She told Hannah to wrap things up, not to forget to go to the store after the wash was wrung and hung. Mrs. Hunsberger followed the hired man out the door.

Hannah pulled an express wagon that had been Jonathan's when he was little. In it was a basket with two dozen white eggs and one dozen brown. She walked up to Ebey's door, but there was no sign of life at the big gray house except for Jezebel sunning on the doorstep. She knocked and waited and knocked some more, then slowly continued to the store.

The overly warm store reeked of leather and kerosene and stale pipe smoke left over from the card games played nightly in the barbershop down back. As usual, Keimey was warm and congenial.

"Hey, what have we got here, young lady?" he said, slapping his baggy thighs when Hannah set her basket of eggs on the counter. She asked if he could use them. "You bet I can! These'll come in handy. I have some new customers, and they eat me out of house and eggs." He laughed at that and counted out sixty cents from the cash register, while Hannah transplanted the eggs into a crate setting on the bench in front of the counter. She put the coins in her left apron pocket, and took Mrs. Hunsberger's money from the other pocket and placed it on the counter. "Now, what else can I do for you today?" he asked.

"They're coming to thrash next week so we're going to be doing a lot more baking than usual. I'll be needing sugar, salt and," she checked Mrs. Hunsberger's list, "about a quarter pound of raisins if you have them and...."

"Raisins? Did someone die?" It was the way of the Pennsylvania Dutch to serve funeral pie in the home after a loved one's burial. Hannah didn't know what Mrs. Hunsberger's plans were for the raisins. But no one died that she knew of.

"Oh, I almost forgot, we need molasses, too." She hadn't forgotten. It's just that it wasn't on the list. Hannah handed over the empty kettle she'd brought along, then selected chicklets from the globe on the counter. She liked the green-covered ones best. They held the flavor the longest after she packed her tooth. She had a decayed hole in one of her lower molars that she was certain showed black whenever she smiled, and a gum patch worked quite well to conceal it, thank you, Mary Hepner. It stuck in the cavity for a day or so, sometimes three, before having to be replaced. She kept chicklets on hand for Sundays and for when company visited the farm.

Hannah smiled fondly as she watched Keimey dig down deep with his dipper into the molasses barrel. He reminded her of the polar bear in her geography book. He had a small peaked head capped with unruly white hair. His girth was wide at the middle, and his legs, seemed heavy inside his pants and gradually narrowed by the time they reached the floor. Then she caught herself. She shouldn't notice such things.

"Bet you're making shoofly pie," he said as he handed over the kettle of molasses.

"Actually, no. I'm going to make moszhy candy to take along to the fair. Are you going to the fair, Mr. Keim?" She'd become bolder with time.

"*Yah*, you bet. That's one time I close up the store. No customers here that week anyhows." He rubbed his bushy white goatee, snickered, then said, "Wonder if that gypsy woman will be there?"

CHAPTER 9

It was a crisp Monday in mid-September. Opening day of the county fair. Hannah lit her coal oil lantern, and, holding it up to her bedroom window, raised the shade. A light frost painted a dainty pattern of little dancing crystals on the windowpane. She shivered, not from the morning chill, but for the excitement that lay ahead. It was decided early on that she and Jonathan take the display goods to the fair. Mr. and Mrs. Hunsberger would attend the final day, returning with displays and, hopefully, prizes. The hired man would go sometime in between. This day was hers. How great was that!

She poured cold water from the china pitcher on the wash stand into the bowl and splattered a handful in her face. Oh, how she wished well water would make the bothersome freckles disappear. Some rainy day, she'd sneak back to the small graveyard behind the woods that had been there since the land was settled and wash her face. Meanwhile, the freckles remained. She guessed it a small price to pay for the freedom of sun, wind, and rain on her skin when she was a young-un. Today, she was a grown-up, and she was going to the fair with Jonathan Hunsberger. That's all that mattered. She brushed through her abundant hair and, using a hairpin, cleaned the dirt out from under her finger nails. Not bothering to do up her hair just yet, she donned her weekday dress and apron and went downstairs for morning chores.

Breakfast was earlier than usual. Afterward, Hannah cleared the table, prepared a pot of beef stew for dinner and put it on the back of the stove to keep warm, then washed the dirty dishes.

When this was done, she changed into her "going off" clothes— the paisley dress and blue jumper over it, and decided on wearing the straw hat banded in pretty pink ribbons. It was late into the season for wearing a straw hat. Still, it protected her face from the sun. It was a long trip. Too, it helped to keep hair in place, which today she braided into one long thick tail hanging down the back. This seemed to be the latest style, least ways that's how Mary Hepner wore hers last week in church. Hannah raised the hat to her head and with a slight lift of the chin and a sideways glance, she smiled approvingly at the mirror. Mrs. Hunsberger said the early morning ride would be chilly and lent her a black muslin cape. She wrapped this around her shoulders and left the house.

Out in the driveway, Samuel checked the east horizon. It didn't appear like any rain this day. The buckboard would do just fine. The men loaded baskets of new red potatoes, MacIntosh apples, pancake squash, and two gigantic neck pumpkins on the back. A wooden crate filled with jarred goods, which Mrs. Hunsberger had done up special herself just for the fair, were placed in front. The four quilts the Ladies' Aid women worked on during the past year were wrapped in a large patched coverlet and spread over the top of the other goods. Bringing up the rear was Henrietta, the most promising Holstein in the Hunsberger barn. The young heifer watched unhappily at the goings-on from her position behind the tailgate. It was a different morning.

Up front, Jonathan gave horse and harness a final check as Hannah came to join them. The handsome young farmer boy bowed deeply, sweeping his cloth hat before her like he was the gallant Sir Walter Raleigh himself. "*Ach*, my fair lady, won't you have a seat in my fine carriage?" he said.

Hannah flushed up warmly. She tilted her face, nodding regally in response, and gathered up her skirt. Accepting Jonathan's hand, *ach, how sweet was that,* she hoisted herself up on the running board and to the rough wagon bench. Jonathan climbed in next to her.

"Onward, m'lord!" Hannah commanded and gestured so with her right hand, then found a space underneath the seat for her candy tin of moszhy.

With a click of the tongue and a flick of the reigns on the well-padded haunches of Sergeant—the bay gelding used for road excursions—they were off. "County fair, here we come!"

"Be sure you're home for milking, you hear!" called out Mr. Hunsberger after them. With ears pitched forward, Sergeant trotted at a snappy gait down the lane, his path cleared of chickens and ducks by the advancing and responsible Froch Een. Out at the road, he turned in the direction of Redding just as the tip of a yellow sun peeked over the meadow.

———

Jonathan and Hannah, for all their boldness at the start, rode on in silence except for the harness flapping rhythmically and the pitter patter of the horse's hooves on the brown gravel road. From somewhere nearby came the musical whistle of a Bob White, while in the distance a train whistle shrieked. After they crossed the river through the red covered bridge, they came abreast of the old Schade property. It had been several weeks since Hannah saw Ebey. She strained hard to look past the iron wicket gate. Jonathan noticed.

"Oh, that's the old Schade place," he said. "They say a gypsy moved in there and that she's *ferhexed*." Hannah didn't know what to say. She said nothing. Jonathan went on. "The Schades farmed this place until their barn burnt down."

So, it was a stone barn foundation she crawled through at Ebey's. "*Ach* now, whatever happened?" Hannah asked.

"The saying goes that there was a paper nailed to the side of the barn one morning that said the barn was going to burn and that there was no need to watch for it. But the family did watch for a few weeks. But when they stopped, the barn burnt down to the ground, including five cows that were inside. It still *grizzels* me when I think of it."

There was silence between them as they drove on by, then Hannah asked, "Didn't they have *hex* signs on the barn?" *Hex* signs were painted on Pennsylvania German barns to protect from evil spirits, a rural superstition brought over from the Fatherland. Or so she heard.

"*Yah*, they did. But he said the signs did no good and no sense putting up a new barn 'cause whoever did it would do the same thing all over again, *hex* signs or no." He puffed on his pipe and suddenly chuckled.

"What's so funny?" Hannah asked. This was hardly a laughing matter.

"Did you see that outhouse back there?" He held the reins in one of his hard brown hands that had earlier touched hers and pointed backwards with the other. She faintly remembered seeing an unpainted shed with its slatted roof worn down to the rafters in spots. A one-roomer outhouse was attached to the side. "Old man Schade lived all alone toward the end, and he had his ways, you know. Me and the Miller boys, we live neighbors next to them, we walked past here every morning to go to the school over. Old man Schade, he come out to the road and grumbled we made too much noise and scared his chickens. "*Du macht tsu fiel zucht!*" (You make too much noise.) Jonathan mimicked, pointing the whip, which he never used. "Why, one Halloween we spooked him. *Yah, but gute!*" The eagerness in his voice made Hannah think he'd been just waiting for the right opportunity to tell her this. He started to laugh and could hardly get out the next sentence. "We turned over the outhouse!"

"*Ach*, you didn't!" Hannah said in shock.

"*Yah*, and he was in it!" Jonathan let out such a boisterous holler that Sergeant bolted, knocking Jonathan's pipe out of his mouth and under the dash. Seconds later, he had the horse back to a placid gait, and Hannah straightened her straw hat that had fallen sideways. They both laughed. All constraint vanished between the two.

They began to talk easily and simply. They spoke of everyday things, of the prospect of good weather for the fair week, of the next church social and the upcoming Thanksgiving Day dinner with the preacher as guest.

Some topics took on a more serious note. Hannah, at Jonathan's query, told him about the many moves the family made in the past to keep up with her father's numerous jobs. She'd touched on that once before. One evening when she helped him crack corn for the chickens, they got to talking about the fire and how the Balthasers came to live at Uncle Thurman's, but that was all she'd said. Now, she'd tell him more. But as the words moved toward her lips, they died. Definitely not a memory lane she wanted to stroll down. Tears rose in her throat and quickly burned their way upward. She reached for her linen handkerchief, neatly starched and folded in her pocket, and played with its crocheted corners. Jonathan was silent for a long awkward moment and glanced sideways at Hannah as she sniffled.

She said, "We must be getting on to some goldenrod, sure enough. It always makes my nose run something awful."

"Did I ever tell you about the time I helped my Pop cure the chicken flock?" Jonathan said with levity in his voice. Wondering what that had to do with the moment, Hannah quickly wiped her eyes and stashed the handkerchief back into the pocket.

"I don't think so." *Of course, if you had, I'd certainly remember. I remember everything you say.*

"I was only knee high to a grasshopper when I went with Pop into the chicken house one day to do what he told was weeding out the sick chickens; it's not good for the healthy ones. There was a hen crouched in the corner with its head down, and Pop said, 'Here's one that looks like it's sick' and he picks the chicken up and chokes it to put it out of its misery, then he put it by the door to take along out when we'd leave. 'And here's another sick one,' he said about a hen that lay next to a feeder with its head drooping. He did the same to it and threw it on top of the other one."

Hannah wondered where he was going with this.

"You know what I did then? That same day I went back into the chicken house, and suddenly all the chickens looked sick. I was about to do the same thing, but then Pop found me out. Hannah looked aghast at Jonathan while he let out a din of laughter like it was the funniest thing he'd ever done. *Or not done, praise the Lord.*

As they neared the outskirts of the city, the traffic on the pike was heavy with all types of conveyances—buggies, gigs, carriages, dreys, carts, hay wagons, spring wagons, buckboards—most with rubber wheels such as their own, and noisy motorized vehicles that hastened Sergeant to a faster pace much to Henrietta's regret. And bicycles. Lots of bicycles.

After a while Hannah asked, "It wonders me how much longer?"

"Pretty soon." Jonathan inspected his pocket watch he normally carried for church and flashed it toward Hannah. "It's five minutes past the hour of ten."

Although the time had gone by fairly quick, the journey nine miles start to finish was especially long today because of frequent rest stops for Henrietta. On one of these, they parked off the road overlooking Ritter's Hollow German Tramp Camp.

German tramps were becoming suspect by *Englischers* due to the war in Europe. More than once, the men came home after playing *Haasie* cards at the store with reported rumors of America's probable involvement in the near future. There was discontent ever since a German sub torpedoed and sank the *Lusitania* the year before—a ship suspiciously carrying ammo for the French and later proven as fact. A ship on which a hundred and twenty-eight Americans were killed along with a thousand other passengers. In spite of this growing military aggravation, and, in spite of U.S. allies Great Britain and France being actively engaged against the Hun, many Americans were not in favor of the United States entering the war. Hence, President Wilson defended U.S. neutrality.

Enter the Swiss-Germans who settled in southeastern Pennsylvania prior to the Revolutionary War. In spite of their similar language and culture, the Pennsylvania *Deutsch* owed no allegiance whatsoever to the *fodderlond* and were considered loyal Americans in all aspects. On the other hand, German tramps, though blending in well with their Pennsylvania cousins, were the antithesis in a growing anti-German hysteria in America.

Jonathan said that German tramps, who most likely immigrated during the Industrial Revolution, frequently walked the railroad tracks in the rural countryside, coming from and going to where no one knew. They begged farmers along the way to work a day in exchange for a good meal or two. They were hard workers. Hannah knew that for sure because Mrs. Hunsberger said so. She always made certain their bellies were full before they continued on to wherever they were going.

Here at Ritter's Hollow, Jonathan led Henrietta, and Hannah led Sergeant to drink water from the creek that flowed through the camp. Two *Bettlemann,* as tagged by their distant blood relatives, cooked out of tin cans over an open fire close by. Although these men spoke in *Hoch Deutsch* and sounded like the *Parrah* Schweitzer when he read from the Good Book, the language was close enough to Jonathan's and Hannah's dialect for them both to understand. One tramp had said to the other, "That young farmer and his wife must be taking their cow to market." Embarrassed, they pulled out immediately.

"We should get to the fairgrounds in twenty minutes or so if we don't stop no more for Henrietta," said Jonathan. They both turned around simultaneously, checking on the unhappy black and white heifer. The rope that tethered her to the tailgate hadn't the slightest slack to it. She looked longingly at both of them for the tread of the soft meadow floor back home.

"Poor Henrietta," said Hannah.

Jonathan smiled down at her and nodded. "*Yah*, poor Henrietta's not going to be so poor though by the end of the week. If she's like her ma, she'll reign for sure as princess in the Holstein heifer category before the week is out."

Now, that would be something. Hannah's stomach did flip flops. She'd never been to a county fair before, let alone display a tin of hard candy, which would also be judged sometime during the week in the grange building. Five or six years earlier, when they lived on the other side of the mountain, she went with her father to a medicine show in the village. A wild-looking man stood on the back of his loaded wagon, shouting over the crowd about all the wonderful things his bottled snake oil liniment could do. It was a remedy for healing anything. Anything from curing flat feet to mending a broken heart, it seemed. The man also sold boxes of candy that sounded like "Catunka" as he barked it to the audience. The candy had miraculous cures, especially for youngsters.

Ever since Hannah could remember, her family was poor and there was never money left over for frivolous things. She'd never forget what her father did just then. One of the medicine man's helpers pushed through the crowd holding boxes of Catunka high in the air. Her father raised his arm and called out loud and clear, *"Eener box do iwwer fer mein gleina anchel."* (One box over here for my little angel.) He had exchanged with a dime the hard, dark, and sweetened candy, just for her. It tasted just like the moszhy candy Granny Moyer made at Christmas. After that medicine show, whenever there was any sugar in the larder and molasses in the kettle and her mother gone from the house for several hours, though usually rare, Hannah secretly cooked a batch of this miracle candy just like Granny's. Just like the Catunka. She hid the results in an empty lard can behind a wood box in the washhouse where it hardened. When doing the Monday's wash, she'd sneak a nibble now and then until it was gone. Hannah checked underneath the seat. The tin was still where she placed it.

It was going on eleven when they entered the fairgrounds. There were throngs of people and horse-drawn and horseless carriages rushing in all directions. Schools did not open until after fair week, so children, too, were everywhere, many helping grown-ups carry goods to the grange buildings and cattle sheds. Some carried chickens, rabbits, lambs, and baby pigs. Others baskets of fruit, vegetables, and baked goods. Still, others came only for a good time. A makeshift parking lot was erected behind the grandstand for machines and horses. Row upon row of ropes and posts were available. Jonathan tied Sergeant to one of these.

Hannah stayed with their buckboard while Jonathan walked Henrietta to a cow stall over in the livestock shed. When he returned, they made several trips between the parking grounds and the hand-crafts pavilion and grange building, carrying their several stuffs for display. When they finished, Jonathan untied Sergeant, and, without much enthusiasm, they climbed back into the empty wagon.

Jonathan gathered up the reins and squinted at the sun that had climbed high into noon of the day. "My belly's growling. We have time yet. Should we go back and eat something?"

Hannah nodded. *Of course, Jonathan Hunsberger. Whithersoever thou goest, I will go.* In seconds, Sergeant was tied again. They headed toward the midway.

The fairgrounds lay on the banks of the Schuylkill River outside the city of Redding. Though a rainy spell was a week or so in the past, mud puddles had not completely dried, and eager feet of early-comers to the fair made the ground rugged and uneven. As they picked their way, Hannah tripped over a gutter and grabbed at Jonathan. Tinkling sensations sped up and down her spine as she leaned against the coarse fabric of his coat. She heard his breathing. She felt his arm around her. She heard him say, "Whoa! *Bischt du gute?*" (Are you good?)

"*Yah. Ich dancke.*" (Yes, I think so.) *People must be watching. What would Dawdy say?* Hannah fingered her brooch. It was still in place.

When Jonathan let go, silence and distance fell between them. By the time they got to the midway, they walked a couple of feet apart.

"Oh, look!" Hannah shrieked. "Over here, Jonathan!" She pointed to a huge wired cage. Inside, an orange-suited man with high, black, polished boots snapped a whip at a black and yellow-striped

Bengal tiger. The big cat snarled at the brave man and pawed the air viciously with its lethal claws, then jumped up on a metal cone. He sat there just as calm and contented as a farm pussy with its belly full of warm cow's milk. "It's a real, honest-to-goodness tiger, Jonathan! Imagine that!"

Jonathan pulled her away to stand in front of huge mirrors. Jonathan looked very tall and very skinny in his. Hannah was short, fat, and dumpy in another.

"I don't like these," she said and moved over to a stand next to the mirrors. A young man shot at a moving target of ducks with a sawed-off shotgun anchored to the counter. In the background, a huge something or other rose up into the air with chairs and people swinging to and fro like they were having the time of their life. Hannah pointed to the curiosity.

"Jonathan, look! Whatever is it?" There was so much to see and hear and do. Oh, the wonder of it all!

"That's a Ferris wheel, and I ain't going on it," he said with fervor.

They passed a tent with a raised platform out front. On it stood a dwarf, a giant, and a fat lady with a beard. A man with tattoos painted up and down his arms barked something into a talking machine. From somewhere, a Victrola played, and a male voice sang, "Ain't she sweet, here's she's coming down the street...." Happy music also floated from behind and drew the two to what was the main attraction on the midway according to the long lines at the ticket booth.

On a circular platform that moved counter-clockwise were people in colorful carriages. Some sat in sleighs or carts or chariots pulled by armored wooden horses or other animals. Some stood next to fancy ponies with their arms around happy children in saddles holding on to posts that rose up and down, up and down. Still, others straddled brightly-painted horses tacked in fancy saddles and bridles with feather plumes that bopped in time to the music as they galloped in place around the carousel. In the midst of this curious sight, a pair of long arms extending from behind a stationary wall pounded on huge snare drums, giving a snappy beat to the happy music. A steam engine puffed out smoke from somewhere. Hannah was awestruck.

"It's a merry-go-round. *Ach*, you never seen one before?" asked Jonathan.

"No, never like this!" Not even at the carnival that she went to with Dawdy. This was so amazing!

"They used to use draft horses to power it, but now they got modern and have a steam engine."

"Do you think we could ride it?" She brought coins from her savings for just such an occasion.

"Not if we don't get in line."

They pushed through the crowd and reached the end of a long line to buy tickets. It seemed forever before they reached the booth. One ride cost a nickel. They waited in yet another line. When they finally got on the carousel and into saddles, it seemed only seconds before things slowed and it was time to get off. A man came around to help Hannah dismount, but she already reached into her pocket for another five-cent piece. Jonathan saw this and laughed.

"*Nay, nay, nay,*" he said as he dismounted from his blue and white painted steed. "We must go on now, or I'll never get home in time to milk. Maybe you can come back on Friday when Mom and Pop come down."

Hannah didn't think that would be much fun without Jonathan. She slid off her horse and followed him. Further down the midway were two men pitching loops that looked like the wooden frame rings Mrs. Hunsberger used to cross-stitch. The one customer's loop encircled one of the milk bottles set up in crates in the center of the stand. The man behind the square stand wore a heavy burlap apron with huge pockets. He held a teddy bear in one hand and a stick of sorts in the other and yelled out in English to the watching crowd, "We have a winner!" and gifted the player with the stuffed teddy bear that was bigger than the little boy next to him screaming for joy. *Oh, Howard would just love that*, Hannah thought. She followed Jonathan.

Next to them and in the center of the midway, a group of spectators surrounded an organ grinder, winding out a melodious tune. A little brown monkey was leashed to a foreign-looking man with a long black mustache that curled up at the ends. It wore a little red cap shaped like an upside down soup bowl. A black strap hooked under the chin kept the cap in place. A striped red and white shirt flapped generously up and down over a curling, hairy tail as the adorable little creature trotted back and forth on hind legs to extended arms. Donors dropped pennies into the cup, and the monkey graciously tipped his cap in return.

"Oh, Jonathan, he's ever so cute!" She had never seen a real live monkey before, only photographs in her geography book depicting jungles in Africa.

Jonathan dug into his pocket and gave her a penny. "Here. Give him this."

The monkey's soft little fingers felt smooth as baby's skin as they picked up the penny from her white calloused palm. She reached for one of her own pennies in her pocket, but Jonathan stopped her again.

"*Ach,* now. We stayed so we could make full our bellies," he reminded her.

They found a food pavilion off of the main midway. Jonathan ordered a sausage sandwich with onions and *catsup*. Hannah had no appetite for sausage, here or at home, knowing how it was cooked scrap meat stuffed inside pig's intestines. The very thought of eating some such disgusted her. Instead, she opted for *schnitz und knepp*. They ate and shared a small pitcher of sassafras while sitting at the far end of a table where sat two young men in soldier uniforms. They were likely volunteers with an American unit assisting the French army.

"Boy, I sure wish I could go in the war," Jonathan said around a mouthful of juicy bun.

"But there is no war!"

"Not yet for us there ain't, but there will be soon. You just wait. Just the other night at the store someone said they heard that a German submarine torpedoed another one of our ships in the Atlantic."

"But the president won't go to war. Teacher said so."

As if he hadn't heard, Jonathan went on, all dreamy-eyed, staring past her shoulder. "I like to shoot. And I could travel. Maybe even get to Germany. Pop wouldn't let me go, though," he added sadly, between bites. "He thinks because his *grossdawdy* bought Pap's way out of the War Between the States that I shouldn't go to war neither if it comes to that."

"Yet, might you have to?" she asked softly. She didn't know about such things.

Jonathan shook his head. "No. They say railroad workers and farmer boys won't have to go if we get in the war." His chin tilted and his shoulders squared. "But I could, you know. If I took a real wanting to." He nodded, smiling, obviously pleased with such courageous thoughts.

"Jonathan Hunsberger! It's a sin to think so! Why, you'd be breaking the Fifth Commandment!" Not to mention the break in her plans to marry as soon as she was confirmed. She fingered her brooch thoughtfully. She'd turned fifteen in August. One more year to go.

"*Yah*, I guess you're right," he said with some resignation. He gulped down the last of the sassafras. "Now we best get on with ourselves."

They each shelled out coins for dinner, and just as they re-entered the midway, a familiar voice called from behind.

"Why, Jonathan Hunsberger. Fancy meeting you here." It was Mary Hepner. She was hooked arms with Leatrice Hamm. Both girls looked past Hannah.

"Why, uh, I brought down stuff here for show." His right hand caressed his shaven chin before finding his pants pocket.

Hannah could've been amused when she saw Jonathan's face turn beet red if she hadn't been so annoyed at this interruption in her beautiful day. And of all people, Mary Hepner! Curiously, she stood off to the side, straining to spot the darkened tooth with its chicklet patch. But, that was no never mind because Mary's smile was directed only toward Jonathan.

"Are you enjoying the fair?" This time from Leatrice.

"Oh, *yah*, it's very exciting, don't ya think?"

Both girls giggled.

Mary said, "Why don't you join us on the merry-go-round? It's such fun. We've been on three times so far."

"Well, yes, I guess so," he said.

Hannah would pay none of them no never mind and just keep right on keeping on. "Jonathan, we must get going, remember?" she interrupted and walked off into the crowd in hopes he'd follow. He did. This time, they passed the cattle stalls to bid farewell to Henrietta and to give last-minute instructions to her caretaker, then circled around the race track where harness horses were exercised.

At the far edge of the track where the parking lot began, they came to a group of small teepee-shaped tents. Smoke rose from the center of the first one, and outside the curtained entrance and under an awning of violent green sat an old woman. The woman wore a long dress of darkish design, and her shoulders were covered with a faded flowery shawl fringed at the ends. A short-haired, long-legged mutt spread lazily at her feet. Dangling gold earrings swayed ominously through long frizzy black hair as the woman said something in foreign to the hound. When Hannah and Jonathan approached closer, the woman's eyebrows lifted, and her sharp eyes settled on Jonathan's.

"I fortune teller. Come, I read!" she beckoned in a scratchy voice.

Hannah suddenly felt queasy and Jonathan squared his shoulders. Holding the woman's stare, he covered his mouth at an angle and whispered to Hannah, whom the weathered-looking woman completely ignored, "She's a gypsy."

"Come, young man. I read!" the woman said emphatically this time, coaxing with her right hand. Her wrinkled skin tightened over her drab olive brown cheeks. "I tell you what you do be happy. You not happy. You pretend be happy, but, no!" She flicked her cigarette ashes on the ground next to the dog that still snoozed at her feet and rose.

Hannah and Jonathan exchanged confused glances, then a look of amusement sparked in Jonathan's blue eyes. He shrugged his broad shoulders and laughed. A deep, comfortable, rolling laugh. "Well, why not!" he said and followed the fortune teller and her dog, The three disappeared behind the curtain flap. A candle flickered through the thin walls of the tent, casting shadowy outlines of the two as they sat at a small table that held a burning light. An evil-smelling odor permeated the early afternoon air. Hannah moved in closer to the tent wall, yet, the inside voices were hardly audible. Fifteen minutes later, Jonathan returned. He was alone. His eyes were quiet and serious. A lock of Hannah's hair had fallen from under her straw hat during the carousel ride, and Jonathan reached over and put it behind her ear. She had meant to do that herself, of course, but was glad now she hadn't. His fingers were so nice and warm.

"We best get going," he said, and without any further exchange, they walked back to the buckboard.

On the way home, it was Hannah who opened the discussion.

"What did the old woman have to say?"

"Nothing much," Jonathan answered casually and was silent for a long moment before adding, "she says I must forget about my dream. She says it will be bad luck for me if it comes true."

Hannah fingered the ripples that ran up and down the length of her pigtail that still hung over her left shoulder from the gutter fiasco. Then tried fixing loose strands of hair that had loosened from under her hat, but it did no good, and she gave up. Her fingers were just not working properly. All the while, she wondered what his dream was about. *Going to war? Was it something to do with Mary Hepner? Me?* She was about to ask when what came out of her mouth was, "What made you tell her about your dream?"

"I didn't."

"You didn't? Well, how does she know then that you have a dream?"

"She says it's in the cards."

Hannah stared at his profile. His white shirt was open at the top where it fell away from his neck. The Adam's apple on his sun-tanned throat moved up and down as he sucked on his stubby pipe. While Hannah was curious about the dream, she was just as curious about the cards.

"How's that supposed to tell you luck one way or the other?" she asked.

Jonathan cradled the pipe and removed it from his mouth. "She scammed me out of five hard-earned dollars is what she did," he grumbled below the sound of Sergeant's clip clop.

"I can't hear you! What did you say?" said Hannah in a raised voice.

"I said, she said I'll be cursed if my dream comes true!" he shouted back and gave Sergeant a plucky snap with the reins.

Hannah's attitude changed from one of authority and command to that of a little girl who had just been caught with her hand in the cookie jar. It had been such a beautiful day, but now her mouthiness spoiled it all. She sheepishly looked over at Jonathan and was about to apologize when he took his eyes off the road and turned to her. He was grinning.

"Oh, *Hinkle Drek!* You don't really believe that kind of stuff do you?" he said. "*Hexerei,* I mean?"

"*Nay,* I guess not." Yet, she wasn't so sure. When she was about ten, she had warts on both hands, and Mem took her to a pow wow woman over in Dryville who predicted the warts would fall off if she did exactly as told. The woman rubbed the warts with a raw onion.

It was her own responsibility to bury the onion underneath an eave at home. With the promise of spiritual healing, the onion would rot as the rainwater soaked into the ground. Every one of the warts disappeared in time. She looked down at the folded hands in her lap that were quite strong and healthy except for freckles and chewed-off finger nails. And there was the time little Levi *schlovered* (drooled) at the mouth. Another trip to the pow wow doctor. Mem pulled a fish through Levi's mouth to break the curse, and the *schlovering* stopped. The memory of that event thoroughly disgusted Hannah. She hated fish.

The rest of the way home, Hannah stared at the undulating pitch of the bay's neck until they pulled into the Hunsberger driveway. The cows bellowed from the pasture gate. They were anxious to be fed and milked.

Hannah wrote in the journal: "*September 18, 1916. Except for Mary Hepner and that spooky old gypsy woman, my trip to the fair with Jonathan was the most wonderful good ever! Then Mr. and Mrs. Hunsberger went to the fair today and when they came home this evening, they returned my candy tin of moszhy with a big shiny blue ribbon attached to it. The tag on it says, 'Hannah Balthaser - First Prize for Hard Candy.' Imagine that! Me - First prize! Dawdy would be so proud. It truly is a miracle candy…Mrs. Hunsberger's canned Alberta peaches took a First prize, too, and our Ladies' Aid took Second and Fourth prize for two of the quilts before they were auctioned off. I was so happy about my moszhy, but I couldn't help but feel sad for Jonathan. Henrietta played a nasty trick on him. Mr. Hunsberger walked her around the arena today for the judging. They say she limped something awful and didn't place at all. Jonathan was really upset and didn't think it was at all funny when Mr. Hunsberger said that she was so peppy and sure-footed all the way home that she should have been hitched in the shaft instead of to the tailgate.*"

CHAPTER 10

During breakfast one early autumn morning, there was a knock on the front door. A soft tapping sound. Jonathan answered.

"Well, well, well, *weiscupf!* Aren't you pretty far from home?" Hannah could tell by the inflection in his voice that he recognized someone quite young on the porch. Someone with blond hair.

"Is my sister here?" came a small voice. Jonathan stepped aside, as Hannah raced to the door.

"John, what are you doing here?" she asked, at the same time noticing a wagon leaving the Hunsberger's lane. The boy's pale face immediately brightened when he saw Hannah. She grabbed him up from the porch floor and swung him around.

"Mem said I should fetch you home, Billy dropped me off," he answered in one breath, his small hazel eyes smiling up into Hannah's. But Hannah no longer smiled. Her guard had pushed up immediately.

"Home? Why, what's wrong?" she said in a panic, still holding him.

"Howard's sick, and you're supposed to come home!" he said loudly, then cupped his hand and whispered, "Mem said I should say that. You're to bring money." The door stood ajar, and Hannah glanced back into the kitchen where everyone watched and waited for more.

Mrs. Hunsberger stood and said, "Well, then, you best get on right away, Hannah. Should Jonathan drive you?"

"*Nay*, that's alright." She didn't want to risk Jonathan meeting her mother. Even if she did, she couldn't invite him into the parlor. There was none. "John here's my brother, and he says Howard's not

89

really so bad. I suspect he's more homesick for me than anything else."

Hannah realized with a sigh it had been long before the fair since she'd been home. Maybe it was her duty to do so right away. Half of her didn't mind. After all, she did miss the young-uns.

"How's Howard really doing?" Hannah asked of John in the privacy of her bedroom. She was very fond of all her little brothers, but Howard held her heart the most. Oh, he was hers all right. She and Billy had gotten the Scarlet Fever two years before, and just as they recovered, they passed it on to Howard, only three at the time. He became deathly ill. She spent every waking hour by his crib, praying and willing him to stay alive, eventually nursing him back to health. Although he recovered, he was never quite the same happy out-going little boy he was before the affliction. The disease weakened his nerves, and he was so apt to cry at the least little disturbance that she spoiled him horribly with attention.

"Mem says it's a shame you don't care 'bout him no more."

"That's not true. I do care." She ached to hold her favorite in her arms. "I care a lot. I miss you, too, big John." She bent down and planted a kiss on his warm cheek. "Now, why don't you help me count out this money here, so's we can get going."

She had her own little savings fund building up inside the piggy bank Cousin Emma gave her but that was untouchable. Most of her money was stored in a Mason jar for which she had easy access to withdraw for expenses or add to when Mrs. Hunsberger paid her the end of each week for her services.

Mrs. Hunsberger was very generous and donated some of the egg money to Hannah that was collected from people who walked to their farm from over the hill. And, too, there was extra money she got for peddling eggs to the store. Egg income fluctuated slightly since the chickens went into molt and went through high and low laying periods. Right now, they were laying moderate-to-well. But it all balanced out in the end. As egg production sank, egg prices rose.

Hannah was good with her numbers. According to meticulous record-keeping in the journal, a grand total of forty-eight dollars and ninety-two cents was saved to date. There would be more, but she'd given Mem eight dollars on an earlier visit. How could she pay off Dawdy's debt if she kept taking it home to Mem?

Hannah had learned about the debt from her father's entry in his journal book:

> *"February 4, 1916. I saw Aaron Stitzel today when I was walking to work, and he advised me under no uncertain terms he'd send me off to the county jail if I didn't pay him $300 for the loss of his rental house. Plus, he claims I owe him back rent of $32. I told him I didn't have $332, but that with my new job at the Plow Works, I'd pay him off soon enough."*

There was something written after that, but it was blotted out, and Hannah couldn't decipher the words, even with holding the page up to the lantern's light. After she'd gotten the job at the Hunsbergers, she vowed to herself she'd clear her father's name and pay back every red cent to that mean old Mr. Landlord. The way she saw things, it should have been his responsibility in the first place to insure his property in the event of fire damage. There was such a thing as insurance, she heard.

"Wow!" John exclaimed when Hannah poured the silvery contents of the jar on top of the comforter that covered her bed. He helped her stack similar pieces into piles. The eight dollars' worth she took was already burning a hole in her apron pocket, and it wasn't even there yet. Before leaving the room, Hannah put two dollars' worth of coins back into the Mason jar. Feeling a bit guilty, she rationalized her action by taking a dozen brown eggs along home for Mem. Mrs. Hunsberger said to.

John and Hannah walked to Uncle Thurman's farm. When they approached the yard, John sprang loose from Hannah's hand and ran up to the summerhouse door, shouting, "Mem, Mem! She's home! Sis is home! I brought her home just like you said to."

A heavy-set figure appeared in the doorway and called out in a gruff, Pennsylvania Dutch tongue, "Well, come in! Guess you thinks you need an invitation now that you're at the Hunsbergers!"

Hannah stood facing her mother. Mem said this time, "Well, don't just stand there. Shut the door, and don't slam it!" Hannah released her tensed fists and entered, the door slapping its usual annoyance behind her.

The room was such an ugly one. She hated it anew each time she entered. But it was exactly what it was meant to be, a functional summer kitchen, where the farm family could do their cooking and canning without heating up the big house for sleeping during hot and humid summer nights. It was certainly not meant for regular living quarters for a family of six, now five, as was theirs, to cook, eat, sleep and live in twenty-four hours a day, seven days a week, winter, spring, summer, and fall. She especially hated this place since Dawdy was gone, but immediately felt guilty with her thoughts. Thank God for the goodness of Uncle Thurman's heart.

Hannah was barely inside, when Mem, who'd gone back to peeling turnips at the kitchen table, sniffed, said, "I see you got your nose mighty high in the air now that you're making money." Hannah guessed it was a subtle reminder. She laid six dollars in silver coins on the table.

"Humph! Six dollars," said Mem after counting it up. "We could starve, for all you care! Little you think about me and the young-uns."

John disappeared behind the closed attic stairway and returned with Howard, who looked up shyly at Hannah and then looked away toward the corner of the wood box by the fireplace. Hannah ran to him and grabbed him up, squeezing hard, and planted moist kisses on both of his wet cheeks. But it was of Mem's accusation she thought.

It was Billy's and Ralph's responsibility to pay for the family's daily living needs. That was the deal. Mem had said so herself. It was right after she'd gotten her position at the Hunsbergers, and the family all met in this same ugly room. Mem had said, "Billy, you even more than Ralph, both of you are like your *dawdy* and can't hang on to a darn penny, so you got to pay me regular." Hannah was sure it wasn't intended to be a compliment to her as being the more responsible, no never. But it had almost sounded like that when her mother had looked at her and said, "You, Hannah, you pay your share in one lump sum at the end of the year." That was a yet undetermined figure toward the annual property taxes. Mem and Uncle Thurman agreed on this arrangement shortly after her father's funeral when it looked like they might have to stay on at the Seiferts indefinitely. Fair enough, Hannah guessed, but looked around now in disgust at the small room with its low, dark ceiling. She resented every dollar she'd eventually have to pay toward it.

Hannah picked up where Mem left off. "It's not my responsibility to pay toward your living. You said so yourself."

"Well, your big brothers need things, too. We can't expect them to give over everything."

It was no use arguing. Mem would always excuse Billy and Ralph. Especially Ralph. He was her first born and always got away with stuff. One time she saw Ralph lifting money from Mem's hairpin box she kept on top of the highboy in the bedroom. When Ralph noticed that she watched him, he told Mem he caught her stealing the money. Why, she was only five, for crying out loud. She wasn't even big enough to reach the top of the cabinet standing on a chair. And what did she know about money anyway? No matter, she was the one who got the hickory switch.

Mem went on. "Ralphie has a girl now, and he had to buy her a ring. After all, a man's gotta buy his woman a ring if he's gonna marry." She looked up from her pan. "*Nay?*" When she didn't get a reply, she said, "Well, most men, anyhow. Your *dawdy* never got me any. I shoulda known right then and there that he couldn't save no money. Never did have money, and never would of neither, even if he lived a hundred." She was chopping the turnips more furiously now. When she finished, she dumped the heap into a kettle. "It wonders me he didn't leave us in debt when he died!"

So, her mother didn't know about the landlord's claim, Hannah thought, surprised.

"Well, don't just stand there, fetch some water. These turnips aren't going to cook by themselves." Mem got up from the table and set the pot of turnips on the dry sink and put the peelings in a bucket to feed Uncle Thurman's pigs.

Hannah sighed and put Howard down. "Come, let's go to the springhouse and get water to make dinner." She hadn't been in the house more than ten minutes, and she already missed the modern conveniences and comforts of working in Mrs. Hunsberger's large farm kitchen. Later, when they sat down to eat, Hannah said, "I brought eggs for you, Mem." Hannah dished out the bland mashed potatoes onto Howard's plate next to her and depressed the pile with her spoon. In the hole it left, she spooned stewed turnips. "The potatoes look like they could use a raw egg."

"Sure," her mother mouthed out loud to no one, "what does she do? I ask for money, and she brings me eggs. Get plenty of them from Thurman. Eggs! Hmmph!" She sniffed, wiping her nose with the back of her hand. "Eat eggs for breakfast, eggs for dinner, and eggs for supper. I make something special today, and what does she do? She brings us eggs! No gratitude!" She lifted her eyes heavenward, "*Ach, give me peace, will You?*"

John and Howard wrestled with a spoon and battled over who would assist little Levi sitting in the high chair between them. Each wanted to feed him potatoes at the same time.

"*Schtupp da fechta!*" (Stop fighting!) Mem said. "I'll *britch* you all good, and then you'll have something to *brutz* over!" She sighed, heavily, pinching her mouth into an inverted curve in her wrinkled face. "These young-uns'll be the death of me, yet!" she whined. When the boys continued to fight, she picked up the fly swatter that lay on the edge of the table, and slapped Howard across the mouth with it. He was the closest in reach. The boys settled immediately. Levi cried.

"Mem, it's too cold in here for the baby. That's why he's crying." Levi was two, but Hannah still called him the baby now that Baby Sis was gone. Hannah laid down her fork and wrapped her arms about herself to combat the chilly air in the room and spotted the low ash in the fireplace. At the Hunsbergers, the shiny Othello cook stove burned nice and warm on these crisp autumn days. In fact, mealtimes at the Hunsbergers were usually warm and pleasant—except for Pap's verbal annoyances, but she was getting used to that. The Hunsberger family discussed at the breakfast table what tasks were on schedule for the day, and also at dinnertime. And they oft times used the supper table as a forum to share minor complaints or successes that occurred throughout the work day. She loved working at the Hunsbergers.

"Well, fetch some wood then. Wood box's empty, and the wood's not going to walk in here by itself!"

"Mem, I can't stay. The Hunsbergers are expecting me right back," she lied.

"*Yah*, I'll bet! Just like your father. Always looking for excuses to leave the house. Just like the night of the fire. That fire'd never happened if he'd been home like he was supposed to! He's gone straight to hell, that's fer sure!"

"Enough!" The blood drummed in Hannah's temples. She pushed herself back from the table and stood. She'd heard this accusation a dozen times and waited a moment before she could find the voice to say goodbye to the boys before recklessly facing her mother. She wanted to say that if anyone would go to hell it would certainly be she. Strange, however, what the conduct of years under her father had done, for, she couldn't reduce herself that low. She grabbed the basket of eggs, which set untouched on the end of the table and stormed out of the shanty, making sure to slam the heavy door behind.

CHAPTER 11

A cool brisk wind hurried below a cloud-filled sky and pushed Hannah forward. Instead of going to the store, she went straight to Ebey's. This time Ebey was home.

"Why, Hannah Balthaser! I thought you forget me!" The gypsy lady greeted her with a big hug.

Embarrassed, Hannah drew back and said, "I brought you eggs."

"Mercy, child, are you the wonder!" Ebey took the basket of eggs and ushered Hannah into the parlor and shooed Jezebel out of the rocker. "You been gone long time. I thought you never come back." She disappeared into the kitchen and seconds later returned with a pot of steaming hot tea and two cups and saucers, one stacked on the other. She then made another trip to the kitchen and returned with a sugar bowl and small tray of pastries. Hannah's egg basket hung over an arm. There were three coins in the bottom of it. Ebey took a seat in the wingback chair and said, "Pray, where you been?"

"I just came from Mem's. I was visiting my little brothers," she said hurriedly and cleared her throat.

"Everything right with them?" Before Hannah could answer, Ebey offered Hannah a pastry. "Have seed cake. In my country, we season pastry with seed from poppy flower." Hannah had no appetite for poppy seed pastry nor any other type of pastry and shook her head. A hairpin had loosened in her travels. She tried to finger it back in place but gave it up to work instead on a loose thread in the skirt of her dress.

"Hannah, I help you," Ebey said this time. And then she did a peculiar thing. She opened the library table drawer and retrieved a book and a deck of playing cards and placed these on the tabletop next to the tray of pastry. She pulled her chair in close to Hannah's and in a soothing tone, said, "You kind to me when I need help, now I return kindness by helping you. Jesus help you. I never said before, but I spiritist. Healer. Advisor. With God's help, I guide you in right direction. Make wish, child, your favored desire. We tell from cards how we proceed so wish be granted."

Ebey took three cards from the deck and spread them, face up, on the table. One was a Queen and pictured the Mother Mary holding the Christ child in her arms. Another was the King card with a picture of Jesus. A blood red heart was painted over His smock where His own heart would be. The third was an Ace. This card contained black symbols that Hannah couldn't decipher. After she viewed all three cards, Ebey slipped them randomly back into the pile and then picked up the next top three cards, placing them on the table, this time face down.

Hannah's heart was hardened with resentment for her mother and painfully hurting for her father. It seemed the whole world came crushing down upon her. Even the feelings she secretly held for Jonathan could be to no avail once he'd discover she wasn't confirmed. She bit her lower lip and squeezed her eyes shut tight like she'd done when very young and made wishes to the tooth fairy.

"I wish that Jonathan Hunsberger marries me when I come of age," she breathed. When she opened her eyes, Ebey smiled and held out the deck of cards.

"Now, Hannah," she said. "Pick card and turn face up on table." Hannah's heart pounded so hard in her chest she feared Ebey might hear it. She chose the card from the top and turned it around. It was the Ace with black symbols. Ebey gasped and thrust the book into Hannah's lap.

"Quick, child! Hold card over Bible!" Ebey placed the King card between Hannah's trembling right thumb and forefinger and commanded, "Concentrate hard on card and say after me!"

Hannah *rutsched* to the edge of her seat and echoed the gypsy,

"Jesus, may Sacred Heart of Thee be adored, glorified, loved and preserved, now and forever. Pray for me, St. Jude, worker of miracles, and remove curse placed on me."

Curse?

"*Nay, Nay, s'is net waahr!*" cried Hannah in Dutch, then switched to English. "Not a curse! It's not true! It can't be!"

"God work in mysterious way. You trust me, Hannah, and do what Jesus ask, and you win Jonathan Hunsberger."

Stunned, Hannah nodded slowly.

"First," Ebey cautioned, "we remove wicked curse, which someone place on you. Until we do, you unlucky in winning Jonathan. Jesus want you use money to fight evil spirit."

———————————

Hannah relived the shocking terror of the Ace card's revelation that she was *ferhexed*. This could be so. There was always hardship, ever since she could remember. And then there was Granny Moyer's warning. What was she to do? Ebey ordered her to bring ten dollars, and she'd take it to church and place on the altar in her name as an offering to a St. Jude. She called it an indulgence, whatever that was. St. Jude, whoever that was, would then ask Jesus to work on her behalf to remove the curse. In addition, she must read six scripture verses from the New Testament every night before returning for further instruction.

Hannah earned fifty cents a day at the Hunsberger's plus egg money. But minus the fourteen dollars she gave Mem to date, spending at the fair and buying candy at Keimey's, and, oh, she almost forgot the fifteen cents she put in the offering plate each week at church, she'd now have only thirty-eight dollars and fifty-five cents left after giving Ebey ten dollars for her patron saint. For now, it would have to do.

———————————

Union churches in the Pennsylvania Dutch community administered Holy Communion twice a year, spring and fall. It was traditional to hold Preparatory Services on Saturday afternoon the day before when congregants could make public confession in advance of receiving the holy sacrament. The coming Sunday was Reformed, and Mrs. Hunsberger, the only Reformed member in the family, took off for church in the gig and dropped Hannah off on the way so she could take Mem some money. Hannah walked toward Ebey's instead.

Hannah fretted about giving up this money. Yet, to remove the curse was more important than saving money, wasn't it? The debt could be taken care of later. Dawdy would agree to that, wouldn't he? And then another thought occurred. Dawdy would surely prefer she go on through school, he'd said so one time. She'd need money for that. But then again, she couldn't go to school if she got married. Oh, what should she do? And what did it all matter anyhow? She couldn't win over Jonathan until the curse was gone, now could she? As always, there were no answers. She pushed on to Ebey's.

This was her second visit since the fair. She took immediate note of the upright outhouse and the well-worn path from the house where the lady was walking when she arrived.

"Hello, Miss Ebey," Hannah said when they met at the doorstep. "I brought you the money."

"Oh, child, St. Jude surely bless you!" said Ebey. "Come in. I warm you with hot tea." *That would be good,* thought Hannah. It was a chilly day.

Ebey served the tea, then carefully counted the money Hannah handed over to her in a small cloth pouch. "Let's say prayer to St. Jude, and we see what he says to remove curse."

Ebey placed the money on the small table beneath the Crucifix and, with a match, lit what she called a St. Jude's candle next to the money, then knelt on the floor and motioned Hannah to do the same.

"Hannah, you pray after me," she said and folded her hands. "I, Hannah Hunsberger,"

"I, Hannah Hunsberger, …."

"…plead St. Jude that you come to assistance and ask Jesus release me from curse. Amen."

The room was silent. After a while, Ebey said, "You open eyes now, Hannah. I take money to church and place on altar. We learn what St. Jude further instructs. At home, one night after dark—must be dark outside—go up to attic and read half page in Bible. Then follow with outstretched palms and ask St. Jude for blessing over you and household."

St. Jude? Attic? After dark? And which home and whose household were the questions on the tip of Hannah's tongue.

Ebey stood and continued, "You need bring twenty-five dollar next visit as thank you to St. Jude for work on you behalf." With that, Ebey whisked away the tea cups and on to the kitchen, expressing her regrets that she needed to bring their visit to a close and hurry to church immediately. In a fog, Hannah rose and made the long journey to the door.

The Ladies' Aid Society met this month at Minnie Brobst's who lived in the village of Bern. The men dropped off Mrs. Hunsberger and went on to play *Haasie* in the general store's back room. Warren stayed home. So did Hannah. Hannah had excused herself from attending the Society meeting claiming she had a headache and wished to go early to bed.

Hannah wasn't sure she could follow through with Ebey's latest request. Twenty-five more dollars? She did some quick arithmetic and discovered that would leave her savings at only thirteen dollars and thirty-five cents. Thirteen? Unlucky thirteen? Oh, no! And the attic? At night? To begin with, she'd never been in the Hunsberger's attic. Nor in any attic at night since Mem locked her in. She wondered if the Hunsberger's attic had a soul hole. Granny Moyer said that most old houses had one. The soul of a dead person could rise up through the hole in the attic and make its way to heaven in no time at all. A chill went through her as she considered these things. No, she couldn't follow through with the attic thing. Yet, God willing, she must give it a try. This was too important.

With Dawdy's small Bible in the left hand and the right holding a lantern, Hannah made her way slowly up the winding, creaking steps to the spooky fourth floor of the Hunsberger's big sandstone farmhouse. And spooky it was. Who knew what lurked behind the shadows surrounding her from the moving lantern. Having never been up before, she had no clue as to where the paths around the stored items would be or lead to. When she saw a long black dress in front of her it took all she had to keep from screaming. Then she discovered it was only one of several articles of the family's winter wardrobe that still hung on a rack before change of season. She decided this was no time for further exploration in such frightening circumstances. She sat down on the first trunk she came to and, moving a pile of framed pictures aside, placed the lantern next to her.

Ebey hadn't specified what scripture to read so Hannah opened up the Bible at random. Strain as she might, she could not read the small print with such limited lighting. Then she remembered a particular psalm her father had taught her to memorize and recite anytime or anywhere she was afraid. She was surely afraid.

"God, if you're really up there somewhere, please hear me," she prayed. She hugged herself and with trembling lips spoke into the dark, haunting garret space as much as she recalled from Psalm 91:

> *He that dwelleth in the sacred place of the Most High shall abide under the shadow of the Almighty.*

I will say of the Lord, He is my refuge and my fortress; my God; In him will I trust.

Surely he shall deliver thee from the snare of the fowler and from the noisome pestilence.

He shall cover thee with his feathers, and under his wings shalt thou trust: his truth shall be thy shield and buckler.

Thou shalt not be afraid for the terror by night; nor for the arrow that flieth by day;

Nor for the pestilence that walketh in darkness; nor for the destruction that wasteth in noonday....

Only with thine eyes shalt thou behold and see the reward of the wicked

Because thou hast made the Lord, which is my refuge,

For he shall give his angels charge over thee....

She forgot the rest.

When no one was around, Hannah snuck a hammer out of the tool shed and smashed her piggy bank, later burying the shards in the trash pile behind the *kelterhaus*. The next day, when there was a break in the afternoon routine and with a short list from Mrs. Hunsberger for the store, Hannah took off for Ebey's.

Ebey accepted the twenty-five dollars and placed the money on the table beneath the Crucifix. Hannah learned that St. Jude, while he worked hard on her behalf to remove the curse, required forty dollars more to finish the work.

"Forty dollars!" cried Hannah. "I don't have forty more dollars. Whatever will I do?" *And what about the twenty-five dollars I just gave you? And the ten dollars before that? Will I get it back? Surely that wouldn't be more than fair considering all that money hasn't gotten rid of the curse.*

"My pretty child. St. Jude make good success but say demons block completion. Forty dollar would be end and curse be gone. I pray about it." Ebey lit the St. Jude's candle and knelt below while Hannah sat stiff in her chair, waiting.

Minutes later, Ebey finished and, her dark eyes transfixed on Hannah's, said, "St. Jude say jewel okay instead of forty dollar. I take to church to be blessed."

"*Nay, Nay*. Not my brooch!" Hannah clutched her pin. "I can't give up my brooch! I won't give up my brooch! Dawdy gave it to me, and Granny gave it to him. It's precious to me." *Not to mention the special powers it has,* came out of the detached corner of her brain.

"St. Jude say, after blessing, curse be gone, and I return jewel to you."

CHAPTER 12

It was Sunday afternoon. Hannah told Mrs. Hunsberger she'd visit Mem and the boys. Manure spread on the fields the day before lay heavily in the air, as she, with snow still covering the roads in spite of the high sun, slushed her way toward Ebey's. Feeling naked enough without her brooch, she shivered and pulled her coat in closer and quickened her step. Today, she'd get the precious pin back and be told the curse was broken. All's well that ends well, Dawdy used to say.

When she arrived, Jezebel was not in her normal spot on the door step. Nor was she laying on a sunny window sill inside as far as she could tell. All of the shades were drawn.

Hannah knocked on the big heavy door and called out. No answer. Was Ebey at the store? Church? Then she noted the absence of footprints in the three-day-old snow, not even Jezebel's. In a panic, she ran from window to window around the entire house, making her own feeble tracks in the snow, all the while hysterically shouting Ebey's name.

The following week—and what a week the past had been, the Hunsbergers rode in the buggy to church, Pap's shiny black Model T up on blocks in the old shed until spring. On the way home, Hannah sat up front with Jonathan and meditated on the preacher's story about Joseph:

The brothers, out of jealousy, sold Joseph to traveling salesmen on camels who then resold him into slavery in the house of Potiphar, captain of the guard for the Pharaoh, King of Egypt....As the years in captivity rolled by, Joseph, a man of God, was taken from prison one day to interpret the Pharaoh's troubling dreams: Seven starving cows ate seven fatted cows. Seven heads of withered grain swallowed seven stalks of full grain...Joseph forewarned the king to store a portion of the harvest from seven years of great plenty in the land to feed the people and their cattle during the seven years of drought that would follow....Joseph, appointed governor by the Pharaoh and in charge of this program, eventually ended up supplying his brothers and their father Jacob with food, more flocks, land, and a new home during the famine. It was then that Joseph revealed himself to his brothers and forgave them, and said, what they had meant for harm when they got rid of him way back when, God had meant for good.

What the brothers meant for harm, God had meant for good.... What the brothers meant for harm, God had meant for good....kept rolling over and over in Hannah's mind. What Ebey meant for harm, God had meant for good....Then followed the memory of Dawdy's words that, in spite of Granny's warning, the brooch held no special powers. "It's simply a fancy stone with a pin welded on the back. Maybe it best the legacy be broken. Only God has special powers and our trust should only be in Him."

It struck Hannah like a bolt of lightning! There had never been a curse! And what had she been trying to accomplish anyway, buy Jonathan's love? Could it be that God would take this wicked event out of her life and turn it into a blessing? What Ebey did was evil, but God meant it for good somehow?

Suddenly, the weight of a ton of bricks lifted from her shoulders, and an overwhelming peace flowed through her body and mind like she'd never before experienced.

Jonathan, at the reins, turned and interrupted her thoughts.

Said he heard through the grapevine that morning the church was starting something new. Boys and girls no longer needed to wait until they were sixteen to get confirmed as had always been the way. Instead, they were encouraged to do so at any age, whenever they were ready to receive Jesus into their lives.

"...They say Catechetical classes will begin the first Sunday afternoon come spring," he said. "How 'bout it, Hannah? I'll even take you in the Tin Lizzie." He gave Sergeant a slight tap with the line.

"...but the Lord thy God turned the curse
into a blessing unto thee because
the Lord thy God loved thee."
(Deut. 23:5)

CHARLES
AND SARAH

(Nineteen Twenty-One)

CHAPTER 1

S arah regarded both from her spot at the window. One held an empty coal bucket. The other, a full-grown man of muscular-build, spoke urgently with his hands. When Mahlon Balthaser's temper exploded, it was a scary thing indeed. She released the sun-faded curtain and fumbled in her apron pocket for spectacles and a small tattered envelope stamped "U.S. War Department." It was posted 29 August 1917 and addressed in a masculine hand. The fading script inside covered both sides of the sheet, which she read for the umpteenth time:

to my sis

just think i am on my way to Europe   we left camp in Georgia for charlston and from there got on a big boat for England   i got really sick the first coupla days but am ok now   when we get to England we get more combat training and from there to france where all the action is   i ll probably get to see some of that before this letter gets to you   now tell ma not to worry none   you know how she gets   nothings going to happen to me   they say the kaisers force are getting weaker and this war will be over before we are even in it full yet   sis you know that single barrelled shotgun I use for hunting rabits   it hangs on the wall long side the muskrat traps in pa's tool shed   give it to charlie   by the time i get back home i ll be trained at using something bigger and better than that rusting old gun   ha ha   jeremiahs got his own and we both know he don't need another

from your brother

Sarah recalled Charles' lethargy each year when his brothers and the men went hunting. Hunting was the tradition that followed every Thanksgiving Day dinner, regardless of which *freundschaft* hosted— Emerich or Balthaser. Her younger brother James was Ma's change-of-life baby and hardly older than her own brood of five. Yet, he'd teased her unmercifully about holding back too much on Charles' growing up. Said she'd make a sissy out of him yet if she didn't untie those apron strings. "…All young-uns should be allowed to raise some Cain onct in a while, things like hunting…."

Hunting. Guns. War. Is that what it takes to make a man out of a boy?

Mahlon stormed into the kitchen, banging the screen door behind. Sarah quickly folded the letter, returned it to her apron pocket along with the spectacles, and poured cornmeal into the steaming pot on the cook stove near the window.

"What's the big idea?" her husband thundered in Pennsylvania Dutch. "I'm trying to get the rest of that corn husked and into the crib before it makes dark out, and you have the kid fetching coal!" He ran his fingers through the junk drawer of the corner cupboard. "Now where is that blasted extra husking pin?" he mumbled.

When he added a couple of oaths, Sarah mentally shut her ears and looked deep into the pot as if searching for an answer. She stirred the hot cornmeal to prevent its lumping together. By morning the mush would be cooled and stiff so it'd fry in thick moist slices like scrapple.

"I can't cook without fuel, now can I? You like eating as much as your cows and chickens do." The words left her mouth before she even knew she'd say that. How dare she rebuke her husband so. Yet, more boldness came on despite. "Charles works just as hard as the others for his age and goes to school in between. Maybe it's time we lay some of this work stuff alongside." While stirring, she reached for the empty scrapple pan on the table. "*Yah*," she said, nodding, feeling her way. "Maybe it's time he got himself a shotgun like he's always *grexing* for. After all, you started the other boys hunting each before they hit twelve even."

Mahlon jerked his head around, his eyes blinking rapidly. A stubborn look hardened his mouth. "Tend to your own affairs, *Frau*," he snapped. "Hunting is man stuff, and we all know that boy of yours will never be a man like the rest of 'em."

That boy of yours? Sarah bit her lips. It always came to this. She'd pay forever for his misconception of her fidelity. "He's your boy, too," she said softly, but her husband never heard more than he wanted to.

Instead, he laughed, a hollow laugh, as he rummaged through the neatly stacked items on the shelf above the drawer. "A good one to talk anyhow, she is. Always preaching that Bible stuff, Thou shalt not kill," he mumbled loud enough for her to hear. "Yet now she wants the kid to go hunting."

No, she didn't. She'd said that with far more spunk than she felt. Her family would hardly starve without the rabbits and pheasants brought home each fall. Yet, it was the way. Her husband's words were, "A man needs plenty of meat in him to work good, and hunting's good sport at it." Except when it came to Charles.

Sarah received James' letter four years ago, shortly after he was killed in the war. She hadn't shared this with anyone and kept it hidden in a dresser drawer beneath her stockings. Charles' fifteenth birthday was coming up. It was time to honor her brother's last request. Still, it frightened her half to death to think of her youngest carrying a loaded gun.

It frightened her half to death to think of any of her brood of five carrying a loaded gun, for whatever purpose. Enough in life had been taken away, in addition to losing James. Two babies before Charles was born, both girls, both infants, died shortly after birth from no known cause. Charles, she almost lost him, too, as a baby. Whooping cough. He was still her baby. Small and lean compared to the rest of them at fifteen made him seem more vulnerable. No, she could never go on if something happened to her Charles.

"Where's the boy now?" she asked, checking the clock on the mantle. But Mahlon slammed shut the once tidied cupboard and left the kitchen without further word, his heavy *gumshtiva* leaving behind a trail of caked mud on the spotless floor.

Sarah poured the mush into the scrapple pan, covered it with cheesecloth and carried it out to the ground cellar to store overnight. The afternoon was relatively warm for it was Indian summer, the time of year when all the seasons flowed together. The cicadas still sang well into the nights, which grew longer with each day, while the first of the Canada geese honked overhead as they journeyed south. Most of the leaves on the maples and oaks painted from recent frost and an early cold spell showering snow flurries across the valley the week before still clung stubbornly to their hosts.

Might as well fetch that coal myself, Sarah decided. *It'll be dark before Charles gets back if he's helping to husk.* On her way to the wood-shed where they now stored coal instead of wood, a tom turkey strut-ting his stuff intercepted her walk. His aggressive attitude and plump-ness was a sure sign Thanksgiving hung just around the corner. In the field above the shed where the corn stood ripe and ready for harvest, she heard her husband issuing orders.

"*Macht schnell!* (Move fast.) We don't have all day. You, there! Help Harry and Rob husk while Raymond and Nevin haul it out. Well, don't just stand there, Charlie, go...."

As Sarah filled the empty bucket and returned to the house, her thoughts reflected on the past as well as the present. Perhaps James was right. She depended too much on Charles. Coming on behind, and in the absence of any girls, he was such a big help, what with washing and cleaning, cooking. Sometimes even baking. But, it cer-tainly wasn't that he was soft. Oh, no! Charles helped much outdoors as well. There was plenty of work for everyone on their busy one hun-dred and thirty-nine acre Pennsylvania Dutch dairy farm.

Charles' father never gave him credit. Like the time the bull gored Alley Schtamm. Schtammy had no sons of his own to do the work and each of the neighbors in the farm community took turns. The day the Balthasers' turn came, Mahlon decided one of his boys should stay home and plow. A novice, yet eager to please, Charles had volunteered. Early that morning, Mahlon followed the lad and the team to the field above the vegetable patch where she was planting lima beans. Things went fine until they dropped the plow into the soil. Charles was at the handles, and her husband walked behind, shouting, "Watch it! Watch it! I don't want you to miss..." Mahlon pushed, grabbed, and released the boy's neck so often it finally disappeared inside the collar of the old cloth coat he wore, the row by this time resembling a garter snake as it wiggled away from her garden hoe. Afterward, after Mahlon disappeared over the wooded ridge for the neighbor's, she dropped her hoe and went over to her son. "Son, you can't plow this way!" she'd said, taking the line from his hands. "Now you leave me show you how." The rest of the day, Charles made furrows as straight as her lima bean rows.

Then there was the Sunday afternoon a couple of years back when Mahlon's second cousin Hannah and husband Jonathan paid a rare visit. The scene floated dismally before her eyes. Charles, shy and quiet in the presence of company, demonstrated his usual restlessness, continuously fidgeting and twisting on the floor as he worked out arithmetic problems for school. She noticed her husband's annoyance. Soon he disappeared from the kitchen, returning minutes later with the ball and chain, which closed the picket gate to the side yard. "Now this ought to keep you from *rutsching* all over the place," he'd said. After he linked Charles' one leg with the table's, he let loose a long peal of laughter. What he'd just done was the funniest thing ever. No one was amused, especially Sarah.

It all went way back to a particular snowy Sunday morning late February. Elam Metz, hired man at the time, assisted Sarah with tacking up the team for church. As luck would have it, her foot got caught when Elam hoisted the trappings up over Big Jake. The mishap forced her down in the straw and the harness landed smack on top. Being the gentleman that he was, Elam helped her back on her feet, the two of them shamelessly laughing when Mahlon arrived on the scene. He fired Elam on the spot. Within the year, Charles was born.

As the boy grew, one couldn't be sure by looking at him if he was one of Mahlon Balthaser's *kinner*. From Sarah's side of the family came the blond hair and blue eyes (hers paled like the washed-out blue of the hand-made aprons she wore). Charles' skin was fair and sensitive to the hot summer sun, and his frame had a thinness to it that took its time in maturing as he aged. His fingers were long and sensitive and skillful in doing minutely fine work, almost as if the fingers were doing the thinking as they worked. They weren't hard and calloused as were the father's and older brothers'. Or her's.

There was, however, one common trait with the father only Sarah seemed to notice. Charles' facial expression had a certain peculiarity. During moments of intense concentration, his lips, tiny muscles pinching and twisting upwards, then sideways into cheeks not yet shaven, worked at a furious pace, and his eyes blinked rapidly. They shone as bright as the sharp brains hidden behind them.

In the farm community, one measured brains and success in physical terms—like how much yield a farmer harvested from his well-fertilized crops. Or how much milk his herd of dairy cows produced, not to mention how well he managed a stable of fine horses for every occasion. And then there were the pigs, the chickens and other poultry. Sometimes, sheep and goats. These, too, were a farmer's pride. Farmers wore many caps. Not only were they tillers of the land, but experts in animal husbandry. They were weathermen, carpenters, painters, masons, mechanics and the list went on and on.

A burly man of Swiss-German stock, Mahlon was all of these and farmed just like his father and his father's father before him. And if there was plenty of food on the table—Sarah certainly saw to that—and a large family of boys to work the farm, such, indeed, spelled brains and success for the likes of men like Mahlon Balthaser.

There was little need to know anything additional coming from *Englischer* books. Still, Sarah insisted Charles be given opportunity to advance beyond the manual labor expected of him on the farm. This, shortly after he finished at the one-room school two springs back.

"Look how he got it in his young head to hook up a gasoline engine to the wash machine last year," she'd said one time to her man. "Why, it made my washing time most in half to have the machine do all the scrubbing. What a shame not to have him go ahead to school in town with smarts like that one's got, now wouldn't it?"

In turn, he pointed out Charles' failure to run the corn sheller by gasoline. Sarah heard the tale often enough, though she also heard the story differently from two of the brothers who witnessed the scene. Knowing where her husband was headed, she'd changed the subject. "You have enough help now that the other young-uns are so grown. After all, it's me who'll be doing most of the sacrificing if he goes on in his schooling." His response, "*Yah, Frau*, you got that right! It won't be me, that's for sure! Kid's too lazy to do work a man's way anyhow. Always trying to figure how to do things by machine instead. That's cause you're making a city slicker out of him. Fine! Let him go on to school where he doesn't have to use his hands to work!" And they'd go on and on.

———————

Sarah settled into the usual routine and cranked down the ashes in the stove, opened the damper on the pipe, and after building up the fire from embers to a blaze, cooked breakfast. This morning was mush.

While cleaning up afterward, Charlie's final chore before catching the Six Forty-Five out of the Bern Station, he asked, "How comes we never get oatmeal no more?"

Puzzled, Sarah glanced at her son who washed dishes onto a tray at the opposite end of the table. "Oatmeal?" she said, distractedly. With the back of her hand, she wiped away the ash-gray hairs that stuck to her moist cheeks. It was Thursday, baking day. Flour dusted her palms and fingers. "But you're so fond of mush that I make it just for you most."

"Mom," that's what each of the boys called her, "the mush is good. But I thought you might make oatmeal for a change. It's been some time," he said in a voice that was beginning to deepen to that of a man's. Sarah looked at her son with rapt attention, suddenly aware of a diminishing reserve. His eyes blinked rapidly and his mouth worked as hastily as the dish rag swishing around the black cast-iron fry pan in his hands. Shrugging his lean shoulders, he added, "Besides, we weaned another calf yesterday, and now we have extra milk."

Sarah spilled water into the flour pan from a small tin pitcher, set the pitcher down, and watched her fingers as they worked the white paste, like a kitten's paws caressing a teat. "Well," she said, resigning herself, "you'll have to wait until next Tuesday when Pop goes to the mill." She jerked her chin toward the butter crock. "Now put me in a little more water and give me some butter yet." Her son did as he was bid, adding both to the pasty mixture. After kneading the pie dough some more, she formed an oblong roll, and smacked the yellow lump on each side before patting it generously with flour. "Guess I'll make a coupla milk tarts, too. You boys all like 'em," she said and reached for the rolling pin.

Charlie finished drying and put away the dishes. "How does the oatmeal come?" he asked this time, pouring the excess water from the tray back into the dishpan.

"Just let the dish water sit. I'll use it to rev up here when I'm done."

"How does the oatmeal come?" he asked again.

"What do you mean how does it come?" The boy wasn't making sense.

"I mean, does it come in a cardboard box? Or a can?"

The thick, rich dough yielded under Sarah's rolling pin as it flattened into a wide circle on the flowered oilcloth. "Why, in a bag. How else? Why do you ask?"

Charlie glanced at the clock with a startled frown. He dashed up the closed stairway, returning seconds later and grabbed his lunch kettle and school bag, and, finally, his cap hanging on a peg by the door. He murmured a hurried goodbye and left.

What's the boy up to now? Sarah wondered, cutting the dough into pie-shaped circles. *Could it be something to do with that big round cheese box under the bed?* She didn't normally snoop in the room he shared with Harry, but she spared no inch when doing spring and fall housecleaning. After lifting a layer of dough into the first tin pan, she pressed it flat against the side and sliced the excess dough around the rim before going to the next one. Soon, all six pans were lined and filled with slices of MacIntosh apple. It seemed an odd place for a cheese box. She'd opened it, inspecting the strange contents of thin wire strips, short pins, a glass tube of sorts, and a curious piece of something or other that looked almost like a shiny piece of black coal. Now that she thought more on it, the diagram folded up inside said something about an oatmeal box. Not a betting woman, but if she were, she'd bet for certain this had something to do with one of his experiments. She hoped it wouldn't explode like he said they sometimes did in chemistry laboratory at school.

Maybe her husband was right. Maybe Charles was becoming too worldly and should stay more on the farm where life was safe, where one could stay in touch with his Creator instead of doing his own creating. Perhaps she should give the gun to Charles, in spite of her husband's objections and her own misgivings. Hunting out in the fields and the woods might keep his mind off of dangerous experiments and give him something to do for fun with his older brothers. After all, she never heard of accidents over hunting, and she did owe dear brother James his last request. She sprinkled the apples with ample sugar and cinnamon, added another layer of dough, poked generous holes with a fork, and slipped the pies, one-by-one, into the hot bake oven.

CHAPTER 2

Charlie had an hour to spare each afternoon between school letting out and the time the train left the Humberg railroad station, twenty-five minutes before the hour of four. Usually, he hung around the station studying, there being little time for that at home. This particular afternoon, he strolled down Third Street instead. At the directions of Ralph Moyer, the classmate who sent away to Sears and Roebuck for the diagram and crystal, he found the little mom and pop store on the corner of Third and Pine. They sold fruits and vegetables and a wide variety of packaged food stuffs.

A stout, heavily mustached man wearing a white-bibbed apron stained with evidence of the day's sales waited on him. At the clerk's request, Charlie handed over twelve cents from muskrat trapping money he'd brought along. He left the store whistling, a round, two-pound box of Quaker's Oats wedged tightly underneath an arm.

"You sure it's going to make good?" Harry whispered after Charlie dealt his secret in bed that night.

"Of course, I'm not sure. That's why it's called an experiment," returned Charlie.

"What if Pop finds you out?"

Charlie knew well enough what could happen. His father would destroy it, just as he had the corn sheller last spring. It was his chore to shell corn to later crack into feed at the mill for their hundred or so starter chicks. It was time-consuming to hand crank the corn through grinders that too slowly scraped the stubborn hard field corn from the cobs.

He'd built his own model. This he made out of old planks he found on the woodpile. Discarded metal pieces from scrap heaped in an old bushel basket shoved to the rear of the toolshed served as screening plates. The last night, after its completion but just before the trial, he concentrated on fitting the gasoline engine into place when he felt a sharp pain in his right ear. Fingers jerked the lobe. Behind him, his father thundered, "In the time you wasted making this blasted contraption, you could've shelled half the corn in the crib!" He hacked the brand new sheller to smithereens.

"He won't this time find me out," Charlie said to his brother with an edge of bitterness, at the same time covering his hope for success to gain his father's approval. Both stared in thoughtful silence at the dark ceiling.

"Can I help you make it?" Harry asked. Charlie agreed.

Every Pennsylvania Dutch community had a general store. Closest and most favored amongst farmers on the west side of the Schuylkill River was Clarence B. Keim in the village of Bern. Keimey was shopkeeper and barber. What better excuse one had to the wife than to get one's hair cut. Every night? What better place to shoot the bull with neighboring farmers, to catch up on the latest news, and, of course, play *Haas 'n Peffer* if there was enough room at the card table. Sarah was just another store widow. No matter. She enjoyed the silence of the evenings after a busy day's work. A good time to rock and mend. And think.

This evening, Charles came out of the closed stairway carrying a package. Harry followed. He held two long thin wires in his hands. Sarah's hands quit for a time while she observed the curious goings-on. Her youngest son placed the package on the kitchen table between them and carefully removed the covering, a yellowed remnant from a worn-out white shirt, found in her rag bag, no doubt. Somewhat carved to resemble a chicken feeder, a Quaker's Oats box appeared next with all kinds of wires and screws twisted throughout. *Where was the wooden cheese box?*

"I bought the oatmeal with muskrat money in Humberg while waiting for the train home," Charles said, sheepishly.

Sarah stared at the funny-looking contraption, then resumed rocking as her fingers darned one of Charles' socks. His clothes needed more attention now that he was going on to school in town.

"What did you do with the cereal?" she asked.

Charles thought about that and answered with a lop-sided grin, "Slopped the pigs with it."

Sarah taught her young-uns not to be wasteful with food, especially store-bought items. Too many hungry children in the world. "And what exactly are you making with all of this?" she asked.

"It's a crystal set. Marconi radio, they call it."

"A what, did you say? Macaroni?"

Both boys laughed.

"No, Marconi. It's a man's name. He already invented this. I'm just making a homemade model of his radio."

"A radio," she repeated. She heard of some such but was totally clueless what it was. *My goodness, what will they think of next?*

Thin steel wires, wrapped tightly around the box, crisscrossed from top to bottom. They connected two vertical rows of screws serving as knobs. Leftover wire dropped through a glass cylinder until it touched the chunk of black something or other that sparkled brilliantly beneath the spontaneous flicker from the gas lamp centered above the table. Charles identified the something or other as a crystal. It was slotted into the base of this weird gadget. Another set of wires reached Harry's ears.

Sarah's calloused fingers forgot to darn as Charles' agile ones poked around at the crystal. All the while, his mouth worked full speed ahead, eyelashes blinking incessantly.

Harry cried out, "You got it, Charlie! You got it! You got it!" Sometimes Harry seemed the younger of the two.

He removed the wires and held them to his mother's ears. Soon, a scratchy noise came through. At first, it sounded like hens in the chicken house just before feeding time, but then culminated into an audible lyric soprano. All the while, Charles' sensitive fingers searched the crystal for its best reception: "Praise God from .....(static) ..... flow, Praise ...(static)......here...(static)..... Father, Son and Holy Ghost."

Soon, a man's deep crackling voice came over the air, "This is KDKA Pittsburgh, your friendly Gospel..... (static) ....
Sunlight Soap, the soap that not only cleans but ...."

His hands shook so badly he could hardly keep them steady on the same spot. Children's voices cut in and out, "Sun light, sun —, bright————life today with ..... Give your (static)...."

The static hurt Sarah's ears, so did the wires, and she pushed them back toward Harry who gave them to Charles.

Seconds later, Charles unwired himself and the two of them whooped and hollered as they marched around the kitchen table, singing, "Sunlight, sunlight, brighten your life today with sunlight!"

Sarah, her heart overflowing with warm, bright sunshine, picked up the darning needles once more and rocked to the beat of the chorus she'd just heard over her son's latest invention. A radio, would you believe! Then, "What if Pop finds you out," she said, barely audible above the commotion.

A quickened silence fell over the room. Charles' scholarly expression switched to an anxious frown.

"Pop never goes in our bedroom," he returned dryly.

"Speaking of bedroom, it's off you two to your bed now so's you can rest up proper," she ordered with a fake stern voice, giving the sock a final examination. "Charles, you have school in the morning, remember?"

The younger nodded and wrapped up the works in the time-yellowed rag. Both boys took off for bed, leaving Sarah to plan for her younger's future. Creative and brilliant. Child prodigy. Boys like him grew up to be responsible and important men, men like Alexander Graham Bell and Thomas Edison. Why even Henry Ford was a farmer boy who made good. And he even quit school she heard before he was fifteen. No reason why her Charles couldn't handle both the farm and the world.

Yes, it was settled. She'd drive home to her folks and pick up James' gun. She wouldn't mention this to Mahlon, of course. If she acted first, he'd fuss, perhaps for days after he found out she defied him. But the task would be done. Eventually, the matter would go away and be replaced by a more urgent difference, life going on as usual.

Mahlon was not a praying man and seldom accompanied the family to church except for spring and fall Holy Communions. Nevertheless, he took advantage of the Lord's generous Fourth Commandment and stretched himself out on the fainting couch in the kitchen for a lazy afternoon's nap. Sarah welcomed the Sabbath, not only for its restful, rejuvenating benefit, but also as a time to study the Word.

Sarah's Bible was small and worn in comparison to the thick suede-covered Balthaser family Bible with its dry, brittle pages perhaps untouched in a century except for registering births, deaths, and marriages. It accompanied her everywhere on the Sabbath. Usually this was to the parlor, a room reserved for company, Christmas, and, of course, reading the Bible.

Today, her youngest child's fifteenth birthday, Sarah had a different mission in mind. She placed the Good Book in an egg basket, alongside two freshly-baked loaves of bread and a shoofly pie. Her mother would appreciate this token since she'd slowed immensely the last four years.

It all began in 1916. Woodrow Wilson was re-elected as the man who kept the country out of war. But things would radically change in the president's second term. On February 3, 1917, Wilson severed diplomatic relations with Germany. On April 6, 1917, the United States declared war against Germany—the Great War—the War to End All Wars.

The newly appointed Supreme Commander of the American Army in France, General "Black Jack" Pershing, soon realized how ill-prepared the USA was. Supplies, equipment, armory, ships, planes, rations, and especially trained soldiers were needed to fight the Hun. Hence, May 19, 1917, newspapers around the country proclaimed the President's Selective Conscription Law. President Wilson stressed: "...It is a new thing in our history, and a landmark in our progress. It is in no sense a conscription of the unwilling. It is rather selection from a nation which has volunteered its mass...."

On June 20, the first draft began with six hundred and eighty thousand young men selected. Though farmers and railroad workers were exempt from the draft, and though contrary to his parents' wishes, Ma and Pa Emerich's younger son volunteered. He was off to see the world. Off to far-away places one only read about in books. The first American troops arrived in Europe as early as summer, but the American Expeditionary Forces did not fully participate at the front until October, when the First Division entered the trenches at Nancy, France. It was in one of these trenches that James Strauss Emerich made the ultimate sacrifice.

The leaves were turning in color and fluttered in the breeze. A gaggle of geese grazed across the harvested cornfield where it bordered the backyard. Some flew up above, chattering as contented wild geese do, until they became mere specks on the wooded horizon. None of Sarah's boys shot geese. To do so would leave the surviving mate alone for the rest of its lifetime. She hoped Charles wouldn't shoot them either. She called him now and getting no response, called Sheppie who was normally close by the boy. The dog appeared out of nowhere and led her down the wooden walkway, the one leading to the summerhouse cellar where he stopped outside and wagged his tail. Sarah opened the door. A dank, musty air of summertime closeness made sweet by recently filled bins of apples greeted her.

"*Ach, dos is woo du bischt!*" (So, this is where you are!) Charles stood at attention inside, obviously surprised by her intervention. "I'm planning to go over to Grandma and Grandpa Emerich's, and it wonders me already if you want to go with," she said. The four older boys went to a neighbor's fishing, but Charles opted to stay home. Now she knew why.

The boys liked visiting their grandparents, and they were quite fond of their two uncles. Although since James was killed in the war, only Jeremiah remained.

Jeremiah was "not all there" as people put it. He was kicked on the head by a mule when eleven years of age. In spite of Jeremiah's condition, Sarah and her folks went over and above to keep him cheerful, perhaps even "spoiled" as she heard one *Englischer* put it. But, these last couple of years, the parents were the ones who needed the cheering up. Sarah intended to do that today with her Bible reading.

"*Yah*, Mom, I'll go with," Charles answered.

Sarah noticed a mature tone of late that tried to mask her son's youthful years. She also noticed he worked with something laying by his feet. The radio? Her Charles always worked with some gadget or other, so who knew.

"Down here I can get Schenectady, New York," Charles said, lapsing into a student vernacular. "Would you like to hear it?" He reached for the wires.

"Later, son. We best get going off now."

Ma cried like a wild thing after Sarah read the letter. Pa slowly retrieved his coat and cap from a peg above the wood box and motioned her to follow. Outside, Jeremiah and Charlie checked out Fraulein's new litter of pups underneath the wooden porch.

"Happy birthday, boy. Got something for you," said Grandpa. Charlie's face lit up, bright as a lantern on a moonless night. He glanced back down at the puppies, each squirming to find the best place to suckle. "Well, now," Grandpa said this time and took off his cap and scratched his silver head. A twinkle stirred in his blue eyes. "You can have a pup, but they're too young yet to leave their mother. Give 'em six more weeks. For now, got something more immediate out in the toolshed to show."

Just as James predicted, the single-barreled shotgun rested against the wall beside the hanging muskrat traps. Hardly rusting, the barrel was oiled and the dark-stained walnut stock polished to a shiny gloss.

"Here, boy. It's all yours. Uncle Jim and your mom want you to have it." Pa winked at Sarah and offered the gun with both hands.

His grandson didn't move. Neither did he speak. But Jeremiah did. "Hey, you can go hunt now, Chollie." A drooling boyish grin covered his thirty-six-year-old face.

Charlie was dazed. His eyes darted from Jeremiah to his mother and back to Grandpa whose hands still held the amazing treasure. He studied his own small hands, hanging uselessly in front of him.

"*Ach*, don't you want it?" asked Grandpa.

"Mine? Is it really mine, Grandpa?" Charlie's eyes were twice their normal size. A muscle played on the side of his face, and the blinking started as it always did when he got excited. He retrieved the weapon so gently one might have thought it would explode with a heavier touch, then caressed the smooth, glossy stock.

"*Yah*, yours, but not until you graduate from high school," put in Sarah hastily. Grandpa shot her a puzzled look. She'd explain later why she suddenly changed her mind. It was a thought she struggled with ever since reading the key Bible verse in the Sunday School lesson book that morning, when Paul told the Ephesians not to be foolish but, instead, understand what the Lord's will is. She constantly sought God's counsel on this business about the gun. Yet, it was confusing to come to grips with whose will she was following when her fickle self kept jumping from one side to the other. Somehow, this time she knew in her heart it was truly God's will she not honor her brother's request at this time. The part about the graduation gift was her idea. After all, much could happen between this day and three years down the road.

Charlie's mouth pulled down into a pout as he stared longingly at the shotgun. Now I have it, now I don't! Small droplets of moisture pearled in the corner of his eyes. Gratified with her final decision, Sarah was strangely dismayed and pained from the impact her sudden words left on her favorite son.

"*Ach* now, you can take it with today," she said, "but don't let me catch you neglecting your study or it comes right back to this shed, you hear?" She didn't have to threaten the boy. Yet, as a responsible parent, the condition needed to go with the gift, no matter how long-term its official presentation. Grandpa backed up this abrupt altera-tion in plans.

"Yep, boy. Won't be all play, but gradiation'll be here before you know it." He gave his grandson a gentle slap on the shoulder.

Jeremiah, not exactly clear on the goings-on, said, "I know where there's a nest full of bunnies, Chollie." Yellow saliva juice leaked out both sides of his mouth as he pointed toward the field behind the barn. With tired eyes, Pa winked in a sideways glance at Sarah as the two returned to the house.

Jeremiah wasn't very smart Charlie had long ago decided. Any-way, not book smart having never progressed beyond the fifth grade in learning. Not to mention the loss of thinking power the mule kick's impact had made on the brain. Yet, his mentally-deprived uncle was a delight to be around since he usually had a clever trick or two up his dirty sleeve.

This time the trick was a pencil. Not the ordinary sort of pencil, but one with a see-through tube between the eraser and the yellow wooden part where it was sharpened to a point and ready for scholarly use. A woman inside had scaly thighs that looked more like the tail of a big fish than a lady's legs. She was surrounded by water. Charlie rolled the pencil back and forth between his thumb and forefinger, revealing more than was proper behind the woman's long, yellow, flowing hair.

"It's a mermaid," the uncle said with a chuckle. "Now ain't she something!"

"From where'd you get this?" asked the nephew. Jeremiah cast an anxious look toward the open barn door on the other side of the hay mow where they lay flat on their bellies.

"Karl gave 'er to me," he whispered. Karl was Grandpa's hired man. "Tell ya what. You can have it fer a ten-cent piece."

"Ten cents! Why ever would I give you ten cents for something like this now?" said Charlie, still twisting the pencil, still thinking. He owed his friend Ralph a favor. This might be just the kind of thing that would catch his fancy. "I'll give you a five-cent piece if you show me where those rabbits be."

Jeremiah spat a chunk of tobacco through the air, perfectly arched down the hay hole. "*Yah*, fer sure!" he said and jumped to his feet.

Following his uncle, Charlie stuck his newly-acquired purchase in his hip pocket. When they returned, he wrapped his newly-acquired gift in a burlap bag and carefully placed it in the back of the buckboard for the ride home. *Ach, du lieva*, what a day!

CHAPTER 3

A messenger summoned Charlie to the principal's office. As they walked up the hall, Charlie was suddenly aware of the chew Jeremiah had given him. He wasn't sure why he accepted. Tobacco tasted bitter, and it gave him a bellyache whenever he swallowed the dregs. Now the stuff might even get him into serious trouble. But patting his side assured him the tobacco was still rolled up safely in the near-empty Prince Albert package hidden deep within his pants pocket. Or, just maybe, he thought more lightheartedly as they drew closer to the office, maybe someone told the principal of his latest invention?

Ralph Moyer, shoulders slumped, sat on a wall bench inside the office. *Whatever's he doing here?* Charlie wondered. *He looks like the cat that swallowed a sparrow.* Mr. Peribund motioned Charlie to join Ralph then lifted up his desktop and brought out the pencil with a mermaid in its center. The principal gave the pencil an emphatic shake, jabbing at the stale institutional air in the closed room, then made a sardonic sweep in front of the boys. Water inside bubbled around the pretty lady with the long flowing hair.

"They tell me you're responsible for this!" Peribund said, his eyes settling critically on Charlie's. "But I suppose now you're going to tell me that you got it from another student?"

"No, sir, I did not. I bought it. I bought it from a friend." Charlie uncrossed his feet and shifted his weight on the hard seat. "It was from someone not from school," he added in a small voice while staring at the floorboards. Ralph joined Charlie's study of the floor.

"Aha!" the principal said and rose. The baggy dark suit covering the tall lean frame followed him to the edge of the wooden desk where he perched, wagging a skinny finger at the boy. Charlie was reminded of the scarecrow Mom staked in her field garden each spring. "Say, aren't you the same young scallawag brought in here a couple of weeks back for that laboratory explosion?"

While that was true, Charlie didn't answer. He'd been rightfully excused of that incident later, after it was discovered that an honest miscalculation had been made on paper prior to the experiment. And the explosion was small. It had done no damage.

The principal went on, "This is a fine learning institution we have here. We have no room for troublemakers like you, Mr. Balthaser! As of this moment you are suspended from ever again entering the doors of Humberg High School."

———————

Charlie hid behind a corn shock for a good hour or so in the back woods field of their farm when the high sun and pangs in his stomach reminded him of food. But when he ate, his ham sandwich had the consistency of dried-out leather, and the Northern Spy apple tasted as if all of the juice were squeezed from it. The meadow tea, still cool from the thermos, didn't work either to dislodge the tight lump that had formed in his throat. In desperation, he reached for the Prince Albert pouch, pushing the dried leaves deep into his cheek, and began to chew. Satisfied, he lay prone on his back cradled between two rows of corn stubbles, fodder for a pillow, and stared at the blue sky while doing some major figuring on things.

He imagined his father's loud, unrestrained reaction after he'd learn of the eviction, not withholding his raucous comments on failure, of course. How would Mom take the news? He knew. It would disappoint her greatly. And who knew what she'd do, given to fits of temper of her own once in a while. He'd take this whole matter a day at a time. Perhaps Peribund would allow him to return after things cooled off a bit, and Mom would never know. Surely, something had to turn up to straighten out this horrible mess.

Charlie's eyes drifted to the treetops along the fence line, then to the clouds. God was in His hiding place, too. Up there, somewhere, he supposed. No, maybe that was only partially true when he recalled Mom's words that, "God dwells in our hearts." He thought about that and wondered where God was today when he was expelled. Certainly not in the principal's heart. Nor in Ralph's. And to be honest, it was difficult to muster up much love in his own heart for God at the moment. When he thought more on it, he wasn't so sure he felt love in his heart for God even before this trouble over the pencil began. Least ways not like Mom said how it was for her.

Mom never missed an opportunity to talk about God. Although he'd never admit this to her, Charlie had a problem believing her Bible was anything more than a storybook. Like how did religion figure into the real science of things anyway? Then he remembered something Grandpa Emerich said one time about this modern scientist who challenged God. The scientist said he could do everything God could do. God said, "I made man from the dust of the earth. Can you?" The scientist said, "Sure," and bent over to pick up dirt. God said, "Not so fast young man, pick up your own dirt." (J.O.)

He knew that to be funny, because Grandpa winked when he said it. Still….According to Mom, the Bible says man was made in the image of God. And in Biology class, the textbook says we might have evolved from fish. God, a fish? And to confuse matters even more, Mr. Manwiller—an interesting name for a man with an interesting theory—said he believed man may have evolved from the chimpanzee. Charlie thought about that many times since but was too shy to challenge his Biology teacher with, "If man evolved from chimpanzees, then why are there still chimpanzees?" There were still chimpanzees. He knew that for a fact. Ralph said so. He'd seen them at the Philadelphia Zoo. *What does it all matter anyhow? I am who I am, and I'll never return to Biology class again. Nor to Humberg High School.*

A hard knock sounded on the farmhouse door. Through the high window, the tip of a black hat appeared. A tramp, Sarah guessed. They frequently followed the railroad tracks along the river and came to her door for work or food. Usually, the second in exchange for the other. She lay her paring knife aside and took a half-eaten loaf of bread from the pantry, pear jelly, and butter and placed them on the table. The knock came again, this time louder, longer. Wiping her hands on her apron bib, she crossed the long kitchen to the door, opened it and stared at two men dressed in Sabbath clothes.

One was old and scholarly-looking and wore thick round lenses held in place without the help of stems. A black cord hung down one cheek. A cane supported him on the right as his lean lank body seemed to waver on the doorsill. The other man, younger, short and well fed like herself with ample flesh across the bones, had a curious gleam in his shrewd naked eyes. Past them was a black horseless carriage parked in the driveway on the other side of the picket fence.

The elder spoke, "Is Mr. Balthaser at home?"

Sarah shook her head and replied, also in English, "Well, *yah,* but he's yet out in the fields." The younger one whispered something to the other who spoke again.

"Are you Mrs. Balthaser?" Nodding, Sarah still cradled the doorknob. "May we come in?"

Loose strands of hair escaped the bun Sarah wore above the nape of her neck. Brushing them back from her eyes, she stepped aside, silently gesturing the men to enter. They removed their hats, she watching. Then her poor manners fell away, and she rushed forward, taking their hats and laid them on the mantle by the clock that registered a quarter past one.

"What can I do for you two folk?" she asked, nervously. These were surely no tramps.

"Nice place you have here," said the older as he observed her spic and span kitchen. His eyes stopped at the rocker.

"Oh, please do sit it at onct," said Sarah, motioning with her hand. The man awkwardly took his place, hooking the bamboo cane over the rocker's arm. Sarah pulled a table chair back for herself and one for the other, who up until now was silent.

"This here's my father, Mr. Peribund. He's the principal at Humberg High School, and my name's Mr. Peribund, too," he said, snickering as if that were a joke.

Sarah's heart palpitated all the way to her dry throat. "Charles? Is something wrong with my Charles?"

"Mrs. Balthaser," said the elder Mr. Peribund, "it seems your son has come across a pencil." He cleared his throat, twice, and, favoring his one leg, lifted it over the other.

"A pencil?"

"Yes, a pencil. Well, it's an odd sort of pencil, really. Rather hard to describe." He cleared his throat again, uncrossed his legs, and shifted his tall, bony torso in the rocker while tapping the padded arm with his long hairy fingers.

"You see," offered the younger, "the pencil has a pretty woman inside a translucent cylinder that's slotted between the eraser and the yellow portion. When you turn the pencil a certain way, this woman reveals...."

"Nevermind the details, Stewart," the elder said, his voice taking on an authoritative tone. He turned back to Sarah. "It seems this pencil has been circulating amongst the students. Upon some formal investigation, it appears your son, Charles E. Balthaser, is the one to have brought it into the school in the first place. He is your son, is he not?"

Total silence engulfed the room except for the clock on the mantel with its brass pendulum ticking to and fro. Sarah nodded and waited for more, her moist, calloused hands locked in place on her lap.

"What my father is trying to say is that your son has been expelled. He can no longer attend Humberg High School."

Sarah gasped.

"Yes, that's what I've been trying to tell you," the principal said, emphasis on the trying part as he peered at Stewart above his spectacles that had fallen to the edge of his long sloping nose. "I have a bad leg, and my son here had to do the driving. We're going to run along now." The men helped themselves to their hats and walked toward the door. The principal turned, tipping his hat with his free hand and said, "Good day, Mrs. Balthaser." Both men disappeared over the threshold.

After the Peribunds departed, and without further adieu and without letting the whole morbid situation sink in, Sarah searched high and low for the polished shotgun. It was nowhere. Not in the toolshed with the others, or if it was, she wouldn't know. They all looked the same, except some were single and some double-barreled. They were all polished. She checked the pump house, then the apple bins in the old cellar, thinking it might be hidden there from the father. Little did Charles realize he should have hidden it from her as well. Then again, looks like he did because she couldn't for the life of her find a lone gun anywhere.

James wasn't right about the shotgun, but he had certainly been right about her being too soft on the boy. A vulgar pencil, indeed! Why, the bitter shame of it! She couldn't let him get away with such a wicked act. *How could he defy her like this?* And hadn't she warned about taking the gun back if he neglected his studies? Now what was to become of him—a farmer like the rest of them? A laborer? A soldier ending up like James?

Then it occurred to her the bedroom was the likely place he'd hide any personal belongings. She ran up to Charles' and Harry's room upstairs and checked underneath the bed and behind the clothes hanging from hooks on the wall. The gun was nowhere. But, wrapped neatly in that old shirt, awkward steel wires piercing through the cloth at the top, was the radio on the bottom of the chifforobe. Her heart pulsated madly. She grabbed the set, ripped at the wires, slicing her right hand in the process, and tore what remained of the cardboard box, finally dumping the entire works on the floor.

She sat down on the bed surveying the mess her foolish temper had produced and began to cry. Slowly at first. But tears coursed out of control as she pondered the beautiful Doxology straining to reach her ears only a few nights before, "Praise God from whom all blessings flow...."

What if she'd made a mistake? What if there were a simple explanation for all of this? God had surely blessed her son with a special gift. She needed to praise Him for it, not destroy the talent He gifted the boy with. And what if Charles were innocent and had an explanation for being tagged with the pencil? What if...? Who did those snotty Peribunds think they were anyhow for barring her brilliant son from school? After all, there were other schools around that would surely appreciate him. Holding on to this thought, Sarah wiped her face with her apron, blew her nose into the crisp, starched handkerchief in its pocket, and cleaned off the trickles of blood in her palm.

Kneeling on the attic floor, Sarah attempted to reassemble the set she had just trashed. But the oatmeal box was so badly mutilated any endeavor at reconstruction seemed hopeless. She'd deal with this, later, somehow. She picked up the scattered contents on the floor and, this time, lowered each piece carefully on to the yellowed shirt spread neatly in the bottom of the five-gallon lard can that stored her seasonal bonnet changes. It was the same shirt that had once clothed her son, swaddled his tender flesh. Flesh from her flesh and....

Suddenly, a chill quivered through her body. Fearing the loss of something more valuable than a few objects of material worth, Sarah capped the contents and returned the can to its dark place underneath the pitch of the attic roof, dreadfully mindful of the barrier that would come between her and her youngest after he discovered the truth.

In spite of the sun's warmth, the earth felt cold underneath. And cold as Charlie crumbled it through his stiffening fingers. As he raised and lowered his hand, dirt splattered against the lid of his kettle, reminding him of the hollow sound the ground made as it rained over Uncle Jim's empty coffin. Before the funeral, Mom had been real strong-like, saying, "We all die sooner or later, though your Uncle James died much too soon. Yet, we need to think of it this way, 'Where he is now, there are no more wars, no more battles to fight, no more suffering or dying.' The Bible says so." Then she cried.

Charlie agreed about the suffering part. But the part his mother added sometime later was beyond comprehension. She'd said, the *par-rah* says we need to forgive the Germans for what they did. It's hard to do, but we need to forgive others before God forgives us, or we can't go on to Heaven.

Forgive Pop for the time he beat me up, then made me lie to company that my black and blue eye was caused by a bee sting? No, never! I can still smell his dirty hand across my face.

A freight train from down below howled its warning whistle to travelers nearing the Epler's Dahl crossing at Bern. Charlie imagined recklessly what it might be like to jump the train and continue on to wherever. Before the War, long before the government took over the railroads to execute movement of goods and troops, a friend of Uncle Jeremiah's did just that, folks saying he ended up years later as an engineer on the same train line where he made his first hop. Somewhere out in Timbuktu, they'd said. Charlie wasn't quite sure where Timbuktu was located, but quite certain life had to be better there than living near Humberg, Pennsylvania.

Soon, a passenger train in the distance interrupted his muse, announcing the Three Thirty-Five as it pulled into the borough's station two miles away. He had ten minutes and hurried down the hill and onto the railroad tracks where he ran across the ties, carefully dodging occasional crunched-up tissue. Tissue such as the softer pages from a *Sears & Roebuck Catalog* that dropped from a hole in the train's rear compartment. He reached the station's platform just in time to begin the normal trek home from school.

_____

Charlie tossed the flimsy book bag into the corner cupboard and the kettle on top of the dry sink and went about his normal routine of checking the pie safe before changing into work clothes.

"How was your day, Charles?" Sarah asked. She was peeling potatoes.

"Uh, nothing out of the ordinary," he answered through a mouthful of apple pie. "Do you need help with the supper?"

His casual response caught Sarah off guard. "*Nay*, not really," she said. "You best go ahead and help the men get the rest of that corn husked in the back field before it makes dark out." This was not an option she'd considered. Rather, she was expecting an honest confession. Or, a clarification, and they'd go on from there. But as so often happened, she'd spoken before she thought things through. Now, she'd have to wait until later to broach the matter.

CHAPTER 4

The next morning, Charlie packed his lunch while Pop and his older brothers still ate and followed closely behind their heels after they finished.

"Sorry, I can't help clean up, Mom. Have to leave earlier. Almost missed the train again yesterday morning," he said with a funny sideways glance. He was shouldering a hand-made book bag over one arm and the kettle under the other as he slipped out the door.

Earlier? Until recently, Charles did leave earlier. He drove Nell in the spring wagon loaded with the cans filled from the previous evening's milking and cooled in the spring overnight. He unloaded them at the Bern Station for pickup by the train's crew on the Six Forty-Five. The train then made its way to Humberg before heading north to the creamery beyond the county line. Before boarding the train, Charles loaded the five empty cans marked "101" painted on the lid and that had been on the station's platform from the train's previous run. Then he'd put the cans in the spring wagon, tie down the reins, slap Nell on the rump and send her home. This routine worked quite well until the cans more often than not were jostled all over the wagon on the return trip to the farm from the sorrel mare being spooked by the increasing number of motorized vehicles that shared the road. Now, these days, the hired man took the milk to the station for a nine o'clock pick-up. Nell was fine with that. She was no longer responsible for the condition of the cans. Her handler was.

Charlie slopped the pigs and slipped into the toolshed next door, found shells in a box and stuck four into his pants pocket. In the rear of the tiny building, the graduation present still leaned against the wall, blending inconspicuously amongst the other beautiful shotguns. Crooking it underneath his arm as he'd seen his brothers do, he checked once more for light in the cow stable and chicken house and made his way out the lane. Sheppie escorted him to the end where he usually sat watching his master walk in the direction of Bern. Charlie ruffled the dog's hairy neck, said goodbye, but instead of turning left, he turned right. He had enough time to walk the couple of miles by road to Jeremiah's, but decided it wiser to try a route across the fields.

He glanced over his shoulder several times going up the hill to make sure no one noticed. Fading lantern light from deep inside the barn and an eastern sky growing brighter graced his view. Indian summer apparently a thing of the past, an early morning chill spread over the valley, separating night from dawn with an icy frost collecting in every nook and cranny. Each leaf of the dying alfalfa crunched underfoot. Here and there crisp gold and rust leaves laid waste together with rotting and moldy ones along the fencerow where dried-out burdock stickers imprisoned their final catch before winter settled in.

After climbing over the split-rail fence into Clauser's cornfield, Charlie surveyed the valley behind before heading over the ridge. He couldn't be sure at first, but a small dot grew larger and more defined as it moved along the fence he'd just come by. He smiled and humored at Shep's recognition of the break from the regular morning routine. But when he considered the missing dog might arouse suspicion, he scolded, not too loudly, of course, yet sharp enough, and the dog retreated.

Charlie continued his journey northward when a steady stream of Canada geese made their way noisily overhead in the opposite direction. He raised the gun, sighting two members of the flock at the end of the barrel. The geese moved too swiftly. Though, it seemed he could almost catch one by the legs, they flew so low. They followed the river no doubt, as it wound its crazy way southward toward the city of Philadelphia. Checking the cock, first making sure of its safety position like Harry had once cautioned, he returned the weapon to its resting place underneath his arm. He circled Clauser's fields and hugged the outer edge above the orchard.

He stopped to view the vivid sunrise at his back. Streaks of pink and orange intercepted gray vapors above a huge red ball that popped over the tree line. The scene reminded him of a jingle Mom had taught them as little boys:

"Evening red and morning gray sends the traveler on his way. Evening gray and morning red sends the rain upon his head."

He hoped the rain would hold off until later in the day when he'd be back home again. The thick woolen sweater Mom had knitted for him the previous Christmas, unlike most clothes handed down from his older brothers with little cloth left in the knees or elbows, was warm enough on this chilly morning. Yet, it was hardly waterproof. Too, he hated spoiling it. Crawling under a barbed wire fence had already pulled several flaws in the tight brownish-green weave. The old worsted coat would have served much better for this venture, but he'd worn the sweater for the ordinariness of a school day.

———————

Sarah checked the clock on the mantle after Charles left. It said six-ought-five. Things were going too far, she decided. Fighting a fitful night's rest and feeling yesterday's old anger swelling, thoughts of forgiveness and redemption quickly passed. She grabbed her shawl hanging inside the *kumma* door and rushed out to the pig stable in the event Charles might be slopping the pigs on his way to school instead of before breakfast like usual. Inside their stable, the pigs were feeding, grunting noisily. Outside, the darkness of night was lifting. Her son nowhere in sight, she slowly returned to the house.

Cleaning up the breakfast, Sarah hit upon the notion the Peribunds might have been impostors. After all, they certainly were a suspicious-looking duo. Now that she thought more on it, the older one surely gave her kitchen a good onct-over before going into that ridiculous story about a pencil. And that tweak of a son, why she could've guessed from a distance he was not to be trusted. Whatever possessed her to believe either one of them anyway!

By nine o'clock, Nell in the gig, Sarah was on her way to Humberg High School. It was fifteen minutes past the hour of ten according to the hall clock outside the principal's office when she arrived.

"Mr. Peribund is teaching a class right now. I'm afraid you'll have to wait," the secretary said without lifting his eyes from the typewriter. Clicking of keys filled the silence in the small room as he pecked away.

Every now and again a bell rang, followed by a rush of footsteps, like young heifers released from the stable in spring. Still no Mr. Peribund. She looked around, waited, took in the surroundings. It was easy to see from where Charles got his restlessness for she could barely stand the idleness of such a long delay and began scanning the many photographs hanging on the wall. Mostly groups of people, in some cases teachers hardly distinguishable from the pupils. One particularly caught her attention, a face obviously that of an adult's. Upon closer inspection, the man had features similar to the older Mr. Peribund, perhaps in his earlier years.

"Sir," Sarah asked. "Can you tell me onct who this man is on this picture?" The secretary ignored her, continuing to type from handwritten notes scattered all over his desk. Then he rolled the sheet out of the typewriter and came over to where she stood, pointing.

"That's Mr. Peribund, Senior. Ma'am, what is it you want to see him about?"

Now that he'd verified Mr. Peribund, she wasn't so sure.

"Actually, it's my son I come for. There's an emergency at home," she lied, lowering her eyes.

"Who's your son?" asked the secretary.

"Charles Balthaser."

The young man raised both eyebrows in surprise. "Charles Balthaser?" he repeated. "But he's no longer here, ma'am. He was let go yesterday morning."

"*Ich bedankt dich,*" (I thank you) was all she managed to say and left. She reached the farm driveway just as it began to sleet.

Charlie turned wrong once or twice and several times purposely went out of the way to avoid being seen. Suddenly, he felt the loneliness this predicament had brought him to. Branches on the tree limbs along the fence line where he walked swiped at his face every inch of the way. One left a deep painful gouge in the hardwood stock of his beautiful shotgun. This first experience at hunting was hardly the day he dreamt about for so long. Yet, he tried hard to convince himself this was better than school.

School? His stomach churned, recalling the principal's condescension and how life had suddenly changed for the worse. If only he had stood up for himself, reminding that weasel Peribund of his innocence on the first count. Maybe then he'd not have been ousted. And what about Ralph? Was he punished? Probably not. *If justice were done,* Charlie thought, *he'd be expelled, too, for betraying his best friend.*

Yesterday, he hid in a cornfield. Today, he hunted alone. What about tomorrow? He was suddenly tired, tired of everything. Tired of hiding. Tired of pleasing others, even Mom. He was tired of doing sissy work in the house. Tired of always trying to win Pop's approval. Tired of starting over each time his experiments were destroyed, the recent memory of the missing radio rubbing bitterly deep inside.

His spirits lifted somewhat when the sleet that started earlier tapered off. He came upon a huge straw stack in George Miller's pasture that was rubbed cow-high all the way around. It was something cows did to get rid of the pesky flies during the summer, and now something he'd take advantage of to shield himself from the biting breeze. The overhang from the top of the stack provided a spot that in spite of the earlier moisture was dry. Here, he parked himself for dinner. Having long since discarded the kettle and book bag by a fence post he'd retrieve later on, Charlie lay his shotgun alongside and unwrapped a summer sausage sandwich from his home-made hankie. An apple stashed inside his sweater for ease of carrying would finish off the meal.

Afterward, Charlie repeated his actions of the day before. Instead of corn fodder, he used long dry hollow blades of wheat straw for a pillow. Lying on his back, he stared at the closing sky. Clouds played catch and release. Some stayed stagnant like indelible sketches on a tablet. Others moved formlessly with the chilly air and swallowed what little remained of the sun that tried its darnedest to peak in and out.

Many a hot August day, he and his brothers took breathers from their work when Pop wasn't around. They'd sprawl in the shade of the huge straw pile, arms behind their necks and study the clouds overhead.

"D'you see the undersides of a turtle up there?" one would say.

"*Nay*, but I see an Indian chief over there," another said and pointed to a feathered profile that transformed magically to an angel in flight.

"*Ach*," said the other, "that's not an Indian. That's old Saint Nick. Can't you tell by the fluffy white beard?"

"Oh, look. There's a horse. You can make out the shape of its head, and the tips of its ears are looking at each other."

"That's not a horse, stupid. There aren't no legs."

"Sure there are. He's just laying down."

"Horses don't lay down."

"Maybe he's old and tired."

And so they went on and on.

Just then, Charlie noticed a sheep's face, too small for a ram yet too large for a ewe. It was leading similar faces in its flock. One, distinctly a baby lamb, resting, a fleecy foreleg folded underneath, haunches extended to the rear, floated calmly along in a sea of foam. Behind its heels, a silhouette of an animal having no forehead or eyes, its head shaped into a wide snout bellowing out a cloud of dark gray, almost black, smoke from its beak-like mouth, kept gaining speed as if to overtake the reclining lamb. There was no body attached to the head. Below, slightly in front, claw-like feet reached out as if to strike the lamb in passing.

Suddenly, a dual shriek from a freight train in the distance reminded Charlie life went on as usual in the outside world. He had best be on his way if he were to make his catch and get back home at the normal time.

First, he'd quench his thirst. Earlier, he recognized a spring by its three walls just down the hill where a herd of cows peacefully rested. Crisp clean fresh water would be just the cat's meow to wash down his food. Best not to take the gun along, he decided. In case a rabbit ran out in front of him, he might be tempted to shoot. This was no time to cause a stampede in George Miller's meadow.

As he approached the spring, one of the cows stirred and rose from its resting place and faced him. Except the one was not a cow. It was a bull. A bull with pointy horns and snorting nostrils. A bull, now pawing in the dirt, making it quite evident he was out to defend his harem from the stranger coming into their midst.

Charlie stopped in his tracks, turned, and high-tailed it to the nearest fence, the bull pursuing closely behind. He scrambled underneath a line of razor-sharp barb wire and escaped just in time. Oh, no, not another tear in the sweater!

The bull returned to his herd. Charles watched and gave the matter a good thirty minutes or so and snuck back to the far side of the straw stack that was on the flat on top of the hill and hidden from the bull's view, or so he hoped. Slowly, very slow, he made his way to the side of the stack where he'd been earlier, picked up the shotgun and, with a hurried sideways glance, noticed the bull was lying next to his girls again. It appeared things were back to normal for the big fat beast.

Without looking behind, Charlie walked swiftly to the closest exit and was out of there in no time flat. Feeling safe and secure once more, he continued toward Grandpa's fields where he'd shoot himself a bunny.

Something hadn't occurred to Charlie until just now. If he got a rabbit, he'd have to let it lay in waste. It wouldn't do to mess his good woolen sweater with blood, though little would it matter at this point since spools of wool were unraveled from his earlier tackles with barb wire. Nor could he take the rabbit home to Mom. Quickly dismissing thoughts of caring one way or the other, he cradled the gun under his right arm and trudged into the good quarter mile or so he had left before reaching Jeremiah's and the coveted nest above the barn.

CHAPTER 5

Her mind a clutter of recent events, Sarah picked up her mending. Idle hands are the devil's workshop, she reminded herself. She'd stay busy. When her fingers no longer performed, she pushed the pile aside. Leaning forward in the padded rocker, facing the front door, Sarah folded her hands and prayed fervently to the One who always gave her hope.

"Dearest Father in Heaven, Thank Thee for sending us Thy Son Jesus. It's through Him that when our time is over here on earth Thou promises a life forever in a place where there be no more worry, no more wicked temptations, no more anger and foolish tempers. But, oh, dear Lord, my son Charles, well, he's such a young one yet and much too young to leave his mother and has so much more to live for yet. Please bring him back home safe to me and to his Pop, so that we can all make amends and onct again start over...."

I'm rambling, she thought, and decided to finish with formed verses as she so often did for solace...

"The Lord is my Shepherd, I shall not want. He maketh me to lie down in green pastures; he leadeth me beside the still waters...."

Up ahead, a farmer stood atop a wagon. A team of horses waited in the hitch while he spread manure over the fallow field with a fork. A distasteful task that Charlie himself was quite familiar with. It seemed there should be an easier method. Using motor power perhaps. He'd heard tell of a farmer out in Snyder Valley who owned what they called a John Deere tractor. It worked by gasoline and pulled implements back and forth across the field. He wondered if anyone had ever thought of spreading manure that way. Coming to a clearing he had to go through to keep his proper direction, Charlie crouched along the fence like a peddler carrying a heavy pack until he reached the far side of the field where the farmer was lost from view.

The sun, now permanently gone, left the sky raw with moisture. An even layer of steel gray cast a dull gloom over his lone journey. He pulled the cardigan in closer. As he did, a rabbit shot out from underfoot. By the time he raised the gun, cocked the hammer, pulling it all the way back, and squeezed the trigger, the rabbit vanished.

With a keen eye, Charles moved forward, kicking at clumps of grass while spanning the area about him. Excitement mounted when he came to an old stack and post fence bordering what he recognized as Grandpa Emerich's neighboring field. He staked the gun against the fence. First checking for witnesses and seeing none, he began his hurried way over. When the second rail gave out beneath his weight, he lost balance and fell backwards toward the ground. A sickening crack split the heavy air!

The clock struck four. Sarah watched the door, expecting Charles to saunter into the kitchen at any moment. This matter about the pencil would be settled once and for all. The clock struck four-fifteen, then half-past four. With each passing minute, anxiety heightened. *He might be hiding somewhere,* she reasoned. Having no pocket watch, a gift still awaiting Confirmation, he could have missed the time. *No, he would surely have heard the train whistle,* she argued back. By fifteen minutes before the hour of five, Sarah was afraid maybe her favorite child might have run away.

A means of communicating emergency from one farm to another was ringing the dinner bell nonstop. Within ten minutes, the Balthaser men arrived. Harry was first. Sarah asked if he had a clue as to his brother's disappearance. It was then she learned Charles found a radio knob the evening before on the bedroom floor, noticing immediately the whole set was gone from its hiding place.

"It didn't surprise him none, though," Harry told her. "He knew Pop would find him out sooner or later. Yet, he got mad, madder'n all get-out. I never seen him act like that."

She'd been about to ask if the radio could be fixed, but then the others entered the kitchen. Trembling, Sarah informed them of the current crisis and the troubling details that preceded it.

Mahlon took charge. His voice was calm and authoritative as the Dutch words rolled off his tongue, "Nevin and Harry, you two finish things up out in the barn and put the milk cans in the springhouse. Then each of you walk separate sides around the back fields toward Clauser's. Follow the fence rows in case he's hiding and fell asleep. Take Shep. Shep will find Charlie for sure if he's out there somewhere. Rob, you go the woods field over, and go down along the crick. Take lanterns. It'll make dark out before you know what hit you. Raymond, you drive over to Schtammy's and see if anyone there seen him at all today. I'm going over to the railroad station in Bern and send a telegraph just in case they seen a kid hopping a train somewhere along the line."

Mahlon turned to Sarah. A look of concern deepened the frown lines, and his eyes twitched at a furious pace. "*Frau*, you stay right here and if neighbors show up, send them out in any direction. Won't hurt to double track." He turned to leave then spun around, saying, "Ring the dinner bell again in case that crazy kid of ours wanders in on his own."

That crazy kid of ours? Astonished, Sarah absorbed the tender meaning behind her husband's words—a first admission ever that Charles was his son, too. Things would be different from here on in, with her and Mahlon. Mahlon and Charles. But what about she and Charles? And where was he?

"Dearest God," she prayed, "please bring home our boy."

The clock ticked on. The hour grew later. The evening darker. Sarah busied herself with finishing the vegetable soup while she waited. Charles would be chilled after being outside all day long, the weather having turned raw and rainy. It was sleeting again when she fetched more onions that were still drying up on the pig stable loft to put in the soup. After each of the vegetables cooked, she pushed the big pot to the back of the stove and went on to her mending. And thinking.

Her guilt over the radio deepened. How would she ever explain to Charles that it was she and not Pop who destroyed the radio. God would forgive her. Would Charles?

She glanced at the clock for the umpteenth time. It had raced to half past the hour of six and still no sign. Her relief was tremendous when a lone figure brushed by the porch window heading toward the front door. She stood up abruptly. It was Raymond. Tall and broad like his father, his massive shoulders towered well over her inside the doorway. Pellets of ice trapped in the folds of his cap quickly transformed to water, slowly dripping from the brim as she searched his eyes for news. Clearly out of breath, he heaved a deep sigh, his lips thinning to a groove as he wiped the moisture from his ruddy face with a wet coat sleeve.

"No, Mom. We didn't find him yet," he said softly. "But, Shep found his book bag and kettle. The kettle was empty," he added with some enthusiasm.

Sarah hardly accepted this as the good news he meant it to be, making a murmuring sound instead, her voice too thick to speak.

"Moz Grummis," Raymond went on, "said he seen a boy that might've been our Charlie. Said he crossed the northern edge of the field while he was spreading manure. Says he carried a shotgun. Out hunting, he supposed...."

Sarah drew a harsh breath. Raymond clamped his lips together. He'd gone too far.

"Go on, son," she said, fearfully, twisting and untwisting a corner of her apron.

"Pop told me to come back and tell you Charlie was seen and that, by the time I got back here to tell you this, they'll find him asleep somewhere." The corners of his mouth turned up a trifle. Sarah forced a faint smile in return. Her eldest turned and disappeared.

CHAPTER 6

Sarah sliced apples to dry for *schnitz und knepp*.

"Mom?" she heard Charles say, so low it barely caught her attention amidst the many worries. The pan on her lap slid to the floor, apples rolling in every direction as she rushed to the lad. He lay on a cot a neighbor had loaned them. The kitchen's fainting couch was alongside from where she had kept vigil throughout the night. What a long dark night it had been. After Dr. Potteiger left, the pellets removed and wound dressed, Charles had tossed and turned, groaning continually until finally she silenced him with some of her husband's Rock 'n Rye. The strong drink was much to her disagreement, but the doctor's orders prevailed.

"Oh, Charles," she said, relieved he was finally awake. It was hard to believe this same boy who stared up at her, his eyes at half-mast, lips cracked, and blood drained from every pore in his wasted face, had been so joyous nights before, frolicking around the kitchen table with Harry like a frisky colt let out to pasture.

"*Wu been ich?*" (Where am I?) he said, coloring a little.

"*Ach* now, where else would you be but at home?" she answered, smiling reassurance. Her right hand, still sore from ripping the radio wires, gave the boy's an affectionate squeeze. Following his puzzled gaze around the room, Sarah's eyes settled with his upon the calendar hanging from a nail on the cellar door. There, a beautiful winged guardian angel hovered above two young children. A boy and a girl rode happily down a wooded pathway in their little brown wagon as they made their way blindly toward a road. Close by and unseen by the children was a motor machine coming around the bend.

"I thought maybe I was in Heaven," he said. The corners of his mouth twitched upwards a bit.

"Nonsense," said Sarah with a shaky laugh, deciding now was as good a time as any to change the dressing over the wound in his right thigh. Doctor's orders were to change it three times a day to prevent infection. "You forget already what I told you onct? You won't go home to Heaven until Jesus personally escorts you there. Now, tell me quick what would taste good to eat?" She methodically checked the supplies on the hutch to make certain everything was assembled for her strategic task. The boy hadn't had food in him since he cleaned out his school kettle the day before, and, goodness knew, he was going to need plenty of nourishment for proper healing. After folding the blanket to the side, she cautiously removed the thick bandage.

Grimacing, Charles struggled to his elbows after she'd finished unwrapping and carefully turned his right leg inward, exposing the nasty hole.

"Doc Pottie says you were pretty blessed," Sarah said slowly, remembering the doctor's words that he would have bled to death had he been hit just two inches higher up. "He says your leg caught just a few stray pellets otherwise you'd not be here to talk about it no more." The very mention of the gunshot sent a quiver throughout her body. When the men brought him in, bright red blood smeared him from waist to foot like a stuck pig at butchering time. It was awful!

"Well, what is it you want to eat?" she asked again, thoughts of food causing an uneasy churn in her stomach. She washed the area gingerly while her brave youngest lay still and unflinching.

"Oatmeal," he replied somewhat wistfully before a pained expression clouded his face. He sank back onto the raised pillow and uttered a small cough. Guessing Charles' pain had to do with even more than his infliction, Sarah was, nevertheless, grateful for his attempt at humor at such a sordid time as this. His comment spurned an idea.

"Tomorrow you'll have your oatmeal," she said, glancing up at him with a wink. She filled the gaping hole with the thick herb poultice she'd made and, lifting his leg carefully, set about wrapping the muslin bandage around it. "For now I'm thinking vegetable soup I have warming up on the stove for dinner might be better for you." The pot was still full. Nobody touched the soup the night before.

After dinner at noon, Sarah sent Harry to Humberg to pick up a box of Quaker's Oats. Having no idea of the cost, she borrowed twenty-five cents from her small tithing fund. She excused this special mission to the others claiming the necessity to advise the school of the boy's accident. This was no lie. Maybe the Peribunds would have sympathy, thus allowing his return. As for discussing the incident with Charles, it would once more be shelved.

———————

The dry edges around the injury progressed nicely during the following days, no signs of infection evident. Still, Charlie's overall condition worsened. He lay like a flat heavy stone on the sheets. His face white as the pillows he lay against. Again, Doc Pottie was summoned.

"Pneumonia," he said, removing the stethoscope from his ears. "I can hear the rattling in his lungs."

Sarah's stomach lurched. Grempop Strauss had passed on from consumption that started with pneumonia. The disease was, indeed, to be dreaded.

"But there's got to be something we can do for him?" she said. Her angst had widened and deepened during the last three days. Wave after wave of fear constantly swept over her.

The doctor sighed and rummaged around in his big black satchel and brought out a bottle. "Give him this," he said. "It's laudanum. Give him a teaspoon every four hours around the clock and keep him plenty warm to keep out the chill." He put his supplies back into the satchel. When he found another and smaller bottle amongst his many things, he turned toward Sarah and said, "Give him this, too. It's castor oil. Should help to bring the fever down some."

Sarah tried to quiet her unease with a dozen different musings after the doctor left. She thought of James. But hardly in the same sense that usually accompanied remembrances of her dearly beloved, deceased brother. There was a twinge of blame balancing fragilely on the surface. Yet, perhaps she was unfair to his memory. For, if she were not always so set in her own ways concerning the boy, she might have at least listened to her husband. Even though his advice during their argument in the kitchen that morning wasn't intended to favor Charles' well-being, the gun would still rest harmlessly in the back of the toolshed.

There being no escape from pain in such concerns as to what might have been, Sarah switched to thoughts of the radio, and her guilt deepened. If only she hadn't destroyed it. If only she could make things right again. Harry pieced it back together in the new Quaker's Oats box, and, although it didn't work, he hoped for success after replacing the cracked crystal with a new one she ordered from Sears & Roebuck.

Now there was a matter she'd put to right as soon as Charles recovered. It wasn't fair the blame should rest on his Pop, who by now had softened much toward their boy. On several occasions she caught her husband staring at their sleeping son from above the *Pennsylvania Farming* magazine he read late evenings, a painful twitch moving in every facial muscle. She suffered not alone.

Sarah tried hard to force sleep. Yet, sleep would not come. Charles stirred and slowly moved his head from side-to-side in an island of light from the coal oil lantern setting on the kitchen table. Making low bubbling sounds, he attempted speech through tired, intermittent coughs. Sarah sat up and, having only a few inches of space to spare between their beds, edged her legs down through the middle.

"What is it, my son? What is it you want to say," she whispered. She felt his forehead. His hot dry skin nearly burned her own.

Deft eyes paled from fever stared up at her blankly as she bent over him. Soon, through his struggle to breathe, words formed intelligibly, though somewhat slurred and hoarse, "I forgive you…Pop, I forgive you, Pop. I for…." Charles' voice trailed off to silence. His breath continued in short raspy spurts throughout another long, worrisome night.

––––––––––––

Even though the green sweater was completely ruined, the shirt Charles had worn underneath it that fateful day was salvageable, there being only three small blobs of stain below the belt area where you couldn't see them. Ironing between the buttons, Sarah grasped for reasons why this had to happen to her son, when she recalled her own biblical advice to her mother after her brother was killed. "God never allows a difficulty unless He has a divine purpose for it." She still hadn't figured out what that divine purpose was. Even now, this scriptural advice triggered the notion that her son, too, might die.

"No, no, God! Don't let my baby die! You can't let him die!" she cried aloud in anguish, as if her will alone could keep the boy alive.

The outburst awakened Charles. Expressionless eyes responded after Sarah rushed to his side. Sitting on the edge of the makeshift bed, she wept hysterically. Suddenly, a peace enveloped her. Still blinded by tears, she slipped to her knees and went into prayer. It seemed she was always praying.

"Oh, mine dearest Heavenly Father, I lift my son Charles up to Thee. Only Thou hast the power to heal his leg and his lungs and can take away this dreadful fever. Oh, Lord, let him live. Please, please let him live. Forgive me for not trusting in Thy wisdom. Don't let the boy suffer for my

mistakes. He's so young and such a good one, he is. I don't know what plans Thou hast for him, but give me the courage to accept Thy will this time and Thine alone whatever it may be, for to Thee belongs the Glory in all things. Through your Blessed Son Jesus' name I pray. Amen."

She opened her eyes and gently patted the blanket as she rose to her feet. She raised Charles' back, and, supporting him with her arm, held a dipperful of cool spring water to his parched lips. "Is it bad for you, Charles? Son, can you hear me?" she asked after he'd downed a few swallows. Her questions were met with silence, except for the horrible crackling, wheezing noise his breathing made. She lowered him to the pillow once more and pulled the covers up under his chin.

Her weary body forced itself back to the ironing board that lay on top of the kitchen table. There were rolls of sprinkled clothes waiting to be pressed. Little energy left, she ironed until another idea sprung forth. An article on home treatment for lung disease had appeared in the *Old Farmer's Almanac* some time back. She quickly retired the flat iron to the rear of the stove and frantically searched through a pile of old periodicals stored in the corner cupboard. Then she found it.

Removing the three woolen blankets and heavy comforter covering Charles, Sarah carefully shifted him between cotton sheets, then sponged his body with "tepid" water, which according to Webster's dictionary meant lukewarm. She let the water evaporate as she did so and gave him frequent sips of cold water by mouth. To the front and back of his chest, she applied hot and cold applications intermittently. When he showed signs of chill, she stopped, putting rags soaked in hot water to his stomach and covered him with the comforter. But always a cool wet rag remained on the forehead and around the neck. In the course of two hours, Charles' breathing and color vastly improved. A shaft of sunlight crossed the room and ended on his face. A benediction from Above! Yes, indeed!

Sarah continued the treatment several times throughout the next few days in addition to a mixed drink of apple and berry juices from her shelf of jarred goods. Occasionally, a dose of castor oil as the doctor earlier directed.

On a chilly but bright, sunshiny late fall Sabbath morning, the Balthasers, except for Nevin who was goodness knew where and Rob who was out courting Sadie Lesher these days and attending her church, piled into the family's Ford Model T Roadster, Mahlon at the wheel. There he was, squeezed into an old dark brown suit, a strange smile playing about his lips. He turned around and said to Charlie sitting on the back bench with his brothers, "Careful now, son, we're moving out," and gave the throttle a subtle pull.

"…For if ye forgive men their trespasses,
your heavenly Father will also forgive you."
(Mt. 6:14)

JENNIE AT TEN

(Nineteen Forty-Three)

"Jennie, now don't you poke none," Mama says, fussing with a dish towel in her hands. "There's plenty work to do at home yet."

Mama's hanging clothes on a line strung across the long farmhouse kitchen. She hangs clothes in the kitchen to dry when it rains on washday. Or if it's too cold outside and clothes will freeze, like today. Then she mumbles through a wooden clothespin clenched between her teeth what she thinks is to herself. She talks a lot to herself. Call it mind-reading, an echo, whatever, I hear her every word. "The girl has such a habit of dawdling," she says. "She gets so distracted by the goings on around her. Small wonder if she don't take off after some deer tracks along the way and completely forget the purpose of her errand."

"I'll come right back," I say, shrugging my tiny shoulders. They are broadened considerably by the puffy snowsuit jacket Mama has just mended.

Ten years of age and old enough to earn a small allowance selling eggs, I ready myself for a walk through the deep snow to the Ketner homestead. Old Miranda Ketner, widowed and sickly and no longer able to care for chickens of her own, is my first and only customer. I wrap a woolen muffler around my neck and secure the hood that protects my long blond pigtails from exposure to the weather. After putting on high galoshes over well-worn oxfords, I retrieve the round reed basket of eggs ready for the taking on the bottom shelf of the pantry. Good to go!

"Now don't forget to tell Mrs. Ketner that I asked of her," Mama says aloud. "Tell her I said she should take care of that sick toe good." She pins the other corner of Luke's upside-down work shirt to the wash line and reaches into her wash basket for another starched garment.

"I will," I say.

"I saw Daddy making the road open again this morning," Mama says, with emphasis on the word "again."

I know what that's all about. Daddy replaced the steel-wheeled treads on the Allis Chalmers with rubber tires just days before rationing on rubber began. Mama accuses him of using the tractor more than necessary now just to show off. "Go it instead of the fields over. Snow's too deep, d'you hear?"

Gee whiz, Mama, I hear you! I have good ears. Even if covered and you mumble through clothespins. But that doesn't mean I agree. It's much more interesting to go the fields over, then pass Clauser's pond before branching off on the trail through the woods to the valley below where Mrs. Ketner lives. And much shorter. Not only that, I'm still upset about you scolding over the snowsuit last night. After all, it wasn't like I tore it on purpose.

Though I never talk back, I remind myself, I often skate close to the edge. "Don't expect me back so soon, then," I answer, drawing on a mitten. I'm sure my spiteful attitude is not lost on Mama as I pass to go out the door.

The fresh air smacks my cheeks as I begin the forever hike by road. The day is cold and white, and the bright yellow sun and bright blue sky blended together make everything more cold and white and breathtaking. Rocky stays inside the picket fence and barks.

"Okay, you can come!" I call out to my big furry pet, the one who waits patiently at the gate each evening when I return home from school. The St. Bernard grabs the gate's latch with his mouth, slides it back with ease, and lets himself out of the snow-covered yard. Laughing, I point toward the open gate.

"You know better than that," I say. "You must close it, too."

Rocky now remembers. He turns and with his right paw gives the gate a shove until it clicks.

"You don't know a word of what I'm saying, but I know they'd rather you don't go with." My four-footed companion leaps over a drift and comes friskily alongside to hear more. I ramble on, "They say you scare people because you're so big, and your bark is so gruff. But they should be glad you're with to protect me in this heavy snow. This is what you're bred for, ain't?" I recall the story of heroic Barry in the Swiss Alps from a book I got last Christmas from my sister Betty Jane. Barry rescued many people after they'd been dumped on by something they called an avalanche.

Rocky rewards me for that special compliment with generous waves of his big bushy tail. Moving in close, he thrusts his drooling wet muzzle deep into my hand. Thus, we seal our loving trust in one another before continuing our journey down the road.

Snows dumped during the past couple of weeks, followed by heavy winds, lengthens the holiday period. Area schools are not yet reopened. It's just as well. School isn't much fun anyway without Mr. Greenawalt. He's my homeroom teacher in the fourth grade at Wegman Township Elementary but was just drafted into that terrible war going on in Germany.

I don't think it's fair that Mr. Greenawalt had to go off to war. He did enough on the home front to help fight if you were to ask me. He, along with our principal Mr. Loose, was in charge of Wegman's participation in a nation-wide program. Grades from one to twelve in every school district across America are involved in one way or another. We all help Uncle Sam build trucks, ships, planes, submarines, and all types of ammunition—from guns, grenades, mines, and bombs to torpedoes, tanks and so on.

At Wegman, we kids collect milkweed pods for use in life preservers. (My sister Helen and I picked four burlap bags full of the weedy stuff that flourishes in our lower meadow.) We hold drives for scrap metal and paper for recycling. We save aluminum foil from gum wrappers and daddies' cigarette packs.

This Second World War is a popular war and everyone pitches in. Take my classmate Ruth for example. Her father was drafted, and her stay-at-home mom no longer stays at home since he left. Instead, she's moved into the workplace at a foundry in town. They say she works next to Rosie the Riveter. Whoever Rosie the Riveter is I'm not quite sure. But I'm sure she's a good person. Everyone who helps with the war is good.

Manufacturing plants everywhere have willingly switched to war production and fly the "E" flag issued by the Army and Navy for their participation. Local industry turns out parachutes, iron and steel products, and major parts for military vehicles, ships, and planes. Numerous textile and knitting mills provide clothing for the Armed Services.

On the home front, store-bought clothing is not an option. The war slogan is: Use it up, wear it out, make it do, or do without. Buy War Bond ads supporting the war are posted everywhere. Mama and Daddy bought eight war bonds, one for each of us kids and four for themselves.

A fella named George Washington Carver promoted the idea for Victory Gardens, and now families with a yard of any size plant their own. The more food Americans at home grow for their tables, the more commercial food's available for the troops. We Balthasers always keep a large self-sufficient garden, war or no war. Yet, Betty Jane and Helen think it's "hep" to have their own in the upper corner of the big garden just because they can.

And there's the V for Victory sign everyone flashes when passing in hallways at school or on pavements in town, movies, church, or wherever one goes. And there are air raid drills. At schools, we're ushered into "fallout shelters," which at Wegman's is the basement. We're kept down there until the town's siren shrieks an All Clear. Frequent evening blackouts are a given. Outside lighting is off and inside lighting is permitted only if thick curtains cover the windows. On our farm, we milk shortly after sunup and again before sunset. "After all," Daddy quipped, "we might make a big mistake and try to milk the bull if we can't see what we're doing."

No matter what age, everyone is interested in the latest developments overseas. Military exploits are in daily newspapers and school library magazines. (Should you be impressed with my literary expression at age ten of what is going on, I admit I get much of my information from *Current Events,* a weekly publication in our school library that I read from start to finish. I'm really into reading.)

Authorities give lectures in assembly. Teachers, using pull-down maps on the blackboard, chart activities alongside for students to follow. Nine o'clock at night finds every ear pasted to the parlor Philco for Gabriel Heater's latest news from the front. Not to mention President Roosevelt's occasional Fireside Chats from the White House. I penciled some quick notes on his address to the nation on Christmas Day. It's not verbatim but it's as much as I remember or can decipher from my chicken scratch, so here goes:

> *...We celebrate Christmas Day in our traditional American way—because of its deep spiritual meaning—because the teachings of Jesus are fundamental to each of us—because we want our children to grow up to know the tradition and the story of the coming of the immortal Prince of Peace....*

Movie theatres precede main features with black and white newsreels of the war-in-progress. They consistently expose the enemy. The enemy, besides people and their guns, comes in all shapes and sizes, i.e. jungles, arid desert, snow-capped mountains, barb wire, trenches, fox holes, and so on. The enemy is everywhere. Newsreels also show speeches from desks of great statesmen like Prime Minister Winston Churchill expounding on Hitler's warped global vision for Germany under the Third Reich. Chilling scenes of bad people called Nazis in gleaming black jackboots goose-step across the screen. Land mines and torpedoes explode before one's very eyes. It is all very terrifying. I often close my eyes and ears until the cartoons or movie begins.

Oh, something else that Mr. Greenawalt coordinated for our school. One student out of every household received a random address for folks on Europe's allied side. I was the chosen pen pal for the Balthasers making this exchange. My letters, translated by the War Department in transmission, accompany each care package of food and clothing we send a family in war-torn Greece. Our new-found friends are Yiannis, Maria, Sophia, Eleni, Alexa, and Anthony Nicholas.

It is so sad Mr. Greenawalt is gone. Some say he may never return. Miss Hummel has taken his place assisting Mr. Loose in coordinating our school's participation in the war effort. Mrs. Schmidtt substitutes for our studies. We kids call her "The Cat" because of the long black hairs growing between her nose and upper lip. My goodness, I could imagine a mustache almost as thick as Grempop's before he got old.

Mr. Greenawalt had often joined us kids out on the playground at recess. "The Cat" is a stern listen-to-me-or-else teacher and likely to keep us inside and work. Not that she enjoys our company. Rather, she's never sure which particular kid played a trick on her. Everyone suffers just in case.

Seeing "The Cat" stalk through our classroom aisles will come soon enough, I think as I lumber along the snowy road. By the look of things, the sun overhead seems to have forgotten that it's January and is shining high and hard and hot. A school bus with chains can probably manage its way through the township's roads by next week.

Taking a deep breath of crisp air, I return to current pleasantries, wishing I'd thought to bring the buckboard sled and let Rocky pull me along the slick wide tracks the huge Allis Chalmers' wheels made. The buckboard. The problem that got me into trouble with Mama. I'll explain.

Of all the activities Rocky and I share, he exalts most when hitched to the miniature buckboard. This is a contraption of special design my brother Luke made to test my amateur driving skills. It is nothing more than a bench nailed on top of a two-by-four fastened on wheels from an old worn-out express wagon. In winter, the wheels are replaced with a few barrel staves that function quite well as sled runners. I hitch Rocky to this sleigh of sorts, take firm hold with my hands of the leather line I'd made from an old dried-out harness, perch myself on the seat, and be off for a good ride.

Rocky, with his inherent Swiss Alps' mountain fortitude, is energized by the cold, blustery weather of a southeast Pennsylvania winter that runs from Thanksgiving to Easter. He takes great delight in spinning me around the snow-covered driveway that connects the house and barn. Unfortunately, yesterday, a barn cat crossed our path. Very quickly, we veered off course, me dumped mercilessly at the corner of the milk house platform. As fortune would have it, a spike jutting from the corner post claimed a precious chunk of the new snowsuit I'd just gotten for Christmas. (Actually, new only for me. My sister Helen wore it two winters before until she outgrew it.) This hadn't gone over well with Mama as I touched on earlier. I pat my suit where she just fixed it up. Looking good!

Thinking more on it, if we'd brought the buckboard, it might prove a nuisance later if the roads are not plowed all the way to Mrs. Ketner's. Celebrating this bit of wisdom, I set the egg basket down and scoop up a chunk of snow and toss the snowball toward the clear blue sky with the bright sun in its center. Then another. And another. Rocky is quick on his feet for a bulky one hundred and fifty-one pounds. As the snowballs fly up, he lunges into the air and, with the tip of his nose, explodes them. It appears as if angels from heaven float about, showering shiny diamonds and pearls into the air around me. Awed, I fall backwards into the snow bank, licking at the cool moist flakes that end as watery droplets on my warm face.

I make angel wings in the snow with my puffy arms and stare at the clear blue sky. I bet I could have ice cream every day up there in Heaven, I dream, swallowing, tasting the sweet creamy goodness that always slips so easily down my throat.

Rocky's slobbering tongue laps me back to reality. When I push up at him, one elbow comes back down and into the eggs and sort of smashes one of them, cracking another.

"*Ai yi yi!* You big sloppy *hundt!*" I cry, jumping to my feet. "Now see what you did." In reviewing the situation, I decide things aren't so bad after all. Those two eggs will come in quite handy for making snow ice cream later on. Besides, I'd been taught never to waste a thing. Remember the starving children in China, Mama always warns.

Mrs. Ketner, too, remembers the starving children in China and insists on taking the damaged eggs. She pays full price for a dozen. I knot the silver dime and two buffalo nickels into the corner of my clean white hankie with the crocheted edges and say goodbye.

"Tell your Mama I ast about her, too!" the old woman, leaning on a cane, calls from the porch, her scratchy voice following me across the uncleaned walkway.

I turn and wave the empty basket in reply.

———

Across from Ketner's is a path I normally take when there isn't so much snow. It stretches before me now, begging, longing to be tread upon as it teases its jolly way up through the northern wooded side of the big hill.

"It looks to me like the wind didn't much blow here in the woods," I say to no one and test the foot of the trail for its depth against my bulky snow pants. The snow barely comes to the top of my boots. "Whaddaya think, Rock? Should we go up it?" I ask, ruffling the pretty white fur on his neck. Rocky agrees with a short bark and bounds on ahead, blazing a trail for this *gleina maedel* (little girl) to follow.

It's much cooler on the northern side of the valley, the afternoon sun well-hidden now from view. I secure my hood and muffler back into place and put on my gloves I'd long ago stuffed into my pockets. Yet, that probably wouldn't be necessary for it warms me plenty just to know how everything else is nice and comfy underneath the thick white blanket Mother Nature provided. Even the tree branches overhead must have escaped the blustery weather for they are still coated with snow. They look like the frosted chocolate yule logs Mama made for Christmas. I noticed after cleaning up breakfast this morning there was still a good-sized piece in the pie safe down in the cellar. Maybe. Just maybe something to snack on when I arrive back home?

Not everything in the woods is covered. Once in a while, the fuzz of dark green moss shows through at the base of a tree where the snow was pawed away by some anxious foot. It's all so beautiful. Beautiful and quiet and still. Yet there are signs of activity. Various shapes and sizes of footprints zig-zag over the rugged path. It is obvious birds and little furry critters scurry about for food.

Deer tracks mark the same trail for several yards. They disappear into the brush only to continue farther on where they lead out to a small, sunny clearing toward Clauser's pond. I notice some shuffling took place on the shallow bank of the pond before the deer returned to the woods.

"Oh, the poor things! They must of come here to drink, and now they can't get to the water," I confide to Rocky as we both view the wind-swept pond. It's a beautiful shiny oasis in the midst of a great white desert.

I am not to learn until sometime later that wild animals eat snow to satisfy their thirst. For now, though, I am out to save them from their serious plight should they come back to this spot for water. I just need to put the thinking cap on as Grempop does when he needs to solve a problem.

I shift my hood from left to right and suddenly recall Grempop saying how he fished through a hole in the ice when he was a young boy. He made a hole with a pick just large enough to draw a fish through that caught on his line. But I don't have a pick. And there's certainly no time to run home and get one out of the toolshed, drag it back up through the heavy snow, and be back home again without Mama becoming suspicious. There has to be another way. If my memory serves me correctly, there's a dump just inside the woods on the far side of the clearing. Surely, I'll find something there that could serve as a pick.

Here and there an object pokes its ugly head through the snow-covered junk. After the snow is gone, Helen and I need to explore for metal for the scrap drive. Then I find it. A cultipacker. After studying the old implement carefully, I scratch away the snow beneath the rotting wooden bar in front of the corroded driver's seat that at one time held four iron tines in place.

"This will work, Rock. You'll see," I say and brush the snow off one of the rusted, pointy blades. Rocky questions my words, cocks his head, and slowly wags his tail in agreement.

Back at the pond, I step out onto the ice with the iron tine while Rocky remains on the bank. He lowers his head and sniffs the frosty surface. Soon, a whine that started somewhere in the back of his throat ends with a sharp bark. I beg him to follow, but he just looks at me kind of funny and keeps on barking like I'm doing something stupid. Me, stupid?

At the shoreline, the water tries hard to escape its prison by seeping slightly over the brim. A couple feet in, the ice looks thinnest and appears the best place to make a drinking hole for the deer. I lift the tine high up into the air, concentrating at the same time on the intended spot to drill, when I lose my footing. I fall backwards on my tush, and the tine skids well away and across the ice. Uh, oh! What was that? A crack? Then another! A louder more sickening sound follows as I roll onto my belly. When I try to stand, my right foot crashes through the ice. Now I dare not move.

I watch in horror as the thin ice beneath my hands and knees splinters off into a dozen directions. Like how the glass shattered when I accidentally dropped Mama's treasured crystal pitcher while dusting in the parlor. I must put the thinking cap back on. But it is hard to think clearly with my boot filling up like it is with ice-cold freezing water. I cry out to Rocky.

Rocky stops barking and crouches close to the pond's edge. By this time, I manage to free my foot, and, on my belly, carefully inch my way across the ice. Finally, my gloved fingers grab my hero's shaggy coat and find his collar. My faithful pal retreats, slowly at first, and drags me up the bank.

My foot is so numb with cold I never feel the squishiness of the waterlogged shoe inside my rubber boot as I struggle homeward through the drifted snow. Thoughts, instead, zero in on how this recent situation relates to Mama. It would be easy enough to slip into the mudroom unnoticed and hide my one wet stocking with the dry one the bottom of the reed wash basket. Surely, I'd find somebody else's dry pair in the dirty wash to replace them with before sneaking upstairs to the bedroom. And Mama would probably never notice the wet shoe. But what might not be so easy is getting away from my guilty conscience. For, I am well aware that the Fifth Commandment says children should always honor their father and their mother. I'd been reminded often enough. Jeanette Louise Balthaser, when will you learn to listen!

For now, there seems no good reason to trouble Mama about something that is over and done with. I'll simply be more obedient in the future and do what Mama tells me to do.

I make it home okay but skip to Plan B. I'd forgotten it was washday, and the basket is empty. So instead, I tell Mama there was so much snow over Mrs. Ketner's way that it came in over the top of my boots and made my shoes and stockings all wet. Well, that's the truth, isn't it? Kind of?

Mama is sympathetic and allows me to make snow ice cream and finish the last of the creamy dark chocolate yule log.

Jennie's postscript: Mr. Greenawalt never came home. The following *Tribute to a Soldier* is in his honor. (Father Dennis O'Brien, Chaplain, *Good Old Days*, March 1978.)

> *It is the Soldier not the president who gives democracy.*
> *It is the Soldier not the congress who takes care of us.*
> *It is the Soldier not the reporter who gives us freedom of press.*
> *It is the Soldier not the poet who gives us freedom of speech.*
> *It is the Soldier who salutes the flag, who serves beneath the flag and*
>   *whose coffin is draped by the flag.*

BARN FIRE

(Nineteen Forty-Four
to
Nineteen Forty-Seven)

CHAPTER 1
(Nineteen Forty-Four)

I t was August. Dog days of summer. The sweltering heat was unbearable, even in the shade where we rocked gently back and forth in a rusting old iron rocker that had somehow skipped the scrap metal drives. My sister Helen said I was too old to sit on Grempop's lap, but Grempop didn't seem to mind. Neither did I. Anything was better than working in the garden with my sisters. I hated working in the garden.

Grempop's sweaty arm, muscles slightly withered from inactivity caused by the "Itis" boys—Arthur being the worst in Grempop's mind—stuck to my sweaty legs that dangled over the side of the chair. "*Yah*, you don't know what I all went through already in my time, *Yoongie* (Young One)," he said in his thick Pennsylvania Dutch accent. Mama said he called me *Yoongie* because he had difficulty pronouncing J's. "It was *chust* this time of year," he said this time, his hot breath sour from the stuffed pipe that constantly rested on his lower lip. The rocking stopped, and his right hand, scratchy and permanently calloused, swollen fingers knotted at each knuckle, moved to cradle the wooden bowl. As he sucked on his pipe, tiny puffs of gray smoke circled in the still, humid air, chasing after the hundreds of pesky gnats swarming around our heads. He began again, "*Yah*, it was *chust* this same time of year that I lost my barn."

I followed Grempop's stare across the driveway at our barn towering over the meadow where we sisters skinny-dipped in the crick's water hole on hot, moonlit nights. The barn, capped with silver roofing, was draped in a coat of pure white. Pasture green trimmed each door and window as well as a strip down all four corners. *Hex* signs— huge stars, geometrically layered one over the other, painted in all shades of the rainbow—decorated four of the five mows. A black and white Holstein cow illustrated within the outline of a single star occupied the center. At the gable end closest to us, a sweep of golden yellow underlined black and red letters that spelled "Balthaser 1933." The barn and I were born the same year.

Grempop tended to tell his yarns over and over. Even though I heard the barn fire story before, I wanted Grempop to know how carefully I followed everything he had to say.

"This one, Grempop?" I asked, letting my blue eyes go wide with wonder as I pointed toward the barn. I was quite the little actress.

Grempop was pained by memories. Dark weathered lines in his face etched into all directions. Clearing his throat, he struggled for the right words, and said, "*Ach*, no, *Yoongie*. I'm talking about the red barn that was there when I was farming yet."

"How did you lose it, Grempop?" I asked this time. But he talked over me, something he usually did when his mind was set on where he was going with it.

"This guy *Chake* Wagner was my hired man at times. And, well, I shouldn't of done it since he had his reputation for slippy fingers, but I told him I needed help getting my hay caught after before a rain comes along. He said, *yah*, he'd come and help me out. He lived Dan Spatz's over and said you *chust* got me in time or I wouldn't be home no more. I said where did you want to go, and he said he wanted to go off and buy a pair of work shoes."

Grempop's crippled right hand flexed up and down on the chair's arm as was his custom while engrossed in talking about the old days. He came to a halt long enough to cough and spit, then continued with his story. Energy built as he stumbled along.

"After dinner he came. We worked in the back hay field, me forking up and him on the hay wagon. Then we rested for a spell so's I could smoke my pipe onct, and he could smoke his cigarette. Then we talked. Again, he said I was lucky that I caught him cause he was *chust* getting ready to go up the mountain and pick huckleberries when I came along. The dumb liar! That's when I told him we'd finish up this load yet, then he could go pick up his dang work shoes on the way to the huckleberry patch. I had to go anyhow and dress around to take the wife to her widowed uncle's in Perry where she cleaned house always for him on Wednesdays. He said, sure, and said he'd even stay and take the horses home and eat them up full yet before he left so I could go."

A caravan of little black dots drew my attention. It formed between a sandy pyramid near the peony bushes growing by the garden wall and an apple core I'd discarded in the grass. The core, entirely covered in ants, began to move. I tapped Grempop's arm to show him my discovery, but my sister Helen interrupted from the garden.

Leaning against a hoe, Helen fisted the other hand on her bony hip and said, "Hey, Jennie! How about putting these weeds in the basket! You're not doing anything anyhow."

Betty Jane straightened and wiped her face with the bottom spread of her yellow apron. "Oh, Helen, leave Jen alone," she teased loud enough for me to hear. "Can't you see Grempop's saying a story?" Giggling, she returned to hacking and pulling weeds in the onion bed.

I knew the answer, but I was killing time. I asked, "Grempop, how did you lose your barn?"

"*Ach* now, be patient, *Yoongie*, I'm getting to that," he answered sharply, fumbling with his pipe. I glanced up at him, fighting tears that threatened to come, but the twitching muscles in his jaw and the slight sparkle in his tired brown eyes assured me he wasn't angry. He continued. "After I was done doing stuff in town and came back to pick up your granny, we were *chust* ready to go when the fire siren called out. We all watched out from the yard gate to see which way the enchine turned. Why, it turned left!

"I had some apples with me and sold them to some of the neighbors yet so they'd be all. Then we started home. When we turned in toward Bern, I saw flames shoot up the other end of the valley and over the hill. I said to the wife it must be back at Harold Riegel's. Or

Moyer's. But when we came on top of the hill at Unger's, I thought different. Machines were lined along the road for as far as you could see. When we came to the Three Corners, there was so much commotion going on that we couldn't drive no further."

Grempop forgot I was on his lap. His hand slapped my legs, stinging them a little from a sunburn I'd gotten minding cows the day before. Maybe it's time to hoe onions.

Grempop went on, "I asked a guy there what's burning. He said it's a barn, but nobody knows whose it is."

"Whose was it, Grempop?"

Grempop took a long pull on his pipe and stared straight ahead, like he was thinking the whole thing through. A pained expression crossed his wrinkled brow as he puffed more smoke into the air, cooling now from a hefty breeze that had suddenly sprung up. Grempop studied his swollen knuckles and barely whispered, "That's my barn, I says to him."

My eyes jerked back toward the barn. It wasn't so glistening and white anymore. Behind, dark slate clouds clustered on the near horizon. Overhead, advance thunderheads jockeyed for position, trying hard to swallow the sun. They cast a sullen shadow over the painted stars that now looked more like pointy thorns on a silver crown, badly needing polish.

"Did you get to see it then, Grempop? What did it look like? I'll bet it was something, wasn't it?" Oh, I had so many questions at the tip of my tongue wanting to pop out all at once. I was getting good at this.

"*Ai-Yi-Yi, Weiscupf!* You ask too much!" Grempop coughed, then pointed with the stem of his pipe. "*Chennie*, see that maple tree over there?" The wind was blowing stronger now, lifting the branches heavenward. "Why, when you see the white undersides of a maple leaf there's a storm coming fer sure. Now, you best help your sisters quick get the weeds carried out before it makes rain." He pushed me gently forward.

I swiped at the stray blond hairs that stuck to sweat on my brow and pouted, reluctant to move away. Grempop stroked the tip of his beard that came to a point like Billy's. Billy was our goat. A tricky smile played below his thinning mustache when he spoke again. "Maybe we'll continue some after chores."

I helped my sisters pick up the many piles of weeds. We dumped the last load into the pigpen and returned the basket and hoes to the toolshed when it started to rain cats and dogs, as Grempop would always say.

Grempop lay stretched out on the kitchen couch, taking a late afternoon nap. I wondered how he could sleep with all the lightning and thundering racket outside. Bullets of rain pecked vigorously at the west side window. Still, wheezy snores alternated with a frequent cough.

I decided to play with the tin barn set inherited from Luke that had bypassed my domestic sisters. Designing the barnyard on the cool linoleum floor at the foot of Grempop's couch, I made as much noise as I possibly dared. I set up the big red barn first. It looked uncommonly plain and naked. With crayons, I drew circles over each of its four mows and created stars inside to match the beautiful ones on our big white dairy barn. Next, I added the milkhouse, an implement shed, corncrib, a chicken coop and pigpen. The cows and horses I stabled carefully in the bottom level of the barn. Chickens, a lone sheep, and a big black and white Holstein bull with a ring in its nose went inside the barn's yard where stood a huge yellow straw stack. With each addition, I communicated in their respective languages until Mama arrested me.

"Shush, child. What a clatter you make," she said in a low, stern voice. "You wake up Grempop!" *Gee whiz, that's the whole idea,* I thought. *After all, he did promise to finish the story.*

"Yeah, anyhow," piped in Helen. She sat at the kitchen table snapping green beans into a tin kettle that I thought was just as noisy. She whined, "Mama, why can't Jennie help? She's certainly old enough to do this."

Betty Jane looked up from peeling potatoes for supper. Instead of rescuing me, she commented on the wicked storm and how heavily it rained. Mama was pickling the last of the red beets for canning and said she hoped the men hadn't been caught out in the hay field. I ran to the side window, eager to make my contribution as long as it dealt with farming and not with cleaning beans. The men, tractor, and hay wagon were parked in the dry, underneath the *vorschust* where it connected to the indoor shed.

"No, Mama, they made it to the barn!" I said excitedly, then added in a rush, "the *hex* signs must have saved them!" Just saying what I always heard. We all laughed, even Helen, but not our mama. Grempop slept on.

The next day, I overheard Mama and Daddy arguing about the *hex* signs. Mama said they made her feel funny.

"You should of never left your Pop have that *Fraktur* man paint those awful signs on the new barn," she said.

"*Ach* now, Floss, there you go again! You know doggone well stars bring good luck," he said with a smile in his voice.

Quiet as a mouse, I halted my dusting in the parlor next to the kitchen and awaited Mama's response. I could hear her clearing the table from Daddy's mid-morning snack of shoofly pie and black coffee.

Pouring Daddy another cup, Mama said this time, "You call losing a whole herd of cows to the TB test good luck? And what about the barn burning down? You call that good luck?"

"Well, this time we have a barn with a cow painted inside a star," he replied too lightheartedly I thought for the delicate moment it seemed. More seriously, he added, "And besides that, we have lightning rods on this barn. There will be no barn fire from lightning strikes, for sure."

Mama's voice toned down some when she softly said, "Well, it wonders me if it's Christian."

"The lightning rods?"

"No, of course not. The *hex* signs."

Daddy mumbled something in Dutch I can't repeat. His coffee cup came down with a thump, and his chair scraped back across the floor, away from the table. He left the house, the screen door banging loudly behind.

CHAPTER 2

(Nineteen Forty-Five)

I got a doll each Christmas when I was little and unwrapped the last when I was six. She was Shirley Temple, modeled after America's sweetheart, the ever popular child movie star of the thirties and beyond. Even her name carried on into infamy. There were five Shirleys out of twenty-eight students in my Wegman Elementary class.

Shirley was fragile, but oh, so beautiful in her fancy blue taffeta dress—a dress not ordinary like the hand-made, hand-me-downs from my older sisters I usually wore. She had brownish-blondish curly hair, sparkling brown eyes and the cutest smile you ever did see. Try hard as I could by pushing the eraser end of a pencil into my plump cheeks, I couldn't make cute little dimples like Shirley had on each side of her pretty face.

Even though Shirley Temple was solely mine, Mama had put conditions on the gift. I was not allowed to play with her. This special doll was one of a kind and needed to be kept safe, clean, and preserved for the ages. In Pennsylvania Dutch terms, she was "*Chust for Nice.*"

Of course, Mama's condition was disappointing, but when I thought more on it, I couldn't really blame her. You see, I had a history of not taking the best care of my dollies. Like with Raggedy Ann.

Often crops were planted on the farm with a wide strip of grass alongside to prevent erosion. They called this strip farming. If, like in the meadow, there was not enough acreage to allow more than one strip, we'd let the cows feed on the lush grass alongside for a couple of hours a day. Not worth the time and labor to erect a fence around the crop, which was usually corn, it became my chore to watch that the cows wouldn't go into the corn. This task was called "minding cows," something I did from the time I can remember. On the farm, one was never too young to do such things.

While I minded cows, I always found plenty to do in between my vigil. I'd play house in the tall weeds on the high side of the crick bank, or dig out clay in the crick and make pottery to use in my pretend kitchen. One day, Raggedy Ann was a guest in my pretend kitchen, and I'd decided to wash her up good before serving a pretend dinner. She never dried out after the soaking I gave her and, as a result, got moldy and smelly and sick-looking. Mama wouldn't even let me bring her into the house. I eventually buried Raggedy Ann, with a respectable ceremony, of course, behind the summerhouse under the shade tree.

Then there was Sally, my small and fragile porcelain dolly whose arm broke when I dropped her in the corn crib. The crib was an excellent room to play house in summertime when it was empty. But, of course, it had its flaws—like a cement floor! And there was Millie....

Through the years, Shirley Temple was part of the parlor furnishings. She occupied a spindle rocker, painted light green, that had been my mama's when she was little and her mama's mama's before that. Often, I'd sneak into the parlor when no one was around and sit in the small rocker with Shirley on my lap and tell her stories.

Grempop had taken sick and died a few weeks after our rocking together under the maple tree last summer, but the memory never faded. One Friday after school, well before Mama was back from hucking in Redding and my sisters home from high school, I'd decided to run my own made-up version of Grempop's barn fire story by Shirley. This exercise was necessary before writing it down just in case she'd offer good constructive criticism in the process. Sitting in the green spindle rocker with Shirley on my lap, I began:

"When Granny and Grempop came to the Three Corners that evening and could go no further, they stopped their machine off and chust left it set on the dirt road. From there, Granny made the way home on foot,

picking her way between the double row of chalopies and buggies parked along the road, all the while focusing her eyes on the heavy orange mist above the treetops ahead." I sounded just like Grempop in the telling.

"*Grempop cut up through the woods and across the fields. At the top of the wooded hill where an old wild cherry tree marking the edge of his property met the back wheat field, he saw the blaze in full view. From a distance, it was no bigger than the woodpile fires he built each spring after trimming the orchard trees of their dead branches. But as he moved in closer, the fire grew bigger and brighter, and the flames shot far into the air, licking at the sky like a thousand fiery tongues!*" (I loved that description. I picked that up from Mary O'Hara's novel, *My Friend Flicka*.)

I had really dramatized this last part of my story, trying to impress upon Shirley the major importance of this event. I chatted on.

"*By the time Grempop reached the driveway, sparks caused by a painted star falling into the burning pit shot upward, looking as spectacular as the fireworks closing Bern's Fourth-of-Chuly picnics. Except now it's still daylight. The crowd of people scattered around the driveway ooh'd and aah'd onct they saw that. But when splinters of burning wood and ash and sparks rained down upon them, they backed away. Soon, one by one, a few stepped in close again.*

"*In Pennsylvania Dutch, Grempop asked one of these* Englischers *how the fire happened, but the man couldn't understand him. Another bystander who did said he heard from one of the firefighters someone probably took gas out of the gas engine in the shed behind the barn and a cigarette ash dropped in.*"

Shirley slipped off my lap and reminded me I had an audience. Shifting her once more to a seated position, I cradled her tight, and my saga continued.

"*It was hot and humid. Typical for an early evening mid-August. Grempop was wringing wet, but he soon dried off from the scorching heat around him. At least his face dried off some from being so near the burning barn. Why he needed to be in that close, he wasn't quite sure because there was nothing he could do to change what was happening anyhow.*"

I found myself slapping my doll on the knees, so involved was I in my own storytelling. Just like Grempop! Then I paused, considering his circumstance, and glanced down at my sad little girl. Her wide dark eyes had sunk deep into her face. No smile. No dimples. Together, we silently rocked, both meditating on Grempop's feeling of helplessness. Mama always told me to pray to God when I needed help. I wondered if Grempop ever prayed. A thought of hope for Grempop popped up. I began again.

"*Actually, Shirley, there was little Grempop could do. But there were firefighters there a plenty who could help do something about it. Even though the barn was getting lost and also the milkhouse, the animals were safe out in the field, and the firemen saved the nearby pig stable, the brooder houses, the corn crib, the old implement shed and the kelterhaus. These buildings were wetted-down, and they didn't catch the fire.*

"So, you see," I told Shirley, thinking back on Mama's earlier advice, "*no matter what bad happens, there's always much good to be thankful for.* Yah, *Grempop had much to be thankful for. But at the time, he didn't think so. Tears began to form in his unbelieving eyes when he joined his family on the side porch. He and Harry, Grempop's youngest son, and, would you believe, my daddy,*" I whispered, "*had worked hard all spring and summer. And* chust *as they reaped what they sowed, everything now was lost. Two mows of fresh hay, first cutting of alfalfa. A bumper crop of timothy. Clover. Granary half full of oats from July's harvest. This now was all. And* chust *one week before the fire, they stacked a third mow clear to the roof with wheat sheaves, thrashing next to do.*

"But, now, Shirley, there was nothing left to thrash. Not even the thrash machine itself. Not even the horse plows or the cultivator, the disk, or the harrow. Not even the two wagons that had been inside the barn or the harnesses. And lots of other things that it would take months for the men to figure out what was lost.*"

Like me, when Grempop went on and on in his storytelling, Shirley got restless—maybe bored—and more than once slid from my lap, putting me consciously back on track with my story.

"Yes, my little one. God is good! Do you know what the neighbors did then?" Shirley didn't know.

"That same night they gathered around Grempop and offered to build another barn chust as soon as this one was done burning. But Harry, already raising his own family in the big house after Grempop and Granny moved into the grossdawdy's haus, reminded everyone of a more pressing need for now. The cows needed milking."

Since I was coming closer to home in my storytelling, Shirley's interest restored itself. Twice her long dark eyelashes fluttered. I rocked faster and explained how uncomfortable a cow is when she's burdened with a full udder. That it's very important she be milked at regular times, like every morning and every evening. I repositioned Shirley securely on my lap, promising a cool glass of milk and some walnut cookies if she'd please let me finish my story. I hurried on.

"A good thing the horses and cows were still out in the meadow while their inside home was burning to the ground. That same evening, one of the neighbors took the horses to his farm and another penned the cows in the orchard. The orchard that was normally fenced on all sides to keep cows out would now serve as a stable to keep them in. Harry scrambled up buckets and crocks and pitchers and whatever else he could find in the kitchen that would hold milk. He distributed these to the friends and neighbors who were there, and the cows were milked.

"The next morning, he did the same after they showed up bright and early in Grempop's driveway. Most brought tools and a couple brought wheelbarrows. Some had milk cans to store the milk in the springhouse and for taking the milk over to the railroad station. Some brought mended harnesses. Mixed grain feed for the cattle. Lumber. Lots of lumber.

"Three days after the fire, a thunderstorm cropped up and snuffed out the smoke.

"Neighbors from every direction came each morning to help rid up the mess. Harry took charge, but Grempop didn't seem to mind. A spark had gone out somewhere deep inside. But things were soon to change.

Harry told the men to tear down the dry wall at the far end. While doing so, one of the men found a stone with carved initials: FSB 1749."

I looked down at Shirley whose eyes were closing and shook her. *"Ai-Yi-Yi, Yoongie!* Wake up! Be patient," I said. "I'm getting to the part shortly what that means. *Chust* don't you forget what I promised!"

Shirley woke up, sat up, and I went speeding on.

"When Grempop saw the blackened stone, he handled it as if it were from Granny Sarah's china cabinet. Suddenly, he spoke out chust as proud as could be, 'This barn was built by my grossdawdy's grossdawdy's *dawdy. His name was Franck Stein Balthaser. Come on the Ship Molly in Philidelphi from Chermany over and planted hisself right here on this very spot.'"* I sounded just like Grempop.

"Then Grempop stepped carefully over a pile of rubbish by his feet as if he were stepping on holy ground. He laid the stone down carefully and placed it next to two iron cat troughs and a grain scale that were saved from the fire.

"Meanwhile, his son told the men to finish tearing down the dry wall where they found the stone, mumbling something in Dutch that the wall that separated the wagon shed from the cow stable at one end of the first floor was no longer necessary in the new barn."

Shirley got thirsty. Since I was coming up on an exciting part to the story and didn't want to be interrupted, we broke for milk and cookies. Afterward, I caught her up with my barn fire story. *"Now what do you suppose Grempop said to his son?"* Shirley stared at me with a blank look, dimples barely deepened. *"Why,"* I continued, *"he said in the crossest tone I'd ever heard him with, 'Son, this cornerstone laid in that wall to begin with, and that's where it's going to end up at onct this barn is up again!'*

"It was easy to tell Grempop was upset cause he got louder and louder as he talked. His face got red and puffy.

"'We're building the new barn on the same foundation and laying the horse and cow stables out the same way chust *as sure as Amen follows*

a prayer!' he growled. 'And we're not going to do without the wagon shed in the same place neither!'

"Harry uttered a small laugh, but there was no sound of humor in it. 'But Pop, that's foolish,' he argued in dialect, his voice chust as icy as Grempop's. 'Times change. We need to make bigger the cow stable and milk more cows. The old stable's too small, and so's the herd. You know that!'"

Just like Grempop, I found myself slapping Shirley's knees, so involved was I in my storytelling.

"'You're getting too big for your britches,' his Pop yelled back. 'Lest you forget, chust because you paid me some, this Balthaser farm stays in my name until I die! It's the way it's always done.'

"Nothing more was said, but the other men felt the strain between their two good friends and remained quiet. Out of respect for Grempop, they left the wall alone as they continued to clean up. They even replaced other stones they found lying in the ashes, but only after scrutinizing each to make sure they were nothing special. Wagon after wagon loaded with twisted iron, chunks of charred hay, pieces of boards and heavy timber beams, and soggy, heavy metal ash and still more soggy, heavy metal ash were hauled away until it was all, and the big hole up in the woods was all full up. It was probably the same hole where they dug out the stone for the wall foundation in the first place.

"Soon later, a master carpenter was hired. His name was Charle Berger. One day, this fella Charle Berger came by to talk about building the new barn. Grempop wanted everything same as before. But Harry didn't budge an inch on the cow stable. Their argument repeated. To make peace, Mr. Berger suggested a vorschust that allowed shed space as well as enough room for stalling twice as many cows as before. Both men agreed on the new design. Plans were made.

"August poured into September. It wasn't 'til mid-September when drier weather returned that they could start rebuilding the barn."

Shirley was asleep.

CHAPTER 3
(Nineteen Forty-Six)

Helen and I were always fighting, or so it seemed. Typical sibling rivalry. Yet behind the scenes, we were fairly good buds and often co-hosted "you're-not-allowed-to" activities when no one was around. Like hunting down the ice cream *stanner* Daddy hid for obvious reasons. We'd make our own batch of that wonderful creamy goodness, only to get sick afterward from over-indulgence. Or, like the time we snuck Luke's Schwinn bicycle out of the shed and rode out on the road, Helen pedaling, me sitting behind, and, in the process, crashed coming down the steep hill back at Schtammy's. Often, we played the old Victrola in the parlor. One time one of us, I won't say who, broke Mama's favorite record—Country/Western artist Eddie Arnold. When we were found out, the usual ensued: She did it, Mama. She broke it. I did not. She did, and she's just blaming it on me. And so forth. Sometimes we'd write and act out plays in the backyard. Once, Rocky pulled down Mama's new store-bought bedsheet we'd hung over the wash line for a curtain. It was torn to shreds. Another....

Growing up, I was what one called a bookworm. My nose forever in a book. Even when *huptaing* home the cows at night. (*Yah*, more than once I stepped in a cow flop because of it.) Helen disliked reading because she was near-sighted and needed glasses according to an eye exam at school. Mama figured she wanted glasses just to show off and, hence, ignored her request.

Helen gave her reading circles to me. In exchange for my chore of washing eggs for Mama's marketing, I'd read them and report the story back to her. She, in turn, made the required book report to the teacher. My point in telling you this is that constant reading sharpens the imagination. This led to my forever daydreaming, fantasizing, and writing. Always writing. Someday, I'd publish the great American novel.

In the seventh grade, for an assignment in English class, I wrote a fictional story on how I imagined Grempop's new barn was built. I made myself the main character in the narrative and became Grempop's granddaughter and daughter all in one. This piece of "literary genius for a seventh grader"—Teacher Mrs. Kerschner's description, not mine—was titled *Barn Raising*.

(A minor postscript here: When I wrote, I got carried away with the story and where it was going, my handwriting totally illegible because of it. To give you an example of how bad it was, one fine school day, Mr. Alberts kept me in after Geography class because he couldn't read my homework. This immediately following a class in Penmanship in Mrs. Kerschner's room where I received a Star. Helen was in the commercial course in high school and bragged how she could type forty words a minute. I'd put her to the test. She agreed to do my story on the portable Royal Typewriter we had at home under two conditions. One, I'd do her share of cleaning our bedroom—for one whole month. Ouch! Two, I'd dictate the story to her. I read, she typed.)

BARN RAISING

By Jeanette L. Balthaser

On the first day of my second grade at the Balthaser School, a red brick one-room schoolhouse beyond the Reppert homestead, I assumed

the task of making other students aware of how Grempop lost his barn through fire, and how he'd raise it up again. A group of us girls huddled at noon behind the green leafy lilac bushes, eating out of our lunch pails, me introducing the discussion. Before I knew it, the others carried the conversation away from me, each putting on the dog how their daddies or granddaddies each had the best and biggest barn. The debate continued until the boys discovered our hiding place. They pestered us bad until the bell rang and dinner hour was over. The afternoon recess was a repeat of the same and the next day as well. By the third day of school, I got smart and hung out with only Mary.

Mary Kettering was a bashful, homely little thing in my opinion. She had an upturned nose and a rather washed-out face with a smattering of pimples on her cheeks and forehead. Her dull brown stringy hair was not done up in pretty braids or what have you like the rest of us wore. She was not only a new student in my class of four, but also new to the community. An auslander *(foreigner) we called her. Mary became a captive audience for my story.*

"Did it really all burn down?" she asked, her thin lips parted with wonder, eyes big and round as twin moons.

I answered Mary in my most Dutchified voice that resembled Grempop's, "Yah, you should of seen it. It burned nigh unto ten days. They had to bring fire enchines from as far away as Philidelphi to make it all out."

"Golly, that must of been a big fire!" Mary said. "Where's Philidelphi?"

"Oh, Mary, you know. Philidelphi's near Chermany," I said.

"Chermany? Where's Chermany?" Mary asked this time.

"Oh, never mind," I said, just a wee bit niffed. "Chermany's not the point. The point is it's far away!" Mary's pale grey eyes swelled with water, and I knew I'd gone too far.

I quickly added, "Do you think your mama would let you come home with me after school to watch them work on the new barn?" Mary had never been on a farm.

"Oh, could I? I mean, do you think it would be all right with your

mama?" Overjoyed, Mary blinked away tears that by now trickled down her hollow cheeks.

It was good to be back in Mary's good graces.

I detoured from my usual route home from school, taking, instead, a much longer walk down around the orchard so I could show Mary the goings-on.

The orchard was busting out all over with fall apples. And cows. I had hoped we'd get there soon enough so I could show Mary how I brought the cows in from the meadow. But with the crisp fall evenings cooler and shorter now, my brother Luke had already fetched them home. Home these days was the orchard.

"My! Don't cows get cold when it snows?" Mary asked when we reached the outdoors make-shift stable. She opened up her school bag and took out a faded brown woolen shawl and wrapped it around her small, bony shoulders.

"Of course, they do, but it's not snowing now yet," I said, much too all-knowing. I'd completely forgotten how delicate her nature was. "By the time it does snow," I added sweetly, "they'll be safe and all cozy warm in their nice new barn."

Then I showed off a little, going between two cows tied at a wooden rail. "Hey! Watch this, Mary!" I said as I wrapped my short fingers around one of Bossie's thick round teats bulging with milk. I squeezed hard and shot that creamy white stuff directly into the mouth of the tomcat who was hanging around for just that treat.

Mary shrieked and scared the cat, which jumped between the cows on the other side of the grassy aisle where Luke was milking. The cow kicked, and both he and the bucket of milk came flying out into the aisle. I judged this as a good opportunity to leave.

"Come, Mary!" I said urgently. "Let's see what the carpenters did to-day!" We raced up the cow lane hand-in-hand, past the rebuilt milkhouse

and on to the top of the bank where the carpenters gathered up their tools. To Mary, I bragged, "This is going to be another bank barn so's we can back the wagons right out into the barn for unloading hay and what-have-you." That's what Grempop would've said.

Big wooden beams were already in place overhead. I ached to walk on them, arms outstretched, balancing myself like I'd seen the tightrope walkers do at the Ringling Bros and Barnum & Bailey circus last spring in Redding. The thrashing floor was also in place. I bragged to Mary how the thrashing worked.

"The horses back the loaded wagon into the barn, and then this big iron hay hook comes down from out of nowhere and stabs the individual sheaves that are stacked on the wagon. The sheaves are then hoisted up and moved over into the mow by horse power. By one horse power, that is." I giggled, visualizing a horse led out from the barn, while mentally patting myself on the back for such a clever remark. I pushed on.

"I sit on top of the horse that is hitched to a single tree that pulls the ropes that pulls the pulley that pulls the hay hook down, up and over." This was confusing, even to me, so I thought best not to confuse Mary with any more detail and went on with my tour.

"Let's see what we have over here," I said. Then I got side-tracked. The floor looked mighty inviting. I was about to check it out when Mr. Berger, his eyes narrowed and his words coming fast and harsh, scolded in Dutch, which only I could understand.

"Those there are temporary boards. Don't you kinner walk on them! It's not safe!"

Embarrassed some in front of my special guest, I acknowledged humbly in my ferhoodled Deutsch (mixed-up Dutch and English) and led Mary around the outside, past the milkhouse again, to go below. Together, we grabbed a stepladder the workers had left behind, pulled it over to the wall and managed to climb up toward the scaffolding. Me first, Mary behind.

"See! There's Grempop's many great-grandaddy's letters," I bragged, pointing to the corner stone after I reached the top rung. "I heard Grempop tell onct that someone brought that stone all the way here with a boat."

"A boat?" Mary was impressed. So was I when I'd thought more on it. Why, I could see the boat floating up the canal alongside the Schuylkill River. It was headed straight for our dairy farm.

"Yah, a boat," I said and continued. "I bet if they had as much rain then as we did during the past coupla weeks, it would have docked right here on the very same spot where our new barn is being raised." We were both quiet for a spell, me all full of myself and contemplating the marvel of this sudden discovery. We backed down off the ladder, and I gave Mary a quick guide of the new stable layout.

"Here's where the horse stalls are going," I said. Balancing with my arms and one foot in front of the other, I stepped out four stall areas that the carpenters had staked in the east section of the newly-cemented ground floor. "Grempop says it must go here like before cause that's where horses belong."

"Why?" Mary asked.

"Why?" I repeated, surprised that she should question me. "Cause Grempop says so, that's why! Grempop says horses must be closest to the house in case you need to get them ready to go off in a hurry." Mary seemed satisfied with that. But I wasn't finished. I told Mary that Harry said it would be better to put the horses at the other end and divide up that area, making a box stall for calves and leaving only two stalls for horses. "I guess we won't be needing so many horses anymore," I said as if I didn't care.

"Why not?"

Mary hadn't the faintest idea what I talked about. I paused for a moment, played with one of my pigtails then grabbed Mary's hand. While we walked the imaginary feed entry aisle between the horse stalls and the big cow stable, I thought about her question.

"We'll be farming more modern-like in future, and horses are old-fashioned, that's why!" I said this with far more zeal than I felt. I'd heard that told by someone. I loved cows, but I would never get rid of horses, back then, now, or ever. For certain, neither did Grempop. As far as I knew, the carpenters were going ahead with the horse stalls as Grempop originally planned.

After leaving the barn, we went on to the pig stable. There, we watched the little piggies scramble over each other as they sucked at the mama sow's fat belly. The dinner bell rang for supper.

Two days after Mary's visit, I ran into some serious trouble with Mama. My brother and sisters were older than me. I, the gleina bubble *(the baby) coming on behind, had to go over the hill to join Ray and Mildred Clauser the rest of the way to school. This counted as a blessing since the top of the hill was a perfect place to view the men at work.*

Mildred scolded me unjustly a couple of times. She said I made us late with my dawdling over the barn. This particular morning, after a long rainy night, I walked backwards up the hill as usual when I fell over a groundhog hole that hadn't been there the day before. My lunch pail unlatched, and the summer sausage sandwich fell apart. The buttered sides landed in the mud next to my apple and pear. Nothing was left of the shoofly pie but crumbs and dark sticky chunks of crust. By the time I finished reassembling things, my blue smocked dress was as brown as the dull brown cotton stockings I wore. Not to mention the extra time cleaning up took away from my viewing.

Mildred fumed when I arrived at their place. She didn't speak a word the rest of the way to school. Mr. Naftzinger, the schoolmaster, was extra mad, too. He made the three of us stand in separate corners throughout morning devotions and during two whole classes that took us up to recess time. That night Mr. Clauser paid Mama a visit. Mama punished me by making me leave twenty minutes earlier from then on. This allowed more time at the top of the hill.

Toward my left and below the field dotted with husky shocks of corn, the cows, after being milked in the orchard stable, returned to the open meadow in usual fashion. All eighteen of them, one behind the other, Bossie in the lead, old Christina at the tail. Christina was my cow. The only one slow enough and bony enough for hoisting myself up on. I always rode her when I hupta'd *home the cows during the summer. Once she even saved me, her back a quick refuge from the bull we named Napoleon.*

To my right, the finished cement sides of the first floor of the barn could be seen from my grandstand. Above the bank stood the silo with its gigantic frame. It was almost completed though still not erected on its permanent foundation. Nearby, men busily sawed and hammered stuff at the many lumber piles in the field.

I heard talk at supper that what the men were doing was measuring timber to shore the barn's mainframe. They hand-drilled holes so wooden pegs could be driven through to fit the frame. Beams were marked, rafters notched.

Grempop gathered the neighbors together a few days later for an old-fashioned barn raising. It was my good fortune this was Saturday and not a school day. Soon after daybreak, fifteen farmers arrived. Some, entire families. Charle Berger supervised while the men got on with the business of raising the sides of the barn and tacking on the roof. Throughout the day, we youngsters carried cold peppermint tea and ham sandwiches to the men, while the women busied themselves in the kitchen preparing for the feast that would follow.

At the finish, Izzy Engel installed a cable across the roof, connecting pretty white steeples above each mow. Then ran the cable down both sides of the barn and grounded them at each corner. Mr. Engel said that these lightning rods were the latest in modern devices to protect barns from lightning strikes during summer storms and that Grempop's new barn definitely needed this protection. "Yah, Gawiss," Grempop had said. "I don't want to lose another one."

By nightfall, work completed, bellies full, everyone paraded out to the new bank barn. The barn smelled of sweet, new wood, and a faint odor of cows milked an hour before for the first time in their new home. The thrashing mow on the second floor was readied for celebration. Grem-

pop started things off by climbing up several rungs on the ladder built into the frame. From there, he was easily seen and heard over the growing excitement.

"Dos is gawiss wunderbar!" Grempop shouted in the dialect that came easiest to him. Then switching to English, he went on, "Yah, now can we all see what hard work makes." His moist eyes slowly spanned the rafters. One end to the other. At last, they came to rest on the beautiful friends and neighbors who now quieted down and listened carefully to what he had to say. "I thank you all good," Grempop finally said, choking out each word slowly as if he'd suddenly forgotten how to speak in English.

Four men broke the silence that followed by tuning up their guitars and fiddles. With sudden zest, Grempop, still clinging to the ladder, enunciated loud and clear, "We work wonderful hard all day, now we make wonderful gschposs all night!" He nodded to the musicians, and they began playing "Turkey in the Straw." That's what it took to get everybody moving again. We youngest rushed off to one mow over and played hopscotch while the older kids alternated the cranking of handles on two ice cream stanners that would harden that wonderful creamy homemade goodie yet to come. Meanwhile, the grown-ups hoe-downed, and, in between sets, laughed, drank (hard cider for men, sweet cider for women), and exchanged funny stories—each tale taller than the others.

And everyone lived happily ever after with the Balthaser's wonderful new dairy barn!

CHAPTER 4

(Nineteen Forty-Seven)

Oh, no! Please. No! I screamed to myself. I turned around, plumped my pillow and covered my head to shut out Colonel's crows.

Colonel had been one of those cute little painted roosters Mama brought home each year shortly after Easter. More often than not, even before the decorated eggs and jellybeans were gone, frustrated mothers along Mama's market route in Redding gifted us with these chicks they had earlier purchased—a fad as popular for the holiday as fancy baskets, coconut eggs, and peanut butter candy. The chicks were still in their small cardboard boxes with little peep holes on all four sides when they arrived on our Pennsylvania Dutch dairy farm.

We laughed at the reasons for such generosity. Ungrateful kids shirked the responsibility of caring for their new feathered friends. Spilled water from tipped teacups inside the box stained through to the Oriental parlor rug. Or, the host was stunned that these little critters refused leftover mashed potatoes, gravy and pork *schpeck*. The story tickling our funny bones the most was when the youngest customer on Oley Street asked Mama to bring back the eggs the little rooster eventually laid.

We pampered these birds, raising them inside our picket-fenced yard until the color wore off of their fluffy white feathers. (They were always white—White Leghorns.) Only then was it safe for them to absorb into the flock in the chicken house without literally being picked on for their difference. Discrimination in its infancy. Colonel, the last of these roosters, hadn't yet graduated to permanent headquarters.

Nevertheless, he achieved grownup status with his frequent floppings (Ouch!) and early morning crows.

There he went again, tooting his horn beneath the bedroom window, purposely waking me up before the rattler on the bureau went off. I shifted positions again, this time cursed by the yellow glare of the ceiling bulb. My folks insisted on the light so they could see their way as they passed through our bedroom to and from theirs in the back. *Wasn't anybody going to let me sleep?* Then I remembered what day it was.

"Gee, you're up early for a change!" my sister Helen mocked as my feet made their way slowly to the floor. Right. I was not a morning person.

Consistent with my non-verbal attitude upon rising, I moved to the window. The dawn mist lifted, exposing the most beautiful dairy barn this side of the Blue Mountains. Tucked away quietly throughout the night, she slowly returned to life. Within the huge white-walled frame, my brother Luke looked curiously like a mime, pacing back and forth behind squares of artificial light, feeding and milking Daddy's prize herd of registered Holsteins. Underneath the *vorschust*, the semi-retired draft horses Barney, Roy, and Dolly watered at the big iron trough just outside their stable.

Next to the barn, in the dirt driveway spread between our sandstone farmhouse and wooden outbuildings, early morning proceeded like every other Friday. Daddy loaded the red Ford pickup Mama used for market. Potatoes, apples, and onions left over from last year's harvest filled most of the front half of the truck bed. Cone-shaped half-bushel baskets displayed lettuce, spinach, endive, and rhubarb along the sides, allowing customers to see the fresh late spring produce in one solitary sweep of the eye. Bringing up the rear lay a full crate of eggs. Eggs I had gathered and washed during the week. With a heavy load like this, Mama would hardly return before sundown.

Helen held a short-sleeved green cotton dress with little red roses designed in fields of white against her skinny frame and stepped up on the creaking iron bed we both shared. Checking herself out in the mirror above the bureau, she twisted this way, then that, while spirals of mouse-brown hair loosened from pin curls dangled over the edge of her forehead. As she primped, they bopped up and down like yo-yos on a string. She stepped down again and tapped me on the shoulder, saying, "I think I'll wear this one today. It goes good with my eyes, don't you think?"

Sure, the red part. I said nothing.

"Too bad you can't go with, Jennie," she teased this time. "I'll bet you're jealous cause you can't go with."

"Who cares!" I feigned a yawn and returned to my view of the driveway.

Actually, each of us girls vied for the opportunity to accompany Mama to market. Besides the glamour of big city goings-on, these huckstering excursions meant special store-bought goodies along the route. Novelty stuff like pretty little wax ladies filled with colored sugar water. Chocolate popsicles, orange creamsicles, soft drinks, Milky Ways, Hershey bars. The small packaged fruit pies from Karl's Kandy Korner were to die for. Thick, sweet and syrupy. They came in dozens of flavors. Pineapple, lemon, peach, cherry, apple, blueberry…. Yummy. So much tastier than our ordinary home-baked fare.

Then there were the special food stuffs Mama bought at Cassel's mom and pop grocery store on Fourth Street. After selling left-over produce from the day's huckstering to John and Bertha for resale on their produce shelves, Mama, in turn, bought such things as sugar, salt, dry cereals, macaroni in a box, Velveeta cheese, or red and green Jello that came in small packs. Maybe Starkist tuna in a can. Sometimes fresh fish. Ocean fish was a delicacy on our country dinner table. Well, delicacy for all but me. I despised the smell and taste of fish. It started when I saw Betty Jane leaning over the porch rail one evening after supper with Mama coaxing a fish bone to either come up or go down that was caught in her throat.

Betty Jane was off and married now. Helen, a junior in high school, having completed spring term two days earlier than I, had the privilege of going along with Mama this particular day.

A dead flower on one of the geranium plants on the window sill grabbed my attention. Crumbling a dried brittle petal between my fingers, I absently squashed it into the potted ground and allowed the sun-yellowed curtain to fall back against the raised window shade, then reached for my Sunday best.

The dress hung starched and pressed on a wall peg above the bed. Mama had made it from yards of pink organdy, and, with her treadle Singer, created a pretty vision with long ruffles around the skirt. Tiny delicate ones on sleeves and collar. A long white sash for the waist finished the gown. It was much too nice to wear to school. Except today was special. It was May 26, 1947. Graduation Day at Wegman Elementary. Our eighth-grade class had a farewell program prepared to entertain the lower classes, and I wanted to look especially nice. After all, I had the leading role in a skit I myself had written.

"Mama told me I could wear my good dress today," I said in sing-song tone equal to Helen's. It sure beat wearing a cotton dress made of printed material from feed bags Daddy got at the mill. "Besides, she said I could visit the Repperts after school. Maybe see their new twin calves." So there!

"In your good dress?"

"Sure, why not? It's special today!" Actually, the part about seeing the twins wasn't made clear to me by Mama, but it did seem a good idea.

———

Joan and Shirley Reppert were lucky. The bus stop shelter stood practically at the end of their lane. Me, I had a good half mile to connect. Even at a full run in the mornings, it was challenging at best to catch the bus on time. Evenings, the distance seemed shorter, and I could immerse myself more fully in the country sights and sounds when not so rushed. Like this last day of school when I decided to forego visiting with the Reppert girls, opting to head straight for home instead. It had been a high adrenaline day, and I needed to be alone with my thoughts. After all, today was a milestone. My last day after eight years in grade school. My last ride on the bus with Stanley Manger.

It was sad to say goodbye to Mr. Manger. He waited patiently with an open door for that little blond *maedel* with the swinging pigtails running to catch his big yellow bus every morning for eight years. I was always late. He never complained.

There were two bus drivers for grade school in Wegman Township, and I was lucky enough to have by far the better of the two. Mr. Manger held every kid's respect. Never any fights on our bus. Plenty of levity. He always laughed and joked with us young-uns and kept busy making *gschposs* as Grempop would have put it. I was the last pickup on his route. As soon as the door closed on the bus and Yours Truly caught her breath, Mr. Manger pushed in the clutch, shifted, and drove off while at the same time leading us in song, starting with the Doxology. It was a morning ritual. "Praise God from whom all blessings flow...."

Mr. Manger was special, too, in another way. Really special. Here's why. Six years before, a Watkins salesman gave him two puppies in exchange for a burlap bag filled with wheat for the man's backyard chickens. The family kept the female and named her Queenie. The boy puppy they gave to my family. We named him Rocky.

Two perfectly marked St. Bernards, Queenie and Rocky were unique in our rural farm community where most dogs were of the mixed shep or hound variety. But being an outsider didn't bother either of them. At least not Rocky. He adapted well to farm life, chasing cows, nipping them in the heels just like the best of 'em. And ridding the farm of meddlesome groundhogs who dug holes where little girls would stumble over. And rescuing stupid children from icy ponds. And....

Rocky was my "furever" best friend. Man's best friend. And horses', too. Dolly was our semi-retired draft mare with whom I hung out from the time I was old enough to say "I wanna horse" and big enough to sneak into the horse stable. I'd climb from the deep feed trough in front of Dolly's stall and onto her back, and, just like Velvet before she became National Velvet, I relished in a fantastic make-believe ride. I was quick to slide off and hide underneath the trough when someone entered the barn.

Dolly was a constant target for Rocky's attention. When she and the other two drafts, Roy and Barney, were in the back pasture next to the yard, Rocky dared to run inside the yard and bark, but only at Dolly. In turn, she trotted back and forth on her side of the fence, head up, facing the yard and whinny. Whatever they communicated to each other I didn't know, but there was obviously a bond.

Even one of the neighbors enjoyed Rocky. Mr. Unger told Daddy that every night, eleven o'clock sharp, our Rocky walked over their wooden porch. Why? No one new why. When Daddy told him we'd have to pen him up at night, Unger, said, "Oh, don't do that. We get a kick out of him coming by."

Rocky did have one enemy on the farm. Gertrude. Gertrude was Mama's pet goose. Gertrude attacked Rocky one time with her big heavy wings, and he kept his distance forever after.

Tears threatened to appear at the memory of these things that once were, recalling for some dumb reason another time when my cousin Grace visited from town. We played "hide and seek." Rocky and I were "it," and Rocky immediately discovered Gracie's hiding place. In the old apple tree next to the outhouse in the rear corner of our yard, Gracie clung upside down like one of those creeping sloths on a banyan tree I'd seen in a *National Geographic* magazine. It looked even funnier when Rocky came away with his mouth full of her dress hanging out both sides of his mouth.

That was back in the days of youth and innocence. When fun and freedom were dealt to the young like white fluffy dandelion flowers dispersed on a warm summer breeze. Me, a youngster raised in perfect harmony with man and God and the wonderful creatures He entrusted to my care. Yes, those were times when nothing bad could happen. The kind that grown-up folks say were the good ole days.

My folks often spoke in hushed tones at the supper table when someone they knew "kicked the bucket." Or some tragedy befell a neighbor. A friend. A relative. People wondering why God let bad things happen to good people. But me? Wasn't the escapade at Clauser's pond proof enough that Jennie was untouchable?

Then it happened. Less than two months ago. April 5th to be exact. The day that changed things forever. The division between a carefree childhood and coming adolescence when life happens and things start going awry. The time when the good ole days are over. The time when I learn trouble really does exist, and my small perfect and safe world is no more.

Instead of waiting for me by the yard gate when I'd come home this afternoon, my dear four-footed friend lies quietly above the summerhouse in a patch of yard, its cover not yet green as the surrounding terrace. You see, not all the neighbors enjoyed our Rocky. It was from poison that he died.

Thick lilac bushes, cones spent of their purple glory from the sudden heat, tower well over the crude marker where ROCKY is etched into the hard surface. At the time of his burial, I was much too emotional to absorb what Mama tried to say as we all stood around the graveside watching Daddy as he positioned the fieldstone facing east.

"It worries me already that we continue the pagan tradition," Mama had said.

Daddy cringed. "*Ach* now, Floss," he said. "Rocky was only a dog as all of you seem to forget."

"I know," admitted Mama sadly. "I can't help it though. The tradition really bothers me."

A couple of weeks after Rocky's burial, I brought up tombstones again. Mama and I were weeding in the old Balthaser family *graab hof* (graveyard) behind the woods, which out of reverence for the ages, we manicured throughout much of the year. The old monuments, few straight, most slanted at an angle, sank unevenly into the earth. They always faced the east.

"Why is it wrong for Christians to have their tombstones facing east?" I asked Mama.

"Why?" she repeated, thoughtfully. "I guess it doesn't really matter one way or the other. They are after all only stones. But it's the reason for the tradition that's wrong according to the way Ken and Molly explain to me." Ken and Molly are Seventh-Day Adventists whom Mama met sometime back when they went door-to-door selling Christian literature. Mama bought two books from them. *Patriarchs and Prophets* and *The Great Controversy,* both by Ellen G. White. Ken and Molly come to the farm now and meet with Mama one evening a month to study the Bible. Our entire family is invited to join in, but we always have more important things to do.

Mama had gone on, "They say it's not founded on Scripture, Jennie, that's why it's not good." With a table knife, she poked at the deep stubborn root of a dandelion. The weed was so big from the spring warmth it already covered most of the word "*Geboren*" etched above my many great-granddaddy Franck Balthaser's birth date. "The reason the pagans had their tomb stones face east was that they expected their bodies to rise up with the morning sun." Mama paused some, then continued, "The bodies of your daddy's ancestors rest in peace here, and they won't ever rise with the morning sun." She succeeded in working the plant loose, slicing off the root and leaving it to dry out on top of the ground to die in the bright sunshine. The green leafy stems were tossed into a basket with others to be made into a thick, hot sweet and sour sauce to pour over cooked potatoes for supper.

"Wouldn't they already be in Heaven if they were good?" I asked, scratching around distractedly where I worked.

Mama dug out another dandelion plant, shook the ground from the root and said, "Maybe. Maybe not. Ken and Molly showed me where it says in the Bible that the dead sleep and know nothing. But it is puzzling. Just the other night I found a scripture on my own that says to be absent from the body is to be present with the Lord. I write down questions when I come up with them and ask them next time we meet. Your Sunday School teacher should learn you some of these things, too. Better yet, Jennie, read the Bible for yourself."

Oh, sure. Now that Mama was studying the Bible with the Adventists, she figured everyone should read the Bible. I received my own copy of the Good Book when I went through catechetical classes the year before. I never opened it since. No need to. At church in Geigertown where we go to Lutheran services one week, German Reformed the alternate, we do our devotions and readings from a weekly bulletin and never have to open a Bible. Before the service, we meet in Sunday School and use a lesson book. Occasionally, the teacher refers to his Bible for answers. But only occasionally.

Mama dug out another dandelion root, looked over, giving me one of those parental appraisals, then added more wisdom to our conversation. "Ken says we have a choice about going to Heaven. Let me see if I can tell it the way he says it is. The Bible says if you repent of your sins—that means that you tell God you're sorry—and then accept Jesus as your Lord and Saviour, you'll go to Heaven. Those who don't, well, they'll go the other direction." Mama had problems saying Hell.

This was a grown-up conversation. I threw out a grown-up response, "Marlene said when her granny died she most definitely went to Heaven because she was always doing good things for others." Marlene was a classmate of mine from school. "Did she?"

Mama thought about that and said, "I don't know. Ken says we're not saved by our good works. It's up to God to judge. Only He knows what was in her granny's heart before she died." Mama stood, stretched, placing a palm in the middle of her back. A most radiant expression covered her face as she stared right on past me. I turned and saw her focused on three fluffy white clouds in the distance. "The Bible says there will be a great blast of the Archangel's trumpet to wake up all the dead at Jesus' Second Coming." She stopped and faced me. "Imagine, Jenny! In just the twinkling of an eye, just like that," she almost shouted, snapping her calloused fingers. "Those who were in Jesus when they died will all be changed as they meet Him up there in the air!"

I was shocked by this sudden outburst, almost scared, and gave this some chance to sink in. I dug out two dandelion roots as I puzzled. I remembered something in Sunday School one time about Christ's return and asked, "But what if we're still alive when Jesus comes back?"

"Oh, Jennie, if we accept Jesus in our hearts, we'll go up, too!" she exclaimed, still standing, still smiling, still focused on the clouds that moved in closer. It was almost as though she saw Him coming for us in "them thar clouds overhead."

Mama paused like she was giving this whole matter some extra special thinking and adjusted the sunbonnet that had slipped behind her thick brown pompadour. *Maybe that's her thinking cap*, I quipped to myself. *Repositioning helps her to think more clearly.*

We worked on in silence, me pondering about the dead underneath my feet, laying there, perhaps just sleeping. Not burning. Nor flying around up above those clouds Mama was so excited about minutes before. It was just as well. Even my goose bumps had goose bumps at the thought of walking near a cemetery at night with spirits hovering above.

Because Mama was so wise on matters concerning life and death, I dared to push things further. I took a moment to get my thoughts and words lined up before saying, "Will Rocky...." My voice faltered, struggling with emotion. "Will Rocky be in Heaven?"

Mama took a deep breath. "Oh, dear. I don't know," she said, letting the air out slowly. "I have to ask Ken and Molly what they think about that. Better yet, why don't you ask yourself. They're coming Thursday night."

I had to think quickly. I said, "I can't Thursday night. I need to study. I have the final examination in two classes Friday."

"I do know that there will be lots of animals in Heaven. The Bible says so. But I've never seen nothing in the Bible that talks about our pets coming up out of the grave...." Mama stopped suddenly, as if to consider the solemn consequence of her telling. Then a bewildered look crossed her face. "Why, Jennie, thinking more on it, I do believe they might. God promises that Heaven will be so much more wonderful than we can ever imagine, so I believe our pets will be part of that package. Yes, indeed!" she finished with a nod, as if that sealed it. "If that's what God thinks will make us happy, I'm sure He'll see that our pets are there, too." Mama was always right. I prayed this was no exception.

While walking home and reflecting on these things, it suddenly occurred to me I was growing up. Life has arrived. Perhaps Rocky's traumatic passing was God's way of preparing me and strengthening me to face more challenges ahead. For now, though, I'd dwell on today instead of the past or the future and focus my attention on what still is during my final walk home from grade school.

Spring floated through quickly this year, the warm and sticky air promising an early summer. We'd already put away first cutting alfalfa and timothy. The sweet aroma of freshly mowed clover drying in the sun permeated the afternoon air as I walked by the field. Barring rain overnight, hay would be made tomorrow.

To my left, the corn Daddy planted three weeks before pushed vigorously up through the rich, dark soil. Their tender shoots reached skyward for God's sunlight and rain. I swear I could hear the crackle of the tiny stalks, growing taller, greener by the second. South of the upper meadow, below the pear trees, our cows lay satisfied along the creek bank, chewing cud while drowsily switching at flies. In a couple of hours, they'd stand by the bars inside the lane, *blahing* madly. Impatient to come in. To be fed. Milked.

After I made the hard bend in the road, I noticed a sudden calm in the air that precedes a storm. Ahead, dark clouds piled up behind our barn. Then my focus switched from the threatening skies to the colorful *hex* signs on the barn's front. Awed, I felt a strong statement of defense and authority by the center one. Like a matriarch, supreme and unmovable, a cow's head painted within the borders of the huge star front and center kept vigil over our Holstein cows feeding in the meadow below, just like Daddy implied. At the same time, I was reminded of the unsettled feeling about *Hexerei* that remained in the back of my mind since eavesdropping on my parents' argument. Though, it wasn't something I paid much attention to until the subject popped up in History class.

Mr. Alberts said *Hexerei* was a carryover from Europe's Dark Ages and actually a form of witchcraft. The Swiss-German farmers brought this superstitious culture with them from the homeland when they settled here in Pennsylvania. They decorated house furniture, barns, and outbuildings with *hex* signs to charm off evil spirits in the name of love, prosperity, fertility, and for "chust plain old good luck."

Instead of taking afternoon recess that day, I had stayed in to talk with the teacher and asked him about *hex* signs, stars in particular. Mr. Alberts said stars are the most popular design amongst Pennsylvania German farmers since it's believed they protect farm animals inside the building from harm. Not only that, but the building itself is protected from the powerful effects of lightning.

So, was Daddy right? Granted, losing all the cows in a TB test wasn't good luck, just like Mama had said. But then neither had a cow been painted within any of the *hex* signs on the first barn like Daddy had said. Nor was lightning the cause of its burning.

Confusion mounting, I felt compelled to further explore this matter of *Hexerei*. It was obvious Mama and Daddy had biased views. I'd continue my research elsewhere.

"The Pennsylvania Dutch paint signs on their barns because it's tradition," said Mr. Yoder when I'd spoken to him of my dilemma. Mr. Yoder was my Sunday School teacher. "*Hex* signs do look pretty in all their frilly designs and colors. But I tend to agree with your mother that any form of *Hexerei* might be evil. Take for example, a painted star on a building maybe looks symbolic of the Star of Bethlehem, when actually it could mean something else. Lucifer, who the Bible calls a 'morning star,' was cast out of Heaven and he brought one-third of the stars, or bad angels as we'd say, down to earth with him. Who's to say then that a star always means good luck like we Pennsylvania Dutch tend to think?"

I remember how his words sent a chill up my spine after I had a chance to digest them. Especially the passages he referred to in his Bible, "Any form of spiritism, which *hex* signs are, is evil. Rather than putting our faith and trust in silly colorful signs for good luck and protection, we should instead put on the armor of God's Word and pray through Jesus Christ." Wow!

CHAPTER 5

A distant rumble drew me back to the present. How rapidly the air had thickened. Fast-approaching angry clouds painted black as stove polish wrestled between a break in the huge maples between barn and house, trying hard to blot out the late afternoon sunshine that stubbornly hung on. I wondered if the cows would be brought in from pasture to the safety of the barn if Luke and Daddy were home. As usual for Fridays, I'm sure they'd gone to Green Dragon, big auction grounds in Ephrata where "plain Pennsylvania Dutch" like the Amish and "worldly Pennsylvania Dutch" like us Balthasers engaged in common dialect and trade. The men would hardly be home until later. Closer to milking time.

I passed through the gate where Rocky always waited for me and on into the yard and up the pavement leading to the porch. In the house, first retrieving two uneaten sand tarts, stuffing both into my mouth at once, I pitched my lunch pail in the kitchen sink. Next, my empty schoolbag found its way to the corner cupboard where it would remain until fall. I changed from my pretty Sunday best into my everyday work duds and a pair of old anklets worn thin at the heels and put on high black galoshes over my old Oxfords. Bring on the rain!

The sun completely disappeared. Slivers of light splintered the sky and alternated with rolls of thunder sounding louder with each passing second. By the time I'd driven the cows into the barnyard, lightning broke in great zigzags across the heavens. Just as I tied the last cow, it began to rain, pelting against the tin roof over the *vorschust* in the form of hail at first. Hailstones clattered to the concrete flooring beneath and rolled around like marbles spilled from a box. Leaning up against Grempop's old wall at the far end of the cow stable, the one that still held the "FSB 1749" stone in place, I listened to the raging storm and thought back to how the barn was built.

I remember it well when the truth of my storytelling hit me for what it really was—just storytelling. It was disappointing that I hadn't actually experienced the building of the new barn first hand. "Yet in a way you have," Mama had said when I shared this with her. "Look at it this way. With all the modernizing and improvements in farm equipment and methods of farming these days, it's kinda like experiencing the building of a new barn, don't you think? Barns are made of more than sticks and stones. It takes people, too. Daddy and I couldn't possibly make a go of this farm without you *kinner* helping out, especially now that Henry's gone." Henry Seaman helped on the farm after Allen Reiter left for war, but he and his family moved up country just last year. "Especially you, Jennie. Your sisters never liked working with livestock, and, besides, Betty Jane is off and married now. Helen, well, she's busy enough helping me in the house and with the gardening. And Daddy and Luke, *ach* now, they could never make a go of it without you, Jennie."

It was true, perhaps. We no longer needed a hired man. My brother Luke was fully grown now. Registered as a farmer, he was exempt from the draft that was still going on even though the war had ended. Now that I was older, I helped more, too. Not to mention all the sophisticated power equipment these days. Harvesters, combines, balers, you name it. Why, with just a little twist of a switch on the wall, a conveyor belt cleaned the manure gutters. This alone saved hours of manual labor each week.

Daddy took sole charge of the pigs and poultry. I and Luke, the cows. Together, we milked thirty-two cows the modern way, using Surge Milking Machines, me helping out evenings during school and weekends. A fancy, shiny stainless steel tank truck came by every morning. The driver hosed the milk from our electric cooler to his tank and then went on to deliver the milk directly to the processing dairy up country. No more need for milk cans. No more need for a springhouse to cool the milk in milk cans like in the old days. No more need to haul milk cans to the train that transported the milk to Brokhoff's.

Between the two of us, Luke and I fed the barn stock, including the dozen or so calves and heifers we raised, plus a bull we kept for mating purposes although I heard that would soon change. The modern way to breed these days was by artificial insemination. Poor Napoleon. He'd most likely end up in roasts come next December.

———————————

Barney kicked against the side of his stall after the latest crack and woke me up from my daydreaming. The storm had gathered momentum and lightning flashed with blinding intensity. I was grateful the cows were safe inside and dry. So grateful, too, that we had lightning rods on top of our barn, unlike the unfortunate farmer one township over who lost his dairy barn just two weeks before. A violent thunderstorm had raged through the area and the five-mow bank barn burned to the ground as well as most of the cattle inside.

As is the custom in the rural community, people came from miles around, if not to help, to nose poke at the farmer's tragedy. Including us. Mama, Daddy, Helen, and I stopped on our way to the annual church picnic to view the terrible disaster from the day before.

Smoldering piles of rubble and soggy debris were everywhere. The pungent smoky smell was awful, truly nauseating. I almost lost my supper because of it. One had to be extra careful where one stepped. Yet, that didn't keep me from wandering off the beaten path. Consistent with my daring and nosy nature, I checked out the manure pit that by now was filled to the brim with water from the numerous fire hoses. There were planks across the top, and I ventured on to one of these. Why? Well, why not? To quote my brother, "Jennie always has to be different." The board was wet, of course, and I slipped, my size five-and-a-half's splashing feet first into the stinky mess below. I clung for dear life to the side of the cement wall, managing to keep my head above the muck of cow pee, poop, and stinky water that was up to my shoulders by the time I was rescued.

My family didn't know what to do with me. They somehow managed to get burlap bags from somewhere for me to sit on inside our almost new grey 1946 Ford sedan. With everyone pinching their noses shut, we returned home. After a rugged scrub-down from head to toe in the bathtub, followed by two rinses, then redressed, I was good to go, again. This time we drove directly to the church picnic. The evening went well until a girlfriend sniffed the air at one point and said she smelled something unpleasant, though that wasn't exactly the word she used. Uh, oh! *Sehr net gute!*

Thunder roared louder and closer, followed by numerous yellow streaks of lightning. I had always sensed a special excitement from thunderstorms with their spectacular fireworks sprinting across the sky. Even fetched cows home during t-storms with absolutely no fear. A far cry from a wimpy five-year-old's first experience with sky phenomena when she went with the family to the Redding Fair. The booming fireworks displayed at the end of the evening scared the living daylights out of me. I immediately ran away as fast as I could to get as far away as I could, which was to the top of the grandstand. There, I hid underneath a seat until I was found. But that's another story.

"Hey, wait a minute, Jennie," you interrupt. "Earlier, you went on and on about how when you were eleven your Grempop's barn fire story was the most spectacular thing ever. You even compared the sky at the time to beautiful fireworks on the Fourth of July. Now you tell us you were frightened to death of such when you were five? What's happened since then that changed your perspective on sky phenomena?"

"Gee whiz, Dear Reader! What can I say? Chalk it up to fantasy I guess, or maybe it's just part of growing up and dealing with life as it comes. As for now, I'll continue if you don't mind."

———————————

This storm was different from any I'd previously encountered. It was certainly no ordinary storm. Ominous actually. Oh, how I wished someone were home and shivered in spite of the sweat pouring off my body from the thick humidity. Even Lassie was scared. Lassie was our new puppy, a boy dog named after the famous collie in the movie *Lassie Come Home*. (Betty Jane said she read somewhere in a Hollywood magazine that Lassie's role was played by several collies. Two of them were male.) Lassie was penned in the feed entry that separated the horses and cows. He whimpered, yelping off and on between the sharp claps of thunder.

Waiting for what I'm not quite sure, I stood in the aisle between the two rows of cow stalls, watching buckets of water pour off the overhang outside and spill into the barnyard below. It looked like Niagara Falls on the postcard Mama kept wedged inside the vanity mirror as a honeymoon keepsake. For certain, the clouds had burst all of their rain at once.

CHAPTER 6

AN EXPLOSION SHOOK THE BARN! Loud and vivid as the most violent cannons in war-time newsreels! Yellow was everywhere!

I screamed and froze in place with my arms wrapped around me. Shortly, a veil of gray smoke drifted over from the horse stable. I screamed again, but there was no one to hear. My brain fumbled with this new numbing reality, and, in a panic, I ran across to the horses, my head spinning, chest burning. The straw pile in the rear of the stable and behind Dolly had already fueled a blazing fire and crackled fiercely. Audible even over the constant roar of thunder and commotion from the frightened horses! A bellowing monster spewing smoke and heat and snatching all the air!

I stood there, shaking, heat singeing my face, smoke burning my lungs, not knowing what on earth to do. The terrible heat sent me backwards. With trembling fingers, I untied Barney, stalled closest to the opening, and tried in vain to back him out. Mary O'Hara's Wyoming ranch novels taught me that horses always return to the fire unless their heads are covered. I was wasting time.

From somewhere I heard a thump. I thought it might be the sound of my heart amplified by terror until Lassie came running to me. He had jumped over the feed entry's Dutch door.

No time to spare, I grabbed the pup and ran for the house. Still no one home. Still alone. The five-party phone line, usually busy, was dead. I ran for help.

Poor Lassie. He grunted continuously, me nearly smothering him with my tight grasp as I dashed through the torrential downpour on the black-topped road toward the Reppert's. Even with my water-filled galoshes and air thick with rain, the half-mile distance compared to my early morning school runs was fleeting and effortless.

I was so distraught I dumped out my boots on the kitchen floor. Whatever was I thinking? The trouble was, I wasn't thinking at all. I couldn't think. Good person that she was, Clarabelle didn't say a word about the mess I just made on her nice clean linoleum. Just mopped it up and that was the end of it. There was more to worry about than spilled water.

Clarabelle, her girls, and I watched Homer from the front window of their big sandstone farmhouse as he headed up the steep lane for a telephone at Bern's general store. But it rained so hard his Chevy flooded out before it even touched the road.

Miraculously, from somewhere, a good neighbor with a working telephone must have seen the fire, for soon, though it seemed hours later, shrilling sirens sounded. A bright red firetruck accompanying those sirens raced past the Reppert home where I remained until sundown. That's when I picked my way between double rows of parked automobiles, listlessly heading homeward, all the while focused on the dreadful orange haze above the treetops at the'end of my destination. Just like Granny Balthaser fourteen years before.

What a homecoming it was! My family, in spite of all the trauma, was overwhelmed with relief when I showed up safe and sound. They hadn't known where I was, maybe even in the burning barn? It was then they told me Warren Clauser had been the "good neighbor" who, after calling the Fire Department in Humberg, ran over the hill and rescued our horses and cows. All except for two cows who appeared to have been electrocuted, perhaps drinking from the metal water cups when lightning struck.

I watched the goings on from the side porch. There were two firetrucks parked haphazardly on the gravel area between house and barn.

Engines rumbled. People shouted. Closer to the burning barn, firefighters manned hoses, their water trained on the spreading blaze. Our big beautiful white dairy barn, now engulfed in flames, was disappearing before my very eyes.

This could not be real. This was just another one of my stories. Something I made up. Yet I could see and feel the embers, soot, and ash that swirled around me like snow in a driven blizzard. The stench of burning wood and a myriad of other burnt materials clogged my nostrils to the degree that I found myself coughing for lack of oxygen. This was no figment of Jennie Balthaser's imagination. This was no story. This was real.

I heard a "whoosh!" Two or three, maybe four, heavy timbers collided around the central star. It was easy to see from my vantage point how the star had lost its artistic rendering except for a hideous reddish glow surrounding the animal's head. Ominous eyes glared past dancing ribbons that twisted angrily, like red long johns flapping in the wind on Mama's wash line. Triumphant until this moment over the barn it was meant to protect, the *hex* sign crashed dramatically, tumbling into a pit of hellfire.

Stunned and in grief for all that was lost and burning, I strangely recalled the engraved stone. I wondered weakly if in the cleanup the men might be fortunate enough to retrieve it yet a second time. Though that hardly seemed possible considering its burial beneath mountains of soggy, heavy metallic ash.

(Author's Note: Following are the first and last verses, with my narrative in between, from "Memories of an Old Barn" by Dorothy Shaw Heckathorn, *Good Old Days* Magazine, Nov. 2000):

A hundred years ago men came,
Laid my foundation, raised my frame,
Roofed me over with loving pride,
Then they build some stalls inside...

Through the years, I overlooked fields of wheat, oats, barley, corn, pasture. And saw orchards busting out all over with apples, plums, peaches, pears, and cherries. Inside, I stored hay, straw, grains, fertilizer, seed. I housed cows, calves, bulls, steers, horses, pigs, goats, and chickens. I watched cows being milked, horses harnessed, calves born, cats chase mice. And children balancing on overhead beams "chust for the fun of it."

...(But now) when you stand and look at me,
A pile of rubble's all you see.
This barn made out of stone and wood,
Stood tall and did the best it could.

ON THE ROAD

(Nineteen Fifty-Three)

CHAPTER 1

"**S**o, what have you decided to do after graduation? Will you marry Billy, or what?"

Or what, my mind echoed in frustration. I'd been asking myself that same question over and over, but she needn't rub it in.

From the time we learned to walk and talk Gloria and I were bosom buddies. Raised in the same church, we did our share of playing Christian missionaries through the years. We preached the Gospel to imaginary audiences in every far-away place one could think of, always giving glory to God with our sincere and avid witnessing. Yet, now, in real time, God rescinded my calling. Our congregation sponsored one student from the high school graduating class to train for missionary work the following fall. This year, the call was a mission outpost in the Peruvian Amazons, and the church elders had selected Gloria, a three-year Spanish student, to serve.

Disrespecting my thoughtful silence, Gloria spoke again, "Remember, we talked about this. If God closes the door for either one of us, He'll surely open a window. Maybe that window has a better view for you, like your heart being with Billy and raising Christian children?" She took a breath and looked me straight in the eye. "Oh, Gracie," she said. "I'd love nothing more than to have us go away together like we always dreamed. But, we're grown up now, and maybe we can reach more people by working independently. There are many forms of mission work, you know. In the spirit of Jesus, we Christians must be committed to bringing others to Him whenever the opportunity presents itself, no matter where we are."

I hear you, girlfriend. You're preaching to the choir, I thought, but didn't say. We sat across from each other at a table in the Perryville

High School library, supposedly studying for an English exam when I responded in a like low tone, "I haven't made up my mind yet." End of story.

With graduation only two weeks away, it seemed I was the only one in our circle of friends who lacked certainty about life after the big day. Not that I hadn't thought about it or prayed about it plenty since my major disappointment. But God didn't seem to hear.

It was during our Commencement Baccalaureate address that I totally dismissed any thoughts of marriage and diapers or taking care of the elderly. "Whether you bloom where you were planted," the minister preached, "or whether you go out into the world to make ripe the seed that's planted within you,...." I blanked out the rest of his message and began formulating my own plans for ripening of the seed. Since God wasn't showing me what to do with my life, I'd take matters into my own hands.

Having three sisters younger than I to help with the house and garden chores, Mama felt it her Christian duty to farm me out. It was the right thing to do. After I turned eleven, a couple of days a week including Saturdays, I cleaned and cooked for the Wentzels, an old, ailing couple who lived two doors up from our pretty three-story red brick house on the eastern edge of Perryville. I dearly enjoyed caring for Tom and Tamah. They, in turn, grateful for my help, were charitable and contributed generously to fattening my piggy bank. This was much appreciated by Yours Truly, yet much more was needed to purchase a car.

To help with that, I joined Gloria and Rachel Friedman, another student from Perryville's Class of '53, and did what so many other teenagers from southeastern Pennsylvania did in the early Fifties. We weaned ourselves from the home front and spent the summer between our junior and senior years waiting tables at the Jersey Shore.

We stayed at a rooming house on the corner of Third Street and Atlantic Avenue in Atlantic City and worked at the huge and busy Come Again Sea Shore Restaurant located one block off the boardwalk. Gloria and I worked the breakfast through lunch shift seven days a week.

During off hours, we donned bathing suits, lathered bodies with baby oil and iodine, and baked in the hot Jersey sun. Gloria was an attractive brunette with a smart pageboy cut that surrounded her lovely face like parentheses. She was blessed with a five-foot-four shapely body that tanned beautifully on the beach, while I, *au contraire*— tall and skinny, fair top to toe, freckled and burnt, peeled and paled quickly afterwards, thanks to a touch of Irish in my German genes.

We swam in the ocean, flirted with boys on the beach, rode bicycle, and strolled the boardwalk munching on sticky pink cotton candy or gummy salt water taffy. At night, we treated ourselves to entertainment on the Steel Pier or danced in its ballroom. My middle name being Dance and Gloria's almost, we did the "Swing and Sway with Sammy Kaye" thing, or jitterbugged to Ralph Flanagan, Ray Anthony, Stan Kenton, or whichever big band was in town at the time.

At least once a week, we attended the outdoor show at the end of the Pier. We watched in awe from our bleacher seats seals balancing balls, dolphins leap through hoops, and divers and acrobats do their crazy thing. The main attraction and the reason I attended this show so frequently was to see that daring horse and rider dive from a platform forty feet in the air into a twelve-foot tank of ocean water. Wow!

Rachel had the more lucrative shift at the restaurant of three to eleven, which included dinner and bigger tips if you were to hear her tell it. What she did in her off hours was somewhat of a mystery. She never told. We never asked. But we did assume. Often her bed was empty and looked untouched when Gloria and I got up and readied ourselves for work in the morning. Yet, who were we to point the proverbial finger? We all sinned one way or another.

———————————

Gloria wasn't scheduled to leave for training until after Labor Day. Since I had no solid plans of my own after graduation, we agreed to go to the shore. Again, the three of us, Gloria, me, and Rachel. Again, by train down through Philly since none of us had a car...yet. Fortunately, we each got our jobs back at the Come Again Sea Shore Restaurant. The summer was a delicious repeat of the one before. Well, almost. This time, I harbored secrets.

One afternoon after work, I banished apron, hair net, and side-kick Gloria, and took a Federal Civil Service Exam. I was shooting high. My eyes on either Washington, D.C., or California if I passed. I passed, qualifying for a GS3 grade entry-level secretarial position.

The nice man in the exam office said D.C. didn't look too promising. Instead, he gave me names and numbers to contact in Los Angeles. There were stenographic positions opening up within the Border Patrol Section of the U.S. Immigration and Naturalization Service should I be available by end of September. Location: Terminal Island south of Los Angeles. Now I, too, had plans. Hallelujah!

Nevin J. Balthaser, my father, owned and operated Balthaser's Ford Dealership on Perryville's main thoroughfare, eight blocks past our house. As a graduation present, he gave me a two-door tan, rather shabby-looking, 1949 Studebaker that was on his Used Car lot going on several months. The car, traded in on a new four-door Ford sedan, obviously needed some serious fixing up, which my father did in his spare time throughout the summer.

After miscellaneous mechanical repairs to the body and engine and replacing a right front fender, detailing the interior, a new paint job, and four brand new white side-walled tires with a spare in the trunk, the car was good to go. And the prettiest on the lot by the time I came home from the shore. When Daddy handed over the keys, I whooped and hollered, "California, here I come!"

"What?" Daddy said in return. Well, there it was. The news was out of the bag.

———————

"Los Angeles!" Gloria said too much above a whisper during church services when I told her of my plans. "Why, that's just about as wicked a city there is next to New York!"

"Fancy you saying that!" I said in return. "I thought wicked places are where missionaries should be going." Immediately ashamed that I spoke so to my best friend, I mused instead, "Just think, in California one can swim in the ocean, ride in the desert, visit a cowboy set in the mountains, and see a premiere at Grauman's Chinese Theatre. All in the same day!" I was very much into movies and movie stars and had four fat scrapbooks to prove it.

I watched Gloria carefully from the side. She shifted her shapely frame in the hard balcony pew where we worshipped, then fixed her attractive gaze down on the preacher momentarily before turning back to me.

"Are your parents going to let you do this?" she asked.

Her question irked me. While she travelled to a strange, primitive continent on the other side of the Equator, I'd simply be going to the west coast. "Sure, why not? I convinced them if I were responsible enough to work in Atlantic City two summers in a row, I should be grown up enough to visit a big city by myself." *So there!* "And in this country," I added with emphasis.

Mama and Daddy hadn't given in nearly as easy as I made it sound. Truth being, the lofty decision shocked and hurt everyone—my family, my friends, and Billy. Especially Billy.

Billy, a somewhat handsome young man with a clean-shaven face and full mane of wavy brown hair, was two and a half years older than I. We met at a church social after our Youth League's annual hay ride two years before. Ours was a casual relationship. We'd bowl or roller skate with the Youth Group Sunday nights, hike in the Blue Mountains spring and fall. An occasional drive-in movie if the weather was favorable. In winter, we ice skated on the canal and played ice hockey Sunday afternoons on a nearby farmer's pond. And there were the cowboy movies at the Strand in Humberg we went to Friday nights with the gang. Occasionally, we hoe-downed at the community hall in Leonard on Saturday night.

His barn work done, Billy often visited me evenings, and we'd sit on the front porch glider, watching the squirrels run up and down the maple tree across the street. And we'd chat. Few knew he'd popped the question. Though never answered, it was assumed by everyone we'd be Mr. and Mrs. William Snyder some fine country day.

"Nice girls don't go off alone like that!" Billy scolded after I'd told him of my plans.

"Gloria's going off alone. Even to another country, let alone another continent. Betty and Ruth. They're both going away to colleges that are out-of-state. They're all nice girls. What's the difference?" I argued.

"But what about us? I thought we were getting engaged as soon as you graduated." There was silence between us. Moments later he looked away. "And then you went off to Atlantic City again," he said in a soft, bewildered voice that trailed off to a whisper. He clearly hurt. "My father's waiting for me to take over the farm, and I can't do it alone."

And so we went on and on.

CHAPTER 2

The morning of my departure, September 3rd to be exact, I briefly hugged each member of my family. This was uncomfortable for all of us inasmuch as we Pennsylvania Dutch are not the touchy-feely type. All the while, I listened for the familiar sound of Billy's old blue Ford pickup honking its way through our few chickens that usually loitered in the alley behind the garage. But Billy never came. I left then, folded road map in hand, and steered my precious "Beulah" toward the west.

But first, I'd make a stop on the other side of town. You see, there was one more secret I withheld until the very end. Rachel was going along. Rachel Friedman, cute, pert, petite Rachel. Someone with a somewhat questionable reputation. Someone I considered only a somewhat good friend because our personalities frequently clashed. Nevertheless, I'd honor the deal we made at the last minute. I'll explain.

The Friday evening after we returned home from the shore, we had a girls' last night out. I and Gloria went with Rachel and another friend of hers to a USO dance at a naval base in New Jersey, the name of which escapes me at the moment. Rachel drove us in her family's sleek and covetous, almost new 1953 Chevrolet convertible. It was a beautiful two-tone green with enough shiny chrome trimming front to back and side to side to light the way even after dark. That was the good news. Here's the bad news.

Rachel and Jane reeked of cigarette smoke and were both drunk as a skunk when we left the ballroom. Neither I nor Gloria drank, but I was the only one familiar enough with driving, me having grown up around cars and all that. I had at least four years' experience behind the wheel and learned to operate a car efficiently long before I was legal. (Though Mama murmured, I got lots of backroad training when the family went for Sunday afternoon drives and Daddy let me take over.) Rachel wasn't too happy when I grabbed the keys from her in the parking lot and insisted on driving home.

It was one in the morning. Only five more miles to go. After driving through the dark, sleepy little village of Leonard on Route 32, a two-lane interstate highway, I ascended the steep hill at the west end. When I came over the crest, I saw much to my horror a head-on collision waiting to happen. In the opposite lane and speeding down the hill toward me was a tractor-trailer with a car passing on its left. A split moment later, I was in the dip between two hills and in direct line of fire.

As if recovering footing on thin ice, I swerved sharply to the right. I'd like to say that because I kept my wits about me and was cool in the face of a crisis, I, hands at nine and three, managed a series of delicately performed maneuvers, jerking and turning and rolling the car until coming to a smooth halt right side up somewhere in the middle of a cornfield.

Yeah, I'd like to say that, but it would probably be a lie. Truth be said, I have no memory of what happened except for hearing an overpowering, noisy, undulating roar and clamor, like a percussionist caught up in his own dream world. It all ended with a bomb-like thump. I faintly recall my door opening and falling out onto the ground like a brood mare dropping her foal. Then, total silence!

None of my passengers knew what had happened because they were each curled up and sound asleep, two in a relaxed drunken state that obviously protected them through the horrible trauma that ensued.

Gloria, in the passenger seat—the most vulnerable for casualty per police statistics, miraculously survived unscathed. Not even a scratch. Rachel mysteriously lost her shoes. Jane had a bleeding lip that, after the state trooper woke up Dr. Specht in the nearby town, was immediately stitched, and she was good to go.

Me? We're talking here of the days before seat belts, harnesses, and air bags. From the harsh bangs, twists, and turns my body endured in that short, split moment in time, I, too, unbelievably suffered little but for minor aches and pains.

We were taken from the accident scene by someone whom I don't recall. I was still in shock when we gathered at the Humberg Diner on Route 32 just outside the town of its name. When we arrived, Eddie Fisher crooned on the juke box, "It Isn't Fair." Amen to that, my brother!

Maybe two, three in the morning, the state trooper came into the diner with Jane and gave us a full report. He removed his wide-brimmed bulky grey hat with a chin strap and ran a hand through jet black hair, all the while shaking his head in disbelief. "If I ever witnessed a miracle on the road," he said, "this one was it."

That's when he told us I had knocked over a telephone pole, and the convertible rolled not once but twice before landing right side up. Also said the car was a total wreck and that only through divine intervention could anyone have possibly survived such an accident, let alone no serious injury. He also relayed that the driver of the tractor-trailer supported my story that a passenger car passed him illegally. There were no witnesses, and the police were unable to catch the guy who flew the scene.

I don't recall what I admitted as my speed at the time of the accident, but judging by the fact that I knocked off a thick hardwood pole at its base, I must have been going at a pretty good clip. Daddy always said my biggest problem behind the wheel was my heavy foot on the floor.

As luck would have it, I did not get a violation, but I did get a thorough balling out from barefoot Rachel when we all met at the diner. Cute, pert, petite little Rachel was by this time completely sober and had much to say.

"My father said before I left home to be very careful, that he wouldn't get one red cent if something happened. There's a clause in his insurance policy that says it won't pay claims if the driver is under twenty-one."

What could I say? It was evident my upcoming trip to California would end before it even began.

I said earlier, this accident was the bad news. It surely was. But there was good news attached as well, besides the fact that all four of us gals walked away from this tragedy to see another day. Turns out the father had made up the failure clause as a warning to his teenage daughter to be extra careful. The car, only five months old, totaled of course, was fully covered by insurance. Rachel used bribery on me nonetheless.

"I think you owe me a trip to California," she said. "After all, you have a car and now, thanks to you, I have nothing to drive anymore."

Oh, that's great, I thought. *Imagine me driving three-thousand miles cross-country with you and your sassy attitude alongside. I truly love you, Rachel, but I don't like you if that makes any sense. Why, we'd be at each other's throats from start to finish.* Then Sunday School lessons kicked in. "Okay," I said. "California's a long drive, and company might be fun. But there is something else to consider here. I have the wheels, but how about gas, food, and motels along the way? What about that stuff?"

"We can split the costs, and maybe I'll even do a little bit more than my share." She smiled. It was gracious, but, knowing Rachel, I was certain it was also phony. "Deal?"

"Deal." I agreed, though it was a stretch. We sealed our agreement with a hurried hug.

The next morning, at Rachel's suggestion, we visited a second-hand shop that sold camping equipment.

My despondency over Billy lasted only a short while, my strong desire for newness and adventure taking over completely by the time Rach and I hit the road.

Daddy, a semi-experienced traveler before he and Mama got married, had helped me map out the trip. He suggested I take Route 32 through Pennsylvania, then Route 40 into and through Ohio, Indiana, and all the way to St. Louis, Missouri. There, I'd pick up Route 66 and stay on that for the remaining stretch to California. Route 66, America's two-lane asphalt and concrete Main Street that curved and rolled and rambled over two-thousand miles through eight states, numerous elevations, and three time zones.

For starters, he said Route 32, though slower, was a more scenic route than say the Pennsylvania Turnpike. Safer, too. I was all into safety at this point. Cheaper, too. Gas, food, and lodging would be less costly on the minor interstate. And, thanks to Rachel's suggestion, we could cook and bed down at campgrounds instead of paying for fancy meals and touristy motels.

First evening on the road, Rach and I gassed up at a small filling station outside Grandon. We purchased a couple of soda pops, used the restroom facilities, and, with the nice owner's consent, parked Beulah behind his building for the night. All for a total cost of two dollars and twenty-five cents. Then dug into fried chicken, hardboiled eggs, and Apple Streudel Mama had packed.

The second day, we drove through the beautiful forested Allegheny Mountains of western PA, Rachel at the wheel, when she complained the brakes were failing. I got defensive and told her it was all in her head, that my father did a thorough check on every single part of this car. Silence.

While on an upgrade, Rachel pulled over to the side of the road, took off her glasses, which she wore only for driving, and suggested I take over and see for myself. My attitude was certainly not at its best at this point. I pulled out and continued the switchback ride up the mountainside, gradually climbing higher and higher. And higher. All the while, I fumed internally that this person sitting next to me had the audacity to insult my precious Beulah.

Well, what goes up must come down. And down we went. I wasn't this frightened since the first time I rode the roller coaster, a.k.a. Jack Rabbit, at Hershey's Zoo and Amusement Park. My stomach rolled, and my chest filled with acid as my young life flashed before me, my eyes on a desperate search for survival. Around each bend, braking for everything I was worth, I barely kept from losing it.

Then God showed up! I came to a cleared area banked on the far side of the road that I later learned was specifically prepared as an emergency stop for vehicles losing control on ice. On ice? I was never so relieved in my entire life as the moment I turned the key to off and reminded myself that life would go on if only I started to breathe again.

Swallowing my pride, I looked over at the gal beside me who, hazel eyes pinched shut, embraced the dashboard with two hands. Both were soaked in nervous sweat.

"Rachel, are you okay?" I said as casually as I could fake it and elbowed her in the side.

Rachel turned toward me. Surely, she saw through to my stressed inner being as clearly as if I were a screen door. Yet, her heart and lungs now working, she managed a weak smile and said, "Yeah, I think so. But I was so afraid that I found myself praying Hail Mary's, and I'm not even Catholic!" The Friedmans were the only Jewish family in our Pennsylvania Dutch community. Her father owned and operated a small successful shirt factory at the far end of town.

There was a knock at the window. Still shaking, I cranked down the glass. The man introduced himself as an off-duty police officer. He and his family were driving through the mountains, enjoying the early autumn scenery. I looked away and saw a black car parked alongside the road about forty feet down. He asked what happened, and I said the brakes aren't working. He asked if I had the car in overdrive.

Overdrive? I just then remembered my father telling me about the stick marked OD and what it was for. Here I was, free-wheeling down a five-thousand foot elevated mountainside without any compression!

The good officer pulled the stick out of overdrive. A teachable moment to say the least, but I was still too scared to drive and followed close behind the officer the rest of the way down the mountain.

Talk about guardian angels! No chubby little cherubim babies with haloes circling their heads and wings protruding outward as they strum on mini harps or shoot love arrows at one another. No, my angels were big, strong, powerful. And omnipresent. Twice within one week's time, The Great I Am saved both of us gals from a horrible near-death experience.

I couldn't speak for Rachel, but what was God saving me for? Was He saving me for missionary work on the road? For Billy? Fight future battles? Writing this run-away bestseller?

After our latest encounter, neither my trip companion nor I were in the mood to finish out the day on the open road. We stopped at the first campground we came to in this Something or Other State Park and settled in a quiet primitive area away from the trailers.

Rachel was an experienced camper. She collected wood and started a fire for a stew she'd make from victuals her mother sent along. Meanwhile, I set up our new old army cots and arranged on them our second-hand sleeping bags, each with rolled-up towels for pillows. Goodness knows, we needed something soft and comfortable for the stiff necks we both endured.

After supper, we strolled through the campground and located restroom facilities. Outhouses actually. Two holes in each individual booth of which there were three. A semi-enclosed shower stall stood next to these. Though it wasn't Saturday yet, kidding, we both decided to bathe. Rachel went first as I stood watch.

She lathered herself with a block of Dial and pulled the rope that tipped the wooden bucket overhead that poured water down over her naked body. The water was comfortably warm, she said, apparently heated by an earlier sun that penetrated the trees. Talk about creative plumbing!

I was next and, thanks a lot, had only a quart or so water left in the bucket to rinse off all the grit and sweat I'd accumulated from two days on the road. Echoing Dial's radio commercial, "A little dab'll do it," a full shower was simply a fond memory.

Weren't sure whose responsibility it was to fill the bucket for the next person's shower, but that would be their worry, not ours. We went back to our campsite, fully refreshed. Attired in clean clothes, we were set and ready for the next day when we'd wake up in the morning and hit (not literally, I hoped) the road again.

That evening by the campfire, I smoked my first cigarette. That evening, Rachel tasted her first Ben Gay toothpaste. Toothpaste? We both brought Ben Gay along to rub over our body parts that were sore in places we didn't even know we had places. But, Rach, not as neat and organized as was I, ahem, had apparently thrown the BG tube in with her toiletries when packing. At dusk, she went to the creek that flowed through camp to brush her teeth when suddenly a wild shriek "Oh, no!" pierced the night air. This second day on the road had certainly turned into quite the adventure for both of us. But the day's not over.

The trip so far was exciting to put it mildly. After all, what's the thrill of adventure without some screw-ups like Ben Gay or rim-of-the-world scare tactics to keep the adrenaline flowing? I'm sure Gloria's mission in Peru couldn't compete with excitement such as this. Nor Marian's and Arlene's hitting those boring books in the country's halls of learning, something I secretly envied them for earlier on. (That was before I realized I was smart enough without furthering my education. After all, I knew how to spell Czechoslovakia. And, really, how much more did one need to be taught about how far participles dangled before considering misplaced gerunds or some other darn thing?) Sometime in the future, married or not, I'd go on to college. For now, much to do, places to go, and things to see.

My thoughts turned to Billy, as they always seemed to do. *What about Billy?* Mine was a platonic relationship. No lightning bolts. No butterflies. But Billy's was serious. What about his wanting to get married? Was their time in my life for him? Time for love, marriage, and raising a passel of kids? Was Billy even in the plans that God had for me? Was God in my plans? Like a rocking chair that rocks back and forth but never gets anywhere, I had no answers.

For now, I'd pull a Scarlett O'Hara and think about all this tomorrow instead. "...After all, tomorrow is another day."

This wasn't the first time I slept outdoors, but it was the first time without a cabin roof or tent overhead. I loved it. I was happy as a lark and cozy as a clam in its shell nestled in my sleeping bag. Though, I did leave the bag partially unzipped to allow more freedom of movement, my muscles still being bruised and all that.

It was a beautiful night. The fire crackled lazily as it chewed up its last embers, while a blended chorus of cicadas and crickets chirped away in the darkness. I locked my arms behind my head and stared wide-eyed at the sky through a clearing in the trees.

They aren't kidding when they say the further you get away from the metropolitan east coast the more beautiful the night sky. The moon was no longer in sight, and the cloudless sky was pitch black, leaving the stars plentiful and startlingly brilliant. Just like the old cliché, "The darker the night, the brighter the light."

I found the big and little dippers with ease. Their individual stars hung perhaps from the beginning of time when God spoke the heavens and the earth into being. (The Bible says six days and six nights though I had a feeling He spent most of the week with His feet up!) They blinked down at me now and glistened like jewels studded on a black velvet cloth when they finally chanted, "Beddy-bye now, Gracie. We'll watch over you until the big bright morning sun takes over."

I rolled onto my side and fell asleep.

During the night, something sniffed at my face, and I sat up with a jolt. Like a deer caught in the headlights, I froze in place and watched a big black bear that I'd just scared away go bounding off into the dark. I lay the rest of the night as wide awake as could be until the sun peeked up over the horizon.

CHAPTER 3

The following morning, I cleaned up camp and packed while Rachel made a final trip to the toilets. I kept checking my Bulova wrist watch I'd gotten for Confirmation four years back and wondered what on earth was taking so long. Having inherited the Balthaser predisposition for impatience, I murmured to myself: *Time to get going, girl.* This was our third day on the road, and we were still in Pennsylvania. We'd never get to California at this rate.

"Hey, Gracie!" It was Rachel waltzing up the path, all cutesy smiles and giggles, her sun-bleached ponytail swinging to and fro like the pendulum on a grandfather's clock. Three strangers followed behind. Three young men. Not a surprise, really. Rachel drew men like flies to a pot of honey. They were cleanshaven with crew cuts and dressed in tee shirts, shorts, and sandals. One of them carried a bucket of fish that smelled like a gym bag.

Turns out these guys stayed in one of the trailers we'd seen the night before and had an outboard motorboat docked at a lake located within the park. Eisenhower ended the war in Korea in July, and these warriors had just come back from overseas. They were vacationing here in the park a few days before starting their first year of college on the GI Bill. Rachel met them at the restroom facilities of all places when they'd invited her and her girlfriend, that would be me, to join them for a boat ride. And water-ski, if we were so inclined.

Water-ski? I was reluctant for several reasons. One, we'd push this trip out to day four and still be in Pennsylvania. Two, the clothes I'd conveniently put on the night before for travel were not appropriate for a day in the drink. Three, as always, I was concerned with what Billy might think about such unprecedented behavior on my part.

Four, and most significantly, I didn't know how to water-ski. Even my swimming skills were not the greatest, having spent most summer days taking care of the Wentzels while my friends were at the pool.

Bottom line, we stayed, donned pedal pushers over swimsuits and joined our new-found friends and boated. And, first for me, we water-skied.

───────────────

Ron gunned the engine. The boat jerked upwards, and we were off. Me, literally. This experience was somewhat akin to lying on the table in OR, and the surgeon looks down and says, "I never did one of these before." (Guess that's why they call it "Practicing Medicine?") I sank each try pulling out from shore. Surely there was a pigeon hole in my cerebral cortex labeled "How to Water-ski," I just had to find it. Until then, I'd be the main attraction of the day for Ron and Rachel, no matter that I was about to drown. Hey, we're talking here before safety vests kept one afloat!

Even when my body did obey, my mind critically digressed, evaluating there was little use for such a senseless sport. Finally, my get up and go had gotten up and went. I had it with all that water sloshing up my nose. Not to mention my ears filling up with same after the chin strap to my rubber swim cap came undone. I was about to give up, when, after the umpteenth pull, I suddenly managed to come out and maintain.

Holding on to the tow rope for dear life, Yours Truly skimmed over the wake behind the boat like the best of 'em. You'da thought I was Esther Williams on parade at Cypress Gardens as I zigzagged back and forth. I was actually getting good at this.

At night, we had hot dogs and toasted marshmallows around their campfire. And beer. I accepted a beer but spit out the first mouthful. How could anyone enjoy such a bitter-tasting beverage? No, thanks! I'd get my kicks from Pepsi Cola instead.

Rachel, more sociable than I, enjoyed herself immensely as she always did when men were around. During our fireside chat, she mentioned that a bear smelled at my face the night before. This prompted Nick to tell a funny story:

> *These two guys were out hiking in the mountains, and the one said to the other, "What would you do if a bear came after us?" "Run," said the other. Number One said, "You can't outrun a bear." Number Two said, "You're right. I just need to outrun you." (J.O.)*

Lions and tigers and bears, Oh, My! Everyone's a comedian.

I excused myself early to hit the hay. It'd been an active day. I was beat and had a long drive ahead. Back at our campsite, my flashlight caught the eyes of a big fat raccoon raiding the pantry box. Leftover stew from the night before was spilled on the ground, and Northern Spy and MacIntosh apples rolled in every direction. The black walnuts from our backyard I'd brought along for snacks—gone. So were the remaining Streudel and hardboiled eggs. Even the shells. I guessed the park was serious about their signs DO NOT LEAVE FOOD EXPOSED. Lesson learned.

A bear. Now a raccoon. I hate when that happens! What next?

What was next was the dreadful drone of Pennsylvania's national bird zeroing in for attack. The Good Lord didn't create anything without purpose, but mosquitoes come close. The air was unseasonably warm and muggy compared to the previous night but, despite that, I covered myself completely with my sleeping bag except for my head. The nasty things buzzed around my head like entrapped bees circling in a jar with no place to go. As much as I hate the smell of fish, I'd have given anything to coat my face and neck with fish oil like the American Indians used to do. And the itchiness, oh, the wretched itchiness. Much worse than the scratchy long woolen underwear I endured as a kid. I was totally at their mercy, and the whine around my ears about drove me crazy.

Rachel was sound asleep on her cot in the morning while I once again broke camp. I shook her awake. Wouldn't you know, she tried talking me into hanging in for yet another day to which I quickly replied, "You can stay for all I care. But Beulah and I are hitting the road in thirty minutes from now whether you come along or not." It felt good to say that, like the satisfaction one gets when scratching a mosquito bite.

After we left the mountains, we stopped at a filling station with a telephone booth on the corner. We called our folks and gave them a synopsis of the trip to date. Minus some of the details, of course. Then we jammed down a quick breakfast at the little café next door.

From there, we drove through the rest of western Pennsylvania, then Ohio, Indiana and on to St. Louis where we, fortunately, in spite of the increased traffic, found Route 66 with relative ease.

An hour or so south of the city, we stopped to refuel. As usual, the one who shall remain nameless conveniently visited the restroom when it came time to pay. Each time I brought the matter up about sharing expenses, she informed me she kept track and promised to pay up as soon as she changed her twenty-dollar bill.

When back on the road, I broached the subject from a different angle.

"There's a verse in the New Testament that quotes Jesus saying we should do onto others what we would have them do to us. Is there a similar scripture in the Torah?"

Rachel threw me I-know-what-you're-up-to look.

Oops! There was one thing I'll say about Rachel. She was astute. (In case I hadn't mentioned before, every day I chose a new word at random from my pocket dictionary. This would expand my vocabulary and thinking capacity, if only to impress myself. Astute was my word for the day.)

"I know what you're getting at," Rachel returned with sarcasm. "Like I told you before, I'll pay you as soon as I change the twenty."

Shortly afterward, Rach scratched around the floor under the dash like she was searching for something, then turned her attention to the back seat where my suitcase lay and clothes were hanging on a rod. With a sigh, she looked over at me sheepishly, her tanned face turning pink.

"I want to prove to you that I really do have a twenty, but I can't find my purse," she said. "I hate to tell you this, Gracie, but I think I left it in the Colored toilet back where we last got gas."

"What?" I said. "And what on earth were you doing in the Colored toilet?" I myself hadn't seen it, but it seemed here in Missouri they had separate facilities for black and white, inside and out.

"Just nosy, I guess. Wanted to see if it was different from ours."

That figured. We happened to be in Missouri. It's the Show Me State. "Well, was it?"

"Different? No. It had two holes inside and the only thing different from outside privies back home was a sign on the door said 'Colored.' There was an outhouse next to it that said 'White Only,' but it was boarded up."

Obviously, that one was no longer used since there was indoor plumbing at the gas station. I had visited it, and I did recall now that it had a sign on the door that said "White Only." Welcome to the South.

"Rachel," I scolded, sounding a bit more than just slightly irritated. By now, I'd had it up to here (and you should see where I'm pointing) with this gal's excuses. "We're an hour away from the pumps. But I guess what you're telling me is we need to turn around and go back and get your purse. That's if it's still there!"

We did. It was.

——————————

Driving through the Ozarks was a bit daunting. The higher we drove the more sky appeared until the mountain was only a small tent of earth against an enormous blue background, then we'd dip below again. Fortunately, a rock-cut, modern four-lane highway somewhere between Lebanon and Rolla lowered the elevation for the motorist.

Yet, even though these downhill grades paled in comparison to the Alleghenies, paranoia prevailed. I doubled, tripled, and quadrupled my check of the overdrive stick, like one constantly checks the safety when trekking through woods with deer rifle in hand—something I frequently did when hunting with Daddy. (Hunting? How can you shoot a deer? you say. It has such beautiful, big brown eyes. I say, so did the cow in that beef burger you're munching on.) More than once, I reached the bottom of a steep hill when I realized I'd been holding my breath for a very long time.

Sometime later, it was goodbye Missouri. Y'all come back now, hear?

Hello, Oklahoma! Getting closer. Three more states to go, and we'd dip toes in the blue Pacific.

Rachel wore a white sailor's hat that she acquired from one of her suitors at the USO dance. Pitched at an angle, it covered her sandy-colored hair which, as usual, was pulled back into a ponytail. I had a good hair day, and my recently permed strawberry blond hairdo, parted on the side and held in place by a pretty rhinestone-studded barrette, hung thick and loose to my shoulders. We were dressed in dark slacks and over-sized white cotton button-down shirts, mine with sleeves rolled up to elbows.

Leaning against the front fender of a lopsided Beulah, we both viewed the road through green-framed sunglasses that were trendy at the time. Surely, we'd attract some good-natured soul to fix a blowout. I knew how to change a tire. But, if there were an alternative at my disposal, I'd certainly be good with that. Three cars motored on by with drivers who had no soul. A single-axel tractor-trailer coming toward us slowed and pulled over across the road.

The trucker came to us with a determined swagger in his walk. (Not sure anymore how Webster defines swagger, but it sounds good here anyway.) He was a fairly good-looking guy, casually dressed in denim and had on a tie-dyed tee shirt that exposed bulging biceps and colorful tattoos up and down both arms. He looked like a walking art gallery.

Not tall, but not short either, our saviour was somewhere in between. He sported the latest fad in male coiffure called a DA. (In more polite English, that stands for duck's tail). And the man had a great sense of humor.

"I thought you were a sailor and his wife," Mister Swagger said, winking at Rachel.

Oh, sure, the all-American couple! Me, five-foot-nine in saddle shoes and skinny as a string bean (but, strong as an ox I might add). And my sailor mate husband barely stretches to half my size. I totally got it, though. I always attracted shorter men. Billy was not necessarily short, yet, when we kissed, our noses touched.

Rachel mimicked a salute and giggled. "We have a flat tire, sir," she said to the man, as if he couldn't tell.

I removed Rachel's suitcase and shoe bag from the trunk in order to get to the tools needed to tend to this latest crisis. The bumper jack, the lug wrench, hand pump, spare tire, inner tube. Daddy told me I could count on at least two flats during the journey—if I were lucky, that is. He sent along two new inner tubes. The damaged tire could be patched at a garage along the way.

"Where're you headed?" the man asked when he was finished. He pulled out a pack of cigarettes, shook one out and put it between his lips.

"California," I said. "How 'bout you?"

"Just came from Tulsa." He lit his cigarette and pulled a long drag, then said, "I'm hauling a load of fifty-five gallon drums of re-fined petroleum to New York."

When he placed the blown tire and tools back into the trunk, he pinched his finger. The words coming out of his oral cavity were enough to make a sailor blush. A real sailor, that is. He smiled it off, then asked, "Would you two be interested in joining me for some sup-per? There's a truck stop with a greasy spoon back a quarter mile." He pointed in the direction we had just come from. The road sign with an arrow said Venita. "Been there several times. They serve a great steak."

My travel partner never let a crisis go to waste. She pitched in and said, "Sounds good. We were planning to stop soon anyway."

We were? It was easy to feel the chemistry brewing between these two.

There was a wide clearing behind the restaurant where travelers were welcome to sleep in their vehicles, pitch a tent, or throw down a sleeping bag on the ground and call it a day, which is what the three of us did.

During the night, a sudden gale-force wind swept through the area with a wicked thunderstorm close behind. Skies rumbled. Jagged lightning bolts ripped a bruised sky, illuminating ghostly outlines of swaying trees. Rachel and Mister Swagger grabbed their bags and ran for his truck, while I struggled out of mine and reached Beulah just before rains of Genesis proportion came pouring down.

Next morning, I woke up to a brilliant sun shining through the windshield. I looked around to get my bearings and, much to my cha-grin, noticed the truck was gone. So was Rachel. And thanks to my giving her a spare key, so were her shoes and suitcase. And the infa-mous green bill with Andrew Jackson in its center. Get this, not even a "thank you for the lift" note was left behind.

Setting aside anger-management issues, I put accelerator to floor. I'd keep right on keeping on. After all, as Mama once said, "You can't be blessed with a sunny day until you've gone through a rainy one." Mama was good with clichés.

CHAPTER 4

Cruising along on America's mother road, I had a windshield tour of a highway corridor that too often included foxes, deer, coyotes, raccoons, rabbits, gophers, and other wild critters that met their demise on Route 66.

There were also plenty of pleasant roadside activities to entertain and capture one's attention as well. Almost like reading the funnies in the Sunday paper. Crazy stuff. Stuff like giant jack rabbits or dinosaurs and armored reptiles to attract the tourist to the premise. Or shrines of gigantic balls of twine, or the world's largest bundle of barbed wire....

On the outskirts of a small town, a front yard sign said, "Drive like these are your pets living here." I liked that. A sign outside a service station said, "We fix flats and make 'em round." Funny.

All too frequently, a motorist who'd suffered from the common curse was changing a flat. Or a vehicle was being hitched onto a tow truck because of some mechanical failure. Occasionally, whole families crouched in high grasses roadside, doing what nature forced them to do. Lots of house trailers on the move. Those reminded me of the romantic comedy, *The Long, Long Trailer,* with Desi Arnez and on-and-off-screen wife, Lucille Ball. Lucille Ball, the gal who was told by some jerk producer she'd never be an actress.

Let me backspace to the giant roadside jack rabbit. One would wonder, I know I did, why a jack rabbit was significant in this state or even in any other state. Well, I think I mentioned before that I was a Hollywood buff. A year or so before this trip, I believe it was down at the Jersey Shore, I saw a black and white titled *Grapes of Wrath* that was based on John Steinbeck's novel of the same name. The movie starred Henry Fonda and showed how violent dust storms back in the Dirty Thirties impacted most of America in one way or another. Majorly so in the areas of rural Oklahoma and the Pan Handle of Texas that were later dubbed the Dust Bowl. Barely surviving an eight-year drought and nothing but dust in their fields, buildings, air and lungs, desperate farmers packed up families and belongings and headed west, resettling in work camps throughout California.

Both intrigued and disturbed by this motion picture, I later researched the Dust Bowl era in the library's *Encyclopedia Brittanica*. Turns out the Dust Bowl was America's most tragic man-made ecological disaster ever. Here's why. Following the invention of the tractor and combine by John Deere in the Twenties, one-hundred million acres of the Great Plains were cultivated and planted with wheat. One huge problem with all of this. Prairie grass, because of its long deep roots that up until then thrived and survived in spite of wind, flood, drought or whatever nature presented down through the ages was now destroyed by man's modern cultivation. Wheat, on the other hand, with its short roots could not survive the drought that persisted for eight long years and, hence, withered away. On top of all this (pardon the pun) came the humongous wind storms. Tons and tons of topsoil were carried in storm clouds and tossed around for hundreds of miles in every direction. Result: Cultivated fields were left completely barren of life except, for some odd reason, thousands upon thousands of jack rabbits.

Well, that's my story, and I'm sticking to it.

A family in an old sedan had a running board picnic. This made me hungry. Beings that darn four-legged masked bandit stole my black walnuts, I had purchased a can of Planter's Salted Peanuts when I got my last gas fill and munched on them as well as on an apple. Mama reminded me that, according to Pennsylvania Dutch folklore, "An apple a day keeps the doctor away." She put two pecks of same from our backyard in my trunk before I left. Goodness knows, apples were not only a handy food source, but also a mandate out here in no-man's land where there was hardly a doc around every corner. Whatever, these snacks would tie me over until evening when I'd have a proper sit-down meal and refurbish at some nondescript roadside coffee house.

Reading Burma Shave jingles along "66" also helped to pass the time. Being ambidextrous, having been born left-handed but re-trained in the early grades to write with my right, I scribbled a couple of them down as I drove:

> The bearded devil
> Is forced
> To dwell
> In the only place
> Where they don't sell
> *Burma Shave*

> This cream
> Makes the Gardener's daughter
> Plant her tu-lips
> Where she oughter
> *Burma Shave*

> No matter
> The price
> No matter how new
> The best safety device
> In your car is you,
> *Burma Shave*

When I could, I listened to the portable radio Rach left be-hind. For the most part, it offered nothing but static along the lengthy stretches of highway. When I came near the outskirts of a town or city, there was usually a wide range of honky-tonk, bluegrass, or country/western to choose from. (Did you know? If you play country/western backwards, you get your job back, you get your sweetheart back, your dog comes home....)

On rare occasions, dance band or jazz came through. Or rhythm and blues—coincidentally, I came across Nat King Cole's latest hit celebrating the very road I was driving on. I tapped the steering wheel and sang along, "...*If you ever plan to motor west, Travel my way, Take the highway that is best, Get your kicks on Route 66....*" It was like Beulah had become my own little private record booth. Just like those I frequented in Zeswitz Music Store back home.

A large flock of sheep baa'd and blah'd their way across the highway in front of me. (I guess to get to the other side?) They were herded by two Border Collies running back and forth. A pickup truck followed close behind. Who'd a thought—a New Zealand traffic jam right here in the middle of Oklahoma!

Soon later, I took my eyes off the road for a second to observe nature in its most submissive state when suddenly two skinny, moth-colored canine mutts locked together in romance filled my windshield. Of all the five billion people on this planet earth and of all the roads and of all the dogs, these two chose this moment to cross this road in front of this person and this person's car to propagate another generation of skinny moth-colored mutts. Everything in the back of my car made its way forward after I made a one-hundred-and-eighty degree swerve to avoid another near-death experience.

Still in Oklahoma. So far so good, but matters began to change, the thought of heading back east occurring to me more than once. Before I get into that, I'll backtrack to the night before.

Feeling a critical need for an honest-to-goodness bath in an honest-to-goodness tub in an honest-to-goodness bathroom, I stopped at The Cherokee Trading Post and Motel. The flat-roofed, rambling one-story structure painted in a riot of pastel colors looked inviting and clean were it not for a couple of mangy, flea-bitten hounds that messed around in the dirt out front. This state had lots of free-range dogs!

A huge hanging signboard edged in jagged cuts with foot-high letters announced the Post's activities. Inside, a rattlesnake show took place from two to three—missed that—and two skilled artisans of Native American heritage entertained tourists. One weaved baskets and the other stitched or whatever one does in making blankets. Next to them were shelves and hooks with displays of finished products for sale. As well as a whole array of hand-made crafts. Indian moccasins and buckskin shirts. Western curios. Trinkets. Stuffed rattlesnake skins (Imagine that!) and other miscellaneous artifacts.

I splurged and bought a poster featuring an upcoming Wild West Rodeo in Tulsa. I'd take a picture of it and prove to a friend back home that the west was still considered, well, wild, but that's a story for another time. I also purchased penny postcards, one of each state I'd pass through down here in the Great Southwest, and a hand-made bracelet and matching necklace strung with alternating orange and turquoise beads. The jewelry would look smart with the two-piece beige nylon outfit I'd purchased at the shore for special occasions. Like maybe an interview?

In the rear of the curio shop was a small dining area with three sets of wooden tables and chairs. The menu listed malts, tacos, burritos, enchiladas, refried beans, and Chili Con Carne. Unfamiliar with all of these culinary dishes except for the latter, chili became my meal of choice. The waitress spoke like Minnie Pearl.

Later, by the time I finished unpacking my car and settled into my motel room, I got sick as a dog and spent most of the night in the bathroom instead of in the bed. And what a night it was!

The next day after being sick and tired of being sick and tired, I tried my best at getting on with life. I'd lost my wrist watch the day I water-skied and since then used an alarm clock we called a rattler back home. Since Rachel left, I kept it on the passenger seat next to the radio and my map and purse so I could keep track of time as the hours rolled by. I'd forgotten to take the clock along into the motel room the night before. Forgot or either too sick to care. Because of this, I didn't get on the road until well after eleven. At the rate things were going, I'd never get to California in time to take a job with the Border Patrol. Border Patrol—the carrot that dangled before me.

The sun was already high in the sky when I opened Beulah's door. The heat hit me like a blast from our coal furnace back home in winter. It gave me thoughts that one should do whatever it took to prepare one's self for an eternity in Heaven instead of landing in Hell (unless, of course, one wants to). Wow, it was hot! Even the steering wheel was untouchable. I used a wash rag in each hand so that I could drive.

Other than an accident, the worst nightmare one can experience on the road besides a flat tire is having two flat tires. No sooner back on "66" when, much to my dismay, I heard a familiar bang, and my steering wheel swung a hard left. I'd just blown another tube! This time in the rear. Turns out a nail I picked up along the way had punctured through the wall of the tire. Well, no worries. A nice, smartly-dressed elderly gentleman in a brown and yellow station wagon was soon on the scene and changed it for me. Grateful for his kindness, having not enough change in my wallet to equal fifty cents, I generously tipped him a dollar bill, which I later discovered had been a five. Ouch! Like Murphy's Law, if anything could go wrong, it did.

Texas is the only state, according to the American History book, that came into the Union by treaty and retains its right to secede should it ever so decide. This largest state has absolutely no physical unity (except for the people—once a Texan always a Texan?). Its topography ranges from high mountains in the west, barren flatness in the north, beaches to the east and a very long river bordering the south. Hundreds and hundreds and hundreds of miles of desert spread in between.

Route 66 cuts straight through the top of the state they call the Pan Handle. Even in that supposedly short distance in comparison to the rest of Texas, time as well as flat earth stretched endlessly for this lonesome driver. My goodness but this was a big state. And a prideful one. To prove my point, I share the following:

> *Traveling reporter sees sign by phone booth outside churches upstate NY and PA: "Long distance call to God $10,000." He drives nonstop to TX, crosses state line and sees sign outside phone booth by church: "$.25 to call God." Asks minister, why only .25 here? Minister says, "You're in Texas. It's a local call."* (J.O.)

Giggles aside, how on God's Green Earth could people call this God's Country and survive in this vast hot and dry desert environment? But that was the problem, wasn't it? The earth was not green here; neither was the earth. Nothing but dried out dusty dirt (leftover from the Dust Bowl era?). No water. No green. Just miles and miles of tumbleweed, prairie grass, and brown sagebrush. And oil wells—those big black monsters that keep pumping away with no human in sight.

No cowboys on horseback in sight either. Occasionally, long-horn cattle grazed, on what I wasn't quite sure. They often roamed next to the shoulders of "66," sometimes with a windmill or water wagon nearby. That "figgers!"

Whether or not it was my own dire need for water to cool things off, I saw ahead a river of the wet stuff flowing across the highway. As I grew closer, just like Alice who dropped down the rabbit hole, it disappeared. Turns out what I'd just experienced was an optical illusion. A mirage. Something they say happens when you combine heat in the atmosphere with the driver's concocted state of weary/bored/lonely—AND HOT.

Running low on gasoline, I pulled in at a Texaco service station in the middle of nowhere and asked for a fill. The uniformed attendant busied himself pumping gas, then checked the oil, and wiped the windshield that was peppered with big bugs and insects, me wishing to share the water on my burning skin that he had in a bucket. My goodness, the sun at the Jersey Shore was nothing compared to this Texan sun. Maybe it had something to do with being closer to the Equator?

I asked the attendant, "Is it always this hot?"

"No, ma'am," he answered, with a chuckle in his Texan twang. "It gets much hotter." Guessing that to be funny, I smiled and paid my fill of gas at twenty-five cents a gallon. It was back on the road again.

CHAPTER 5

This trip was tiresome. Granted, Rachel's filling my nostrils with vapors of smoke throughout the day was a constant irritant. Despite that and despite her immoral compass, just between you, me, and the road sign up ahead, I missed her and would make things right between us if we ever ran into each other down the road. I even missed her cockiness and silly banter that kept me moving forward during this long, very long journey west. The windshield is bigger than the rearview mirror, yet, visions of back home crept into my mind more and more as the grueling miles ground on.

Along the way, I saw steam rise from beneath the hood. Thinking at first it was just another optical illusion, I ignored it. But when the needle on my dash pointed to HOT, I knew I had a problem. Now what? I practically crawled with Beulah until we finally came to a service station, aptly named Phillips 66. The station manager checked the overheated engine and convinced me a canvas water bag would make all things right again.

"That'll keep 'er cool," he said after he affixed the bag with ropes to my front bumper.

Eighty-five cents later, buyer's remorse set in. Eighty-five cents for a little bumper bag? Really? Everything in Texas was BIG, even the price tags!

On the outskirts of Amarillo, a funeral procession stopped traffic from moving forward. A crowd of mourners dressed in black stood on the street corner, mingling with one another in bear-hug fashion, while pallbearers carried a coffin down the church steps. A hearse out front waited with a row of cars behind. Their lights were on and little flags of something or other were suctioned to each roof.

What ceremony! *When I die, they'll probably just throw me in a ditch somewhere, shovel dirt in my face, and go back to the church to eat potato salad.*

A man wearing black cowboy boots sketched with frilly white designs came to my open window. He was dressed in a black suit, white shirt, and ribbon bowtie of sorts. His head was topped with, you guessed it, a ten-gallon cowboy hat. It was the great southwestern trademark.

He nudged his hat back with his thumb. "If ya don't mind waitin', it'll just be a coupla more minutes, ma'am," he said in a friendly drawl, dragging out ma'am. "We'll be movin' on only for a short distance, then we'll be outa yer way for good." Short sounded like shirt with two syllables.

I waited some more and wondered about the body in the casket. Had he died of heat exhaustion? Had he succumbed to the challenges of life itself? Were he to relive his life, would he do things differently rather than living up to others' expectations? Or, maybe he raised a family instead of fulfilling his dreams to see the world, like with George Bailey of Bedford Falls in the movie, *It's a Wonderful Life.*

After things go downhill, George wishes he'd never been born and decides to end it all. His guardian angel Clarence comes to the rescue and reveals the drama that is current life in Bedford Falls had George Bailey never been born. With this short review, George suddenly realizes the positive impact he'd had on others. From the snow-covered town bridge with the dark river swirling below, he shouts to the world, "I want to live again! I want to live again!" And he did and went on to fulfill his father's earlier prophecy, "All you can take with you when you leave this place is what you have given away." (You mean there's no hearse pulling a U-Haul?) George Bailey had much to give away. So did Jimmy Stewart.

The funeral procession proceeded, and so did I.

I said *Adios* to the Lone Star State and drove through a Welcome to New Mexico arch with a US66 shield overhead. Near Glenrio, per the road sign. Getting closer. Only two more states to go. Hollywood, here I come!

Soon afterward, I picked up a hitchhiker. A soldier on a three-day leave was headed for Albuquerque to be with his wife and four-year-old little girl. He took over at the wheel and, now that I finally had company, I snoozed. Go figure. Late afternoon, we pulled up to a telephone booth on the outskirts of the city where he called his wife to come pick him up.

I continued on for a mile or two and drove into Katson's Drive-In Curb Service and parked. A pretty car hop dressed in short shorts, cowboy shirt and hat roller-skated up to Beulah with a friendly welcome, window tray, and menu.

I ordered a California Burger. Another first. What made the California Burger different from a normal beef burger back home was that it came with lettuce, tomato, and onion. And salsa instead of ketchup if the diner so desired. I thoroughly enjoyed this delicious burger, salivating particularly over the healthy salad veggies included inside the bun.

FYI: I was really into good health ever since I learned my body is the temple of the Holy Spirit. Ironically, my lowest grade achieved, or I should say dis-achieved, in all four years of high school was in tenth grade when I got a "C" in Health and Phys. Ed. on my report card.

Maybe it was because I didn't get the food groups in the correct order on the pyramid? Or maybe the bandage I wrapped on a supposed victim didn't stay put? Performed CPR the wrong way on my partner? If I were to guess, it was because, even though tall and strong, I didn't do well in sports involving that round thing they call a ball. No matter that I excelled in track and at archery (a forty-pound pull no less). Whatever, my Dear Reader, Mrs. Weiss, Perryville High School health teacher and gym coach, showed favoritism for girls who played on her basketball, softball, or volleyball teams, leaving those less inclined to be discriminated against even before discrimination was a household word. Sorry, I digress.

While I enjoyed my fantastically delicious and juicy burger, a driver pulled out from the row ahead and backed into my front bumper. Not hard, not even hard enough to knock over the vanilla milkshake on my window tray. It was inconvenient to get out and inspect at the time because of all the stuff hanging on my door. When I checked later, there was nary a scratch.

The following day, this driver was in and out of panic mode. Desert, mountains, nosebleeds, Continental Divide, high cliffs, rock formations, more desert and still more desert. A couple thousand miles in my rearview mirror and many more to go! After hours of ups and downs, over and arounds, and straight aheads, steam came out from under my hood. What the heck? This isn't supposed to happen. Not with an eighty-five-cent water bag cooling the radiator. When I got out and checked, I noticed the sack was wrinkled with barely any water inside. Then I spied the problem. There was a smaller than dime-sized hole near the bottom.

Oh, *Caca*! That man did it! I screamed out loud to no one but Old Man Sunshine overhead. That idiot of a man back at the Drive-In last night did it! He bumped into my car and punctured my water bag. I was furious!

I may not be the sharpest pencil in the box, but I can certainly hold my own. Time to get creative here since who knew how long until I'd be back into civilization. I searched for rags in the car and came across a dirtied white shirt Rachel had thrown on the back seat. A man's shirt labelled Friedman Shirt Company, Size Small. I soaked the shirt in water sacrificed from my thermos jug filled every time I filled the gas tank and placed it on the inside of the radiator and closed the hood. *Fait accompli!*

A mile down the road, Beulah stuttered, coughed and shook, doing her own little version of rock 'n roll. Then she stopped. Stopped right there in the middle of Route 66! Right there in the middle of New Mexico! Right there in the middle of the great United States of America! This was beyond ridiculous.

I got out and opened up the hood and much to my horror saw Rachel's shirt wrapped around the fan belt. Bits and pieces of same were strewn in every nook and cranny throughout the engine. Two men of Mexican descent popped up from nowhere.

"Holla, Senorita," one of them said. The other said, *"Ocupa usped alluda?"* which in my limited Spanish I figured was asking if I needed help. Gloria, where are you when I need you? One year of Spanish and two of French were not going to help me much. Just then universal sign language kicked in, and communication prevailed when I pointed out the disaster beneath my hood. Number One's eyes lit up like light bulbs. Number Two scratched his head in puzzlement and said something to his buddy. They laughed. Both had teeth that were small and crowded.

Funny or not, it was obvious my situation was not a good one. Following these angels' sign language, I put Beulah in neutral and steered while they pushed us a piece way and then off of "66" and in front of a dilapidated run-down feed mill. One hour, one dollar, and four apples later, Beulah was all cleaned up and good to go. *Gracias, Jesu.*

I stopped to buy another bag at the first filling station I came to. This time the price was ninety-two cents, which included three cents tax collected by the state. No way, José! This was highway (66) robbery, for crying out loud! Why, I could fill up my gas tank for little more than that. No more canvas water bags! No more watered-down shirts to cool the radiator! If it comes to that, I'd drive at night and sleep days. Better yet, do a one-eighty. For those of you geometrically-challenged that means turn around and go home!

Flashing lights and black and white-striped gates blocked passage at a railroad crossing in Gallop, New Mexico. A steam engine pulling a string of boxcars across the highway stalled on the track. No problem. I'd gladly wait with the other motorists and watch while the engineer got things back into gear.

You see, trains fascinated me. Especially freights. Often on Sunday afternoons, our family took drives in the country or visited Uncle Harry's farm on the other side of the river. We'd wait at a crossing and wave to the proud engineer in his steaming, glistening black locomotive as it pounded north or south along the Schuylkill River, always pulling an endless string of clickety-clacking cars behind.

I wondered about names of far-away places like Chesapeake and Ohio, C&E, Northern Pacific, Topeka, Boston, Maine.... Names, eventually replaced by graffiti, were giveaways from where these trains originated or where they might return. It was a curiosity how cars from diverse places hitched together into one single train went in one single direction.

Coal was king, and open cars on our Redding Company line were either loaded with anthracite from Schuylkill County to the north or empty ones returning to the mines. (Did you know? Prior to the Civil War, the Redding Railroad Company was the largest corporation in the world.)

What was inside those multi-colored boxcars? (Since I have some wait time here, allow me more useless trivia: On a truck or boxcar, its content is called a shipment. On a ship, a shipment of goods is labeled cargo. Hmmm.) What stories did these boxcars have to tell? These were questions to contemplate as one waited at a railroad crossing when a train rumbled by. Then, it was like watching an exciting travel adventure on film. Now, it's just an interruption in one's rush to be someplace else....

Well, there you have it. Everything you ever wanted to know about rail transportation in the Commonwealth of Pennsylvania but were afraid to ask.

Now, as before I got sidetracked (pun intended), we're still in Gallup, New Mexico, waiting on a stalled train at a railroad crossing around mid-September in the Year of our Lord, 1953.

Every now and then the train gives several fits and starts and thrusts forward with decided gumption, only to stop again, all the while creating a noisy and hazardous domino effect.

Watching these goings on, I try to see where the boxcars are from. Yet the names aren't entirely visible because of a pickup truck in front that impedes my view. All of a sudden, the driver, who sports a large cowboy hat, jumps out and runs over to the track and rescues a woman, obviously drunk, who'd been trying her darnedest to climb between two cars. Moments later, the woman climbs between the cars again. Again, the cowboy gets out of his multi-horse-powered pickup, runs over and pulls her back. This time, he remains by her side.

Fifteen minutes later, according to the rattler on my seat, the train's engine shudders and belches black smoke from its stack. After a sudden hard jolt, the train slowly pulls away and clears the track, enabling traffic to proceed. Meanwhile, the driver in the car behind me exercises early signs of road rage and barks at the indigenous humanitarian still standing with the woman but who then immediately jogs back to his truck. A few seconds fly by, and the drama is history.

Pressing on.

CHAPTER 6

T
wo men in uniform inspected my car from front to rear, inside and out, at the Arizona border. They searched for fruit and other fresh produce and requested I pull over. What the…? Talk about upsetting the apple cart—literally. Five succulent apples in the pantry box? You got to be kidding!

I ate two right there and begrudgingly let them confiscate the remaining three before I was allowed to drive into the great Grand Canyon State. Oh, how I wished I'd been more generous with the good *compadres* who removed the rags from my engine. But shoulda/woulda/coulda was not an option. However, keeping charitable thoughts in mind, I asked one of the inspectors for a small favor in exchange for my apples. I requested he snap a photo of me smiling graciously in front of the Welcome to Arizona sign. After all, as the song says, "I May Never Come This Way Again." When I'd get to Los Angeles, I'd have the film developed and impress the heck out of folks back home with all the interesting things I'd seen along the way. My goodness, there were enough notable sights to shoot a roll in Arizona alone.

I was surrounded by all manner of interesting, picture-worthy historical markers, ranging from prose on statehood and former Pony Express routes to recognition of famous, or, more correctly said, infamous train, stagecoach, and bank robberies. Even a black sign carved in the shape of a handgun and etched with huge bold white letters read, "Bonnie and Clyde were here." I pulled to the side of the road and snapped a couple of pictures. When I turned to get back into my car, I saw a photo op to top all photo ops. At first, I saw voluminous dark clouds on the distant horizon to the northeast. Turns out they were actually the incredibly beautiful, eye-popping, jaw-dropping, majestic Rocky Mountains. *C'est magnifique*!!! I love mountains. I just don't like driving in them.

Allow me to shift gears here for just a moment. With my first paycheck from the Border Patrol, this frustrated photographer is going to buy herself the latest in 35mm SLR technology—a camera that has a couple of interchangeable microscopic and telescopic zoom lenses. Maybe a tripod or two. Then I'll donate Old Box Brownie to the Salvation Army.

On the road again. Again, more notable billboards and signs. Two were stenciled, "You Are Driving through Apache Indian Reservation" and "Navajo Indian Reservation," each with a real live arrow pointing wherever. One wooden, weather-faded sign said "Grand Canyon," directing the driver north of Route 66 and due west toward the Southern California border, a side trip I intended to make before leaving this state. There was also a small sign, "Death Valley That a Way." With all due respect, I don't think so.

Further on, a billboard advertised the Wigwam Village—cabins furnished with Navajo and Apache rugs and blankets. The sign said "50 Miles Ahead." Perhaps too high scale, yet how great would that be to sleep in an actual teepee? Something indeed to write home about!

Hope you're not getting bored with all of this sign business. Allow me one more, and I promise that's the end of it. I hadn't driven too far before I saw one that said "Petrified Forest." Whichever way the arrow pointed, I'm not exactly sure anymore. My soldier friend I dropped off in Albuquerque was an Arizona native and suggested this park was a must-see while I was in the area.

When I came to the crossroad, I extended my arm out the open window to signal to the driver behind that I was turning off. I was getting more excited by the minute as I drew closer and closer to the Petrified Forest National Monument. (The Monument has since been designated a National Park.)

I came away with three beautiful chunks of petrified wood that I'd cherish forever. I found these roughed-up and layered red stones at random as I walked around the grounds (something you were allowed to do at the time). I also purchased three rolls of film at the Visitors' Center and picked up a brochure.

The brochure said the Petrified Forest is made from fossils 225 million years ago and is part of the Late Triassic Epoch and Chinle Formation, whatever the heck that is. (Source: Petrified Forest, 928-524-6228.) Unless one aced Geology 101, it's impossible to understand the scientific history of this World's Eighth Wonder (Eighth? Sorry, I made that up) or of any other geological formations throughout planet earth. I know this flies in the face of the secular scientist, but, according to my Sunday School teacher, Mr. Hendricks, there's a Creationist View that vastly differs from the Scientific View and subscribes to biblical authority; i.e., …In the Beginning, God created the heavens and the earth… in six days…six-thousand years ago…. Based on the Bible, mountains, rock, soil, seas, and fossils as we know them today have been formed by the Great Flood and the post-Flood Great Ice Age that followed. Check it out for yourself in the Book of Genesis.

(Author's Note: Steve Austin, head of the Geology Department for the Institute for Creation Research, studied Mt. St. Helens in the state of Washington as a committed evolutionist and switched to the Creationist View following the volcano's eruption in 1980. He and his cohorts had found that within hours following the eruption, studies revealed geologic phenomena that the mainstream scientists have been saying takes millions or billions of years to evolve. This discovery called into question the many traditional theories such as carbon-14 dating methods, and so forth. If you're interested, read: *Strong Evidence for Creation* dated March 20, 1992, by Steve Austin.)

Well now, that was an interesting bypass to *On The Road.* Do you agree?

Not sure how it happened, but, when I left the Petrified Forest, I found myself in the middle of nowhere without one Route 66 sign in sight. Zip. Zero. *Nada.* Is it this road that I should take or is it that road up ahead? Or was it the one I saw way back there? Whatever, none seemed like they would take a body anywhere, so desolate and lonely everything was. Meanwhile, the sun sank lower in the western sky. Surely, it's time to go home and forget my recent plans.

Neither parent had liked that I was going to California. "It's so far away!" they said. But they wouldn't say no to their eldest cutting the cord and spreading her wings. Mama said that if you keep a bird in a cage, it'll never learn to fly. Now she'd put that to the test. Through tears the morning her fledgling left the roost, she'd said, "Grace, you must trust in the Lord to do the leading when things don't go right for you, remembering His promise that all things will work together for your good."

Well, Mama, things are not going right for me. Thoroughly frustrated and leaning over the steering wheel while Beulah idled, I called out, "Okay, God. I give up, now it's Your turn. Lead the way!"

One road led to another with an occasional crude sign that meant nothing to me. Clearly, I was lost. But how can I be lost when I don't know where I'm going to begin with? And why isn't God telling me which way to go?

I was hungry and tired and mildly frightened that dark should come before I found a town. Finally, I randomly chose a road with the late afternoon sun in my eyes.

Lots of land. Land without a tree line or hillside gracing it. Nothing like our green, rolling Pennsylvania Dutch countryside with pretty dairy farms like Uncle Harry's back home, which I was beginning to miss more and more as time wore on.

I drove for miles alongside a post and wire fence on my left when I came to a break with a sign overhead. Iron letters hanging from a bar spelled "Last Chance Dude Ranch" and swung eerily to and fro in the desert wind.

Wow! A dude ranch! I immediately perked up and imagined rides into the sunset, barbecues, and, like in the Friday night cowboy movies, group singing around a campfire. And a bed! It'd been days since I had a decent night's sleep. My body certainly felt the effects of it.

CHAPTER 7

Beulah rumbled cautiously over the bumpy, wide-spaced steel rails I later learned was a Texas Gate (Arizona Gate?). The dirt lane went on forever. Dust swallowed the gravel behind while, in front, swirling eddies of red sand made fluttering pinwheels on the car's hood before bouncing and dissipating on the windshield.

Big black horse flies entered the open windows and buzzed around me. A gopher sprinted across my path, giving assurance of at least some life in this lost and forever wasteland. No more fencing, no trees, no creeks. Nothing but flat, slightly undulating land and red sand. Where were the cattle? Where were the horses? Where was the end of this long, very long, dirt road?

Finally, a form took shape in the distance. As I drew closer, a grand Victorian house loomed out of the wide horizon looking oddly out of place in the midst of the rustic Arizona landscape trying to dwarf it. Elaborate cornices painted a weathered yellow appeared everywhere. Below each, red shuttered windows closed out the blinding desert sun like the burnt eyelids of a pagan giant performing its morning ritual. An iron-pillared veranda surrounded the first story and connected with a low, flat building that stretched throughout the treeless yard.

From there, an old wooden shed with a bay spilled out into a corral. A windmill, its blades slowly turning, stood alongside a shattered one that had seen its better days. The wheel was splintered into numerous pieces at a dilapidated base.

I crawled between this skeleton and what I assumed a bunkhouse and stopped the car. A man, six foot and more, came out the door from the big house. He limped towards me, his alternate boot heel sharply accenting the weather-beaten floorboards of the wooden porch before hitting the dirt. This tall silhouette in the western sky peered down at Beulah from under the wide brim of, what else, a huge ten-gallon cowboy hat.

I stepped out of my car and extended a shaky hand. "Grace Balthaser," I said.

Staring at the license plate, the middle-aged cowboy mumbled something like, "Northeasterner." His thumbs never left his pockets. Withdrawing my eastern courtesy, I leaned back against the open car door as my eyes searched for other activity in the yard.

"I lost my way," I said to fill the silence. "I left Petrified Forest earlier and was on my way back to Route 66 when I discovered I was lost. Boy, was I ever glad to see your sign out there!" I pointed in the direction of the long lane entering his ranch.

"Name's Jim Bartlett," the man said, focusing his double-barreled blue eyes' stare at me.

Again, I looked around nervously. Except for an old grey dented pickup parked alongside a rusty hand pump in front of the bunkhouse, no other vehicles appeared in sight. Yet, I asked, "Do you have any vacancies for tonight?"

The man shifted his body weight left to right, relieving the leg he'd favored crossing the length of the porch. He removed his hat and scratched his head.

"Y'all'll have to sleep in the back room upstairs in the big house," he said as if apologizing for this concession. "Can fix some vittles later if yer hungry." It seemed a long speech for him. There was silence except for the pranks the wind played in the yard.

Brittle tumbleweeds drifted about, gathering momentum when they somersaulted back and forth against the dark drafty opening of a shed close by. Something moved inside the darkness of the shed while, in the loft above, a door flapped carelessly back and forth on iron hinges.

I swallowed some hot, dry desert air and exhaled audibly before my eyes turned back to Mr. Bartlett. I heard myself saying, "Oh, good, I'm famished."

"Harlan!" the man barked, scaring me to pieces.

A younger man came into view from the black shadow of the shed. He was tall, lean, and lanky and dressed similar to Bartlett. High boots, tight, faded denims and, despite the heat, he wore a snug-fitting, long-sleeved cotton shirt with button-down pockets on the chest, the type we called a cowboy shirt back east. Now I knew why. And, of course, he was topped with the typical native headwear that shields out the oppressive sun.

"Take this young gal's bags to the house," Bartlett ordered. The corners of his mouth turned down when he talked, exposing slightly crooked teeth, stained yellow. Instead of staying to make introductions, the man returned to the main house.

"Howdy, ma'am," the younger said as he tipped his big hat. Standing downwind, I detected an aromatic mix of sweet hay and aftershave that reminded me nostalgically of Billy. But, with that, I remembered, too, the sparring Billy and I had done during our final days together.

"Hi!" I returned in my friendliest east coast manner, not bothering to shake hands. "I'm Grace Balthaser. Lost, tired, and starved!"

"Pleased to meetcha, ma'am." The cowboy's sky-blue eyes sparkled while he spoke in a flat, lazy, barely discernable drawl. He stooped, looked into the loaded interior of my car and let out a shrill whistle, like the kind Roy Rogers used when teasing Dale Evans. "B'lieve yer stayin' for a long time wherever it is yer headed."

I laughed and said, "I'm headed for Los Angeles."

"Los Angeles?" He whistled again and shook his head. His sun-bleached eyebrows raised generously. "I'd say you got a wee bit side-tracked."

"I did, a little." Next, I said, "Am I lucky enough to be your only guest?"

The man paused, thought about that, then with a small chuckle, said, "Sorry, ma'am, what's thet you just ast?"

"Am I your only guest?"

"Guest? Ya mean like a caller?" he puzzled and added, "Oh, ma'am, this ain't no dude ranch if thet's what you 'spect. Ain't been for quite some time. Just never took thet thar sign down out thar."

I began to protest, but, losing no time, he yanked my Samsonite suitcase from the back seat of the car like it contained only down from a duck. "I'll take yer bag up to yer room like Bartlett said, and we'll feed ya some real grub that sticks to yer ribs, Miz Balthaser. So don't you worry none 'bout nothin'."

"Grace," I corrected, relaxing a little.

"Where y'all from, ma'am, uh Grace?" said the man with the awkward grammar and funny accent.

"I come from back east," I said, not exactly speaking the King's English either according to my co-workers in Atlantic City. Pennsylvania Dutch people, up to my generation anyway, are birthed into households where English is a second language. Outside the confines of our rural countryside and small towns, we are labeled "Dutchified" and something to be ashamed of. "I'm from Pennsylvania," I added, not totally relieved from the tension I felt spinning inside.

Part of me wanted to tell this young man to put my bag back into the car, while the other part of me was ready for the adventure I'd set out to have.

Maybe no dude ranch, it was still a ranch. These were real live cowboys, and the adventure part of me won out. I picked two of the four ironed blouses still hanging from a broom handle that served as a clothing rack above the rear seat. Also, a pair of maroon cowboy boots with frilly designs packed in a Sears and Roebuck box still smelling of new leather.

We made our way across the porch and toward the veranda of the main house, me hurrying to keep pace with Harlan's long legs that in spite of the permanent bow at the knees extended artfully wide in their stride. Glancing sideways at one point, he paused long enough for me to catch up. When he relieved me of the box cradled under my arm, his hand felt comfortably warm in the exchange.

Harlan asked what brought me to where I was right now, and I briefly explained how I'd gotten lost. He shook his head as if he found my story hard to believe.

"Still can't quite figger why a young gal come all the way out here alone. Sure got yerself some spunk!" he said.

I smiled and blushed, embracing the theory that heat rises to the top. Suddenly, my whole situation seemed warped and ludicrous. I straightened and added another inch or so to my already too tall body and changed the subject. "Are you and your father the only ones living here?"

"Oh, thet's Bartlett. He ain't my father."

"Who is he then?" Maybe he hadn't heard because he didn't answer. That was okay. My goodness, I sure was being fresh.

We came to a huge door with elaborate designs carved in its heavy frame. Freeing one hand, Harlan opened it and led us through a parlor furnished tastefully in dark Victorian.

"We don't get much company in these parts, so's yer a mighty beautiful surprise to come our way."

Beautiful? The word hung fragrantly in the dry air like the swirling, flowered fabric draped over each of the parlor windows. I might be halfway attractive, but much too tall and skinny to be beautiful. My nose too sharp. Nonetheless, I found Harlan's remark quite flattering.

"And why is that?" I asked, frivolously. "I mean about not having company anymore." From the parlor, we walked up a winding set of stairs and entered a dark corridor that seemed to echo from its spaciousness.

"Dunno, 'cept word's gotten 'round, I guess." He added barely above a whisper, "Folks here say that ole Jim's out of the head. Y'know what I mean?" No, I didn't, and questioned what I was doing here in this forsaken place. When I didn't answer, he went on. "His wife hailed from back East. Spent all Bartlett's money making this here ranch into some sort of tourist getup. Well, 'bout fourteen years ago, she ran off with one of her male customers, that being the last anyone'd ever heard from thee Mrs. Bartlett." He kicked open a door to a room smelling dusty and close. "Bartlett holds against all women now, so don't mind his manners none."

I shivered. "I can live with that," I mumbled. *Could I?*

Harlan flipped on a light. He placed my suitcase on a padded stool inside the door and set the box on the dresser.

The room was mammoth and so were the furnishings. Coarse, yet daintily decorated with obviously a woman's touch, including a colorful tiffany lamp on the nightstand and its twin on top of the chifferobe. On the wall behind the bed hung two Renaissance paintings. Both showed beefy people, a man in one and woman in the other, scantily draped and lying on couches. These were hardly what I considered a westerner's taste in art. Nor, in this northeasterner's perspective. In fact, they were pretty ugly to use a dichotomy of terms. I don't care for Renaissance.

Except for a thin layer of red dust covering the massive head and foot boards, the double bed under its ruby silk spread looked welcomingly clean and cool to this young, frustrated, and tired guest. Dropping myself down, I tested the resilience of its springs, kicked off my penny loafers, and stretched my travel-weary legs. I told Harlan, watching me from the doorway, I'd like to refresh before supper.

My chaperone's handsome freckled face, framed by curly copper hair escaping generously beneath the Stetson hat worn high over his forehead, showed pleasantly of humor and good graces. His mouth had a nice crooked smile on it when I could actually watch him speak, although there was no way to be sure what thinking went on behind his words. Mid-twenties or so, I guessed. Strong like Billy, his muscles had contracted hard and tight beneath his snug cowboy shirt when he carried my luggage up the steps. Actually, built somewhat like Bartlett, it suddenly occurred to me.

"Bartlett's the cook," Harlan said. "Give 'im an hour. Kitchen's down below. Just follow the scent, and ya'll find it quick enough." He touched the brim of his hat, saying, "Now if ya'll pardon me, ma'am, I've gotta git along." With that he disappeared.

Harlan's so nice, I told myself and wondered why he stayed here with that surly Mr. Bartlett. Well, I had more important things to think about and things to do. Although my stomach cried out for nourishment, the long wait before supper gave additional time to explore.

I changed from my wrinkled dress, and, after washing myself at the sink closeted in the corner, slipped into my only pair of dungarees. Of the two blouses I'd brought in, I decided on the green as the most complimentary to my appearance and readied myself for an interesting evening on a ranch.

I guessed western country folk were just as trusting as country folk back east, there having been no key in our exchange. I closed the door behind me, and, without the aid of a flashlight, found my way through the windowless hallway, down the steps and toward the parlor and veranda where Harlan brought us through earlier.

CHAPTER 8

An orange sun lowered itself over the harsh landscape. The skyline broke here and there by clumps of dry sage and tall brown grasses clamoring for attention as they waved along the distant horizon. Uncertainty in the rapidly cooling air, a feeling of anticipation, excitement perhaps, seized me as I continued my way along the dirt path in front of the bunkhouse, then over toward the corral.

Three horses loafed in the corral. One of them whinnied softly and trotted up to greet me. I rubbed the little filly's nose, hoping I'd have a chance to ride her before I'd leave the ranch the next day.

"Well, if it ain't Miz Grace from the great Northeast!" It was Harlan, leading a sweating saddled gelding into the corral from the rear of the shed. "Can ya ride?"

For all of my assumptions I'd be able to ride, I suddenly panicked. I'd done some, well kind of. Growing up, I spent a week every summer on my Uncle Harry's dairy farm. I and Cousin Jeanette, both too young to help with fieldwork, rode the drafts as they pulled the hay wagon around the field. My horse's name was Barney. Jennie rode on Roy. We sat on top of the harness and held onto the iron handles attached to the horse's collar and never moved beyond a labored walk. But I did far more than my share of watching how riding was really done from the cowboy movies I saw most every Friday night in Humberg. Toes pinching from the pointy fronts of new boots, I peeked my feet between the bottom boards of the fence and leaned over the top rail. "Of course, I ride," I said to Harlan like I was a real pro.

Not bothering to tie his horse, Harlan swung the reins over the fence near me and disappeared into the shed. He returned, carrying a blacksmith's trough.

"Wanted to check on the cattle in the lower draw and part the ways there ole Colonel here threw a shoe." He took a pair of pincers from the trough. Then picked up the bay's left rear foot, positioning it between his leather chaps, and skillfully clipped at the excess growth.

"I'll be headin' out tomorrow mornin' to give it another try." He clipped some more and added, "Before the sun gits up." He glanced up at me as if expecting a comment.

I sensed an invitation even though he hadn't asked the question, but I asked two just then. I was full of them. "Where are you from? Have you always lived here?"

"The Bartletts took me in when I was still a kid." He threw the pincers back in the trough and retrieved a hoof knife. "My Pa was a bronco rider in the rodeo and got gored to death by a bull. Ma, God rest her soul, died of a broken heart." Thin white slices of hoof splintered rapidly into the sandy dirt. When he finished, he filed the rough edges and placed an iron shoe over the hoof for its fit.

"I saw this lots of times when I was young yet," I said to fill the awkward silence. It wasn't a full lie. I watched a blacksmith demonstration at the Redding Fair a couple of years back.

Harlan was impressed. He dropped Colonel's foot, straightened, and said, "Ya have? And how old might ya be?" A tease danced gaily around the outer corners of his eyes, and a crooked grin lingered deliciously on his lips. For a naughty moment, I imagined what it might be like to kiss them. Now, now, Gracie.

"Twenty-two," I lied, again. Savoring tentative redemption, I hurried on to the next question. "What do guests do...," I stammered. "What does one do for entertainment out here?" I hardly believed it was me asking such a bold thing and felt warm blood filling up my pale Northeastern face. Fortunately, a high clanging noise from a triangle interrupted us from the front porch. Just like in the movies.

"Thet's fer you," Harlan mumbled through healthy white teeth that grasped a couple of shoe nails. "Gotta finish up here first and feed the horses some grain."

I returned to my room, trying desperately to delay going for supper until Harlan finished his chores. I started a letter.

"Dear Billy, I'm fine and hope you are, too. The weather..."

It was silly, like the kind of perfunctory beginning one made to a pen pal at Christmastime. After several attempts, I tore up my failures and went down to supper.

No steak. No barbecue. Chili Con Carne? You're kidding. Thoughts surfaced of how sick I'd gotten on the chili back in Oklahoma. More aptly put, Montezuma's Revenge. Whatever, I'd survive. I'd fake it. I was getting good at that.

The chili was satisfying, and the beef jerky strips served generously on the side were gummy and tasteful. Disappointed when Harlan didn't join me, I asked Bartlett of his whereabouts. "Out," was all he offered. I ate alone, stealing frequent sideway glances at my host between spoonsful of food.

He sat in a rocking chair by the cook stove pulling on a long, stemmed pipe, shooting little puffs of grey toward the high ceiling. A permanent rim crossed his brow where his hat, now hanging from a peg on the wall by the kitchen door, shaded him from the burning daytime sun. His heavy brows, still dark like his thinning hair but hinting at reddish brown, jutted imperiously over a long, thin nose. Across his right cheekbone, he wore a most repulsive-looking scar that seemed to redden and swell when he spoke, which certainly wasn't often. His small dark eyes stared past me into blank space. I wondered if his thoughts included "thee Mrs. Bartlett."

Silence uncomfortable, I finished eating without seconds from the pot on the table and quietly excused myself. Bartlett simply nodded, sending more grey smoke my way, and continued to rock. It looked dark outdoors and not at all like there'd be singing around a campfire, so I returned to my room. I gave the letter another try.

Dear Billy,

Rachel met a friend along the way and left me alone. I've had a good trip so far, and everything's worked out exactly as I planned. I'm currently staying at a dude ranch for tourists— you know, the kind that the Sons of the Pioneers stayed at in Trail with a Silver Lining. *I should be back on the "trail" (Ha! Ha!) by early morning. I expect to be in California the day after tomorrow and will drop you a postcard as soon as I cross the state line.*

(I debated making mention of his absence the day I departed and how rude not to wish God's special blessings upon my trip. But when I thought more on it, I hadn't even asked God Himself to bless my trip, my faith waivering as a result of my bitter disappointment in spite of Him saving my life. Considering all of this, I figured it unfair to pass judgment upon Billy for his shortcomings. I wrote…)

…Hope all is well by you and the family. Say Hi to each one of them for me.

Yours truly,
Gracie

CHAPTER 9

I dozed off. How long, I couldn't be certain, for I'd once again forgotten to bring in the rattler from the car. Smoothing out Billy's letter, crumbled from resting my head on the small dusty writing table, I folded and edged it under the bureau scarf on my dresser as a reminder to mail the following day. I assumed they had postal service way back here in only God knows where. Pony Express? I'm being funny. But, seriously, maybe by plane? I'd heard from world traveler Cousin Jeanette that's how mail is delivered in Australia's Outback.

I donned loafers and a light-weight cardigan I'd bought for traveling and fumbled through the dark corridor that led to the steps. A light shone in a crack above the doorjamb just off the passage to my right so I knew the hour couldn't be too late.

Outside, a full moon shone brightly, casting long thick shadows across the empty yard. The wind had died completely. Except for a cow's distant bellow, the evening lay calm and quiet. The truck was gone. I wondered if Harlan or Bartlett had taken off. I picked up the clock, forced it into my sweater pocket, and walked over to the corral. The same little paint trotted up to me. Patting her gently on the neck, I whispered softly of our assumed early morning rendezvous.

A chill went through me. The air cooled considerably without the hot desert sun. Drawing the cardigan closer, I returned to the house. Butterflies fluttered out of control in my stomach when I saw the slim light still showing beneath the same door. I paused in the hallway outside listening for movement until feeling shame for the stirrings in my innocent body. I hurried on to my own room.

The clock said ten-ten. Whatever time zone that was I couldn't be sure. In any event, the sun would rise soon enough. The room was warm, and I lay down on top of the covers, but sleep would not come. Perhaps twenty minutes or so passed by when I heard a noise coming from somewhere. I raised myself in bed, listened intently but heard no further sound. With a certain uneasiness, I lay back down. Something brushed against my door. The knob turned. There being no attempt at secrecy now, the door swung open boldly and slammed behind.

Although black against black, I saw the outline of a man entering with a long, panther-like stride, half crouching. He straightened to his full height, then catapulted himself upon me. His mouth, a sea of stinking liquor and tobacco, came down hard on mine. I struggled below this monster, pushing with all the strength a hundred and twenty pounds could muster. His arms slackened some, and, praise be to God, I managed to squirm out from under, screaming desperately that he stop. My years of being in the Lord had been such an ingrained part of me that I found myself pleading for His mercy as well. But He didn't hear.

Like the devil himself, this evil human creature seized me and threw me down again. This time, I managed to bring my knees back and kicked. Kicked hard. With both feet. The lamp on the nightstand crashed to the floor. Then silence. A click. Light.

"You shoulda locked your door!" Jim Bartlett shouted at me. He stood fully dressed in the doorway. Shock and fright and confusion blurred, then anger rose inside me. This man standing there obviously considered this brutal act the result of my own negligence.

Through tears, I shot back, "Why don't you supply keys for your guests?" Only then did I notice the black cast iron latch below the doorknob.

A dazed Harlan, sprawled on the carpeted floor alongside the bed, appeared totally wasted. Half dazed myself, I clutched my nightie around me. As if that weren't enough covering, I got up and tugged the scarf off the dresser, scattering my toiletry items in every direction, and wrapped the scarf around my shoulders. Shaking, I sat down on the bed.

"Sorry, ma'am," Bartlett said. "Kid's been strange in the head ever since his Ma left."

Left? But Harlan said she died?

The man who had looked so tough to me earlier sounded contrite and repentant and was now on his knees. He stared at the back of his hands resting on Harlan's shoulders like he was strongly irritated with them. Like he was struggling with some kind of feeling inside, which he wanted to keep from showing anyone, especially me.

Following some shuffling, both men got to their feet. Then Bartlett led the other from the room. Like a cowboy hero doing the routine cleanup after a saloon brawl, the mistreated heroine was left behind to wallow in her own misery.

Only then did I absorb the real-life drama for what it was. Harlan's mother hadn't died. She abandoned him, and he's been in denial ever since. And that part about his father being killed in a rodeo accident, that, too, was a lie. Bartlett is Harlan's father! What a crazy situation. Dangerous, too. I needed to get away from this place and these people—NOW!

No fee had been negotiated. I pitched a five-dollar bill on the bare dresser, snatched my dungarees laying over the stool, and pulled them up over my nightie. Without bothering with socks, I slipped into my penny loafers. The toothbrush, paste, hairbrush and whatever else still on the sink or floor or closet could stay.

I grabbed the suitcase, surprisingly light, and pocketbook, and had my hand on the doorknob when I remembered the letter. I stepped carelessly over the broken pieces of tiffany and retrieved the letter, which had flown to the floor when I pulled the scarf out from under it, and stuffed it into my pants pocket.

CHAPTER 10

Wwhat just happened? What was I doing here, and where was I? Where was I going? There was such a battle raging inside my mind I could hardly maneuver the bumpy road.

What reason could I give my folks for returning home so soon? Did I really want to give in to everyone's expectations? What if I went on to California? Would I be happy sitting indoors at a monotonous desk, typing monotonous letters day after monotonous day? Well, certainly after this night, monotony would be mighty welcome. But who's to say that men in Los Angeles or Terminal Island or wherever the heck the Border Patrol was located acted any better? Gloria might be right about it being a wicked place.

Suddenly, Gloria's earlier advice found its way into my brain, which at this point swam perpetually inside a grey ball of massed confusion. "In the spirit of Jesus, we Christians must each be committed to bringing others to Him whenever the opportunity presents itself, no matter where we are." I wondered if Harlan and his father were Christians. Hardly, from what I'd just experienced!

Where was my Christian allegiance? Was this whole episode for my own edification? Part of the journey? The minister once said, "We know the destination. Life is all about the journey in getting to the destination." Hmm? Should I rise to the challenge of applying my organizational skills and return this back to a dude ranch, demonstrating to Bartlett that not all Northeasterners are distrustful? Nor women? Wow! Could I face Harlan again? What would Billy say to that one? Would Harlan, even in his drunken stupor, have tried to rape me had he known I was barely eighteen?

293

If I stayed for his sake? A gentle warmth floated through in spite of what I'd just experienced, helping me realize the hurt that Harlan suffered all these years by his mother's desertion and denial of his father. Hardly a flattering approach, this young man begged for female compassion.

Don't get me wrong. There's no way I was feeling the same things for this man who molested me as I ever felt for Billy. My Billy. Billy whose relationship I considered platonic, but whom I truly thought of as marrying someday and fathering my children. No, it was different from that. It felt more like a need to befriend Harlan, like a sister. Like I would treat an older brother I never had. Show him trust, be forgiving of his brutal assault, be a living sermon on love somehow, a caring love. Brotherly love. God's love.

No! I could never face either one of these men ever again!

I made a periodic rearview mirror check, and the battle raged on. To stay would compromise my convictions. What were my convictions? And to whom? To God? I wasn't sure. Before graduation, when I became overly perplexed about my future, I prayed desperately, as the Psalmist did, that the Lord deliver to me His promise.

I found myself whispering now His promise to instruct and teach me the way to go and added in humble repentance, "…Lord, You and I go way back, back before you chose Gloria instead of me for mission work. I know that I haven't been exactly on Your side ever since. I was even angry with You, but I know now that I was wrong, and that I need You. Not just for what's happened to me tonight, I need You for always, every day and like the hymn says, 'I need you every hour'—for safety, for truth, for guidance. For love.

"Teach me what's right and what's not right in my walk with You. Forgive me for lying, and most of all for lying and not even feeling guilty about it. I know You have a lot on Your plate right now dealing with millions of other sinners like me, but, please, I beg that You fill me with Your Holy Spirit and communicate Your perfect will to me, that I might plant the seed wherever You lead…."

When finished, I expected to see God's answer directing my footsteps written across the windshield. Nothing except two streams of buggy yellow light pierced the blackness.

For the next crazy mile or two, the battle continued, each option jockeying for first position. Then that "still, small voice" that's mentioned in the Bible said to me, "Use this experience as a stepping stone and not a stumbling block. I have plans for you."

By the time I reached the end of the lane, I'd made up my mind and stalled briefly underneath the sign that welcomed me earlier.

Strange, of all the answered and unanswered questions, it never occurred to me to ask those people what Thee Mrs. Bartlett meant by "Last Chance." I considered this numbly, pushed the clutch to the floor, and shifted. Never in my life had I felt so lonely and so far away from everybody I loved as at this moment. Yet, something inside told me I was doing the right thing.

"...forget those things behind and reach forth
unto those things before (you)...
and press toward the mark (goal)...."
(Phil. 3:13,14)

RED HERRING

(Nineteen Ninety-Three)

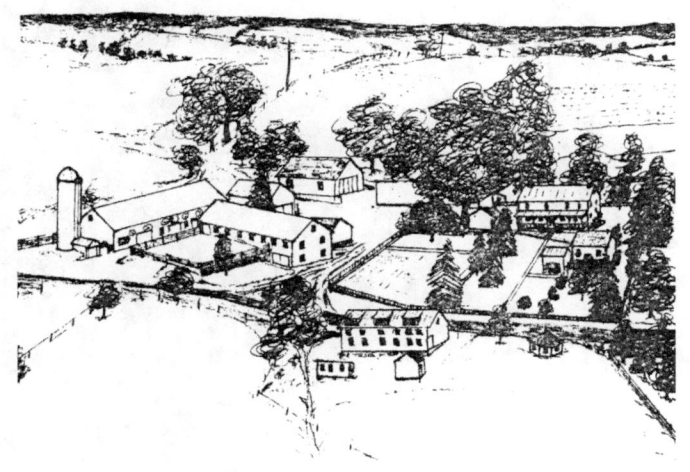

CHAPTER 1

I sat Yoga style on the attic floor, skimming newspaper clippings from the Seventies.

"Look, Nana! See what I found!" said Annie. She struggled with my senior prom gown of long ago, pulling it down over her straight blond tresses. It was a pretty gown. Strapless. White. Full, stiff netting skirt over a three-quarter length crinoline petticoat that was popular in the Fifties. A mammoth, crumbled red rose made out of some type of fake fabric was pinned at the waist, left side. The dress practically drowned the petite figure that hardly favored the large Swiss-German genes of the Balthaser bloodline. The gown cleaned the dusty attic floorboards as Annie twirled and pirouetted on her toes as gracefully as a ballet dancer in Tchaikovsky's Swan Lake. A live performance I was actually privileged to attend at the Kremlin's state theatre in Moscow.

"Annie Mae Geiger! Aren't you just the cutest one! You look like a princess," I declared, my heart bursting over with pride at my oldest grandchild. "So much prettier than me when I wore that to the senior prom." My goodness, that was forty-two years ago.

Annie smiled. She said, "This was yours, Nana? What's a senior prom? Why did you go there? Was mommy with?" She rattled off questions faster than any ten year-old I'd ever known, never missing a step as she primped back and forth in the narrow aisle that divided the huge attic into two.

The attic, or rather garret as people called the top floor of a farmhouse way back when, held great fascination for me, too, when I was growing up. The odd excitement of fear and adventure crept over me each time I climbed the winding stairs that wound along inside the thick sandstone walls. At the top, leftover odors of smoked meats strung on wires from earlier days mixed with the smell of moth crystals, giving the room a musty stillness.

It's a big room. It extends the full length and breadth of my folks' four-story 18th-century home. Tiny, cobwebby windows at each gable end provide the only light besides a single electric bulb extending from a cord in the center of the pitched ceiling above. Closet space in the house is nil except for wooden pegs high on the walls downstairs. Hence, off-season clothing, bed covers, and other periodic household changes are stored in the attic. Abandoned furniture—relics of a past era—keepsakes and boxes of cast-off finery also found their way up here through the years. Including many of my own personal belongings.

"Nana?"

"A senior prom is a dinner dance you go to when you graduate from high school," I said, now giving her my full attention. "It's a formal, dress-up affair. At least it was back in my day. One usually went with a date." I had a clipping in my hand that read "NORTHERN BAERRICKS RESIDENTS gathered last evening to speak out against Metropolitan Electric's plan to…." I knew what was coming and placed the clipping on the floor, next to the grey square cardboard box that once held a store-bought birthday cake. I'd deal with this later.

"A date?" Annie said, stifling a giggle.

It was surely far-fetched in the little girl's mind that her Nana was ever young enough to date. Pushing the big Six O is over the hill in her eyes so I'd let it go at that. At the same time, I give thought to who that old woman was I saw in the bathroom mirror this morning?

"What was it like to go to a senior prom with a date, Nana?" she said with a straight face this time.

I sighed, searching for the best words to describe that memorable evening to one so young and innocent. "See this?" I pointed out a big stain on the side of the gown that commercial cleaning and years of storage had not erased. "Your granddaddy was responsible for this. He was showing off and accidentally tipped a full bottle of Coca Cola on my beautiful gown. It nearly spoiled the evening for both of us because of the way I reacted. But fortunately, my darling, your great-grandma had taught me well. She stressed that we must forgive others before God forgives us. If we do, He'll most surely bless us in return."

Caressing the imaginary silver band that once graced my third finger left, I reminisced briefly. God had surely blessed me that evening. It happened after the prom. Allen Reiter, tall, handsome, Charlton Heston look-alike and eight years my senior, was home from California visiting his folks at the time. I had the unbelievable courage to invite him to be my escort. When the night was over, my long-time childhood crush took me in his arms and kissed me.

Some history here. Allen Richard Reiter, from our Pennsylvania Dutch community, helped out on our farm in summers. They called such as he a hired man. Every farmer had one unless he had his own flock of boys. When the war came along, Allen joined the Marines. I was a kid still wet behind the ears at the time, yet forever infatuated, and swooned big time whenever he came home on leave.

Amidst odd circumstances that included a failed shotgun marriage on Al's part, three years after my high school graduation, Jeanette Louise Balthaser and Allen Richard Reiter tied the knot in Santa Monica, California. There, we both worked at Douglas Missiles and Space Division. Me, a humble department secretary. He, an electrical engineer on the Queen's Skybolt Program. In 1958, our sweet baby girl was born. "Sounds like a race horse," my husband quipped when I suggested "Donna Kym." Hence, the nickname Filly.

For the most part, Al's and my personalities mixed like oil and water, supporting the theory that opposites attract. We rarely agreed on anything. If I said something was white, Al saw black. Me, a Believer, Al, *au contraire.* He read a textbook on Advanced Mathematics like it was a can't-put-down mystery novel. I hated math with a passion, still do. Toothpaste. I squeezed from the bottom. Al from the top. Hang in. There's more.

Al was detail-oriented with the patience of Job. And talk about self-discipline—he could stop after one potato chip. Imagine that! Me? Call me spontaneous if you will, little self-control, impatient. Act now, think later. Always in a hurry, life too busy to sweat the small stuff. Just the facts, ma'am. Give me the big picture.

I'm sure Hubby Allen could add a few things to level the playing field. But who's counting? Moot point. I'm the one writing the story, so it is what it is. In any event, we dealt with our normal everyday husband/wife issues and lived happily ever after, right? Wrong.

Life happens. Alcohol. I didn't understand back then, but I do today. Alcohol was Al's attempted fix for a condition not yet termed or dealt with when exiting the military, not until decades later. Post Traumatic Stress Disorder.

In World War II, our boys put their lives on the line and endured all kinds of hell on two fronts in their fight to keep America free. From the Atlantic to the Pacific, from Normandy to Hiroshima, and every battle in between. But as history teaches, there's no such thing as freedom being free. War changed everything and left heavy costs to pay. After victory, our traumatized heroes were expected to return home to civilian life, hit the reset button and go back to business as usual. But it didn't work that way. My former jarhead's price for his part in seizing Saipan was: a collection of shrapnel, two purple hearts, and the inevitable PTSD. And alcohol addiction.

Al was an exceptionally brilliant engineer, having been trained, thanks to the GI Bill, at two of the country's best engineering schools—MIT and Cornell. In 1960, Douglas made him an offer too good to refuse. He accepted and immediately transferred to Cape Canaveral as Quality Control & Reliability Manager on the Saturn rocket program.

We mutually agreed the long-distance separation would do us both good. I and Filly stayed behind in California while our favorite once-a-marine-always-a-marine fulfilled another mission for Uncle Sam. On July 20, 1969, the Saturn rocket team at the Cape launched NASA's Apollo 11 space capsule, putting the world's first man on the moon.

In spite of the geographic distance, Reiter family relations remained relatively close and civil. Filly and I visited her dad from time to time in Melbourne, Florida. Then Al, who twice committed to "for better or for worse," again remarried. Filly, age 10, attended classes for one semester at Cocoa Beach Elementary where schoolteacher wife Pat taught fifth grade. The reason I mention this is that through Al's connections at the space center (later renamed Cape Kennedy), Pat's students were on-location guests December 7, 1972, when Apollo 17 was launched. This was NASA's final space mission to the moon.

Filly still brags how Dad in his red "Good Luck" polo shirt did whatever he had to do in the pad's control room. Not to mention the thrill of standing just feet away from other VIPs in the viewing stand. For one, John Wayne. (Sorry, Filly. Can't help but expose to my readers cowboy hero John Wayne for whom he really was—a coward. Big tough hombre on the big screen dodged the draft claiming a bad back, yet continued incredulous stunts before cameras throughout a lengthy movie career.)

CHAPTER 2

"**N**ana, Nana! Are you mad at me?" Annie jolts me from my nostalgic state.

"No, of course not." I fidgeted with a front page of the *Redding Daily Times* that I now held in my formerly nicotine-stained fingers. "Why ever would I be mad at you?"

"You got quiet so I thought maybe you were mad about something. When Mommy's mad, she gets quiet and doesn't talk."

I thought about that then said, "I'm sorry, sweetheart. My mind just kinda wanders back in time. Let's see now, what was it we were talking about? Oh, yes, forgiveness." I folded the newspaper sheet, tossed it on top of the growing pile on the floor and absent-mindedly reached inside the cake box for another.

"Do you mean like when Mommy forgives me for something before I go to bed?"

Kudos to Filly! Pleasing to know she passed on to her daughter the same values my mother passed on to me. Mama constantly reminded her youngest, that would be me, that Scripture says not to let the sun go down on one's anger. Still, forgiveness was never easy.

"Yes, like Mommy forgiving you for something before you go to bed," I reached out and patted Annie's little backside still covered with all that bulk. "I'm sure she doesn't want you to finish the day unhappy when there are differences between you." *Like with me and your mother. Filly, clean up your room, NOW! And go and sin no more!*

"Nana." Annie prompted, her focus already somewhere else. *Must run in the family*, I humored to myself. "Is this supposed to be you here?" She pointed to Jennie Balthaser, the pseudonym I used when free-lancing. Netting from the gown's bodice tickled my face as the little girl bent over the top of me trying to read further on the newspaper page I held in my hands.

"So it is, my dear."

"I didn't know you worked for a newspaper? Mommy said you…"

"Well, I don't. I didn't really." I glanced at the yellowed front page of the *Humberg Item* and added it to my pile. Then took another clipping out of the box. "I guess I'm sort of what one would call a field reporter at times."

Allow me, Dear Reader, to backpedal for a moment or two. Maybe more. When Filly started her freshman year at UCLA, this chicken moved home to roost. But not until I had the diploma in hand for my Bachelor's Degree in Business Ad achieved after seven long years of night school. I guess this looked great on my resumé when I applied at American Semi-Conductor Corporation (ASCC). I was hired right off the bat.

They say if you love what you're doing, you never have to work a day in your life. I loved what I was doing. It was more than a career, rather a lifestyle. As Public Relations Specialist, I had a wide range of responsibilities within the company and community. A list too lengthy to spell out.

(Author's Note: This should humor you in the 21st century as to how far we've advanced technologically since the mid-Eighties. My co-worker Lori in PR invited me to attend a PC trade show our ASCC Marketing Division in Philly was holding in Redding. I said, "Sure, I'll go along. What's a PC?" Enter The Information Age!)

Before you judge me all full of myself, let me explain why I bring up all of this. One of my myriad tasks on the job included co-editing the company's monthly magazine, *The Solid Stater.* The really good news is, this latter in my boss's mind qualified me for the corporation's tuition reimbursement program. Upon his authorization, I enrolled and was accepted in a five-semester creative writing curriculum. It was back to burning the midnight oil. Books, pens, tablets, typewriter, and on and off campus study for five long years took me to Vermont, Florida, and even Paris. All the while, I worked full time at ASCC. Ultimately, I graduated with an MFA Degree in Creative Writing from Vermont College of Norwich University.

Writing was in my blood. In addition to articles for the company magazine, I free-lanced and wrote an occasional column of local interest in the *Redding Daily Times*. Also the *Humberg Item*, a small hometown weekly newspaper.

"What's a field reporter?" Annie asked this time as she wiggled herself out of the fancy dress. I smiled at my curious, perky, vivacious grandchild. So like her mother when she was young, sweet Annie bubbled over with energy and enthusiasm. What a lift to my down-hearted spirits to have her stay on during this remorseful period of my life. The morning after we buried my widowed father, Filly, with seven-year-old Thomas Junior and baby Nona Marie, returned to California. Annie had begged to remain. It was reluctantly agreed by her parents she stay another week. She'd then fly home in time for the church's annual youth camp at Lake Arrowhead in the San Bernardino Mountains. The commitment would take her through the remaining stretch of summer, what little remained.

"Oh," I said, "a field reporter is one who is not on the newspaper's staff but occasionally contributes things in writing."

"Mama says you used to write a lot. She said you even scolded in writing."

I smiled, "Yeah, I guess I did once in a while." It tore my heart in two when Filly and I held disagreements. With writing, I was better able to contemplate my thoughts. Though, it was a technique to be carefully accomplished. Words in black and white have a tendency to be bold and direct and not as erasable afterwards as is the spoken word.

But the written word can also be rewarding. As a matter of fact, Filly picked up on my odd method of communication and occasionally responded in script. One note was so meaningful, I still have it in my Bible, re-reading it every now and then as a reminder of the penitent heart and how God wants each of us to come to Him as a little child.

"What do you write about to the paper?" Annie asked, folding the gown.

"Oh, different things. Farmland mostly." Or more correctly said, the disappearance of.

Seemingly unimpressed, Annie was quiet and busied herself with rewrapping the gown carefully in the blue tissue paper before returning it to the coat box where it lay buried for forty some years.

"Nana, I have to go to the bathroom."

"You know where it is, honey. I promise I won't let you miss anything." Annie disappeared.

CHAPTER 3

Little wonder farmland hadn't peaked Annie's interest. In the sprawling suburban community of Los Angeles County where Filly lived with Hubby Tom, who, coincidentally, works in R&D for the same company where his in-laws had worked, seventy-five percent of the land is paved. Still, land is never considered a scarcity to residents of the Golden State. Everything grown or raised is regionalized, making the long state nearly self-sufficient from top to bottom. One need not have a farm next door or even a yard or garden to supply fresh produce.

From the north come fruits and vegetables. The interior valleys are rich with lush grasses throughout the winter and spring seasons for the roaming beef cattle. To the south of LA, in Orange County, numerous twelve-acre-sized feedlots support as many as three hundred dairy cows in each. Hay and grains to feed them come from nearby Imperial Valley. The mighty Colorado River to the east sustains all life—human, animal, and plant—in this ever-growing popular, populous desert country.

No, farmland is not a valued commodity for a little girl growing up on the west coast. It's not even taken for granted. It's just not thought about at all.

But I thought about it plenty. How it used to be here in this prime agricultural area of Pennsylvania that Swiss-German immigrants settled way back in the early 1700s. And how the Balthasers down through the generations, including my father Harry, carried on the farming tradition. And, sadly, how it was now. Sadder yet, how it would be in the future. Alas, that I become mellow with time!

"Hurray, you're back!" I said as Annie cleared the top step. She came over to where I sat reminiscing, again.

"Was Pop-Pop a farmer?" were the first words out of her mouth. Pop-Pop was the name all of my family called my father.

"Why, yes, he was," I said, utterly surprised that she'd been thinking about farmland after all. "And this is his farm." *Or, more appropriately said, it was his farm,* I added silently. "It's where I grew up and actually where Pop-Pop grew up. Even his Pop-Pop. And his Pop-Pop's Pop-Pop and so on."

"Was it this farm you wrote about?"

I considered several replies, none of which included yes. "Yes," I said. "You could say that." I returned to another news clipping from the box. When I glanced up, Annie faced me with a puzzled expression, then put the long cardboard lid back on the coat box that once more held the prom gown. She returned it to the crawl space beneath the slatted rafters.

"Who're these people?" she asked after inching her way back out.

She referred to a framed picture hanging overhead. Great-Granny Balthaser's face revealed rapt attention as she scrutinized our every move. Her hair was pulled back severely from a widow's peak. Her mouth pinched tight below a stout Germanic nose. The woman stood in robust fullness next to a seated heavily bearded man and a standing brood of nine youngsters.

The children ranged in gradual size from a tall lanky boy at the high end to a plump baby dressed in a lacey white dress propped up next to the father on the padded settee. The little boy's eyes widened with surprise as they followed my hands removing the gold-gilded frame from its rusty hanger.

"Those people, dear heart, are your ancestors. Let me introduce you." I stood up and tore an imperfect square from an old bed sheet crumbled on top of a ton of quilts and comforters. When I wiped the beveled glass, I was certain a frightened whimper escaped the baby's short fleshy throat that warned of a sudden disturbance within this familial tranquility.

I pointed to him and said, "This little boy was your great-great-grandfather, actually my paternal grandfather. Grempop, I called him. I was around your age when he passed away, but I remember him well. After my granny died, he lived with us in the big house having moved from the *grossdawdy's haus* or summerhouse as we called it in my time. The summerhouse is where your Nana hangs out since she moved back from California." That is, when she's not working, studying, writing, riding, hiking, skiing, or travelling. I have a propensity for busy, having never learned that "No" is a complete sentence. If you're not dead, you're not done, right? Dear Abbey, I have this problem that maybe you can help me with.... "I spent many an hour on Grempop's lap. He went into story after story of the good ole days, and some not so good, on this once big, fertile Pennsylvania Dutch dairy farm."

I held the portrait at arm's length and checked for streaks. Following inspection, I introduced Annie to each of the other forebears as I knew them and tenderly hung the picture back in its place that time had sketched on the hardwood beam.

"Annie," I said, pointing to another beautifully carved oval-shaped frame hanging from the beam. It held a portrait of a handsome young couple. The man in a light grey pin-stripe suit and matching tie sat on a settee. Next to him stood a pretty woman with short, dark puffy hair parted on the side and dressed in a beautiful light blue silk dress. She cradled an armful of long-stemmed roses. "Do you recognize either of these two people?"

Annie shrugged. "Not sure."

"Maybe Pop-Pop and Nanny?"

"Is that Pop-Pop?" Annie pointed at the man.

"Yes, this is their wedding picture. I know you wouldn't remember your great-grandmother. You were only three when you last saw her, and she died before you visited after that."

"Yeah, the man kinda does look like Pop-Pop. Nanny was pretty," Annie said touching the glass.

"Yes, she was. I wish you could've known her. Everyone loved Flossie. She was a good person. A good Christian. She made sure the family went to church every week no matter what. She had a heart as big as all outdoors and always thought of others. She'd visit the sick and the lonely or cook up something special and take it to a family who grieved the loss of a loved one. It was the right thing to do." I paused, admired and said, "Though, come to think of it, there was something she did one time that wasn't quite so Christian." I chuckled. "Looking back on it, it was actually pretty funny."

"What did she do that was funny?"

"Well, people we call homeless today were called tramps back then. They were men with their life's belongings scrunched up into a sack that they carried on a long stick over the shoulder. They'd walk the railroad tracks and visit close-by farms, offering to work in exchange for a meal. Sometimes just a meal. I was too young for school, but old enough to remember the time I was in the kitchen with my mama when a tramp appeared on the other side of the screen door. She wasn't into charity that day and immediately disappeared.

"The tramp saw me and asked in a High German accent, 'Where is your mother, little girl?' My mama raised me to tell the truth, no matter what. I said, 'She's in the closet.'" I peeked at Annie who smiled and rolled her eyes. Simultaneously.

CHAPTER 4

I stepped over a stack of shoe boxes and paused by a copper apple butter kettle stored against the chimney wall. Inside was a beautiful pair of matched buggy lanterns with ruby glass globes that caught my eye. I polished them with the sheet I still held in my hands, admired them and returned them to the kettle. Nearby was a dome-lidded trunk. "Hey, this should hold some interesting treasures," I said to Annie.

The trunk had a dark green and rust, geometrically-shaped *hex* design painted on the front of it. The inscription "Balthaser 1754" was painted in the center. Inside were neat and wonderful things I recalled from childhood. Glancing up at Great-Granny for her vigilant approval, I lifted the massive dome lid as faint smells of more mothballs and old leather rose up to greet me. A few silverfish darted about.

A heavy cardboard tray held an assortment of colorful documents, obviously designed by a skilled *Fraktur* artist who roamed the countryside back then. The certificates were baptismal, confirmation, and marriage ones. Yellowed and brittle, edges curling. Some were scrolled into cylinders corded by string. They crackled as my eager fingers tried to flatten them. This was clearly memorabilia from Daddy's side of the *freundschaft* (relation).

My mother was orphaned at an early age and never much for attaching herself to material things. She was quick to throw things out. (How well I know. She threw out dozens of manuscripts I wrote in my early years before horses, boys, and other adolescent activities took over.) I supposed, too, the constant task of housecleaning had something to do with this tendency. My father, quite the opposite, saved everything. My mother was denied the opportunity of throwing out anything of his for fear he'd one day require its usefulness.

According to the names and dates on the certificates, most of these people had long since gone to their graves.

I laid the documents to rest once more, allowing each to roll up into its dormant position. Someday, soon, after my sisters and brother had a chance to sort through things for estate distribution, I'd frame a couple for wall hangings in my cozy, antique-furnished private living quarters next door. That is, if there's any room. A plaque that says "What would Jesus do?" occupies the space above my desk and between two deep-sill windows. The rest of the wall space is minimal, including a door to a small attic, and a shelf over top of the walk-in fireplace that houses an electric range. Still, I managed to squeeze in small Monet, Van Gogh, and Renoir renderings here and there. I love French Impressionism.

I removed the entire tray from the trunk. A large Bible, its black leather cover faded to muddy brown from age, topped one of the piles stacked inside. I lifted it out and, opening it up, could see even through the poor attic lighting that the Holy Word was in German script.

"Annie, I have another little story to tell."

"Oh, goodie!"

"Grempop told me of a relative—back then if you had a German surname everyone was a relative if you went back far enough on the family tree—the Reverend Benjamin Schweitzer was a distant relative. He was the *parrah* (preacher) and came every other week to their church. He was especially known for lengthy sermons that lasted well into the afternoon.

"One time Grempop, at the mischievous urging of his youthful pals, played a prank on thee *Parrah Schweitzer*. He snuck up the back steps to the high pulpit before the service began and replaced the German notes with a blank piece of paper. When the minister took his place behind the pulpit, he stared at the blank piece of paper in front of him, then flipped it over and back again. He preached his longest sermon ever on how God created the heavens and the earth from absolutely nothing."

"Oh, that's funny," said Annie, suppressing a yawn.

I put the heavy Bible aside to later check out Births, Marriages, and Deaths inscribed on the foreword pages. I promised Annie I'd bring the record up-to-date with her name posted in it.

―――――――――

Four eager hands shuffled around in the dark trunk for more. Annie's pulled out a pair of flat-heeled, worn pair of dark button shoes.

"Were these yours, Nana?" she asked, holding them toward the light.

I laughed. "Goodness, no, sweetheart. I'm afraid those were the fashion much earlier than my time." Measuring the shoes next to my size seven and a half mediums, they looked quite short and narrow. "These no doubt were Great-Granny Balthaser's in her younger years. Like you, she was unusually petite for our culture I understand." I made a sideward glance at her portrait and, pinching a smile, I winked and mumbled under my breath, "Though I heard she widened some with age."

I received a subtle assurance from Dear Great-Granny. Indeed, it was her tiny feet that for fifteen odd years rocked the large cradle behind the trunk. It was her feet that marched back and forth between garden and kitchen three, four, five, and more times a day during hot summer months, preparing meals that could serve a light army. It was her feet treadling the sewing machine in front of our closed fireplace, probably an open hearth back then. I could picture her on long cold, winter nights, making and mending clothes for each member of her growing family. "Yes, I am thoroughly convinced they were yours," I said, nodding respectfully at the portrait. I placed the shoes back in the trunk and retrieved a handful of books that caught my attention.

I've loved books from the time I can remember. Love to smell them, feel them, read them, write them. My fingers caressed the smallest book on top with its patterned cloth cover entitled *New Second Normal Reader.* I blew the dust off and turned the cover. Another puff of dust escaped as well as a musty smell trapped in the pages for decades.

"Annie, take a look at this." Inside was penciled: Sarah M. Emerich, July 11 (year undecipherable). The tan brittle pages were in English. In the first exercise, students were required to fill in the missing blanks. "Sarah, my paternal grandmother and your great-great-grandmother, completed the first exercise like this: A man has a (*foot*); a horse has a (*paw*)."

Annie stole a glance my way and snickered. "A horse has a paw? Was she stupid or what!" she said and rolled her eyes.

My goodness, I thought. *Kids are certainly expressing themselves in grown-up fashion at an early age.* "Oh, I'm sure Sarah wasn't stupid. She knew better, being raised on a farm," I chided in defense. "You must remember, English was a second language for our people back then. Even as recent as Pop-Pop. I'm sure Sarah never learned English until the first grade in a one-room schoolhouse. Even then, none of the students spoke anything but Dutch as soon as they left the school grounds."

"Dutch? Did she wear wooden shoes? I read a story once about Peter and the dyke and..."

"Dutch was not Holland Dutch like you would think," I interrupted. "Our people were German or *Deutsch*. *Deutsch* was anglicized to sound like Dutch when English-speaking people pronounced it. Annie, say *Deutsch* for me."

"*Deutsch.*"

"Congratulations! You go to the top of the class. Now say Dutch for me."

"Dutch."

"Good. See how much easier it is to pronounce Dutch? That's why we've become known as Pennsylvania Dutch even though our roots are *Deutsch* or German. *Fershtay* (understand)?" I said in dialect. By Annie's facial expression and shrug, I pushed this language thing too far, like driving a nail through a net. Yet, I rambled on. It was fun. "Anyway, I'm certain Sarah never heard the English word for hoof, nor the word for paw, for that matter. But I can assure you her silly answer was not from stupidity. No, Annie. There was no stupidity in the Balthaser family.

"While there was only one semi-educated schoolteacher and one preacher in the *freundschaft* whom I know of, there were many who specialized in trades, and certainly in the field of farming. 'Why, to be a farmer,' Grempop boasted, 'you had to be the smartest of all.'" I pumped out my chest and mimicked my grandfather in his thick Dutchified accent, "'I was a planner as well as a planter, a mechanic, a mason, a weatherman, a carpenter, an *animalduktur* and a *kinnerduktur*. Even a mid-wife if I couldn't get the *duktur* in time.'"

"What's a mid...."

"Mid-wife." I finished for my darling after she'd ignored the un-pronounceable Dutch words. Not knowing how much Annie knew about the birds and the bees, I'd determine her level of understanding before plunging head-on into the topic. "Do you know where you come from?" I asked cautiously.

Annie nodded, but before I give you her answer, I'd like to share a Pastor Joel joke:

> *Little girl asks mother, Where do we come from? Mother says, God created Adam and Eve, and they had children, and the children had children. Girl then asks father. He says, We*

come from monkeys... Puzzled, the little girl asks mother, Why do you and Daddy say different things about where we come from? Mother, Oh, that's easy; I told you about my side of the family; he told you about his. (J.O.)

Annie's answer: "Mommy says you come from Pennsylvania." Her body straightened as she spoke and a hint of pride crept into her voice when she added, "But me and her, we come from California."

"That's right," I agreed. I cleared my throat then said, "Well, Annie, back to answering your question about a mid-wife. A mid-wife was sort of, let's say that she was a woman who....I tell you what, why don't you ask Mommy when you get back home?" While I wasn't sure Filly knew what a mid-wife was either, she'd attempt to find out.

I recall how Grempop's blue eyes twinkled when he realized I didn't know what a mid-wife was. I was even younger than Annie when he'd sprung it on me. Sometime later, I asked my older sister Betty Jane. She said when Mama carried my brother Luke, her first-born, she had absolutely no idea why she was so sick one day. She was *uft gablosa* (blown up) with a bun in the oven, that much she knew. But having never visited a doctor throughout pregnancy, Mama was completely unaware of a tentative due date. Nor, did she recognize signs of near de-livery. Nobody talked about such things. But Granny Balthaser, living next door to the big house, knew well enough what was going on, hav-ing given birth to five healthy boys (and two girls who died in infancy). She immediately summoned her son to bring the doctor ASAP. "If he's tied up, bring Mrs. Grumman." He was. She came.

My thoughts continued to skip about while Annie occupied herself with other pages in the Reader. She especially admired the pretty illustrations of little Victorian boys and girls acting out lively examples for students to follow. One in particular grabbed her fancy. It was a pretty little girl, kneeling by her bed. Below the picture was the prayer, "Now I Lay Me Down to Sleep...." It was the same prayer my mother taught me and the same one I taught my daughter before she learned to form her own words while speaking with God. Now, she did the same.

"TJ says his own prayer, but Nona is learning to say this one," Annie said, pointing to the page. "It looks so cute, Nana. She kneels by the side of her crib and folds her little hands like she sees us do at bedtime. But she doesn't even reach up to the mattress in the crib. Then she says after Mommy, 'Now I lay me down to sweep....'" Annie giggled with fondness. Or maybe nostalgia for her baby sister now three thousand miles away. Nona, my sweet baby grandchild. Nona, who got a head start on grown-up humor at an early age. I asked one time, "What's your name?" She answered with accented emphasis, "No! No!"

I pondered the traditional values we Balthaser women passed on through the generations. Instead of rejoicing in the Lord for this blessing, it made me sad and teary-eyed. My grandchildren lived so far away and were growing up without me.

I was back rummaging in the birthday cake box while Annie paged through another book.

"Look Nana. Here's a funny one. There are cats and frogs in here and some of the words look like they are upside down underneath." She turned the book upside down, and then right side up again. A perplexed expression crossed her face. I got up and grabbed the book. Annie looked up in shock, then tried to get a better look at the book I clutched.

"It's in another language," I said. "That's why you can't decipher it." That was not exactly a lie. Though not sure how the book ended up in my parents' attic, I knew it to be a book Uncle Raymond had gotten his hands on, probably at a farm sale somewhere. It was titled *The Seventh Book of Moses*. It read in both English and German script inside, along with descriptive illustrations I knew to contain the supposed black magic of *pow wow*. Though I'm sure my uncle never practiced *pow wow* himself, he never tired of scaring us kids with *Hexerei* incidents that took place in our superstitious Pennsylvania Dutch farm community.

I needed to burn this book. But now was not the time to bring more attention to it than I already had. Shivering in spite of the intense summer heat on this fourth floor, I casually pitched the book back in the trunk, and picked up another instead. I recognized this as one of my father's journals.

I inherited my gift to write from my father. How do I know this? I took an eighteen-month correspondence course in Grapho-Analysis. For my certification thesis, I studied Daddy's handwriting, which revealed a strong literary leaning toward the art of writing. Now, I have your curiosity stirred, don't I? You can't wait to send me a handwritten review stating what a great read *The Balthaser Women* was, and, oh, by the way, would you please analyze my handwriting? To this I say, thank you very much for reading my book, glad you enjoyed it, but must say sorry to your request.

Handwriting analysis is unbelievably time-consuming, boring, and, to be accurately accomplished, a terribly detailed study. Multiple measuring is involved, comparisons, size variations, spacing degrees. It's above the line, below the line, on the line. It's slant, it's signature versus text. It's this, and it's that....Ad nauseum.

This is Jeanette Balthaser Reiter speaking. If you recall, detail is not my forté. I only do short glances at people's handwriting just to entertain myself. If you're interested, go for an OTC analysis at a carnival somewhere, pay ten bucks for a quick falsified job and have fun with that. Or, if you're really serious in determining who you are, seek out a professional handwriting expert. You can find them through counseling services, employment agencies, legal firms, courts.

Cold winter evenings, my father often sat by the open oven door of our big grey Othello cook stove, clipboard on his lap, writing a judicious statement or two in a journal. Suppressing tears that threatened to come, I flipped hurriedly through its pages. Some were neatly pasted with little single column newspaper clippings. Some written in a small cursive hand.

"Annie, look at this. This was Pop-Pop's," I said tenderly caressing the journal after I realized once more I'd been ignoring my precious granddaughter. I sat down on an old handmade bench painted red that had somehow made its way up to the attic. Pulling Annie down beside me, I said, "Let's see what Pop-Pop has to say here."

I pointed to one of the journal entries. *"Snakes are not wet and slimy as always thought. They are dry and smooth."* It was obviously my father's love for saving stuff that made him collect such trivia. I smiled, yet, at the same time my spine shook at the thought of those slithering, crawly, creeping things. They were certainly creatures of the lowest order. "Have you ever come across a snake?" I asked Annie, recalling in a flash the numerous snakes I encountered growing up on this farm. I hated snakes.

"Yeah, I saw lots of them at the San Diego Zoo," she replied.

"Well, then I think you know that they look pretty wet and slimy, even when they're in cages. But I assure you," I said, shaking my head, "I'd never do any practical research to dispute our Pop-Pop's findings. I myself will always consider snakes slimy. I think it's the way they slink and sneak about so, so undercover. Deceptive, if you will. Are you familiar with the story of the serpent in the Garden of Eden?"

"Yeah. Mommy says it was a snake but that it had legs back then instead of crawling on its belly."

"I guess she also told you the serpent was Satan." With a heavy voice, I mimicked the serpent talking to Adam and Eve that they would not surely die if they ate the fruit. "One has to admit that was the slimiest deception of all time, don't you agree?" Annie nodded slowly as if she understood.

"Mommy says that when you die you go to Heaven if you were good. Or if you never told Jesus you loved Him, you go down to, well, I don't like to say that word. She says Pop-Pop went to sleep and that if he had Jesus in his heart, he went to Heaven. Nana, did Pop-Pop go to heaven?"

"Oh, yes." Of that I was sure. The night before he died, I prayed at his bedside and asked if he was ready to meet Jesus. Eyes closed, and barely audible, he said in dialect, "*Yah*." I noticed a faint smile on his face in spite of the pain he endured from the prostate cancer that had metastasized into every bone in his weakened body.

Annie was once more back into the trunk and found a stack of old comic books that had once been mine. Occasionally, I went with Daddy to Uncle Raymond's feed mill in town. More often than not, we ended up at Miller's Five and Dime. A CMP for him, double dip of orange sherbet and comic book for me. I was really into comic books.

"Look Nana, here's one with Mickey Mouse and Minnie. They're at the fair." She giggled and said it reminded her of Disneyland where the family goes every year.

"I loved Disney characters, too," I said. Disney. Walt Disney, the man whom a Hollywood art director labeled as having no creative ability.

Annie entertained herself, paging through the comic books while I thought back to our conversation on Jesus and how, through a divine shift, He defines who I am today.

CHAPTER 5

I t appeared Filly was doing a good job of teaching biblical truth to her children judging by things Annie said now and then. Surprise, surprise, considering she spent her college and early years of marriage outside the church. Her father's and husband's stubborn scientific views didn't help matters either.

I raised Filly in the church. It was part of Parenting 101. But I learned early on not to pressure her in any way regarding spiritual matters. Why would I? I wasn't sure myself that I leaned the right way. I even resisted the come-forward call at a Billy Graham crusade in Chavez Ravine. Nonetheless, I hoped Filly would eventually make a sincere choice for the Lord. I did the right thing and handed the entire business over to God. When God didn't move fast enough, I took the matter back and gave things a push on my own.

While Filly was still in high school, we had a rare exchange one day on the touchy subject of afterlife. She said, "…C'mon, Mom. When you're dead you're dead, and that's the end of it."

I countered, "That's all well and good if that's the case, but what if you're wrong, dear? What if what you learned in Sunday School about Heaven and Hell is true? What if your belief or non-belief determines which of these two places you go to when you die, and then it's too late to switch? What if…?" Filly changed the subject. Fortunately, God had the final say.

They say Satan is defeated when a mother is on her knees. How it did my heart good when I received that special phone call seven years ago.

"Mom, I'm going to do it!" Filly exclaimed long distance. "I'm getting baptized."

Baptized? But you were baptized at two weeks old, I thought to myself but didn't say. Whatever, this was a good thing. Like a butterfly emerging from its chrysalis. "That's wonderful, Filly! When?" I barely controlled the emotion in my voice.

"A week from tomorrow. And guess what?"

"What?"

"Tommy's going in the tank with me."

This, indeed, was surprising! Tom was a confessed agnostic, and his doubts and skepticism rubbed off on my daughter. "But, how... did...?" I was speechless.

Filly laughed. "I know. I can't believe it myself," she said, helping me out. "For some strange reason, he agreed to go with me to the second last night of a 'Discover Jesus' seminar I'd been attending since going to this little Bible church down in Whittier. Just like that, he got hooked. Oh, Mom, I'm so happy, I'm floating!"

I found myself on the next plane to LA to witness the great event. Though I tried hard not to show it, I was rather stupefied and resistant while attending their make-shift church. No steeple, no bell tower, no stained-glass windows. In fact, no windows at all. The building was converted from a warehouse and surrounded by a huge asphalt parking lot. A wooden sign in the shape of a cross stood on a dock out front and said, "Welcome to New Life Bible Church." Activities and times were stenciled below.

Inside the packed sanctuary, my cultural shock deepened. No pews, only row after row of folding chairs. No hymnals, choir loft, organ. No pulpit except for a small bookstand off to one side of the platform. Spread across the platform were eight musicians leading Praise and Worship with singing, loud steel guitars, a keyboard, and ear-splitting drums. An enthusiastic congregation sang along with lyrics flashed on a large overhead screen:

Amazing grace how sweet the sound
That saved a wretch like me.

I once was lost but now I'm found,
Was blind, but now I see....
(John Newton, 1779)

Seven men and women readied for baptism gave personal testimonies. They told stories of suffering a life of drug and alcohol abuse, brokenness, and other fallen wanderings. They now surrendered their lives to Jesus.

A pastor standing waist-high in a tank of water below the platform said to each, "If you confess with your mouth that Jesus Christ is your Lord and Saviour and believe in Him with all your heart, you are saved for eternal life." Then he lowered each individually into the water. This ceremony, called Born Again, symbolized burial in death. And just as Christ was raised from the dead by the glory of the Father, they, too, were saved for eternal life in Heaven.

Another pastor, casually dressed and no notes, delivered a challenging thirty-minute spiritual message that compared one's best day on earth to one's worst if one went to Heaven; or one's worst day on earth to one's best if going below. This to a captive audience that included the shell-shocked and bewildered Yours Truly. One could only succumb to this type of contemporary service through an acquired taste. Obviously, a generational difference. Only the baby-boomers. Only in California. Ready for a smile?

New pastor in town asks little boy how to get to the post office. Little boy tells him. Pastor says, Come to church on Sunday, and I'll tell you how to get to Heaven. Little boy says, No thanks. You don't even know how to get to the post office. (J.O.)

My friends don't call me The M&M Girl for nothing. I love all things Military or Music. It took little time for M&M to burst her religious bubble and acquire a taste for the enthusiastic, contemporary, and non-liturgical form of praise and worship. It's also a time when I realized I'd been warped with ritualism and worshiped a faraway God. I wanted what Filly and Tom had. Newness of life. Jesus. Salvation.

During a spiritual journey going forward for this child of the Most High God, a deeply personal relationship developed between me and He who loves me with an everlasting love. Studying the Word and going to church were no longer a religious duty; rather, a privilege to look forward to. A blessing. A reward. Joy.

Adventurous, too! Using vacation time from work, I travelled, still do, with our Bible study group on mission trips. On one, we smuggled Bibles into mainland China from Hong Kong. (When communism took over in 1949, the Christian Church was forced underground and has remained there ever since.) Talk about tension at the border as we prayed our heavy bags through customs. Not one bag was opened. No surprise there, really. God was in control.

In summer of '89, just months before President Reagan said the famous words that reverberated around the world—"Mr. Gorbachev, tear down this wall!"—we visited a couple of East European countries behind the Iron Curtain. Specifically, Czechoslovakia and Hungary. While there, we experienced a taste of life in a repressive totalitarian society where the people's voice is suppressed. Our guide on several occasions cautioned quietly, "Be careful what you say. Big Brother is watching."

The Communist Party "uses" cameras, secret police/military, vendors in the marketplace, co-workers, schoolteachers, students, you name it. No one is trusted. No one! A spy's incentive? Ratting out fellow comrades, friends, or even family, gives one a get-out-of-gulag-free card. That's how the game is played.

We visited Russia shortly after the Cold War ended in 1990. By this time, the people moved about more freely. Somewhat. I have many stories about this trip. No room here, so they'll wait until we chat in the Great Beyond. But there are a couple I'd like to share for now.

1) Churches were closed, yet the people were hungry for Jesus. When word got out that a U.S. mission group was in town, a handful

of people risked attending our mini-crusade, including a young man who walked five miles! On crutches! In the rain!

2) One of our translators, Valentina, told how she and her family and friends met secretly in the forest each weekend for prayer and worship.

3) As told by Soviet novelist Chingiz Aitmatov, here's Stalin's legendary demo on how tyranny is accomplished: Stalin held a live chicken in one hand and, with his other, plucked all its feathers. The tortured bird tried in vain to escape. When finished, Stalin threw out bread crumbs, and the chicken followed him across the room for more. "That's how you handle people," he said. "You take away everything they have, then drop a few crumbs, and they'll follow you forever."

4) I can't resist adding another. An analogy, if you will. Let's call it "Socialism Defined." If there were a barnyard election, pigs would vote for the person who feeds them, even though that person's the same one who slaughters them in the end. Hmmm.

Allow me more time on the soapbox. God forbid the day when We the People in proud and arrogant America—LAND OF THE FREE THAT'S SAVED BY THE BRAVE—can no longer worship who, where, or whenever we please. Nor peacefully protest in the public square without dire consequence. Or a time when power brokers controlling student education with socialistic, immoral, and non-ethical doctrine is Standard Operating Procedure.

Such could never happen in our nation, you say. Our founding fathers put a Constitution in place that restricts government overreach. True, I say. But if the D.C. Insiders have their way, that will change. Prophetic rumor has it an encroaching "shadow government," a.k.a. New World Order, works actively behind the scenes on "rules for thee but not for me."

I don't know how to say this except to just go ahead and say it. The time may come when some three-letter agency will ban, silence, censor, cancel, re-educate or even eliminate you—the common ordinary citizen—should you challenge their goals, be they religious or political, domestic or global. Bottom line, it's all about power and control. Majorly control, like a steel bit in a horse's mouth. Conspiracy theory? I don't think so. But do the research and learn for yourself. Meanwhile, stay tuned.

Hey, Dear Reader, I don't mean to scare you. It's 1993 and just calling it the way I see things rolling out in the not-too-distant future. But, again, I digress.

Our mission group also travelled south of the Equator. We visited bush villages in the Peruvian Amazon, Kenya and Tanzania in Africa. We visited homes, small churches, schools, dental clinics, and hospitals. We spread the love of Jesus by giving clothes, toiletries, medicines, and testimonies wherever we went.

A visit to these countries was a blessing on everyone, including us. Interestingly enough, we learned much about our own country simply by leaving it. I say this because the whole experience in third-world cultures made us appreciate the conveniences, the abundance of goods and services, and the freedoms and liberties we still enjoy in America that are constantly taken for granted. Let me count the ways.

When I hear someone complain about a bad shopping day, would it be that they shopped in a restrictive market economy where store shelves and racks leave scanty choice for style or price. One's lucky to find something that fits. Or, one continues driving on the road at five miles an hour because of a mechanical failure and there's no Three A's to call. (Been there, done that.) Or, one goes to bed mid-September in bitter cold Kaliningrad wearing every article in the suitcase. (I counted ten layers.) The city's heat comes on in October. *Da!!!*

Oh, did I mention the absence of lovely little cottages in Russia with green grass and flowers front and back? One views only acres of huge tenement buildings with no landscaping in sight.

How blessed we are to lay our sleepy heads on a nice soft puffy pillow at night instead of a solid log like do the Maasai and Kikuyu tribes in Kenya. Or, sleep on a wooden platform *pas avec* mattress, not to mention next to a smelly side room where young livestock are kept safe from prowling predators in the African night.

Women, how would you like walking miles from a clean water source to your straw hut with a tub of H_2O on your head? All you need to do in the good old USA is adjust the faucet for cold, warm, or hot—your choice. All you want. In seconds. Oops! Forgot step one. Before you enter the kitchen to go to the sink to get to the water faucet, be sure to switch on the ceiling light to avoid bumping into the electric range or fridge on the way.

When you get sick, I'll bet dollars to donuts you simply pop a pill from the local pharmacy instead of drinking a shaman's one-size-fits-all bitter concoction. Toilet? How about a hole in the ground. Shower? Forget it. Or after a long hot day on the savannah, you and your significant other sit around the dung-fueled fire pit drinking milk tea your hostess served. But, you can't stop coughing and wheezing from all the smoke inside the heated hut. Oh, for the twist of a switch, a fan, a thermostat for a time such as this!

Bottom line. Quit complaining, murmuring, whining. Be grateful for all God has blessed you with here in these great United (sometimes Divided) States of America. America, where you have A/C, pizza around any corner, and a car at your proverbial fingertips. The Bible says...Sorry, I'm preaching. Enough.

Oh, one more thing before we journey back to the attic where I'd been enjoying myself immensely with my pretty little house guest. My cousin Grace, who works for the U.S. Border Patrol and lives in San Diego County near Camp Pendleton, came up and attended Tom's and Filly's baptism with me. Cuz Gracie, too, was impressed with the new form of praise and worship and now attends Shadow Mountain Church in El Cajon, which is a mix of traditional and contemporary. Her Marine-career husband is not quite into the church thing yet, but we're praying for him.

CHAPTER 6

Annie tired of comic books, or, maybe it was my silence. She picked up Pop-Pop's journal that lay dormant alongside me on the bench and put it on my lap. A ploy for attention, like my dog Brandy with a ball.

"Nana, can we read some more in here?" asked Annie. There were all kinds of interesting things in the huge trunk here in the attic to capture a ten year-old's attention. A train set we ran around the Christmas tree each year. A wooden barn complete with barnyard animals I inherited from my brother Luke and still loved to play with at Annie's age. A wooden erector set Luke practically wore out from erecting over and over and over again. Yet, Annie's interest navigated toward books. An upcoming writer in the Balthaser's crystal ball?

"Nana?"

"Sure, we can." I opened the journal again and flipped through a couple of pages. "Here's some history for you. Do you like history?"

"Oh, yes. History and English are my favorite subjects. Mommy taught me something funny about history. D'you wanna hear it?"

"The floor's all yours."

"Yesterday is history. Tomorrow is a mystery. Today is a gift. That's why it's called the present." She laughed. I laughed, remembering that I taught Filly that silly little ditty.

"My turn." I read from the journal, *"August 14, 1945, I and Florence—*'Florence was Nanny, Pop-Pop's wife, remember?'" Annie nodded, and I read on. *"I and Florence were in New York City the day that the Japs surrendered and the War ended. I saw first TV and was on it."*

"What do you mean he saw first TV, and he was on it?"

"Just that, Annie. They were in New York City with another couple to see a burlesque show and…"

"What's a burlesque show?"

I ignored her question and moved on. "It just happened to be the day the war ended with Japan. I remember them saying they were in Times Square when the news flashed over a huge TV screen above, and the cameras spanned the growing crowd below where he and Nanny watched." It was the same time Corporal Allen R. Reiter prepared for homecoming from the Mariana Islands.

"Here's another historical event, Annie." I read, "*November (22) 1963, I was trimming trees up in the orchard and came into the house to get another cigar when I heard on the radio that Kennedy was shot.*" I myself was sitting behind a desk in Santa Monica when one of the other gals announced the news. We all thought it was a sadistic joke.

"Who was he, Nana?"

"Jack Kennedy was our 35th president. While in office, he was assassinated by Lee Harvey Oswald, who in turn was killed by Jack Ruby. You'll learn all about this someday in Civics." Or so I hoped. Modern-day teachers and professors were beginning to rewrite history, so who knew.

Journal entries were randomly posted since there seemed no chronological order. "Oh, here's something amusing," I said after spotting an entry dated August 28, 1945. "Pop-Pop says here, and I quote: '*We and the Manger's went to Canada, and the* fer domm'da (whoops!) *customs guys held me inside their border patrol office for 2 hours because they thought I was a German escapee.*'"

"A what?" asked Annie.

"An escapee. Let me explain. When the war ended in 1945—Europe it was May 8 and Japan in August—gas rationing stopped and people started travelling again, but our country still held prisoners of war who weren't yet returned to their homelands. We're talking about traveling at a time no passports were required to cross into Mexico and Canada. Since Pop-Pop's accent was so Dutchified, the Canadian Border Patrol suspected he might have escaped a German prison camp within the United States and was entering their country illegally. They asked him all kinds of questions.

"I remember two being, 'What model was your first car, and what year was it?' Pop-Pop told them, and then the next question was, 'How much did you pay for it?' Pop-Pop answered, '$1,648.' The agent looked at him and said, 'Yeah, that's about right.' My father in anger shot back in his thick *Deutsch* accent and said, 'That's not about right, that's exactly right!' The agents let him enter." I laughed and added, "What's funny about this, Annie, is that Pop-Pop was mostly upset afterward because they interrogated only him. I remember him saying, 'Stanley Mancher is *chust* as Dutchified as me.'"

"Nana, it says here," Annie's finger following along as she read, "*1939 summer was about as dry as we had for a long time. Potatoes, oats, grass was failure, a shower rain in July about, just to turn corn to be over 1/2 crop toward normal yields.*"

I looked at the journal and silently read the parenthetical note that followed, "*(I guess the Almanac was right. If it doesn't make rain on St. Swithers Day it won't rain for forty days. It didn't neither.)*"

I chuckled at my father's naivety in such nonsense and marveled briefly how superstitious Pennsylvania Dutch farm folk were, be it on weather or whatever. They believed in *hex* signs on barn fronts. A horseshoe nailed over a door kept away evil spirts; if fastened with open end down, it spilled out the good luck as you walked through the door. A *Himmelsbrief* on display protected the room from evil. Walking beneath a ladder yields bad luck. Be careful with a mirror; a smashed one causes seven years of illness to its careless handler. If you have a tumor or other threatening growth, stroke same with hand of corpse, and it will disappear as corpse decomposes. Remove freckles by washing with water of baptism or water collected from tombstones. That mysterious bump in the middle of the night is surely the boogie man, so watch out! Do twelve or fourteen of anything, and never, never unlucky thirteen. Thirteen unlucky? How many people were present at The Last Supper?

Before you judge, allow me to add that Germanic Protestants were not the only God-fearing people who believed in superstitious charms. How about Roman Catholics with their crucifix and holy water, St. Christopher medals, and any number of other devices to ward off evil? And how about Buddhist and Hindu? I read somewhere that where there is religion of any kind, you'll have superstition, and that one need carefully attune one's self spiritually to God in determining where one stops and the other starts.

While I floated, Annie read Pop-Pop's added note for herself and asked, "What's St. Swithers, Nana? Pop-Pop says here 'It's St. Swithers Day.'"

"I'm not really sure," I answered. "Actually, I never heard of it before this. It might be a carryover from the Roman Church. Do you have any Catholic friends?"

"Tammy's Catholic, and she's my best friend."

"Good. Why don't you make a mental note of these questions we're coming up with, like mid-wife, St. Swithers Day, and I'm sure we'll come up with some more during your visit that you can ask someone about when you get back home. Questions that your Nana is too dumb to answer." This made her giggle.

I wiped Annie's beaded brow with the bottom of my tee shirt that had ASCC AMBASSADOR emblazoned on the front, then wiped my own. It sure was hot in the attic!

"Hey, my dear, this should cool us off." It was from a pasted clipping in the journal. "*In the Blizzard of March 1888,*" I read, and to Annie, said, "That was over a hundred years ago, before Pop-Pop was born even. Let's see what it says. "*…the Humberg stage arrived shortly* *after noon and couldn't leave until 2:15 the afternoon of two days later because of the snowstorm's fury."*

Memories of clear, white winter days following a snowstorm came back to me with a nostalgic stab. I briefly explained to Annie how it was in my day. She loved my storytelling.

"…While my older sisters and brother shoveled out a network of navigable paths to and from the house and barn, pig stable, chicken houses, and sheds, I dug tunnels in the snow.

"During heavier snowstorms, two or three feet followed by strong winds from the north soon became drifts that reached as high as six, seven feet outside our lane. Even with the front-end loader on our Alice Chalmers, the men couldn't clear the road well enough to allow our pickup to travel through. Yet, we couldn't risk holding the milk until the township plow came by, which might literally be days from then. In desperation, but sheer delight for us kids, my daddy harnessed up the retired drafts we kept for occasional tasks around the farm. He hitched them to the two-horse wagon sled we kept block and tackled on top of the old implement shed. That's how we hauled the milk to the railroad station. From there, it would be shipped to a processing dairy upstate.

"I can still hear the clear, brassy tone of sleigh bells harmonizing with the crunch of hooves as the horses, their noses snorting frosty streaks of grey steam into the cold air, made their way through the heavy snow."

"Mom and Dad take me and TJ skiing at Lake Tahoe," said Annie. Northern California's beautiful High Sierras above Lake Tahoe is where both Filly and I learned to ski. "One time we got caught in a snowstorm and couldn't get home when we were supposed to. It was such fun! I missed three whole days of school because of it." Annie, too, was having a memorable trek back in time.

"Say, do you know the song 'Over the River and Through the Woods?'" I asked, changing the subject while continuing to page through the journal.

Annie shook her head, watching attentively as my lips formed the words from one of my childhood favorites. I sang, *"Over the river and through the woods to grandfather's house we go. The horse knows the way to carry the sleigh through the white and drifted sno-ow…"*

"Teach me it. Teach me the song, Nana," Annie begged, tugging on my arm.

"I will, Sweetie. Later. Here's another one of Pop-Pop's entries that evokes some memories," I said after I eyed, *"1946. The preachers on both sides came for New Year's Day Dinner."* Oh, this was so cool to put it in Annie's terms. "Annie, you'll get a kick out of this one."

"Tell me, Nana. Tell me another story."

"It's about something dumb your Nana did. I was your age, maybe a year or two older. Certainly old enough to know better," I chuckled and went on to explain. "Next to Christmas, New Year's was my favorite holiday. We went to a Union church. Pop-Pop was Lutheran, my mama German Reformed. Both denominations shared the same building and alternated their services weekly. Our family attended each service faithfully and, as annual tradition would have it, we had both preachers for dinner to start out the New Year, my father figuring it good luck to do so. I'll never forget one of those special times. In the afternoon, after the dishes were put away and everyone visiting in the parlor, I got bored with grown-up talk and went upstairs.

"I snooped through the pile of hats and heavy coats laying across my sister Helen's and my bed in the first room above the closed stairway. Then I came across a pretty blue and white knitted hat that, with ribbons, tied under the chin. It belonged to Lavonda, the Reformed preacher's cute little three year-old. I plopped it on my head and checked myself out in the small mirror above the bureau."

Annie pinched a giggle.

"Wait," I said. "It gets better. I snooped some more, experimenting with other fashionable combinations that were at my disposal. Well, Annie, of all the silly things, I'd forgotten to remove that ridiculous baby bonnet and went back downstairs to be greeted by incredulous stares and laughter."

Annie's face lit up like a Christmas tree. "Does Mommy know this?" She doubled over with laughter.

"I don't recall if I told her or not," I said and, with a wink, added, "but I think she's going to know soon enough, won't she?"

CHAPTER 7

I got all serious with the next of my father's journal entries. *"On December 2, 1939, I slaughtered a bull, weight 1288 lbs dressed (3 yr. old) and Tom Wagner one 1319 and Elias Stein one of 1380 the heaviest bulls for the season."*

My eyes slowly drifted from the page. This entry evoked unpleasant memories, for sure. In the winter, usually early December, after the corn was husked and weather consistently cold, a butchering crew of twelve or more friends and neighbors arrived at our farm early one weekday morning. Before leaving for school, I'd plant myself in front of the corncrib where I had full spectrum of barnyard and driveway activity. Why I did this I have no idea because the same scene played before me year after year. I screamed after the first pig was shot, and, through violent tears, cried out, "Daddy, you won't let them shoot again, will you?" "No," he'd promise. Moments later, another shot. That's all I have to say.

Butchering did have a few pleasant moments, however. I could hardly wait to get home after school on butchering day. That was after all the killing was over and the blood and hair and bones cleaned up. And the dog out of sight where I couldn't see him chewing on the raw, red skeleton of the bull's head discarded above the woodpile.

While I'm hardly nostalgic for the smell and sight of all that raw fresh meat covering the summerhouse kitchen table, I do still miss the hustle and bustle that took place during those early evening hours. The women cooked liver pudding and scrapple in big steaming black iron kettles in the smokehouse, while the men, telling tales in Dutch—each tale taller than the other—cleaned the pigs' intestines and stuffed them with raw meat for sausages that would be eaten fresh or hung in the smokehouse for curing.

In the big house, my sisters along with Dorothy Reiter—neighbor, oft-times house maid, and later sister-in-law—busied themselves preparing the evening meal. The room smelled of fried scrapple and fresh sausages to be served with thick brown milk gravy for dipping. Piles of potatoes fried in peppers and onions with a choice of warm, freshly made applesauce, dried corn, or buttered peas to cover them would be served as well.

I was charged with setting the table—the five-legged kitchen table with all of its wooden slats inserted. I dished out cole slaw, chow chow (a jarred sweet bean relish), pepper cabbage, horseradish, ketchup, cottage cheese, applebutter, red beet eggs, stewed apricots and placed the small dishes here and there, leaving room for large steaming hot platters and bowls still to come. Baskets of Freihofer's bread at each end stood at the ready for a quick pass-around.

Hot coffee and tapioca pudding, an assortment of fruit pies, and one or two walnut layer cakes on the sideboard topped off the feast. Oh, yes, almost forgot the mincemeat pie flavored with rye whiskey—the only alcohol my mother permitted in her house.

(A Pennsylvania Dutchman's invitation to his supper table? *Come eat yourself full up for the day is almost all. Yah, gawiss!*)

These were aromas, visions, and tastes of butchering day suppers I deny myself today in the name of calories, good health, and animal rights. Don't get me wrong. I'm no PETA activist should you judge me as such. Simply put, animals are my friends, and I don't eat my friends.

"Nana, Nana!" Annie pushed at my arm. "You're thinking about something again, aren't you? What's it about? Tell me!"

Uh, oh, the Thought Police! "I was just deciding between tomato soup or peanut butter and jelly sandwiches for lunch."

Another entry read: "*Dec. 5, 1941. Today it is twenty years since Charlie died.*" Charlie was Daddy's younger and favorite brother and, according to the family tree, my uncle. Uncle Charlie at age fifteen had a hunting accident in the fall of '21. He recovered from the gunshot wound and from pneumonia that followed, only to be struck with a nasty infection soon afterward that took him to the hospital and ultimately his grave. My father never got over this.

Here's a little side story how his loss affected me. On one of my frequent trips with Daddy to Uncle Raymond's feed mill in town, this cowgirl wannabe slipped away to Western Auto. I purchased a replica Roy Rogers six-gun pistol and holster set for $5.79. It was money saved from my wild bluebell flower sales on Mama's city huckster route. Soon afterward, the gun disappeared. No guns for little Jennie, fake or real.

Another: "*I paid the farm in full from Pop. $3,500. The wife and me started farming right away.*" My father had several major setbacks after he took over the farm, but none so bad in my mind as how things ended up. I was sure there'd be an entry posted somewhere in the journal, but I couldn't chance upon it at this particular moment. Nor did it matter. I knew the details well enough.

This wandering conjecture depressed me. I closed the journal and placed it inside the birthday cake box, then checked my watch. "It's getting late," I said to Annie, with a hint of impatience. "We've forgotten why we came up here."

"Why did we come up? I thought you said we were going to look for stuff."

"Yes, sweetie, I sure did. And I found it." I stooped and picked up the newspapers and clippings scattered at my feet and put them back into the cake box. "This," I said, tapping the lid as I replaced it on top.

"I know. You want to read all those things that you wrote the newspaper, don't you?"

"Yes, ma'am." That and much, much more.

My goodness it was hot. I welcomed the excuse to leave the attic and *outened* the light, grabbed a couple of *National Geographics* from a stack next to the mortared chimney and tucked them under a sticky arm. Someday, I'd browse through these after my Things To Do list was over and done with. Goodness only knew when that would be.

We worked our way back down. The last few steps were so cluttered with items to be transferred to the top, we barely kept from tripping. You couldn't tell, but my mother had gone through the typical Pennsylvania Dutch housewife ritual of spring and fall housecleaning from top to bottom whether needed or not. She also worked side-by-side with the men in the fields when she was younger and one day slipped off the hay wagon and fractured her hip. It mended in time but pained her in the final years after arthritis settled in the old injury. Hence, that and other ailing joints prevented the long, narrow climb up the winding stairs to the fourth level no more often than necessary. Another item on my Things To Do list.

CHAPTER 8

My beautiful Brandy, a stray German Shepherd who found me a few years back, greeted and followed us to the small stone house on the far side of the yard. I slept, bathed, and sang and played piano in the big house. The summerhouse was where I parked in between.

"Why do you want to read those things you wrote long ago? Did you write all of them? Was it a long time ago? Can I read them with you like we did Pop-Pop's journal? I'd like to know about farmland and those other things, too. Please?"

"Hold it! Hold it!" I said as we entered my small but comfy living quarters. Annie was a breath of fresh air, which she never ran out of. "How can I answer your questions when you ask so many at one time?"

Inside, I placed the magazines and cake box on the huge walnut desk I bid and paid two-hundred and fifty for at a public *fendue* (farm sale). It held my PC, ink jet printer, and a number of other office accessories: phone, stapler, maroon coffee mug inscribed with Vermont College and filled with an assortment of pens and pencils, a tape dispenser, scissors.

"Now, let me see," I said trying to recall each of Annie's questions. "Yes, we can do all those things. As a matter of fact, you can even assist me doing research for a special project." Yay! Help is on the way, quote unquote!

"Oh, goodie!" Annie flushed her pleasure, a deep dimple showing in each cheek, dimples that came from her grandfather Allen's genes. "Daddy does research. That's why he spends so much time at work in the evenings. Mommy gets mad when she has to keep warming up dinner for him, then she gets quiet." Out of the mouths of babes.

"Well, now that you mentioned food, why don't I make us some lunch?" I checked the fridge for ideas. Eggs, sprouted multi-grain bread, carrots, celery, fruit, hummus, cheese…. "Also got another idea," I said as I took out the bread loaf, box of Velveeta and tomatoes. No counter, I placed the items on the hardwood table that stood squarely in the center of my little old-fashioned kitchen, then grabbed a black cast-iron fry pan hanging from a beam overhead. "You can work on the project while I make us grilled cheese sandwiches and a pitcher of fresh lemonade. How does that sound?"

"Oh, goodie! What do I do?"

"It's not difficult, but you need to stay focused. Do you remember the newspaper articles you caught me looking at up in the attic?"

"Yes."

"Well, this box we brought down from there," I said, going over to the desk and removing the lid, "it holds all kinds of editorials and pictures that I saved from newspapers. We'll make two piles," I pushed aside the *National Geographics* and desk calendar and picked up two manila file folders and put them inside a bottom drawer to make more room. "The one pile we'll call land and the other is the scrapbook pile. Okay?"

"Okay."

"Now, starting with the top of the pile inside this box, take out each newspaper or clipping. One at a time. At a glance, if it looks like it has to do with any of these key words," I said writing them down on scratch paper, "land, agriculture, farming, METEL, nuclear power plant, you put it on the land pile, okay? Oh, and SOIL," I added as an afterthought. SOIL (Save Our Individual Lands) was a local citizen group formed specifically to preserve agriculture here in Wegman Township. "You should be able to tell just by reading the headlines where they go."

"But what if I don't see those words or don't know how to say them?"

"I'm not finished yet, sweetheart. If you don't see anything that looks like those words then it doesn't belong in the land pile. Put it on this second pile we'll call scrapbook."

"Why?"

Hmmm. Time to buckle the seat belt. Bumps ahead. "The ones that go on the scrapbook pile are going to, guess what, they're going in Nana's scrapbook someday when she has time to do it."

"Will I get to see the scrapbook?"

Is the Pope a Catholic? "Of course, dear. The next time you come visit." Hopefully by then.

"What about the land pile? What are you going to do with the stuff in that pile?"

"I'm going to review the pieces I wrote and that other people wrote and then write a summary for a magazine." Here it was, fourteen years after Three Mile Island. I'd been contacted by the editor of the most widely-read rural magazine in our state called *Pennsylvania Farming*. They commissioned me to write a feature article summarizing events that took place in the late Seventies right here in RD#1, Humberg, Pennsylvania. And those things that took place since the accident near Harrisburg sixty miles west. The quarterly issue would circulate in October.

I went back to preparing lunch. Annie was quiet for a few minutes, then said, "Nana, here's one with you in a big hat. It looks like you're kneeling down, and there's something in your hand."

"Does it have land, agriculture, farming, METEL, or nuclear power in the headlines? Or SOIL?" I asked over my shoulder. I buttered four slices of bread and layered them with cheese and slices of tomato and placed both sandwiches in the pan heating on the stove.

"No, it says 'Digging into Bible History.'"

"Then that goes on the scrapbook pile, okay?" I said reaching for the lemons I had in the salad drawer of the refrigerator.

"What are you doing? Why was your picture in the paper? Did you write it?"

Annie's contribution to this project was not going to be as quick and easy as I thought. Nice try, Jennie. I cut the lemons in half and began squeezing the juice into the pitcher. I said, "No, dear, I didn't write it, and, yes, that's me underneath that big sunhat. Where I was the sun was very strong and very hot. I was on an archaeological dig." Then, the question I knew was coming.

"What's an archaeological dig?" Annie asked, stumbling over the words, yet not doing too badly considering.

Sigh. Let me camp here for a moment. I always thought it would be exciting to go on an archaeological dig. One day I came across this opportunity that someone had mentioned at church. After some research and phone calls, I hooked up with a Christian university team from Walla Walla, Washington, that goes to the same Tell in the Middle East every other year. Their goal? To authenticate Bible history through excavation discoveries.

The 120-member team I joined was made up of people from around the world representing multiple disciplines, cultures, and religions. There were archaeologists and professors and college students of history, geology, or some such accruing credits from life experience. And there were some like me who came along just for the ride. It was the Madaba Plains Project's 25th expedition to Jordan to dig deeper, no pun intended, into Tel Al-Umayri. The Tell had been an ancient Moabite community near present-day Amman that existed centuries before Christ was born.

"An archaeological dig," I answered Annie, "is what they call it when they use small garden tools like the one you see Nana holding. They scratch around in the ground looking for shards or scraps of pottery, glass, or iron. Even bones. Or whatever. They do that to find stuff that proves that people and their stories in the Bible actually existed and were not simply legends or fairy tales handed down through the ages.

"Did you find something?"

"Yes, actually, I did. That's why my picture was in the local paper." I wiped my hands on my pants and came over to the desk and pointed. "Do you see that stone in my left hand?"

"It looks like a baseball. TJ and Daddy play baseball and…"

"Yeah, somewhat." Actually, more like a hand grenade. "It was the one and only artifact your Nana personally discovered in the two weeks she was part of the six-week dig. Experts identified it as a basalt stone grinder, dating back to the Second Iron Age, 1200 to 587 B.C. That's a very long time ago, Annie. Way before Jesus even."

"Can I see it?"

"Oh, no. Our Project was hosted by national dignitaries in Jordan, including King Hussein's beautiful niece, Princess Sumei-a. While they were good enough, God Bless 'em, to let us dig for antiquities, we were not allowed to take any findings out of their country. Every artifact we discovered was catalogued, then celebrated through their national press and put on display in the Royal Museum.

"But the good news is, we were permitted to take with us broken pieces of pottery called shards. We found lots of shards. I have a small basket a local Jordanian crafted that is filled with them. I'll show them later. I might even give you one to take home. Maybe three, one for you, TJ, and Nona."

This subject was too deep, and I could tell Annie wasn't really understanding. Or maybe she was? She said, "If you were digging in ground, that's the same as land, isn't it?"

You have a point, my precocious one. I thought about this and said, "Well, sort of, but let's just for now put that clipping on the scrapbook pile. Okay?" I went back to the stove.

"Nana, here's one that says nuclear in it." I turned and pointed to the land pile. Then, "Nana, here's another one with you on it, and you're with a donkey. It looks like Poncho. Is it Poncho?" She held up a front page of the *Redding Sunday Times* with the headline: "A Palm-strewn Pathway." There was a picture of me wearing a light blue gown walking alongside a Sicilian donkey. A man who looked like Jesus sat on the donkey's back. A group of people, also robed, followed behind as we walked the crowded main street of downtown Redding during a Palm Sunday procession.

"That's our Poncho alright," I said proudly, and, with the spatula, patted the tops of the sandwiches that were still frying. I set the table for two and made a cursory glance toward the piles on the desk, if that's what you'd call them. There was a maximum of maybe four clippings on each. At the same time, I saw the stack inside the box. There was barely a dent.

On top was a picture of me along with thirty-four other women and men from the Philadelphia business community. We posed standing on steps that entered a humongous C-131 cargo plane with MILITARY AIRLIFT on the side. This MAC clipping was another for the scrapbook, a.k.a. Jennie's Brag Book. I could only guess the questions Annie would raise on this one.

Before she'd ask, I said, "Hey, you got a good head start on this project for Nana, so how 'bout we put it aside for now and eat. Then after lunch we can give Poncho some much-needed exercise. Okay?"

"How cool! Are we driving him around in the cart again?"

"Yes, ma'am." I shoveled a grilled cheese sandwich out of the pan and slid it onto Annie's plate. One onto mine. I poured us each a glass of lemonade and sat down.

I put Annie on a plane at the Philadelphia Airport for a non-stop flight to LAX. During the two-hour return drive, I mulled over in my mind various ideas for the article promised to *Pennsylvania Farming* on Wegman events since the Three Mile Island accident in '79. I had two and a half days left before it was back to work at ASCC following my leave of absence for Daddy's funeral. This gave sufficient time to meet the magazine's September 4 deadline. At home, it was back to the birthday cake box.

I sorted out the newspapers and clippings. The ones that didn't pertain to my current project, I put in an expandable folder for the scrapbook I'd do down the pike. After a cursory review of the remaining, I selected a couple I considered referencing in the article. One of these read:

> *"RESIDENTS DIG DEEP TO LEARN INTEREST BY NY REALTOR. A group of Wegman Township residents called SOIL organized to determine why the recent interest in farmland in their area. It was learned, but not confirmed, that a NY realtor is acting on behalf of Metropolitan Electric Company (METEL), the…."*

Spirits plummeting, I buttered two more slices of Ezekiel sprouted bread. Rehashed accounts of how the electric utility raped our Pennsylvania Dutch farm community made me eat. Not from hunger, rather frustration, anxiety, pent-up anger. Too, a great degree of helplessness, hopelessness, and other varied "lessnesses" overwhelmed me ever since the land robbers victimized my father.

You may be curious as to what the heck is going on, things I reference but never explain. For the "rest of the story," read the following pages—a snapshot of what happened during the late Seventies in Wegman Township near Humberg, Pennsylvania.

CHAPTER 9

This whole sorry business began in 1976, the year before my return home from California. Several men were seen drilling on Marvin Konradd's farm and two other properties near Bern. Bern is a hamlet bordering the eastern edge of the Balthaser boundary line where it once followed the Indian Creek that dumps into the Schuylkill River. Scuttlebutt around water fountains, in supermarket check-out lines, barber shops and church lobbies guessed these excavators represented a steel company. They were drilling for iron, and these properties seemed a prime source for this precious ore. Some speculated a uranium field was discovered and that approaches were made by the Feds to purchase land rights for this scarce and valuable element. Some rumored housing developments of major size.

When you learn or hear something second or third hand, there's usually a certain disconnect. Turned out none of the above speculations were correct. Wegman, my home township, was one of ten proposed sites in the nation's Nuclear Regulatory Power Commission's Master Plan for eastern Pennsylvania and western New Jersey. Did you get that? In case you didn't, I'll run it by you again. Watch my lips: "Wegman Township was one of ten sites considered for a nuclear power plant!"

In 1977, following the purchase of Konradd's farm and two adjacent properties, Metropolitan Electric Company, the corporate power source in *Baerricks Kounty*, now moved openly from door to door and farm to farm like Ramses' men searching for the Hebrews' firstborn. My father, Harry Emerich Balthaser, was one of their victims. The buyers pressured him under the threat of an imminent Eminent Domain law when he'd have no choice but to settle for a lesser price. There was little resistance from my mother who was admittedly tired of a heavy commitment to farming. My brother Luke welcomed the excuse to avoid the traditional father-to-son hand-me-down of the family farm. He opted for a career in flying instead. At the time my father was approached, my two older sisters, Helen and Betty Jane, lived outside the area, neither with husbands who were into tilling the land.

Then there was me, Jennie. The *gleina maidel*, the baby. I was the only one perhaps who could have influenced my father's decision not to sell. Knowing me, I would've figured out some alternative. But I, too, was not around. While officially living back in Pennsylvania at this time, I'd decided to travel before settling down to my promised position at ASCC. Jeanette Balthaser Reiter was horse riding (that's what Europeans call horseback) and having the time of her life, trotting through Grecian olive groves and cantering over grassy trails and sandy beaches along the Aegean Sea when METEL made its fatal attack.

Bottom line, my father sold his 139-acre dairy farm. As with other sales thus far, he was allowed to remain as tenant on the property for a stipend. Of course, no longer able to till the land or operate a dairy, hog, or poultry business. Exit the family farm. Enter the corporate farm.

Growing up, I eagerly performed minor farm chores alongside Luke and Daddy as well as my childhood crush and future husband, Allen Reiter, whom I've mentioned before was our hired help in summers until the war took him away. Cleaning, ironing, cooking, and toiling in the yard and garden were jobs best left to my more domestic sisters. Fast-forwarding to decades later, I was still attached to what once was, the saddest time in life being the day of the public farm sale.

It was heartbreaking to watch the cows paraded around the barnyard, lips parted to show their teeth. Milk was squirted from a teat while the auctioneer rattled on in Dutch until a winning nod closed the bid. Pet calves went under the auction block as well. And so the poultry and pigs.

Allow me to back up. Even though I moved away shortly after graduating high school, I flew home frequently from California to keep in touch with my parents and the farm. And, of course, the animals.

I was an animal lover from the day I exited my mother's womb. But when it came to livestock, my feelings second to horses were greatest for the pigs. Nothing cuter in my mind than a row full of squealing piglets climbing over each other to get to the best suckle on mama's belly. Dairy cows were bred, raised, and fed in exchange for their milk and cream twice a day. They'd live on in comfort, peacefully grazing pasture from dawn to dusk. Chickens gave eggs, horses their labor, whether under harness or saddle. But the poor, poor pig. Its fate was none other than man's to kill and eat. Like it or not, butchering was an annual event and just one more important source of revenue for the Pennsylvania Dutch farmer. It's what farmers did.

This butchering business is certainly not a humorous topic as I touched on before. Yet, I need to share something that might put a smile on your face. If not for you, at least for me. I need it. Like Mary Poppins says, laughter makes the medicine go down.

Following is what I wrote for a class assignment in Marketing while still at UCLA. It academically explains the difference between Involvement and Total Commitment:

> *One silly day, a minister and his wife were invited to breakfast at one of the church members' dairy farm. Word got around, and the farmer's animals decided to participate. The cow said she'd contribute rich creamy milk, and the hens promised their finest eggs. Dobbin offered to fetch the pair from*

town and bring them to the farm. The pig stood off to the side while all the negotiating went on and said not a word. Then Bossie noticed her silence and suggested she provide either the bacon or ham and sausage. "Yeah, sure," Miss Piggy complained. "You guys are willing to be involved, but, with me, it's total commitment." (J.O.)

Stick a fork in me. I'm done.

Moving right along, on July 20, 1978, a public meeting arranged by SOIL had been held in Humberg High School's auditorium. Lines outside stretched as long as the wait at the pumps during Jimmy Carter's gas shortage. Minutes after the doors opened, every seat was occupied as well as every inch of space along the walls. Local residents, foaming at the mouth, protested a nuclear plant under more than the basic premise, "there goes the neighborhood." There was tension, fear, angst, confusion. Questions. Us versus them mentality. A swarm of bees at the hive. Private sector on the front lines. Boots on the ground, energized for battle. Nuclear power was the enemy. This electrically-charged audience, no pun intended, hoped and prayed that before the night was over a red herring would alter the utility's plans.

On the stage off to one side stood a narrow table. Seated were two news reporters. One had a camera around his neck, and the other was already scribbling rapidly in a notebook. Next to them sat a court stenographer ready to charge at the strike of seven.

The front center rows of the auditorium were reserved for the rank and file. All decked out in full regalia and looking important were: Wegman Township's municipal officials, members of SOIL (*moi* included), Sierra Club, *Baerricks Kounty* Planning Commission, and a team of executive, legal authorities, and proponents of nuclear energy representing Metropolitan Electric Company, each creased and starched, each with bulging brief case. Latches clicked, zippers zipped. Let the fights begin!

Following introductions, METEL's bespectacled CEO, Richard Stanley, stood and walked up to the mic with great purpose, buttoning his dark pinstriped suit on the way. He was a huge man, both directions, and had thinning hair and rusty sideburns. I whispered to Janice who was one armrest to my right, "Batten down the hatches. Here comes the wind." Janice is my second cousin thrice removed or something like that. In simpler terms, she's the granddaughter of Hannah Balthaser Hunsberger, deceased, who figures somewhere on the Balthaser family tree. The Hunsberger homestead is located across the river from the proposed nuclear plant site in Wegman Township. Hence, the family's concern "beyond a reasonable doubt."

Obviously not his first rodeo, Mr. Stanley articulated well-prepared arguments and the whole nine yards in support and defense of nuclear power. "...Nuclear-powered energy," he expounded, "is the late 20th-century's cutting-edge technology that runs rings around coal, water, wind, and solar. Not only for electrical generation, but also in comparative economic and safe strategies that...."

"Safe? Sure, just like the *Titanic*," I whisper to Janice.

The man burdened with two first names added his verbally stamped approval on safe disposal methods of hazardous waste that was sure to, his words not mine, "stifle fearmongering that's obviously wreaking havoc in your community............Blah, Blah, Blah." No worries. Just go home, folks. Relax.

"Fine," Janice whispered behind a cupped hand. "Everything's great as long as this horrible crap's not in HIS backyard. The whole thing is a recipe for disaster if you ask me."

On the other side of the aisle, figuratively speaking, was Mark Schwoyer, Wegman's legal representative with several initials next to his name. He was smartly dressed in a brown scotch plaid blazer. His tie had Monarch butterflies flying throughout. (Maybe a symbolic statement of what was lost should nuclear power take over?) His greying hair conveyed wisdom and experience, which he'd soon apply on behalf of We the People who were present—the local "Dumb Dutchmen," if you will.

Attorney Schwoyer, standing in place with a hand-held mic, counter-attacked Stanley's narrative with an apocalyptic forecast, stating that nuclear power is undeniably an unsafe alternative for creating electricity. To solidify his argument, he referred to notes on a yellow legal pad, citing problematic examples of accidents that occurred in the past and, not if, but when, would occur in the future from a malfunctioning nuclear reactor. His warning about a change in the system—"If it ain't broke, don't fix it"—spoke volumes.

So, was the glass half full or half empty? Depends to whom you talk.

There are usually two sides to everything, often a good and a bad. Like a strike. In the bowling alley, a strike is a good thing. In a ballgame, it's bad. Here, neither side was on my priority list. From the very core of my being, I perceived a no-win situation but kept that opinion to myself. What I could say is nuclear power is cleaner than fossil fuel in producing electricity. This might appease environmentalists including my friends from the Sierra Club. Or, I could make a compelling argument that nuclear power negatively impacts the coal industry, eliminating tens of thousands of jobs within the great Keystone State of Pennsylvania.

Yes, I could stand and say these things, but this was generic conjecture on my part with no hard data supporting either view. Actually, the whole topic was above my pay grade, period. There's no question we were headed for uncharted territory here and in a dangerous place no matter how one approached it. The word "dangerous," of course, defined differently depending upon whom you spoke to. Like fighting fire with fire!

What's your point, Jennie? You're all over the place. You're even skeptical of your skepticism.

My point is that METEL never intended to be the chosen one for a nuclear power plant in its service area. Their plan was profit-motivated from the beginning. This was all about the money. Not exactly sure why I felt this. No think tank scholar. Just something that permeated the air, like the rotten stench one smells after manuring stand-in heifer pens in spring. Or, maybe it was based on something a former road supervisor let slip early on at a SOIL meeting. Something that made me scratch my head and go "Hmmm!"

My parents raised no idiot. I put pieces of the puzzle together until they fit:

1. Board of Supervisors met in private session with METEL long before land acquisitions began and the nuclear power plant project was publicized.
2. Township fathers at that private meeting speculated development would be end result and would ultimately yield tax revenue for the municipality.
3. I learned through connections I had with the BK Planning Commission that Wegman's site on the Schuylkill was the least favored of ten sites proposed in NRPC's Master Plan.
4. If I knew this, METEL knew this. Yet, they took advantage of the situation and continued purchasing land just because they could.
5. Unfortunately, their move was legal. Applicants in the Master Plan allowed purchase of land in advance of "and the winner is" announcement. For now, let's just call this "delayed gratification" for METEL and move on to the next puzzle piece.

6. I'm no legal expert, far from it, but I believe METEL's purchases would not hold up in a court of law if it were to come to that. Being of sound mind, I know that I know that I know neither municipality nor utility can legally invest in real estate without an approved plan ultimately benefiting the public.

7. Good or bad, and as surely as God is in good and evil in Devil, at the time the Township and METEL had the private meeting way back when, I'd be willing to bet no approved plan was in place. How do I know this? I don't. But I worked with corporate execs and political officials often enough to be highly suspect of things that eventually supported respective treasuries.

8. It was illegal for Wegman Township to meet behind closed doors. Period. End of story. Pennsylvania's Sunshine Law mandates all municipal meetings be open to the public. Transparency is key.

9. Here's the largest hole in the donut. Wegman landowners were pressured into selling under threat of Eminent Domain. But until a site's actually chosen by NRPC, no Eminent Domain law is in place. Therefore, a court would, or more accurately said, should under due process of law rule that the purchase of land from property owners was made under false pretense.

The Prosecution rests.

Interesting points when you sort out the evidence and connect the dots. But do they compute? If you're in the arena, you need to be ready to punch. I stood up during the public meeting's Q&A and said, "Mr. Stanley, I actually have two questions for you, the first being: If the NRPC denies Wegman as the chosen site for a nuclear plant, what will you do with the land you've already purchased, land you've purchased under the threat of Eminent Domain, I might add?"

Stanley removed his horn-rimmed glasses and glared down at me. Totally ignoring my sarcastic comment and, as if it were a given, replied, "The land holdings will be turned over to a realtor." Before I could shoot the next arrow in my quiver, "Will the land be offered back to the original owners and at the same price you paid them?" Mr. GIGO (Garbage In Garbage Out) stonewalled me and reverted back to his own agenda: "…Installation of a power plant requires the low-lands along the Schuylkill River as well as all tributaries flowing into the Indian Creek that flows into the river…." He paused long enough for this to sink in, then revealed the Utility's "…brilliantly conceived strategy is to dam the entire valley, supplying enough water for two cooling towers needed to operate the plant…."

What the hay? All this over-the-top relentlessly ridiculous rhetoric while I'm left standing and look like a stooge! I was furious with this blithering idiot's diversionary tactics and sat down, fuming like the smokestacks on top of Henn Steel's foundry in town. Jeanette Louise Reiter on steroids! *Sehre net gute!*

I actually engaged in anecdotal prattle with my electric appliances the next morning.

I poured a cup of coffee, added cream, and sat down at the breakfast table, all the while grumbling to the percolator and toaster. They both agreed that things looked pretty hot. I didn't mention anything to the mini-wash machine standing in the corner of the kitchen as she, no matter what, always put a different spin on things. And certainly not to the fridge as he'd been acting mighty cold and distant lately.

Afterward, while sprinkling my dress for work, the iron straightened me out, saying my steamed attitude was much too pressing to carry on like this; all was sure to end well. With that encouragement in mind, I felt oodles better and proceeded to clean up the crumbs on the braided rag rug Mama made that covered my kitchen floor. But the vacuum was very unsympathetic and told me to just suck it up. Humming above this mixed commotion, the ceiling fan said, "Not to worry, Jennie. This whole ludicrous situation will blow over before you even know what's happened."

Wait, I'm not done. When back in the big house and putting on my makeup in the bathroom, I noticed the toilet looked a bit flushed when I asked its opinion on the matter. To my regret, it had nothing to say. But the bathroom door knob did. It said, "Jennie, you need to get a grip on this, and then let it go again." And to top it all off, when I was leaving, the front door said I was definitely unhinged so the curtains on it told me to, yes, you guessed it, pull myself together. I left for work.

With the help of an anonymous contributor, I'm obviously messing with you. A little bit of levity never hurts. In fact, it's necessary when dealing with a circumstance as serious as a nuclear power plant (or daunting facsimile thereof) that dovetails with one's own backyard.

Such was the case in Wegman Township during the year of our Lord, 1978.

All Hell broke loose on March 28, 1979. BREAKING NEWS headlines that crossed the nation:

...AMERICA FACES WORST NUCLEAR ACCI-
DENT IN ITS HISTORY....SLEEPY LITTLE MID-
DLETOWN ALONG THE SUSQUEHANNA RIV-

ER NEAR HARRISBURG, PA, 40 MILES WEST OF A PROPOSED NUCLEAR PLANT SITE IN WEGMAN TOWNSHIP, BAERRICKS KOUNTY, IS FOCUS OF NATIONAL ATTENTION......UNIT 1 OF THREE MILE ISLAND'S NUCLEAR POWER REACTOR THROUGH HUMAN ERROR FACES PARTIAL MELTDOWN..........FEAR, PANIC, CHAOS, HYSTERIA PREVAIL....

The rest, as they say, is history.

As a result of the TMI accident, the NRPC cancelled all proposals for future nuclear power plants in the country. This included the ten sites in the Master Plan for the east coast. And all Wegman's people said "Amen!"

CHAPTER 10

I stuck a tape of Dave Brubeck on piano with Paul Desmond on sax in my cassette player and booted up the PC. I sipped mint tea and stared at a blank screen all the while coaxing the right words to begin. My brain was at a standstill. Like a plane on the tarmac without fuel, I could not move forward.

Beginning is the biggest challenge of writing anything. At least for me. Whether it's a book, letter, or article. The key, of course, is to just start and let the writing take you where it goes. Anyway, that's what academia suggests. But that wasn't working for me.

Maybe I couldn't start because I feared the end or maybe the beginning of the end. Maybe I needed to reconnect with the past so I could understand the present to prepare for the end, whatever and whenever that would be? Like "go through to get through," if that makes any sense? Put up the bridge before trying to cross it?

Or, perhaps in Prime Minister Churchill's words after the victory in Egypt against the Germans: "This is not the end. This is not even the beginning of the end. It's the end of the beginning."

Lots of conjecture here. While we're quoting political heroes, allow one more. President Reagan: "The best thing for the inside of a man is the outside of a horse." *Voila!* My best thing was getting out of Dodge and ride my best bud up to Riverview Lookout.

What better place to marshal my thoughts—to ruminate, to reminisce, to love, to hate, to sort things out, to evoke old emotions tentatively suppressed—than Riverview Lookout. Up there, at the top of the hill I called a mountain when I was a kid, stood a huge boulder overlooking the river valley. Like Loreli—Lady of the Rock guarding Germany's River Rhine.

Many a time on summer weekdays, chores hastily done, the others working in the fields, garden, or wherever, I'd sneak up to the rock. There, I'd bask in the warm summer sun as it tanned my soft fair skin exposed around brief shorts and halter. I'd read or dream the lazy, hazy time away. I dreamt not of fame and fortune, but dreams to travel and see the world. And to write. Little did I think back then that someday I'd write about the demise of Riverview Lookout. Take pause. I'm getting ahead of myself.

I changed into jeans, a thin sweat shirt, and my favorite riding boots and threw some things together and hurried to the stable where I tacked up Bourbon. Bourbon was a gorgeous five-gaited American Saddlebred I purchased as a three year-old in '81. He and Brandy were my dearest companions. Life-saving companions, as a matter of fact.

Brandy slept with me up on the second floor of the big house. One night, her wet nose poked in my face and awakened me to a bedroom filled with smoke. The volunteer fire responders said there was no fire anywhere, but the oil furnace malfunctioned and did what furnaces do when they malfunction. It contaminated the air. Fire or no, this accident caused enough fear that my father, should Brandy not always be around in the future, installed smoke alarms throughout the house.

Bourbon? I was leading him across the road from barnyard to pasture one fine country morning when a pickup truck appeared out of nowhere and knocked me down. Equine fight-or-flight took over. Bourbon dragged me twenty feet across the road else the truck would have squashed me like a big old dirty cockroach underfoot. The worst that resulted from this scary episode was a fractured spine, which fortunately healed with time.

Life-saving companions? Yes, indeed!

Linda, a dear friend of mine who rode western, never missed a beat teasing me about riding up steep trails on a flat English saddle. I'd been airborne often enough that falling off the back end of a horse was no big deal. Yet, I kept her tease in mind and gripped Bourbon's sides, riding crop in hand to swat flies from Bourbon's ears, as he and I, Brandy leading the way, climbed the switch-back, washed-out, guttered wagon road to the Lookout's summit.

On top, I slapped a big thanks on my chestnut's lathering rump, loosened the girth on the saddle, raised the stirrups, and tied my special friend to a tree.

Trees were abundant. In spring were the trailing arbutus, flowering white dogwoods, and sweet-smelling honeysuckle. Summer had its shady elms, oaks and maples that spread into a spectacular spectrum of color come fall. Too, there were plentiful walnut trees—the last to leaf in spring and first to shed come autumn. Right now it was in between seasons.

In the saddle bag was a dark red-checkered linen, folded neatly into a small square. I spread this over the rock and took out of the bag a crystal goblet I'd wrapped inside burlap and filled it half-way with a sparkling burgundy I'd brought along. A fine rich red wine from California. An end piece of French bread, grapes, and a round of Gouda completed the gourmet setting. Even though I'd just eaten a couple of hours before, I refurbished in style since my visit to Riverview Lookout would probably be the last. Wedge of cheese in one hand, glass of bubbly in the other, I stepped to the edge of my table.

The Balthaser "has been" farm lay before me. In tears, I recalled my father's words when he spoke at an annual *Ponsylfawnisch Deutsch Fersommling* a few years back. "…I just LOVED farming," he said in dialect to the audience. And that he did, despite the awful setbacks he endured since taking over the family farm.

With Grempop's assistance from a rocking chair, Daddy farmed five years on his own when a devastating fire burnt down the original Balthaser barn. Suspicion, though never proved, was that the hired hand at the time smoked a cigarette inside the shed behind the barn where he stole gas from an engine standing ready for use. Discouraged but not defeated, Daddy rebuilt and restocked. No pain, no gain.

Ten years later, his entire herd of cows failed a tuberculin test and was put down. Four years following, lightning struck the new white barn and burnt it to the ground. How well I remember. I was inside when it struck. So were the cows and horses. Praise be to God, we each escaped, well most, but that's another story.

Daddy was grossly depressed. Yet, "can't" was not in his vocabulary—neither Dutch nor English. Was it Thomas Edison who once said, there's no success without failure? Like with Edison, my father, with a passion and unwavering commitment to the trade, once more grabbed the bull by the horns and made the arduous climb to the top. He not only raised another five-mow barn on the original stone foundation, but also a smaller cow barn next to it. Yes, in spite of the major setbacks, life went on for this *dickeppiche* (stubborn) and unyielding Pennsylvania Dutchman. Farming was in his blood. Farming—The Great American Experience!

Unlike conservative farming methods of the Amish, the "worldly" Pennsylvania Germans' farms and farming techniques have gradually evolved and greatly diversified during the past three hundred years. In terms of effectiveness, one could even make the silly comparison of the "plain" versus the "worldly" method to the proverbial toothpick versus dental floss in getting the job done.

I, Jennie Balthaser Reiter, "worldly" Pennsylvania Dutch gal, give you here an amplified version of farm life in northern *Baerricks Kounty* where I grew up in the mid-1900s.

Die Bauerei (farms) in my youth were moderately-sized, numerous, and prosperous-looking. Stone-walled and wood-framed, locally sourced, *die scheirer* (barns) were painted "barn red" and later fresh white. They were banked from behind so wagons could drive onto the top floor to thrash and to store hay and straw in the mows and grains in the granary. Vents at gable ends circulated air to prevent internal combustion—a tragedy that often happened as the result of hay not sufficiently dried. Some of the vented areas were large enough to allow barn owls to enter. Barn owls and barn cats were essential to control rodent population from eating the grain.

A *vorschust* (forebay) extended forward from the threshing floor and above the front entrances of the ground floor below where livestock were stabled. At the far end of the barn closest to the house for obvious reasons were the horse stalls. Black and white Holstein cows, with usually a Guernsey or Jersey added to the herd to increase milk fat content, occupied the major part of the ground floor space. A *futtergunk* (feed entry) separated stables for convenience of feeding. After electricity in the early Forties, drinking cups were installed inside the cow stable at each stanchion, and manure gutters were cleaned by automatic conveyor belts.

Outside the stable areas was a fenced-in, stone or wood-walled, barnyard with a large iron water trough and a huge straw stack that the cows loved to rub around to rid themselves of pesky flies.

Barns were designed with family names and colorful stars, animal portraits, or *Distelfinks* (*hex* signs that were thought to protect the buildings from evil) and always faced south. And, for reasons I'm not quite sure, the barn overlooked a meadow. By the 20th century, a farm wasn't complete without a silo or two standing next to the barn where corn fodder that ripened into silage was stored for cattle.

Numerous outbuildings surrounded the barn. Most importantly, a milkhouse. With the advent of electricity, farmers no longer placed milk cans in the spring. Now, a steel tank cooled the milk until a huge shiny steel tank truck picked up the milk in the morning and hauled it off to a processing dairy. There were the *kelterhaus* (ice house years before refrigeration) and sheds for horse-drawn conveyances that were converted to garages for the pickup truck and family automobile. In fact, there were numerous sheds that stored wagons, tools, and small and large implements, including a tractor or two. Tractors had replaced the horse and now pulled spreaders, planters, harrows, cultivators, balers, combines, harvesters that also needed to be stored inside when not in use. There was always a corncrib or two and a wood bin that eventually stored coal. Chicken coops, brooder houses, turkey shelters. And, of course, no farm was complete without a pigsty or two or three.

Sandstone, limestone, or wood-frame farmhouses were large and well kept. Always nearby stood a summer kitchen or small house for summer cooking, eating, and canning. A brick or stone smokehouse for butchering, a pump or springhouse, a ground cellar to store food items. In my youth, the refrigerator replaced the ice box, the electric range replaced the cook stove. Washers and dryers replaced the washboard, wringer, and sometimes even the wash line. Regardless of what decade, a huge garden was inside a yard that was fenced—usually with whitewashed pickets—to keep out chickens and goats.

———

Webster's Dictionary is the only place I know where success comes before work. To achieve success, the Pennsylvania Dutch farmer works hard twenty-four/six and rests on the seventh. Always busy. On his farm, cows, horses, pigs, poultry are bred, raised, and well-tended. Field fences are built, mended, and trimmed. Machinery oiled and maintained in running condition. Orchard trees yielding an abundance of fruit are pruned, trimmed, and sprayed. Grass is mowed and sun-dried for hay. Fields fertilized, limed, plowed, and harrowed.

Crops planted, cultivated, and harvested. Grain thrashed. Are you tired yet? An old Pennsylvania Dutch adage is, "If you take care of the land, the land will take care of you."

And so it does. I grew up during the Great Depression that was followed by the war years. We were probably poor compared to modern-day standards, yet we never knew it. Like most farmers, we grew a variety in wheat, oats, rye, barley, corn, timothy, and alfalfa to sustain numerous household flour bins and livestock. Livestock in turn gave labor, milk, eggs, and as much as I hate to admit, meat. We planted acres of potatoes (Ugh! Many back-breaking memories thereof.), sweet corn, and multiple other "truck" vegetables in both field and garden for city huckstering and home cooking.

The thrifty Pennsylvania Dutch farmer, independent businessman, and jack-of-all-trades, "sells the best and keeps the rest," as the saying goes. If you starve on the farm, it's only because you're lazy.

Oh, need to mention something else. Something majorly important. In addition to hard work, a farmer's prosperity is greatly dependent upon nature's cooperation. If it rains, crops will grow. If it rains too much, crops will rot. If it doesn't rain enough, crops will fail. If it doesn't rain at all, forget it.

Farmers as a rule are self-reliant and roll with the punches; i.e., fat years, lean years, like in Joseph's Egypt. But that's not good enough for the Pennsylvania Dutch small family farm farmer. He subscribes to the wisdom: "Don't keep all your eggs in one basket."

A variety of crops that require a variety of weather conditions are planted to sustain him and his family regardless of weather extremes. This usually results in great success with one crop and possible failure of another. For example, in a wet season the grass grows fast, thick, and lush resulting in first, second, and third cutting hay. (That is, if one can get three consecutive dry days with abundant sunshine to "make" it.) Conversely, a rainy summer is bad for grain crops, which prefer drier weather toward end of growth. In contrast, sporadic wet weather favors corn harvest in fall. And then there's crop rotation from one year to the next to maintain nitrogen and other nutrients in the soil. *Yah*, you get the drill, don't you?

My goodness! I've just shared more with you about farming than I thought I ever knew. Time to celebrate the *beaucoup* blessings of what once was.

CHAPTER 11

"H ere's to the good ole days," I toasted to no one and took a generous sip of wine. The mid-afternoon sun faded through streaks of grey and crimson behind billowy clouds overhead that cast a crawling shadow over the hillside, stopping only as it reached the empty barns. There, the orchard, fields, pastures, and meadow alternated like colorful squares in Mama's patchwork quilts. Sighing, I took another sip of wine and once more retreated to the past.

On summer Sunday afternoons, my sisters and brother, along with the Clauser and Moyer kids from over the hill, and often the Riegel boys, found all kinds of things to do down there in that meadow. First, my brother always teased his little sister, that would be me, with, "Watch out for snakes!" I hated snakes.

The youngsters played hide and seek in the fescue where its creeping rootstocks and reddish spikelets camouflaged the hunted from the hunter. Avoiding cow flops, the older boys and girls played kickball in the drier clearing on the far side of the creek where the cattle pastured.

Allow me another sense of *déjà vu*. Our faces and fingers were smeared like the canvas from an artist's contemporary brush as we raced rampant through wild strawberry patches and thorny raspberry bushes growing throughout, doing whatever kids our age would do. When the wild cherries were in season, we held pitting contests. (Spitting?) Funny, I can't recall if I had oatmeal or dippy eggs for breakfast this morning. Yet, I specifically recall five decades past when my cherry pit made it two barefoot lengths ahead of Bobby Riegel's, the tallest member of the gang. My prize? They dunked me in the swimming hole, clothes and all. Imagine that! But, no matter, it was all in fun. Town kids had their pools, pee-tainted and smelly, no doubt. In retrospect, we country kids swam in cool, crystal clear, clean water that, before the word pollution was invented, was even safe enough to drink.

In autumn, during corn harvest, my siblings and I split open watermelons found here and there within the rows. We'd sink our faces deep into the sticky red boats, enjoying the delicious sugary flesh as well as the welcome break in the husking routine. Not to mention the contented honk of Canada geese as they puttered nearby, searching for stray kernels to refuel for the long journey south. Often, a mockingbird hidden somewhere in a tree along the fence line entertained with its noisy, but pleasant, repertoire. And the songbirds. Those lovely songbirds would've brought down the house in today's cultural halls. *Thank you for the birds that sing, Thank you, God, for everything....*

In winter, behind the big barn, an icy crust covering the snow made various shades of red and pink from the setting sun that dazzled one's very eyes. Even the phenomenal Aurora Borealis—God's light show from Alaska—moved in the night sky one time, something I didn't realize the true value of until it became a memory, like now.

It's strange how much you remember when you allow your mind to return to the old places. One thing reminds you and then that reminds you of something else. I took a nibble of cheese and thought back to the school years when I carried a chip on my shoulder.

In my youth, you were low man on the totem pole if you had a rural address. A nobody with humble beginnings. The kids at Humberg where I went to high school gave us farm kids negative labels like hicks from the sticks, country bumpkins, Dutchified Dumb Dutchmen coming to town to learn how to talk right. Eleanor Roosevelt once said, "No one can make you inferior without your permission." Too shy to do otherwise, I gave permission. With time, geographic relocation, and *mucho* travelling, my Dutchified accent disappeared but for occasionally *ferhoodled* v's and w's. (Weather vane? Veather wane?) But in spite of that and in spite of achieving maturation and self-esteem, I still have problems dealing with discriminatory memories. They say the best defense is a good offense, so here we go.

Let me tell you, town kids were ignorant of the relationship between a farm and mom's life-sustaining kitchen table. They knew nothing of the enormous hard labor involved in a crop's journey from seed to human consumption. Like what does a farm have to do, if anything, with juicy hamburgers, onions, and ketchup? Or the wheat buns that sandwich them? Not to mention fries and garden salad alongside. How about those delicious pancakes with tons of butter on top? Steamed apple dumplings? Potato filling, Chicken *Bot Boi*, baked ham, vegetable soup, you name it. Cherry cheese cake smothered with whipped crème? (Yumm. Are you hungry yet?) Maybe ice cream if the jolly old ice cream man came around that day?

Ach now, dear Suzy, what's the difference between field corn and sweet corn? What's the relationship between sweet corn and those conveniently packaged cornflakes you (or Mom?) poured into your cereal bowl each morning? Or the *Fasnacht* you munched on as you tore off for school? Or the relationship between cows and the milk or cream you poured over your cereal. Let me guess, you thought chocolate milk came from brown cows.

Tell me, Big Little Johnnie, have you the faintest idea what an omelet is made of? From whence cometh the barbequed spare ribs you helped daddy grill in the backyard summer evenings? How about those succulent apples you bobbed at Halloween? How about it, Johnnie? Tell me.

God had specially blessed me growing up to savor the smell of fresh sweet country air after a mowing. And to feel the earthy touch of cool, clean dirt between the toes after a summer rain as I drove the cows up the lane for milking. How soothing it felt to tickle my cheek with a fluffy little peep after it hatched from mama's egg. Life on the farm was where it was at. But things would change. As Peggy Lee sings, "Is that all there is?" Yes, ma'am. Memory is all there is.

I step to my left. Toward the west and behind the larger of the two barns are endless rows of field corn. The stalks stand in linear formation, like a front line waiting to advance at the first command for harvest. Above the corn and slightly to the north, a field lays fallow. In a normal year, that same field was planted in fall with winter wheat, green blades pushing up thru the ground come spring. Combined and thrashed in August. Fast forwarding to spring of '94, that field awaits a different newness of life when weeds will grow up between slabs of concrete instead.

Thoughts kept darting in and out of reality as I took another swig of wine. Dorothy, you're no longer in Kansas, I say to myself. You might've known it would come to this. You see, Dear Reader, there was a precursor to METEL's invasion. A turning point, if you will.

It started in the Forties. The countryside gradually changed in the post war years after the boys came home and started families of their own. Soon, a demand for housing encouraged people to build ranch houses here and there along country roads where farmers conducted business as usual around them.

Before the Sixties, town folk and city slickers would not have been caught dead living in the country. Now, suddenly, they, too, wanted a piece of it. By the Seventies, development spread away from the cities and suburbs like the Bubonic Plague. Come the Eighties, subdivisions inched closer and closer to our rural township and then into it, prompting my father to say, "We don't plant corn anymore. We plant houses." *Sehre net gute!*

Like campers bringing their fully-stocked RVs to the woods,

these new homeowners brought the city with them to the country. They made no bones complaining about snow-covered driveways and roads in winter, strong animal waste aromas in spring. Not to mention noisy and bothersome tractors and harvest equipment spring, summer, and fall while they entertained on backyard patios.

Equal thanks to METEL, these people were grabby fingers and out-front probers, a premonition of things to come. Big box stores like Cabela's, Lowe's, and Walmart plus a string of fast food restaurant chains and hotels are on the waiting list. Welcome to the Nineties!

CHAPTER 12

E nough doom and gloom. I needed to recharge. I slipped off the rock and gave Bourbon and Brandy a couple of Oreos I'd brought along. They loved their sweets. Grapes in one hand and crusty French bread in the other, I returned to the rock and viewed the scarred landscape to my right. A pair of cackling crows lifted toward the late afternoon sky as more memories floated to the surface.

Up river was the railroad crossing. The locals still refer to that railroad crossing as the Bern Station even though its platform and office have long since been torn away. By the time I went to high school, I walked a mere half mile to a bus stop shelter, then bussed the rest of the way. My brother had pedaled his Schwinn bike over hill and dale. My sisters, born in between, were the most privileged. They'd commuted to Humberg High by train from that little railroad station up ahead.

The station is no longer there, of course, but with all due respect, I can't blame METEL for that one. It had happened back in the Fifties already. People started travelling by car, and tractor-trailers took over America's hauling, well reducing the number of trains, both freight and passenger, left on the run. (I loved trains. Still do. Can you tell?)

From my vantage point at the summit, I could visualize to the left of the has-been station the old gristmill. It stood intact inside a sharp bend in the road where it bordered the Indian Creek. Except for a small barbershop at one end that was later moved across the road to Keimey's general store, the mill, its water wheel dry and the rolling stone silenced, was abandoned years before. Still, a constant hubbub of activity prevailed in its shadow.

This monstrous sandstone structure with its boarded entrances was a temptation to every youth growing up. We all broke into the mill at one time or another to explore its awesome depths. Parents none the wiser, of course. In winter, skating parties held on the mill's raceway ended with hot cocoa served in the general store across the way. I can still smell damp woolen mittens as they dried on a line hanging over the crackling potbellied stove. Norman Rockwell at its best.

A memorable trek back in time deepened my sentiments more than any other when I spotted the little red church and the one-time one-room schoolhouse. They stood side-by-side at the northern edge of the valley where the Blue Mountains stretched along the horizon behind. It was not the log building the Goettlers had built in 1742 on that site. Rather, one dubbed the Red Church because of its later brick construction.

The one-room school, in accordance with local tradition, was named after the donor of the property. Grempop Balthaser boasted how he attended a school of his name when a wee lad. The Balthaser School was also where my father and his siblings attended. And, in my active childhood imagination, where I pretended to have attended.

Late Twenties, the one-room school went out of business so-to-speak. The building was since used as a Sunday School room. Now, the church doors are closed, this after METEL resold the property earlier purchased. It was rumored a modern community hall, large enough to accommodate bingo for senior citizens, wedding receptions, fire company parties and such, would replace both red brick structures. I grimaced when I imagined the soon drinking and gambling where the fine mahogany altar once stood with its carved-in German letters, "This do in remembrance of me."

Anger burnt inside. I decided here and now I'd title my article, "The Red Herring Boomeranged." Maybe it hadn't boomeranged for others, but for me it certainly had. Because of the reactor meltdown at Three Mile Island, NRPC banned construction of all proposed nuclear power plants within the United States. As a result, METEL turned over the entire two thousand acres of land they earlier purchased in Wegman Township, not to previous property owners, but to several real estate firms. Prophecy fulfilled!

That was the bad news. The somewhat not quite as bad but hardly classified as good, much of the land now fourteen years later is still tilled by the corporate farmer. But it is just a short matter of time this newer tradition, too, shall pass.

Soon, this entire valley will be stripped of all types of farming, as well as the Indian Creek's natural flow and the dam. Stripped of cherry trees and berry bushes. The railroad station as it were, the old mill, the little red church and schoolhouse. The Balthaser's "Riverview Farm." No, it is too much to give up. Too much to sacrifice for the good of all.

A red-shouldered hawk tipped its wing toward me as it screeched and soared aloft the florid valley beneath. It was late summer. But autumn was just around the bend and on its way when the hawk would migrate south. I wondered how this valley would greet the bird on its return flight in spring. I shivered. It might be from the coolness of the evening. Or maybe the thought of those huge yellow caterpillars I passed at the foot of the summit. Yes, there would be newness of life in this valley. Soon. A housing development. One of many!

———————————

At home, it was back to the drawing board. I rebooted the computer and began:

PENNSYLVANIA FARMING -
OCTOBER 1993 Edition

RED HERRING BOOMERANGED
By Jennie Balthaser

Nuclear power plant construction in the U.S. came to a halt 14 years ago following the disastrous Three Mile Island nightmare. The accident that occurred on March 28, 1979, near Harrisburg, PA, was a game-changer, causing major civil unrest for both opponents and proponents of nuclear energy. While expectations fell short for some, it was boost or bust for others....

"The grass withereth, the flower fadeth;
but the Word of our God shall stand forever."
(Isaiah 40:8)

ACKNOWLEDGMENTS

Kudos to my daughter Nona Riedel Geiger. As I wrote, she read and edited, keeping me on track with each story's time era and lingo, what should be cut, what should not be cut, and critiquing the story line from a reader's perspective. To you, Nona, goes my deepest thanks, both professionally and personally. I love you.

Thanks to Pastor Joel Osteen (Lakewood Church, Houston) who begins every sermon to millions of viewers worldwide: "I like to start with something funny..." I've borrowed touches of his humor and splattered them here and there within the manuscript. Thank you, Joel, for your uplifting and positive messages. You're a ray of sunshine in a dark world.

A special thanks to my good friend Anne Marie Scharf for lending her amazing talent to this project with her insightful cover art and images posted throughout the book. You are awesome, Anne Marie. I'm so grateful for your help and your friendship.

How I wish my brother, Marvin C. Zweizig, now deceased, could see his amateur artistic talent displayed in this book. On the "Red Herring" title page, you'll see a miniature of a sketch of the family farm he did from memory while serving in the U.S. Army and stationed in Germany. His detail is incredible!

I give credit to the Pennsylvania German Society for its literature on Pennsylvania Dutch sayings, folklore, etc. (PGS, Birdsboro, PA 19508) Credit for the Hex Signs on the book's cover goes to Jacob Zook, Paradise, PA. (In the old days, Six, Eight, and Ten-Pointed Stars were thought to protect barns from evil. Distelfinks were meant for good luck. All Hex sign decorations in the 21st Century are meant to be "Chust for Nice.")

Last yet foremost, my humble thanks to Jesus Christ, the Creator of the Universe, who, when I was down and ready to give up, whispered, "Do it for me, do it for me, do it for me." He cared. He encouraged. He loved. To you, Jesus, be given all credit, honor and glory!

PENNSYLVANIA DUTCH SAYINGS
AND THE ENGLISH

1. *We meer's mocht, so hut meer's.*
   As we make it, so we have it.

2. *Aga lob shtinkt.*
   Self praise stinks.

3. *War net heart, mus fela.*
   Whoever disobeys must feel.

4. *Wos mer net wase, mocht em net hase.*
   What we know not, burns us not.

5. *De kinner un de nora sawga de woret.*
   Children and fools speak the truth.

6. *Wos mer net im kup hut, hut mer in de fees.*
   What we don't have in our head, we have in our feet.

7. *War net kumt zu rechtich zeit, mus essa wos ivrich bleibt.*
   Whoever does not come in time must eat what remains.

8. *We es lond, so de leit.*
   As the country, so the people.

9. *Won der goul g'shdola is, shlest mer der shdol.*
   When the horse is stolen, we lock the stable.

10. *Won ich geld hob gah ich ins wartshous,*
    Won ich kens hob, bleib ich drous.
    When I have money, I go to the hotel.
    When I have none I stay out.

11. *Meer mus net en kots imma sok kawfa.*
    We must not buy a cat in a bag.

12. *Unna druwwel hut mer niks.*
    Without trouble we have nothing.

13. *Neia basem kara gut.*
    New brooms sweep clean.

14. *Won mer shbawrt in zeit, hut mer's in note.*
    When you save in time, you have it in need.

15. *Zu wenich un zu feel fardarbt olla shbeel.*
    Too little and too much spoils everything.

(Pennsylvania German Society, Birdsboro, PA 19508)

"Whether your foxhole buddy was black or white, it made no matter, just as long as we shot in the same direction."
- This is Walt, Over and Out

"At the core of all great stories is human experience. Zweizig has captured the drama, wonderment, and heartbreak of war in this insightful retelling of one man's journey from farm to battlefield."

- Christopher Klim, author of *Jesus Lives in Trenton*

The 25th moved to Korea within hours after the North invaded the South on June 25, 1950. All combat units of the 8th Army arrived in Korea within those first thirty days. Only a handful of officers and enlisted men were veterans of WWII and well trained for combat. The rest of us were mediocre at best. Most felt there would not be another war. After all, we had the bomb. Everyone knew of its destruction capability. Who would dare to confront a country with such potential?

Walt enlisted in the U.S. Army in 1948, trained at Fort Dix, and spent two years in Occupied Japan prior to the outbreak of the Korean War. In his journey, he experiences disappointments and joy, hardships and adventure, and reflects on his growing-up years on a Pennsylvania Dutch dairy farm, contrasting them to the Japanese and Korean cultures in which he finds himself.

Available at Masthof Bookstore, Barnes & Noble and Amazon. Author's proceeds on book sales go to PVA and DAV.

ABOUT THE AUTHOR

Shirley Zweizig Nestler's love for writing began at an early age. When still a child, she secluded herself Sunday afternoons at a huge straw stack in a back field on the family farm and scribbled, to her heart's content, fantasies, dreams, stories. Tablet after tablet. Through the years, her love for writing matured into co-editing *The Solid Stater,* company magazine at AT&T where she worked in Reading, PA. She wrote numerous articles and columns in local newspapers through the years and published *One Infantryman's Journey: Pennsylvania Farm Boy in Korea*, an excellent read on the Korean War as well as a cultural study of the Koreans, Japanese, and, last but not least, Pennsylvania Dutch.

Shirley grew up in a Pennsylvania Dutch household where English was spoken as a second language. Sad to say, the German dialect as well as rural customs and lifestyles are fading out. Through stories of the Balthaser family, a time period spanning 1916 to 1993, the author shares with the reader how the "worldly" Pennsylvania Dutch culture evolved through the years, how it was then and how it is now.

Nestler received an undergraduate degree in Business/Marketing from Albright College and an MFA in Creative Writing from Vermont College of Norwich University. She lives out retirement from a corporate public relations career on her small animal rescue farm near Hamburg, PA, and operates Rivermeadows Farm Kennel in her spare time.

Available for purchase at
Masthof Bookstore or Amazon.

www.Masthof.com
610-286-0258 | orders@masthof.com
219 Mill Road, Morgantown, PA 19543

www.ingramcontent.com/pod-product-compliance
Lightning Source LLC
Chambersburg PA
CBHW060311100726
47907CB00002B/370